TROPE-ING THE LIGHT FANTASTIC

OTHER BOOKS BY EDWARD M. LERNER

- *Probe*
- *Moonstruck*
- *Creative Destruction (collection)*
- *Fools' Experiments*
- *Small Miracles*
- *Countdown to Armageddon / A Stranger in Paradise (collection)*
- *Frontiers of Space, Time, and Thought (collection)*
- *Energized*
- *A Time Foreclosed (chapbook)*
- *Dark Secret*

InterstellarNet series

- *InterstellarNet: Origins*
- *InterstellarNet: New Order*
- *InterstellarNet: Enigma*

Fleet of Worlds series (with Larry Niven)

- *Fleet of Worlds*
- *Juggler of Worlds*
- *Destroyer of Worlds*
- *Betrayer of Worlds*
- *Fate of Worlds*

TROPE-ING THE LIGHT FANTASTIC

The Science Behind the Fiction

Edward M. Lerner

an imprint of

MANOR
Rockville, Maryland

ISBN: 978-1-61242-365-4

www.PhoenixPick.com

Library of Congress Cataloging-in-Publication Data

Names: Lerner, Edward M., author.
Title: Trope-ing the light fantastic : the science behind the fiction / by Edward M. Lerner.
Description: Rockville, MD : Phoenix Pick, [2018] | Includes bibliographical references.
Identifiers: LCCN 2017061847 (print) | LCCN 2018010380 (ebook) | ISBN 9781612423661 (ebook) | ISBN 9781612423654 (hardcover : alk. paper) | ISBN 9781612424019 (pbk. : alk. paper)
Subjects: LCSH: Science fiction--History and criticism. | Science in literature. | Science fiction films--History and criticism. | Science in motion pictures. | Science fiction television programs--History and criticism. | Science in popular culture.
Classification: LCC PN3433.6 (ebook) | LCC PN3433.6 .L47 2018 (print) | DDC 809.3/8762--dc23
LC record available at https://lccn.loc.gov/2017061847

Published by Phoenix Pick
an imprint of Arc Manor
P. O. Box 10339
Rockville, MD 20849-0339
www.ArcManor.com

For Abby.

Because the multiverse is the best toy *ever*.

CONTENTS

by Trevor Quachri

had been working at *Analog* as an editorial assistant for about a year when I first met Edward M. Lerner. He had sold a story, "Dangling Conversations," to the magazine's then-editor, Stanley Schmidt, which I had worked on, and upon meeting Ed at one of the various professional mill-'n'-swills, my never-less-than-stellar social skills kicked in. I told him: "You know, I *really* thought 'Conversations' was going to be boring...but it wasn't!"

Clearly that's the kind of thoughtfulness that gets you invited to write a foreword fifteen-plus years later.

In my defense, Ed knew exactly what I meant, bless his heart. If you were going to hear the elevator pitch for the story, its appeal would only be immediately apparent to a select few *cognoscenti*: "Humanity finally makes First Contact, but realistically. No physical travel, since the distances are daunting; it's just communication. In fact, we never even see the aliens in person. So communication leads to trade, and there's a lot of time spent on the repercussions and implications of that trade."

Boy, interstellar economics. Gripping, right?

Except it is. Ed's execution is everything. In almost anyone else's hands, there might have been some temptation to clumsily "spice it up"—add some teleported-in extraterrestrial assassins or saboteurs, or at the very least, a shoot-out or two between humans; failing that, it could easily have wound up as dry as sand.

What Ed does in that story is something you're about to see him do repeatedly in the articles that follow. It's the skill-set of the best teachers and journalists: making something compelling without sensationalizing it; considering the implications—but resisting the urge to go for cheap thrills. And because the resulting pieces are so carefully considered, they're more relevant than they would be if they were blatantly fantastic.

That, as far as I'm concerned, is at the heart of the best hard science fiction. So it's easy to see why Ed has been a frequent *Analog* contributor for so long, and it's no surprise that when Ed pitched me a series of fact articles, I listened very intently.

Now, *Analog* is a hard science fiction magazine. We run regular science articles and columns, and our readers have a certain degree of scientific literacy that we can take as a given. But it's not *Nature* or *Scientific American* or *National Geographic*. We're not a peer-reviewed journal. "Straight" science articles that don't inspire the imagination or present possibilities aren't necessarily a great fit for the magazine. That article on a new breakthrough in genetics or physics is probably interesting in its own right, but if it doesn't ask questions or provide some thoughts about what comes next, it won't be enough for us.

So Ed, responding very directly to my edict that the fact articles be relevant to science fiction in some way, said, "What about exactly that?" What about articles that look at *the science that's relevant to science fiction*? How would those familiar genre tropes work, exactly? Why not look at the ways they're used, the assumptions, the places where a "What if" turned out to be right, and we're just now starting to see it?

They're the flip side of the same coin as "Dangling Conversations" (as well as Ed's other fiction pieces, really); making complex concepts easily digestible without watering them down is at the heart of Ed's fact pieces just as much as it is part of his fiction. And make no mistake, they *are* science articles, akin to Isaac Asimov's approachable non-fiction science books or Brian

Stableford's seminal *The Science in Science Fiction*, not "How to Write SF" pieces, like you might get in a writer's workshop.

Still, only a fool agrees to buy something sight unseen, so I was going to consider the articles on a case-by-case basis; I wouldn't commit to a lengthy series that I might have to constantly wrestle back to my vision of what I wanted if Ed didn't get "it."

I needn't have worried. In the end, I bought all of them anyway. And I hope you'll do the same; they're worth your time, your money, and your consideration, whether you're interested in accessible science, looking to understand trends in science fiction, or—optimally—both. Ahead, you have essays about time travel, artificial intelligence, alien biology and worlds, and more. Quite a few of them placed highly in *Analog*'s annual *Analytical Laboratory* readers' award. (Did I mention the generally high standards for this kind of thing among *Analog* readers?) Give them your attention, and you'll be amply rewarded with the best workout your imagination has had in a while.

And if you ever bump into Ed, having read this, and you tell him that you were unsure about these articles at first, but they turned out to be really interesting, it's okay; he's heard it before. He'll know what you mean.

(Trevor Quachri began as an editorial assistant at *Analog Science Fiction and Fact* and *Asimov's Science Fiction* in 1999, and is currently the editor of *Analog*.)

A NOTE TO THE READER

Footnotes, identified by symbols (*, †, ‡, and the like) expand or comment upon specific passages in the text. Footnote identifications restart with * on every printed page.

End notes, consecutively numbered, identify the sources of particular details. End notes are collected at the end of the book. (Caveat: a superscript number alongside another number, as in the ^{9} in 10^9, is an exponent, not an end-note identifier.)

"To read further" sections, at the end of each broad topic, suggest more general reference material.

LINK DISCLAIMER

This book includes URLs which point to external websites. The publisher and the author made every effort to confirm these URLs were correct and active when the text went to press. The publisher and the author are not responsible for those websites, and cannot guarantee that referenced material on those external websites will remain live or relevant.

INTRODUCTION

All Troped Up

When people first meet, a predictable part of the interaction is, "So, what do you do?"

"I'm a writer," I'll say. (No surprise there: you have a book of mine in your hands.) To the customary follow-up question ("Oh, and what do you write?"), my answer is "Mostly science fiction."

And then inwardly, hoping it doesn't show, I wince. Because, too often, the response will be along the lines of, "Oh. Like Harry Potter."

No.

Popular culture conflates everything from horror to comic-book superheroes to wizardry to space opera to science-based storytelling into the amorphous collective known as "sci fi" (or, as one cable TV channel would have it, "SyFy"). I've read and viewed across that expansively defined genre, but what I generally consume—and the fiction that I almost exclusively write—is *science* fiction. Fiction without elements of fantasy. Fiction in which, absent the science, there would be no story.

Is there a difference between science fiction and fantasy? Absolutely. As book reviewer (and SF author) Don Sakers summarized it:

> "One quick and dirty distinction between science fiction and fantasy is this: sf deals with things that are possible, while fantasy is the realm of the *im*possible."[1]

15

You may be wondering: what about the many clearly impossible things upon which so much science fiction relies? Faster-than-light travel. Time travel. Telepathy. Aren't they impossible? Which is to say: aren't they fantastical?

True, faster-than-light travel, as one example, *may* be a mere storytelling convenience. FTL allows an author to set a story somewhere, or to move along star-spanning action at a pace, that would otherwise seem impossible. By analogy to literary tropes, words used other than literally, such "science"-based assumptions can be deemed science-fictional tropes: that is, *science* used other than literally. In the *Star Wars* universe, no one attempts to justify the all but instantaneous voyages from star to star—we just accept the FTL jaunts as narrative convention. As a trope.[*]

An SF trope often works in the background, rather than front-and-center in a story. By way of analogy, suppose that wind-powered sailing ships had yet to be invented. A science-fictional *Robinson Crusoe* might treat the ship as a trope. The vessel served its purpose in the story when it sank; the mechanics of sailing don't matter. In contrast, consider science-fictional versions of *Moby Dick* or *Two Years Before the Mast*. Those stories can hardly be told without showing the technology of sailing ships.

It's not 100% clear-cut when a story premise is a trope. Science-fictional time machines are usually tropes, ways to shift a modern character—someone with whom the reader will empathize—to the time(s) of the story. But suppose I encounter a passage such as:

> "Early in the 22nd century, physicists succeeded in dependably stabilizing entangled quantum particles.

---

[*] As if to ensure that no one take seriously the "science" of such space opera, we were offered early in the original (1977) *Star Wars* movie the boast that the *Millennium Falcon* is the ship that "made the Kessel Run in less than twelve parsecs." The parsec being a unit of distance (equal to about 3.26 light-years), Han Solo's boast conveys as much about speed as would, "I'm the runner who did the 100-meter dash in 100 meters."

When the entangled particles were tachyons, quantum teleportation became time travel...."

I'm put on notice that the mechanism is meant to be taken literally. In this story excerpt, the nature of the supposed time-travel mechanism and its underlying constraints are apt to become central to the story.

One way to think of an SF trope is as a willing-suspension-of-disbelief contract between author and reader. As with any contract, of course, both parties must agree.

Some readers—and some authors—won't sign that contract. "Mundane science fiction" deems FTL travel, or anything else beyond the ken of current science, off-limits to storytelling. The mundane SF movement would have authors write as though every technology that may ever be possible (including by intelligent aliens whom the mundane-ists also rule impermissible) is already known.[2] Consider such people misan-tropes.*

FTL travel is *such* a common SF trope, it gave this book its title. But faster-than-light travel, and time travel, and many other great storytelling devices needn't be mere tropes. In the corner of the genre known as "hard science fiction," authors see science as a storytelling element to be embraced. Hard SF takes its name by analogy to the rigor of the so-called "hard sciences," such as physics and chemistry. The adjective *isn't* an editorial comment about difficulty for readers—even though it is sometimes taken that way.

Hard SF acknowledges current science *and* goes on to look a step or three beyond. Hard SF doesn't ignore what we (think we) have learned about the Universe—but neither does it limit itself to that. Hard SF is big on considering the possible implications of the many things we know we don't yet know, and of pondering what it could mean were we someday to overcome present-day limits. Hard SF is most of what I write. But not all....

---

*   I take my science seriously. Myself? Not so much. There will be the occasional wry aside ahead.

Since 2011, for the hard-SF-friendly pages of *Analog Science Fiction and Fact*, I've written essays exploring, one by one, the common tropes of science fiction. The science that might justify those tropes. The science *behind* the fiction. Throughout, I offered examples of how science fiction—on the page, the screen, and, occasionally, the gaming console—has explored these ideas.

In *Trope-ing the Light Fantastic*, I've collected, integrated, expanded upon, and updated those essays. Trope by trope, this book reviews the latest related science and illustrates it with a broad range of genre examples. Some scientific topics, such as relativity and quantum mechanics, recur, both because they relate to more than one trope and to make trope-specific chapters more self-contained (i.e., more useful as standalone references).

As for the genre examples I picked to illustrate my topics, I had a *lot* from which to choose. When a story, movie, or whatever, gets mentioned more than once, illustrating more than one plot device, that's a testament to the author and not from any shortage of candidates. I tried to include both genre classics and more recent examples.

Many of the cases in point are award-winning or widely popular, and often both. Other examples, I suspect, many readers will find unfamiliar. That, as software engineers say, is a feature, not a bug: an opportunity to discover new material and authors. And while my own stories and novels contributed only a small fraction of the examples, neither did I shy away from naming my own. There's an advantage in knowing *exactly* what the author had in mind.

If this book helps genre readers to better appreciate the underpinnings of hard SF or inspires even a few readers to careers in science or technology (as SF pointed me to my first career), or proves useful as a reference—or a source of story ideas—for SF writers, I'll be most gratified.

On, then, to science and tropes. We'll begin with a trope that applies broadly across the genre: the ability to communicate with beings from other times, places, lines of evolution, and dimensions....

SAY, WHAT?

Ruminations about Language, Communications, and Science Fiction

Vanguard's *bridge was a lonely and boring place, but as a matter of tradition watch officer Joan Miller served her shift without complaint. To come upon more than a mote of dust or fleck of ice here in the depths of interstellar space would make the shift eventful indeed.*

Only suddenly something was *out here, and it was no mere fleck of ice.*

Eyes wide, Joan studied her sensor array. Gravitational waves had drawn her attention. Something was making those waves. Something massive, moving fast, exploiting technology far beyond that of Earth. Something heading straight at her.

A ship?

Her heart pounded. At long last, humanity might have found a companion intelligence.

Before Joan could decide how to share the momentous discovery with her shipmates, an LED flickered on the comm console. With a trembling hand, she accepted the hail. Her holo tank filled with what brought to Joan's mind the crossing of a walrus with a lobster. It wore an ornate garment of some sort, replete with sash, braid, buttons, medals, and gold epaulets upon its (four) shoulders.

"I say," the creature began, its chitinous mandibles sliding over one another, its brush-like mustache wriggling, "Jolly good show meeting here, eh wot?"

·· ◆ ··

19

Threw you right out of the story, didn't I?

Why does the walrus/lobster know English, let alone speak English like a refugee from a Gilbert and Sullivan operetta? With chitinous mandibles, how does it even make sounds reminiscent of human speech?

We'll chalk up that dreadful story snippet to making a point. To wit: in science fiction, language and communication details matter. In this chapter we'll look at how language and communications can enrich an SF story—and at ways to bypass the related complications when communications details are less than central to the tale. (Our topic goes beyond human-alien encounters. As we'll see, languages can change over time. Stories set in any era besides our own [including, but not limited to time-travel stories] should consider language issues, too. Ditto alternate-universe stories, even those set on a parallel "Earth.")

Let's begin by considering how different from English even human languages can get.

Variability in human languages: the view from low Earth orbit

No overview can begin to do justice to the range of differences among human languages.[3] If you've studied any second language (or English is your second language), you already have a window into the many ways that humans differ over the nature of languages. Without exhausting the range of variations from English among human languages, consider:

- How many tenses should there be? Spanish has two past tenses, one for events that definitely occurred once and another for events that repeat or continue.

- What's the domain of gender? French and German assign genders to inanimate objects.[4]

- How many pronouns are needed? English, since it (mostly) eliminated *thee* and *thou*, has nearly eliminated the distinction between familiar and formal pronouns. The exception—most evident, one supposes, in the UK—is the royal we.

- What building-block sounds comprise a language? English lacks the guttural "ch" of Scottish, German, and Hebrew. Western languages lack the clicks of southern African languages like Xhosa and Zulu.

- How should languages be symbolized? Humans haven't agreed, with billions of us embracing alphabetic systems and billions more using logographs and syllabaries.

With such variability among human languages, how likely is our walrus/lobster friend to speak English?

Let's get physical

Humans evolved to communicate via modulated sound waves. Fair enough: the noises we make can cross moderately long distances through the atmosphere, are reasonably non-directional, and can encode complex messages. But what other methods might have worked?

It requires no great stretch of imagination to suppose communication by modulating emitted (or reflected) light. Terrestrial life offers early steps in that direction. Pit vipers have infrared sensors apart from their eyes.[5] Octopi and squids camouflage themselves and signal emotion through changes in skin color.[6]

And why limit ourselves to visible and near-visible light when the electromagnetic spectrum is so broad? Aquatic life as varied as sharks, lungfish, and catfish have rudimentary electric-field sensors.[7, 8] Many migratory birds orient themselves with magnetic sensors.[9]

Other terrestrial species communicate by gesture (the dance of bees[10]) and chemically (ants leaving pheromone trails to guide foraging expeditions[11]). Human sign languages demonstrate that a gesture-based language can convey information in as nuanced a manner as voice. As one example among many, consider American Sign Language.[12] And while chemicals released into wind or water seem an unreliable means of communication, chemical packets physically delivered to a receptor—no different, in principle, than handing someone a written note—could be quite reliable.

It's far from certain that language-capable aliens will use sound waves for their communications.

Picture this

Humans evolved to communicate with sounds, but (mostly) we perceive the world visually. "I see" is synonymous for "I understand." How different would languages be if communication and primary perception shared a medium?

Consider dolphins and their sonar-based navigation. Their sonic pings return a 3-D representation of the nearby ocean. Can dolphins imitate those echoes? If so, they can directly communicate 3-D images to their pod mates (as do, for example, the enhanced dolphins in David Brin's Uplift universe).* And if dolphins can emit sonic images of real scenes, why not also sonic images of imagined items?

---

* Written SF appears in many formats. For clarity, references to written examples are shown as:

- *Italic* for novel titles (including novels that appeared only as serials).
- "In quotes" for titles of fiction at shorter than novel length.
- Mixed Case for names of fiction series, whether a series of novels, or shorter fiction, or a combination.

As an example, Nancy Kress expanded her 1991 novella "Beggars in Spain" into the 1993 novel *Beggars in Spain*. The latter became the first novel of the Beggars series (or as listed in some venues, the Sleepless series).

Hopefully not too confusingly, the names of magazines also appear (as per customary usage) in *italic*. Ditto, TV series and movies. Individual episodes of a TV series, when cited, are named "in quotes."

It's not a big step from envisioning sonar-imaging dolphins in Earth's oceans to radar-imaging aliens on another planet.

A familiar adage has it that a picture is worth a thousand words. Certainly human languages require many words to describe a visual scene. Our languages would be quite different if we could directly "paint" pictures.

Where am I?

Languages encapsulate, among other things, our understanding of the world and our relationship to it. How might languages differ if our sense of the physical world differed?

Proprioception is the sense by which we relate the position of our body parts to each other and to the external world.[13] Humans are bilaterally symmetric, with sensors that favor a particular direction (i.e., define "forward").* Reflective of our physiology and proprioception, our speech is rife with references to that which is in front of, next to, and behind us. We place quite different values on what transpires to our faces and behind our backs.

Creatures with body plans other than ours might perceive—and describe—the world quite differently than humans do. Imagine a trilaterally symmetric alien, with limbs and sensory clusters spaced every 120° around its body. It walks, reaches, and senses equally well in any direction. Front/back and left/right distinctions do not apply. *No* reference solely to its body suffices to locate an object—or a fellow alien—relative to itself.

In my 2005 novel *Moonstruck*, the Krulirim have this body plan. I had to give these aliens a magnetic sense. A Krul locates an object in part by reference to the angle between a line toward the thing and a line toward the nearest magnetic pole.

---

* Most of us aren't even quite bilaterally symmetric—we're left- or right-handed. And so (righties being chauvinists), English offers us *gauche* (from the French word for left), as a synonym for tasteless and vulgar, and *sinister* (from the Latin word for left) as a synonym for threatening and creepy.

With my left/right, front/back relationship to the world, it's natural for me to locate an item as (for example) "three meters in front of me and four meters to my right." A Krul (ignoring its use of meters and degrees as units of measure) might say in that circumstance that the item is "five meters distant from me and in a direction thirty degrees east from my bearing to the North Pole."

Now imagine the Krul relating the relative positions of separated objects or describing those objects' positions to another Krul. The Krul's propriocentric sense—and so, its language—necessarily deals with trigonometry.

Consider group minds like, but more intelligent than, the bees of a hive.* What sort of proprioception—if any—might the collective mind have? How might its propioceptive "read-out" change as the collective's members disperse and re-gather? How would one such collective mind describe the position of an object relative to itself? To another collective mind?

A moving target

Languages evolve.

Vocabulary changes. We don't exactly speak like characters in a Shakespeare play. ("Who would fardels bear?" Hamlet asks in his famous soliloquy. A *fardel*, it turns out, is a Middle English term for a burden.) Or consider end-of-year "top word" lists (a couple of recent examples: H1N1 and [as a verb denoting concise communication] twitter). Consider the flood of terms entering the language from:

- Company names (like Xeroxing and Googling).

- Acronyms (like RN, UFO, SAT, and AIDS).

- Commercials and popular culture (like "Where's the beef?")

---

* Or less extreme (from a human perspective) than an intelligent hive, the Tines: intelligent packs of dog-like, ultrasound-linked creatures in Vernor Vinge's 1992 *A Fire Upon the Deep*.

24

- Cultural evolution (like "Ms." as an honorific and "they" as a gender-neutral singular pronoun).[14]

- Science and technology (everything from a veritable bestiary of subatomic particles* to such neologisms as dark matter, blog, and carbon footprint).

- Current events (such as anything with the -gate suffix, from the name of a hotel that saw "a third-rate burglary attempt").

Expressions go in and out of vogue. (Is "out of vogue" yet out of vogue?) "Hold your horses" is, to be charitable, on the dated side. "Too big to fail" is a recent coinage reflecting events that we would all be happier not to have experienced. Verbs become nouns, and vice versa, such that dynamite and telephone can be either part of speech.[†,‡] Idioms borrow from literature (say, "Catch-22") and from mythology (say, Pandora's Box) in ways that don't translate.

Pronunciations change, too, sometimes for no better reason than that people can't always be bothered to enunciate clearly. English is full of anachronistic spellings: time capsules. And so it is that "rough" rhymes with "tough," but neither rhymes with "though."

Languages fragment and diverge. For example, around 500 B.C. Proto-Germanic split off from Indo-European. About a millennium later, one of Proto-Germanic's many offshoots split into High and Low German—high and low being geographic distinctions—on the figurative road to modern German and Dutch (and amid that split, pronunciations shifted, too.) The

---

* Even subatomic particles can have nicknames. The Higgs boson—a manifestation of the Higgs field, which provides many particles with the attribute of mass—is sometimes referred to as the "God particle."

† As a *Calvin and Hobbes* cartoon would have it, "Verbing weirds language."

‡ Dynamite can even be an adjective, as in: that was a dynamite party last night.

fallen Western Roman Empire's onetime European territories evolved various "Romance" languages (such as French, Italian, Spanish, Portuguese, and Catalan) by blending Latin with the local vernaculars, the local vernacular being variable, too, as Goths, Huns, Franks, and other ethnic groups shifted about Europe.

Languages collide. Redundant terms speak to successive conquests of England. Think house (from the German "haus") and (upscale, from Old French, because the Normans were the last to conquer England) mansion.

Languages borrow from one another. You can travel Europe ordering a hamburger (in English, French, German, and Italian), *hamburguesa* (in Spanish), or *hampurilainen* (in Finnish). (As much as I enjoy hamburgers, I don't recommend this course of culinary action.)

National authorities also sometimes try (with mixed success) to resist such borrowings. Thus the "English" neologism *telephone* (from Greek roots *tele* [far] and *phone* [sound]) gave way for a time, by official decree, to the German neologism *Fernsprecher* (far speaker).[*] The English neologism *computer* was rejected in favor of the French neologism *ordinateur*.[†]

---

[*] My college German instructor, a grad student from Germany, taught that the Nazis purged many French and English technical terms. I find similar anecdotes on the Web, but nothing definitive—perhaps because I retained too little from that long-ago class to read articles in German.

Google Language Tools offers the following German translations for English telephone: *Telephon, Telefon, Fernsprecher, Apparat, Telephonapparat, Telefonapparat,* and *Fernsprechapparat.* Germans didn't simply adopt the (classically derived) term from the inventor's English.

[†] The French government has long taken an interest in language purity. *L'Académie française* (http://www.academie-francaise.fr/) was established in 1635 as the official arbiter of the French language. Enforcement of language standards is very real, as GE Medical Systems learned to its dismay in 2006 when a French court ordered translation from English of all internal technical documents.

So note: *L'Académie française* prefers that you order *viande hachée* in lieu of that proverbial hamburger.

How quickly do languages change? Without attempting to quantify change, conversation with adults merely one generation younger or older than I suggests an answer. Very. For one fascinating fictional example based on historical language shifts, see the 2009 short story "Come-From-Aways," by linguist Tony Pi.

In short, human languages reflect more than our physiology—they reflect our history, technology, and sociology, too. Aliens' languages may have similarly complicated origins.

Time out

What about stories set in Earth's future? Humans aren't evolving so quickly we need to worry about changes to future humans' sense organs or body plan.* Or we can set our stories in the past to preclude changes to human nature.

As we saw earlier, languages transform over time. Set a story in another era without addressing the language differences ("Chill out, dude," Socrates said) and something is apt to seem amiss.

Communicating with strangers: the easy cases

If two languages—and the beings who created them—are sufficiently similar, the difficulty can be finessed. After all, people *do* learn new languages. A story that opens long after humans and aliens (or whomever) first met can credibly assume that at least one side's linguists previously figured out the other's language.

Translation programs are common even today, although the current state-of-the-art in translation software is as often humorous as helpful. Correct and complete translation requires an understanding of both languages, their historical contexts, idioms, and literary traditions. Translation software, at its core, is

---

* Or do we? In the not-so-distant future, we might learn to gengineer gills or new senses, enhance our natural senses with implanted prostheses, or upload our minds into (among the possibilities) a virtual reality, robotic shell, or cloned body. We look at "Human 2.0" later in the book.

a matter of artificial intelligence—and AI is certainly a staple of science fiction. (Also, the subject of two chapters toward the end of this book.)

Stories dealing with travel to the past have a lower language hurdle. (Have you kept track of the metaphors that keep intruding? Pondered whether they're apt to translate?) Our Hero can research the historically appropriate dialect of the language he'll find spoken at his destination before jumping through time. Even then, the time traveler may, and probably should, be surprised once he arrives by idioms and pronunciation shifts absent from the historical record.

So much for the easy cases. What happens when the others' languages, native environments, or worldviews are very different from ours?

Language-related tropes

SF authors use many tropes to circumvent the problem of human/alien communications.

The simplest science-fictional language trope, so deeply embedded as to go unnoticed, is the *universal language*. It's not that everyone suddenly adopts Esperanto.[15] Rather, future (or alien) science has discovered principles that—unknown to human science today—underlie all communications. Anyone knowledgeable of the underlying principles of the universal language can readily master any other language.

Does the universal language exist? No one has disproven it, so its use remains fair game for SF. That said, it's difficult to imagine what underlying principles could encompass the many historical and physiological differences between human and all alien languages.*

---

* A *universal language* goes far beyond any hypothesized *universal grammar* (an overly broad term for any language-learning capabilities hardwired into the human brain, à la Noam Chomsky) and *linguistic universals* (supposed building blocks common across all languages, à

Humans, with the advantage of a common physiology, have yet to achieve a global language.[*][†] Technological shortcomings might once have precluded convergence on a single human language, but with radio, television, the Internet, and on-demand publishing, we could—at least among the high-tech societies— standardize on a single language. I don't foresee that happening anytime soon. That begs the question: how many languages are apt to be extant within an alien civilization? If only one, that discovery alone would suggest interesting cultural differences between those aliens and humanity.

If a universal language exists, that's no guarantee everyone is physically able to receive or express a particular species's realization of it. One may still need a *universal translator* to convert between such disparate formats as aroma blends and modulated sound waves. The universal translation device is only as plausible as the language skills and technological mechanisms by which it has been implemented.

The *Star Trek* franchise makes frequent use of a universal translator—or a not-quite-universal translator when plot logic requires a bit of misunderstanding. Viewers accept the (il)logic because a new linguistic puzzle every week would get tedious.

---

la Joseph Greenberg). Proof even of the latter, among merely human languages, is hard to come by—and controversial.

See "MIT claims to have found a 'language universal' that ties all languages together: A language universal would bring evidence to Chomsky's controversial theories," Cathleen O'Grady, *Ars Technica*, August 6, 2015, http://arstechnica.com/science/2015/08/mit-claims-to-have-found-a-language-universal-that-ties-all-languages-togethert/. (And I agree with you, that headline ought to have named Greenberg, not Chomsky.)

[*] Or we had a global language and lost it, if you take literally the Tower of Babel story.

[†] If George Bernard Shaw is to be believed, even a shared language has its limits. To wit: "England and America are two countries divided by a common language."

Perhaps we or the aliens can bypass the incompatible-language barrier through *telepathy*. Setting aside (until the chapter on "Alternate Abilities") questions of how—even at the handwavium level of a trope—mind reading might work, this hypothesis raises questions about the relationship between thought and language. Unless thought operates independently of language (which doesn't seem to be the case in my head), or thought uses the undiscovered universal language, it's hard to see how telepathy can overcome language barriers.

What about a form of telepathy that bypasses language by directly transferring images, sounds, smells, or sensations of touch? Even among humans, that would be disorienting! Neuroplasticity enables each of us to adapt to idiosyncratic sensor shortcomings, such as degrees of color blindness, any loss of acuity to particular audio frequencies, and the like. We're also idiosyncratic with respect to which and how many aspects of a scene or soundscape or olfactory background we focus on or tune in, with varying tolerances for distraction.

Inter-species information transfers (seeing and hearing in different frequency bands? Using different sensory suites altogether?) could only make raw-data-based mind-to-mind transfers *more* problematical.

Whether in words or pictures, for telepathy to work across species—especially species with disjoint neural mechanisms and biochemistries—requires an additional leap of faith. Consider the range of possible data formats. If analog: modulated onto the strength/weakness or prevalence/scarcity of what underlying medium? If digital: using what symbol set, and with what type of error-correcting coding? If neural, which chemical(s) are involved, at what concentrations? Is information localized, as in familiar digital storage, or distributed, as in holograms and our own neural wiring? That's only a small sample of the variability we might encounter among independently evolved biospheres.

(And you thought HD-DVD vs. Blu-ray was a thorny problem.)

Finally—and not for the faint of heart—we come to the shush!-we've-all-agreed-to-look-the-other-way language trope. The *Stargate: Atlantis* franchise features remote worlds whose populations descended from humans abducted thousands of years earlier. Pegasus Galaxy humans speak English even though their ancestors left Earth before there *was* English. It's an impressive feat that certainly moves along the storyline. Just try not to think about it....

Putting it all into words

So: your fictional aliens, alternate-Earth residents, and humans from other eras have language(s)—or at a minimum, pronunciation(s) and vocabulary(ies)—different from our own. By technology or by trope (this expression is hereby offered as a replacement for "by hook or by crook"; reasonable terms available) the human or human-empathetic characters establish communications. An important question remains: how, within the story, do we represent that communication? Writers have used many techniques:

- Foreign words or short phrases rendered into a familiar character set sprinkled into otherwise English text. Items without human equivalents, like advanced technologies of the aliens, retain their alien character. (For example, the bigger-than-worlds artifact that is the Ringworld is constructed from a substance so strong and dense that it blocks a substantial fraction of solar neutrinos. That's amazing stuff, without any human equivalent. And so, throughout Larry Niven's Ringworld series, that material goes by the natives' term: *scrith*.)

- As above, but with foreign usages limited to proper names. Guillaume, when he visits London, may speak English, but he doesn't start referring to himself as William. (Of course English readers can pronounce, to greater and

31

lesser degrees, the name Guillaume. What if the alien names are hard or impossible to pronounce? I have it on good authority—read: irate emails—that such words annoy some readers. Should I as an author avoid hard-to-pronounce terms? Perhaps sometimes: when language cues aren't meant to emphasize the alien nature of the nonhumans.)

- Alien concepts sprinkled into dialogue, whether literally or metaphorically. In *Trial by Fire* (2014), Charles E. Gannon enriches the translated speech of the exosapient Arat Kur using metaphors that emphasize their alien/subterranean nature.

- Aliens with great language skills, who have mastered English so that the human characters (and readers) don't have to learn, say, Tau Cetian.

- Arcane word orders that make the English *seem* alien. (In the *Star Wars* universe, Yoda and Jar Jar Binks, think of you will. Better yet, don't think of them. Annoying, they are. Strong, the aggravation becomes. Weirdness, an inferior substitute for alien is. On the fantasy side of speculative fiction, J. R. R. Tolkien used archaic wordings to great effect to give Middle Earth a terrifically *other* feel.)

- Alien speech and writing rendered into non-Roman character sets, even to non-linguistic symbols such as musical notes, with translations offered nearby. (Such as the Mother-Thing alien sings/speaks in Robert A. Heinlein's 1958 *Have Space Suit—Will Travel*.)

Bottom line: the author must fit the technique(s) to the story. And nowhere is that challenge harder than where tropes just won't serve....

Search for Extraterrestrial Intelligence (SETI)

SETI inherently deals with another civilization's communications (a topic we'll revisit in "Alien AWOLs"). Suppose Earth's observatories hunt for extraterrestrial signals, perhaps transmitted our way as microwaves or laser beams. What formats of long-range communication might the aliens use? Suppose a signal is detected. What method(s) might extract the signal's meaning? If a signal seems intended for us, how will we ascertain what the aliens are attempting to convey? If a signal seems accidental—their analogue, perhaps, of *American Idol*, spreading at light speed across the galaxy—what meaning might we manage, through cleverness, to extract?

It's hard to imagine a SETI story that is not at least somewhat concerned with the details of communication. Tropes won't do—there *is* no story without delving into the method by which the signal is received, what within the signal is understandable, or the cleverness with which that meaning is determined. In a SETI story, we can hardly start to understand the aliens by tapping our chests and over-enunciating our names.

How might we find meaning in an alien radio broadcast? It's not as though we can hope to uncover something like the Rosetta Stone.[16]

Except that for some messages *Nature* is a Rosetta Stone. To the extent physical laws are universal—and known to both parties—representations of those physical laws may provide a basis for mutual understanding.

Why *may*? Because common understanding of physical principles does not assure compatible representations. Newton and Leibniz, for example, developed quite different representations for differential calculus. Schrödinger's equation and Heisenberg's matrix mechanics are very different representations of quantum mechanics. And on, and on….

Lots of hard work would be required to establish a mutual understanding of the physical domain.

If limited translation succeeds from clues provided by physical laws, what then? It's less than intuitive how to proceed from a specialized vocabulary based upon shared physical discoveries to the broader vocabulary necessary to discuss unrelated-to-science topics. "Catch-22" is far afield from the periodic table.

I'm hardly the first SF writer to wonder how distant species might establish communications. Nor am I the first to suggest that the universality of physical laws would provide common ground. H. Beam Piper's novelette "Omnilingual" did the latter way back in 1957. The story involves astronauts finding the ruins of an extinct Martian civilization and one explorer recognizing a periodic table—and seeing its value in cracking open the Martian library.

My novelette "Dangling Conversations" (2000) opened with a SETI discovery and went on to delve deeply into interstellar message-coding issues. Expanded and combined with related stories, "Dangling Conversations" provided the opening segment of my novel *InterstellarNet: Origins* (2010). As the term InterstellarNet suggests, the communication mechanisms—and attendant challenges—grow complex over time.

A trail of bread crumbs

Earth's earliest transmissions were likely submerged in the naturally occurring radio emissions of the Sun,* but perhaps aliens with sensitive receivers can make out humanity's more recent

---

* As our discussion ranges across time and space, we'll encounter all manner of astronomical objects. Some object categories (such as planets and asteroids) have labels separate from the name of any particular example; other categories, alas, muddle the general and the specific.

For clarity, therefore, throughout this book I've capitalized the name of any uniquely identified astronomical object, and I've left uncapitalized the category labels for generic object classes. Hence:

- the Sun is the nearby star that warms Earth; a sun could be any star.
- the Moon is Earth's one natural satellite; a moon could be any satellite anywhere (such as, for example, Titan in orbit around Saturn or Europa in orbit around Jupiter).

transmissions. It'd be interesting if visitors were to back-track such signals and come calling already conversant in English (or Cantonese, or whatever).

But can Earth's transmissions teach human languages? Our broadcasts are hardly designed for an alien audience. The transmissions employ a multitude of frequencies (not all of which propagate equally well through the interstellar medium), carrier-wave modulation schemes (e.g., amplitude and frequency modulations), data representations (e.g., audio and audiovisual, analog and digital, "in the clear" and encrypted), and spoken languages. Superimposed over the unending radio and television chatter are powerful radar pulses.

Suppose nearby aliens (including those simply passing through the neighborhood) intercept Earth's transmissions of the past several decades. If their capabilities are sufficiently advanced—if, say, they've been civilized and technologized for much longer than humans—perhaps they will have mastered decoding or translation methods we primitives cannot yet imagine. If so, they may glean everything about us from our broadcast cacophony, including how to tap into the Internet, while en route.

That said, reconstructing video from TV broadcasts seems like a simpler task than extracting meaning from radio broadcasts or TV's audio subchannel. If so, imagine what impression video alone—say, from the evening news—might make. Perhaps humanity should hope that "we're here, and we use technology" is the only significance that distant visitors can attribute to our transmissions.

(My Krulirim discovered Earth by back-tracking TV broadcasts. And encountered, amid all that chatter…*Sesame Street*. Say

---

- the Solar System is the Sun (aka Sol, after the Roman sun god) and its planets, asteroids, etc.; a solar system is any star and its retinue.
- The Universe (or in some instances, the Multiverse—we'll come to that) is *everything*; a universe, while something enormously expansive, is one of many vast things.

what you will about Big Bird, his show might be educational for aliens, too.)

First Contact

First Contact stories up the ante: the interaction is face (or whatever) to face. Where SETI stories look for the commonalities among species that might enable communication, First Contact stories more often focus on our differences. It's hard to imagine a First Contact story in which inter-species differences don't manifest in contrasting worldviews and languages.

For example, the 1998 novella "Story of Your Life," by Ted Chiang, revolves around a linguist mastering the newly arrived aliens' (very alien) language, and the worldview implicit in it. She succeeds only when a physicist in the contact team recognizes an alternative perspective to how human physicists usually formulate physical laws. The linguistics/physics conundrums are laid out for the reader in a very striking story.[*]

Ryan W. Norris, in his 2016 novelette "Not Quite *Taterona Kempi*," offers a DNA-based communications scheme. Would-be readers can interpret its messages only by recourse to an Earthly ecosphere for reference. Long after humanity is gone, such messages might be translated by alien passersby or our evolutionary successors. In Norris's story, the eventual beneficiaries of an extinct humanity's time capsule had evolved from mice.

But from the Department of Special Cases…the SETI discovery or First Contact situation can itself be a trope, the author's way to make us think about ourselves and our culture. Challenges in translation, or the detailed process of learning a new language, are downplayed because the focus is on (a) the message *content* or (b) the unexpected *truths about ourselves* that the existence of aliens forces the human characters to confront.

---

[*] "Story of Your Life" is the basis of the 2016 movie *Arrival* (which omits the physics element of the story).

For example, consider *Planet of the Apes*, by Pierre Boulle. In this 1963 novel, far more than in the many subsequent movies, the ape/human reversal is blatantly allegorical. Major worldview or language differences would only have obscured the point.

From which we conclude

Tropes and translations, alphabets and aliens, worldviews and walruses...this chapter has covered a lot of ground.[17]

But for a particular story, what does this all mean? Should an alien-featuring story entail an alien language, complete with lexicon, syntax rules, and odd idioms? Should a time-travel story feature classical Greek or Elizabethan English? Or should authors gloss over the complexity, sticking with tropes?

It depends. The needs and logic of the story outweigh the alien creatures and the temporal displacements.

Back to our story

So why *does* our walrus/lobster friend speak like a Victorian English gentleman? Because parody is one more reason to break the rules—

And (check his uniform) he is the very model of a modern major-general.

I GOT THE LONG-DISTANCE BLUES

Why Interstellar Travel is Hard

There is a reason why faster-than-light travel appeals to the storyteller. In a word, because the Universe is *big*.

Suppose I wish to set a story on a planet of a star other than the Sun. The setting nearest Earth is the three-star Alpha Centauri system. Alpha Centauri C (aka, Proxima Centauri) is a red dwarf star ~4.22 light-years (LY) from Earth; its companions are a bit farther at 4.36 LY.

That 4.22 doesn't sound far, but only because our unit of measure, the LY, is so vast. Traveling at about 300,000 km/sec (186,000 miles/sec) in a vacuum, light goes about 10 trillion km (6 trillion miles) in one year. Using more precise numbers (9.46 trillion km/year) the distance to Proxima Centauri is ~39.9 trillion km. In scientific notation, that's 3.99×10^{13} km.

A *long* way to move my characters.

For comparison, consider "merely" the distances that separate Earth from more familiar objects.[18] The average distance between the Earth and the Moon—the limit, to date, of in-person human exploration—is only 3.84×10^5 km. The average distance from the Earth to the Sun, also known as one astronomical unit (AU), is ~1.5×10^8 km. From the Sun to Mars, the average distance is ~2.28×10^8 km, or 1.52 AU. (Earth and Mars approach each other more closely, on the order of 5.5×10^7 km

38

[or 0.37 AU.]) From the Sun to Pluto—only recently visited for the first time by a human-built space probe—is, on average, 5.9×10^9 km (39.5 AU).

Thirty-eight years after launch, NASA's *Voyager 1* probe—the fastest-moving object ever launched from Earth, having gone farther than anything else ever built by man—is ~20.1 billion km (134.3 AU) from the Sun.[19,*]

Let's contrast *Voyager 1*'s epic exploration with the distance separating the Sun from next-door neighbor Proxima Centauri. That's (20.1×10^9 km / 3.99×10^{13} km) ~ 5.04×10^{-4}. *Voyager 1* has traveled only a small fraction of one percent of the distance to the nearest star.

Past nearby stars, the numbers become yet more daunting. The Milky Way Galaxy—and who among us hasn't a soft spot in his heart for sagas of galactic empires?—is, loosely speaking, a disk measuring 100,000 LY in diameter and 1,000 LY thick.[20]

Storytelling without FTL

There are great science-fictional stories that embrace these challenges in distance and time. Some involve generation ships, like Brian Aldiss's *Starship* (1959) (in the UK, *Non-Stop* (1958)), Robert A. Heinlein's *Orphans of the Sky* (1963), Harry Harrison's *Captive Universe* (1969), and Kim Stanley Robinson's *Aurora* (2015). Other stories exploit the extreme time dilation of near-light-speed travel and the associated one-way trip to the future, in-

---

*   Fastest relative to what, you ask? *Voyager 1* is the fastest object headed away from the Sun, a bit faster than her sister spacecraft *Voyager 2* and than the *New Horizons* probe that recently streaked past Pluto.

    But not the fastest spacecraft of all. The *Helios A* and *Helios B* probes, long out of service, are in highly elliptical orbits around the Sun. At their closest approach to the Sun, or perihelion, these probes clip along at about 70 km/sec (versus about 17 km/sec for the outbound *Voyager 1*).

    See http://io9.com/5786083/what-are-the-fastest-spacecrafts-ever-built.

cluding Larry Niven's novelette "The Ethics of Madness" (1967), Poul Anderson's *Tau Zero* (1970) and Joe Haldeman's *Forever War* (1975). Yet others, like Andre Norton's *The Stars Are Ours* (1972) and Vernor Vinge's *A Deepness in the Sky* (1999), put the crews into suspended animation for the long, slow trip.

Starfaring without FTL: some options

As our *Voyager 1* experience suggests, chemical rockets aren't going to support interstellar travel. Even to loft a satellite into low Earth orbit, at a velocity of ~8 km/sec, burns a lot of fuel. Most fuel serves to carry the fuel to carry the fuel to...carry the payload.

We know how, in principle, to do better. That is, we can conceptualize propulsion technologies that rely upon fuels of a much higher energy density (read: nuclear) and/or in which ships don't carry fuel at all. Examples:

- Solar sailing. Light from a star pushing against a large surface yields a slow but steady acceleration over a long time. The Japanese *Ikaros* probe successfully demonstrated the technology in 2010.[21]

- Photon-beam propulsion. Sunlight dims rapidly with distance (a pesky inverse square law is at work), so substitute a high-intensity laser beam. The beam diverges slowly with distance, and so the overall system performs better than strictly solar sailing. (Quite possibly, a space-based, solar-powered, phased array of lasers would be used. Atmosphere would then neither dilute the sunlight powering such an array nor scatter its beam.*) And in breaking

---

* But be careful where you situate any such interstellar-grade energy projector. A powerful space-based energy beam, laser or otherwise, when suitability mis-targeted, becomes a weapon of mass destruction.

  In my 2012 novel *Energized*, the boon-turned-bane system was the high-intensity microwave beam intended to down-link power generated aboard a miles-square Earth-orbiting solar power satellite.

news during my final edit pass: a Russian billionaire has pledged $100M to develop a swarm of gram-scale probes for an Alpha Centauri flyby. The Breakthrough Starshot project envisions using ground-based lasers to speed its tiny solar-sail probes on their way.[22]

- Electric sailing. Replace a gossamer sheet that catches sunlight with a few miles-long high-voltage wires. The fast-streaming, positively charged protons of the solar wind push against the electric field projected by the positively charged wires.[23]

- Magnetic sailing / mass-beam propulsion. The magnetic field projected by one's ship reacts against an incoming beam of electrically charged particles. The complication, of course, is that charged particles repel one other—they won't stay in a tight beam. So: a mass projector must propel vast numbers of electrically neutral pellets at high speed toward the starship. Shipboard lasers vaporize and ionize the incoming pellets *just* before they arrive.[*,24]

- Nuclear-explosion propulsion (aka Project Orion). Lob a nuclear device behind your ship. The explosion presses against a pusher plate (remember to put a *big* shock absorber between the plate and crew portions of your ship). Repeat.[25]

- Fusion rocket. Fuse hydrogen into a very hot (read: high speed) helium exhaust.

- Bussard ramscoop. Your fusion rocket projects magnetic fields to sweep up hydrogen fuel from the diffuse inter-

---

That satellite was constructed, mostly by robotic labor, from materials mined from an asteroid captured to Earth orbit.

* A ship's magnetic field can also push against planetary and solar magnetospheres, but (as with pure solar sailing) the propulsive potential diminishes quickly with distance. On the other hand, repelling the solar wind at a voyage's destination can help a starship to decelerate.

stellar medium. Fuel collection increases with the ship's speed and (the somewhat variable) density of interstellar gas. Onboard fusion fuel is needed for preliminary acceleration and final deceleration.[*]

None of which is to suggest that building a starship and/or its external propulsion system will be easy. And for anything other than a flyby mission, all the energy that went into accelerating a vessel to high velocity must (somehow) be shed at the other end. It might be prudent, for reasons beyond advanced scouting, for the first mission sent to another star to be robotic. That pioneer—or the robot swarms whose construction it would oversee—could be tasked (in part) to build deceleration infrastructure, such as a powerful laser battery or mass-beam projector, for use by any vessels to follow. (Robot hordes that disassembled asteroids with which to build vast solar-powered structures in space will have played a role in getting the starship launched in the first place.)

As a quantitative example, consider Project Daedalus: the British Interplanetary Society concept for sending an unmanned probe to Barnard's Star. Barnard's Star is, after Alpha Centauri, the Sun's closest neighbor, "only" 6 LY away.

The Daedalus mission envisions using a fusion rocket. Setting off with fifty thousand tonnes—one tonne, a metric unit, equals 1.1 American standard tons—of helium-3 and deuterium as fusion fuel, reaching a peak velocity of 12% of light speed, the spacecraft delivers a 450 tonne payload into orbit around its target star after fifty-six years.

---

[*] Or a ramscoop might not work at all. Much of the interstellar medium takes the form of hydrogen ions, and a magnetic field moving through a sea of ions experiences drag. You can find arguments on both sides of whether a Bussard ramscoop is practical.

For people in the "won't work" camp, a silver lining: magnetic wings, such as a Bussard ramscoop would deploy, may offer an excellent way to slow down at the end of an interstellar journey.

Why interstellar travel is hard

No matter the propulsion technology, we are adding energy to an object to impart velocity. From Newtonian mechanics (that is, at velocities too low for relativistic effects to manifest), the kinetic energy (KE) intrinsic to an object of mass *m* and velocity *v* is:

1. $KE = (1/2) * m * v^2$

If we aspire to cross interstellar distances in less than millennia, that velocity-squared factor is problematical. Consider spacecraft A and B, with B moving twice as fast as A. B has *four times* the kinetic energy of A. (Read: B's propulsion system must impart four times the energy.) If spacecraft C is three times as fast as A, C has *nine times* the kinetic energy of A. And so on.

How much kinetic energy is in a one-kilogram mass moving at one-tenth light speed?[*] By equation (1), and expressing light speed in meters (not, as before, kilometers) per second,

$$KE = (1/2) * m * v^2$$
$$= (1/2) * 1 \text{ kg} * (0.1 * (3 \times 10^8 \text{ m/sec}))^2$$
$$= 0.5 * 1 * (9 \times 10^{14} \text{ kg m}^2 / \text{sec}^2)$$
$$= 4.5 \times 10^{14} \text{ joules}$$

A joule, more familiarly, is the energy that produces one watt of power for one second. A typical nuclear power plant has a capacity of ~1 gigawatt (10^9 watts). So: the kinetic energy of a one-kilogram mass moving at one-tenth light speed equals the energy output of 100 nuclear power plants running at full

---

[*] Coasting requires no new energy. The challenge is to *accelerate* the object up to its coasting speed. No energy transfer is 100% efficient, so the actual energy expended will always exceed the kinetic energy of the accelerated object.

capacity for 4500 seconds (75 minutes). That's not an easy amount of energy to impart to an object.

It's more than 4 LY to the nearest star. A ship and crew will weigh much more than one kilogram. And a ship expends as much energy to stop as to start.

Interstellar travel is challenging.

Why relativity makes things *really* hard

Albert Einstein's special relativity takes as axiomatic—it does not derive—that the speed of light is constant (in a particular medium). Acceptance of special relativity demanded a revolutionary shift in physicists' worldview: for the speed of light to be always and everywhere the same, space and time must be malleable. But Einstein's insight served to explain the otherwise enigmatic results of the Michelson-Morley experiment.[26]

(Here's a quick overview of that enigma. In algebra texts and Newtonian physics, speeds add. A car northbound at 60 mph and a car southbound at 60 mph converge at 120 mph.

Earth has an orbital velocity of ~30 km/sec. Send light beams in the direction of Earth's orbital motion, and perpendicular, and behind. This time, we do not see velocities adding: all three light beams have the same measured speed. Speed = distance/time, and to make the math work out, time and/or distance must change. Hence, relativity speaks of four-dimensional space-time.)

From the constant-speed-of-light axiom, by fairly straightforward math, flowed consequences that could be—and have been repeatedly—verified.

Special relativity predicts that the faster an object moves, the more massive it becomes. Consider a mass m (measured at rest) moving at a constant velocity v (relative to you).* The speed of

---

*   Situations with an accelerating frame(s) of reference fall—pun intended, if you get it—into the domain of general relativity (GR), and are quite messy mathematically. Exact solutions wouldn't change my basic points.

light—relative to anyone—is denoted by *c*. The relativistic mass *M* for that object is:

2. $M = m / SQRT (1 - v^2/c^2)$

To date, humanity's space ventures have involved v << c. (*Very* much less. *Voyager 1*, its speed boosted by the gravitational-sling-shot effect of its Jupiter close encounter, is tearing away from the Sun with a relative speed of…less than 18 km/sec. That's about 6×10^{-5} of light speed.) In these circumstances, the v^2/c^2 term is effectively zero, the square-rooted quantity is effectively 1, and so M~m. But if we plan to travel between stars within, say, a human lifetime, then v needs to be an appreciable fraction of c. And as (2) informs us, the faster a mass moves, the larger its relativistic mass:

v/c	M/m
0.1	1.005
0.2	1.021
0.5	1.155
0.9	2.294
0.99	7.089
0.999	22.366

With each increment of velocity, the object becomes yet more massive. (That statement is not mere theory: relativistic mass is a factor in the operation of particle accelerators, where-in effects on the orders of thousands are observed.[27]) So: at high speeds, the kinetic energy of a moving object increases rapidly with mass *and* velocity.

(A probably apocryphal story has it that in the early days of GR someone told astrophysicist Sir Arthur Eddington that he [Edding-ton] must be one of only three people in the world who fully under-stood GR. Eddington is said to have gone silent—not from modesty, but trying to think who the third person could be.)

And the source of that additional mass? It's converted from (is a transformation of) energy. From the most famous equation of special relativity (or, possibly the entirety of physics):

3. $E = mc^2$

As c^2 is a large number, manifesting even a tiny amount of mass entails a lot of energy.

As v approaches c, the square-rooted quantity in (2) approaches zero—and for any nonzero value of rest mass, M approaches infinity. The energy to accelerate an object (no matter how little its rest mass) to light speed is infinite.

So: no object having mass can reach the speed of light. Photons, the "particles" of light itself, have zero mass. (Neutrinos *do* have mass. That's one reason why the 2011 reports of FTL neutrinos—since debunked; more on that topic in "Faster Than a Speeding Photon"—were so puzzling. How could they have been accelerated to that speed?)

More complications

Suppose we build a near-light-speed starship. As it plows through the interstellar medium, its speed converts otherwise harmless traces of gas and dust into highly energetic projectiles: cosmic rays. Our ship needs yet more mass, as shielding. While ionized particles can be deflected by electromagnetic shielding, not all particles are ionized.

(Here's a plus of magnetic sailing / mass-beam propulsion. The ionized remains of the pellets thrown at the starship get caught up in the magnetic field surrounding the ship. The plasma cloud that thus accumulates ahead of the starship, far denser than the interstellar medium—but still *extremely* tenuous—will intercept much of that oncoming cosmic muck.*)

---

* On the other hand, a magnetic-sailing starship needs some shielding astern to handle the occasional wayward pellet the starship's lasers miss and thus fail to ionize.

Our ship will also encounter...photons. Just as a fire-truck siren sounds higher pitched—of a shorter wavelength—as we drive toward it, the light from the star we approach is shifted to a shorter wavelength. The shorter the wavelength of light, the higher its frequency and the higher the energy of each photon.

The faster our ship, the more dramatic that frequency shift. What would otherwise be harmless visible-wavelength light strikes our ship as ultraviolet, then (as we go faster) as X-rays, then (as we go faster still) as gamma rays. Photons carry no electric charge; like neutral matter, they cannot be deflected by electromagnetic shielding.

Physical shielding, such as a lead sheath, makes our ship more massive—and yet harder to accelerate to high speeds.

And just for completeness

These challenges aside, suppose one can push a spacecraft up toward light speed. It turns out that more changes—as seen from our Earth frame of reference—than the ship's mass. A clock aboard the spacecraft ticks slower than a clock that is at rest. (Time dilation has been confirmed, too: broadcasts from GPS satellites must correct for this effect.) For a ship of mass m traveling at velocity v, a shipboard interval of time T relates to the interval t observed on the ground according to the relationship:

4. $T = t \, / \, \mathrm{SQRT} \, (1 - v^2/c^2)$

For $v \ll c$, the square-rooted quantity is effectively one; shipboard and earthbound clocks measure time's passage similarly. For v of ~0.866 c, the denominator in (4) reduces to one-half. The clock ticks once aboard ship for every two ticks on the ground. Put another way, the shipboard clock runs at half the pace of the earthbound clock. For values of v approaching c, the denominator approaches zero; an observer on Earth sees the shipboard clock at a standstill. (We'll revisit time dilation later in the book, in "Here We Go Loopedy Loop," in the context of time travel.)

Special relativity likewise predicts that a fast-moving object observed from at rest will appear contracted in the direction of motion. Let a ship approach light speed and—you guessed it—to an outside and stationary observer, the ship's apparent size in the direction of travel shrinks toward zero.

Wrapping up

That's some of the basic physics of interstellar travel. (In a later chapter, we'll consider some more speculative—but quite serious—physics that might change aspects of the problem.) Assuming we master the physics, though, can we travel to other stars?

Perhaps—but there's other science, particularly biology and medicine, to be considered.

To read further

- *Interstellar Travel and Multi-Generational Space Ships*, edited by Yoji Kondo, Frederick C. Bruhweiler, John Moore, and Charles Sheffield.

- *Starship Century: Toward the Grandest Horizon*, Gregory Benford and James Benford, editors.

- "A Photon Beam Propulsion Timeline," Paul Gilster, June 24, 2016, https://www.centauri-dreams.org/?p=35862.

Rising to the Challenge

Among the simplest explanations for the Fermi Paradox (right after "We *are* alone in the Universe.") would be that communicating or traveling between stars is simply too hard.* Does that make all science fiction of an interstellar nature merely a willing-suspension-of-disbelief pact between storyteller and audience?

Are we all starship trope-ers?

Perhaps. But in 2014 I spent a long weekend with a couple hundred people, from twelve countries, determined to prove there *is* a way to the stars—and who are working to make that happen within a century.

100 Year Starship

Back in 2011, NASA and DARPA† cosponsored the first 100 Year Starship conference. The purpose of that gathering was "to

---

*   The paradox: if, as some suppose, the vast Universe *must* be home to other intelligent beings, why don't we find any evidence of them? Why haven't we detected their radio transmissions, or seen their starships, or found some trace of their past stopovers?

      For (much) more about the absence of such evidence and many possible explanations, see the upcoming chapter "Alien AWOLs: The Great Silence."

†   That's the Defense Advanced Research Projects Agency, best known—

TROPE-ING THE LIGHT FANTASTIC

begin studying what it would take—organizationally, technically, sociologically and ethically—to send humans to another star, a challenge of such magnitude that the study alone could take a hundred years."[28]

How was such an epic study to be performed? By enlisting, initially with DARPA seed funds, an organization dedicated to that long-term project. That initial conference and its grant competition led to several forward-looking endeavors and follow-on symposia.

100 Year Starship (100YSS) is the organization that came about directly from the grant competition, and whose 2014 annual symposium I had the good fortune to attend. In this chapter, I'll draw (in part) upon that symposium's technical-track and plenary sessions—and from cocktail-party conversations and chance hallway encounters—to give a big-picture look at the challenges of interstellar travel. I won't cite any symposium papers, because the proceedings are quite pricey. I've referenced other supporting material where available.

And expect the occasional SFnal citation. Many among the symposium presenters did the same.[*]

More reasons why interstellar travel is hard

As the proceeding chapter showed, to cross interstellar distances will require both new, far more powerful, means of propulsion and the taming of vast energies. 100YSS certainly includes those topics among its interests. I sat in on, for example, an update from NASA propulsion technologist (and SF author) Les Johnson on the state

---

outside the defense community, anyway—for the R&D that gave rise to the Internet. (The defense interest, back during the Cold War, was in creating a highly distributed, hence highly reconfigurable and fault tolerant, communication network to supplement the very hierarchical, very vulnerable, public switched telephone network.)

[*] Science Fiction Stories Night, a discussion among SF authors, was one of the main events. I was one of the panelists and (full disclosure) the symposium organizers reimbursed many of my costs to participate.

of solar sailing. I also saw a presentation by physicist Jeff Lee on exploiting the Hawking radiation of a quantum-scale black hole.*

Cool stuff, that, to be sure, but the last chapter already considered many candidate interstellar-drive technologies. For now, let's focus on other challenges to be faced on our way to becoming an interstellar civilization.

Staying in the loop

Humanity evolved in a particular environment. We rely upon Earth's air, water, gravity, and narrow range of temperatures. The planet's atmosphere and magnetic field protect us from solar ultraviolet radiation, solar wind, and cosmic rays. We share our world with a rich and varied web of life, upon which we depend for food and the very oxygen we breathe.

All of which must somehow be provided (or substituted for) throughout any spaceflight. Unless the Universe's speed limit turns out to be faster than light (and next chapter offers some possible loopholes), that artificial environment must be sustained, at the least, for years. Quite possibly, the environment must be sustained for generations. As the Biosphere Two experiments and the frequent resupply missions to the International Space

---

* I grant you, a quantum-scale black hole sounds small. It *is* small: far tinier than an atom, or even an atomic nucleus. But small needn't mean insignificant: a quantum black hole masses about three-quarter million tons, and spews out 100 petawatts per second. It will pump out energy for years before evaporating.

And a funny thing about black holes: the more one evaporates, the faster it emits energy. (Until the object has lost too much energy (which—recall your special relativity—is a form of mass) to remain a black hole. You *really* don't want to be around when that transition happens.)

For reference, the U.S. Energy Information Agency reports worldwide energy-production capacity in 2011 (the latest year for which data are available) at about 5.3 petawatts.

Humanity is—for now, perhaps for the best—unable to fabricate black holes.

Station both attest, we're a long way from knowing how to sustain a closed-loop ecosphere.

In a closed-loop, bounded environment, every type of resource is in limited supply. *Everything* must be reused. Tools, repair parts, furniture, and many other items will be produced as needed, then broken down and recycled, rather than tie up scarce room and materials. Whatever the daily shipboard processes turn out to be—perhaps to include agricultural, industrial, machine-shop fabrication, and 3-D printing activities—byproducts and waste, if only in trace amounts, will insinuate their way into the closed-loop environment.

Will the gradual accumulation of such contaminants degrade the ecosphere? Be toxic to crops or crew? Prove carcinogenic or mutagenic? Trigger addictive or allergic reactions?

Kim Stanley Robinson's *Aurora* (2015) does a fictional deep dive into these questions. The novel focuses on the struggle to maintain an ecosystem aboard a generation ship, considering such complications as variable rate of genetic drift among species and the trace losses of key elements (as they bond to surfaces here and there about the starship), all leading to "metabolic rifts." The overarching question of the novel: can life *ever* be transplanted from Earth?

If someday we can build generation ships, will we? A respect for the pace of technological progress might discourage any such attempt. Imagine taking part in a multigenerational trek, only to discover that the pristine world you hoped to settle had been claimed long ago by colonists who left the Solar System—long after your ancestors set out—aboard newer and faster ships. An FTL leapfrog of this sort was the premise of A. E. Van Vogt's short story "Far Centaurus" (1944). A non-FTL leapfrog is the basis of Robert J. Sawyer's short story "On the Shoulders of Giants" (2000).

Staying alive

A major theme of the symposium, with many subtopics, was keeping humans healthy while off Earth. In a summary as abbreviated as this, I can't always attribute a particular concept to a single life-sciences speaker. To everyone thus synopsized to anonymity, I apologize.

Let's consider some aspects of the life-support problem.

Among the health consequences of microgravity conditions is the gradual loss of bone mass. At least one extrapolation from astronaut experience to the duration of a round-trip Mars expedition suggests bone-mass loss similar in extent to two years of menopause. Will the deterioration continue as long as crew are in micro-gee, or will effects plateau after a period of acclimation? That remains unknown. Absent near-light-speed travel (so that, courtesy of relativistic time dilation, from the crew's perspective the journey seems short) or FTL technology, bone-mass loss on an interstellar flight could be severe.[*]

Bone mass doesn't just disappear. Minerals, mostly importantly calcium, lost from bone are processed through the kidneys. That's why astronauts are prone to develop kidney stones.

Nor is bone-mass loss the only health consequence of microgravity. The shifting of bodily fluids under these conditions increases intraocular pressure and can lead to degeneration of the optic nerve. That is, prolonged micro-gee can impair eyesight.

That's microgravity. What about unfamiliar levels of gravity? Will long periods spent on Mars or Europa, on worlds in other solar systems, or in the gravity-simulating context of a large, rotating, *2001: A Space Odyssey*-like spacecraft also impact health? Likewise, to be determined.

---

[*] Bone-mass loss in microgravity conditions (and candidate preventive measures) is itself a complex topic, with outcomes influenced by the extent of exercise, type of exercise equipment, and drug treatment. At least one exercise-and-drug regimen might limit long-term bone-mass loss to 15 percent.

See this chapter's final reference for a more complete discussion.

Of course even the longest experiences to date with microgravity are far briefer than any (non-FTL) interstellar transit.

Does the presence or strength of gravity play a role in the development of fetuses? Gestating in microgravity, at the least, may be problematical.[29]

Then there's radiation. Cancer is an obvious radiation hazard, but not the only one. Sustained cosmic rays can cause all manner of bodily injury, including brain damage.[30] Another danger: over the course of evolution, earthly life has incorporated into its DNA many long dormant retroviruses. If radiation should activate or mutate such retroviruses, we'll have no experience with, or immunity to, them.[31, 32] We already know that the spacecraft environment isn't friendly to our immune system.[33]

Nor will only human genes be at risk. Microbial hitchhikers (our "microbiome") outnumber human cells by ten to one.[34] These cohabiting cells will also be exposed to radiation and other unnatural aspects of the spacecraft environment. New diseases may emerge. Critical symbiotes may die off. Familiar diseases may become more potent and resistant to the pharmaceutical stocks with which the voyage began.[35]

Light-years from the rest of humanity, at risk of these difficult-to-pre-characterize hazards, the journey is certain to be stressful—and prolonged stress is yet another health risk. Among its effects, stress can negatively impact the immune system.

Lest anyone suppose this was a complete enumeration of interstellar travel's medical risks, some humility is in order. Not long ago medical science didn't know that our health requires trace nutrients. Geophysicists had no inkling that an invisible magnetic shield protects us from a deadly sleet of equally invisible solar and cosmic radiation.

Life aboard a starship may reveal things we don't yet know.

You are getting sleepy....

Several of the life-support challenges aboard a spaceship seem more tractable if passengers sleep their way to the stars. Passengers in deep sleep would use less food, water, and oxygen. They would generate less waste to be recycled (and less waste that, eluding recycling, degrades the shipboard environment). They would avoid the stress of years-long travel, and could be more readily sheltered from radiation.

Not surprisingly, crossing deep space in "cold sleep" is an SF staple (as in, for example, the *Aliens* movie franchise). But is cold sleep possible?

Marcel Dirkes, M. D., in his presentation on suspended animation, noted that state-of-the-art hypothermic treatment lowers human body temperature for days to the range of 86 to 93 °F. State-of-the-art cardiovascular support may lower body temperature for hours to the range of 68 to 78 °F. Set aside that those intervals are far too brief for an interstellar journey; at those temperatures, the body is still actively metabolizing—read: consuming food and oxygen.*

In contrast, hibernating mammals (the details varying by species) sustain temperatures of as low as 27 °F for months.

Dirkes cited experiments showing that hypoxia can trigger hibernation in mammal species that don't normally hibernate. Ordinary lab mice don't hibernate—until sealed in a chamber whose oxygen is lowered to 5% (versus the atmospheric norm of 21%). Thermal imaging of these mice shows their bodies uniformly reduced to ambient temperature. That is, the metabolism has shut

---

* That said, small reductions in body temperature may lead to useful savings. Days after the symposium, word came that NASA planners of 180-day (each way) Mars trips are investigating "therapeutic torpor" (in the 89 to 93 °F body-temperature range). The prospective benefit: a reduction in mission consumables from 400 to 220 tons.

   Of course to date, no one has spent more than a week in hypothermia and sedation, getting nutritional support all the while through an IV. Nor (in the scenario that the process can't safely be extended) has anyone gone through the cooling/sedating-and-reviving process over and over and over....

   See "Making the long trip to Mars? Let NASA put you in a deep sleep," by Anthony Domanico, *CNET*, October 6, 2014, http://www.cnet.com/uk/news/making-the-180-day-trip-to-mars-let-nasa-put-you-in-a-deep-sleep/.

down. After a few hours, the mice returned to normal—including their performance in cognitive tests—within an hour of normal oxygen levels being restored. If this process can be carried over to larger non-hibernating mammals—such as humans—especially over longer periods of time, that would be A Big Deal.

Alas, there isn't yet (as I type) evidence that human hibernation is possible. If it is, I wonder how this solution would compound the problem of preventing bone-mass loss. It's difficult to vigorously exercise in one's sleep.*

And on the other side

What about the alien life that might be encountered at the end of the journey?

Because we should anticipate extraterrestrial life whenever an interstellar mission sets its sights on an Earth-like world with a breathable atmosphere. Oxygen is highly reactive. That's why metal rusts. A planetary surface rich with rust—iron oxide—has given Mars its characteristic ruddy color.

The only known way to sustain an oxygen-rich atmosphere is to endlessly replenish the oh-two supply.† On Earth, that process involves cyanobacteria.

There's little reason to expect life on another world will be Just Like Us (and we'll explore that topic soon, in the chapter

---

* But perhaps not necessary for a hibernating person's bone health. The breaking down of bone is an active process that involves the action of specialized cells. If those specialized cells, too, hibernate, perhaps we'll discover that bone loss in humans can be stopped.

We do know that bears don't lose bone mass as they hibernate ("Why don't hibernating bears get osteoporosis?" Ned Rozell, August 21, 2014, http://www.gi.alaska.edu/alaska-science-forum/why-dont-hibernating-bears-get-osteoporosis). Of course, those bears weren't hibernating in micro-gravity conditions. I don't suppose anyone cares to loft a hibernating bear up to the International Space Station for a test there.

† That said, see the chapter "Alien Worlds: Not in Kansas Anymore" for speculation about a possible exception to the rule.

"Alien Aliens: Beyond Rubber Suits"). That said, there's no reason why alien life can't have *some* similarities. For example, biogenesis elsewhere may have favored the same common chemical elements—e.g., carbon, hydrogen, oxygen, nitrogen—that proved workable on Earth.

David Almandsmith observed that amino acids, the basic molecular components of terrestrial life, are often found in meteorites. For that matter, many organic compounds (and *organic chemistry* literally means carbon-based), amino acids among them, have been remotely sensed in distant nebulae. That's not to say amino-acid-based alien life must use the same amino acids as earthly life. Human biochemistry relies upon 20 distinct amino acids (or 22, or 23, depending which source you credit), but the gamut of possible amino acids (again, exact numbers varying by source) reaches well into the hundreds.[*,†,‡]

---

[*] Terrestrial DNA uses three consecutive nucleotide bases, each of which can be any of four types (that is, a three-letter genomic "word" written in four genomic "letters"), to encode for the production of a specific amino acid. 4 * 4 * 4 would seem to permit specifying any of 64 distinct amino acids, but that turns out not to be the case. After disallowing reserved combinations (that cellular machinery recognizes as "stop codes" to terminate a related sequence of amino acids) and multiple three-letter combinations that all code for the same amino acid, terrestrial biology gets down to the twenty-or-so amino acids earlier mentioned.

The four-letter alphabet appears to be arbitrary, given that cells have been altered in the lab to use six bases (which, sticking with a three-letter word to encode for a particular amino acid, allows many more combinations). See "Hacking the Genome Alphabet," John Cramer, *Analog*, December 2014.

[†] Many organic molecules, amino acids among them, exhibit "handedness." Mirror-image versions are chemically stable—but not found in earthly organisms. Could alien life use different isomers (molecules of like chemical formula but different chemical structure) than earthly life? Or use left- and right-handed versions at the same time? Unknown.

[‡] Life using Earth-atypical amino acids is no longer mere theory. Some genetically modified bacteria already incorporate—and rely

(Among my favorite interstellar novels is Brian Aldiss's previously mentioned *Starship*. The root cause of disaster aboard a generation ship is the unfamiliar/alien amino acid that taints the onboard water supply.)

Will alien life, even with somewhat Earth-like biochemistry, seek to eat us (or vice versa)? Likely not. People and any life form from an alien world will have less in common than do people and paramecia. How about infecting us? How about triggering an immune-system response, such as an allergic reaction? Those are also unlikely, though a bit harder to discredit.

None of which lets our hypothetical space explorers out of the metaphorical alien woods.

An escaped-to-the-wild sample of primitive terrestrial life—and starship crew, their crops, and their domesticated animals *will* carry their microbiomes—might out-compete native varieties. Such upheaval at the base of the food chain could throw a native ecology out of whack.

Or some of the metabolites produced by alien life might be toxins—biologically produced poisons—to humans or our microbiome, to one of our crops or its microbiome....

Consider botulinum toxin. The Illinois Poison Center indicates it is "the most toxic substance known to man. It takes only a tiny amount of botulinum to kill a human. The lethal dose of botulinum is estimated to be 70 micrograms for an adult human (by comparison, the estimated lethal dose of cyanide is 200,000 micrograms)."[36]

---

upon—a synthetic amino acid. The engineered dependency is for safety. If such bacteria should escape lab or biofactory, they will starve to death in the wild.

(And yes, chaos theorist Ian Malcolm of Michael Crichton's *Jurassic Park* (1990, basis of the 1993 movie) would scoff at the efficacy of this defensive measure. I never saw the connection between chaos theory and biology.)

"Scientists create 'genetic firewall' for new forms of life," Sharon Begley, *Reuters*, January 21, 2015, http://news.yahoo.com/scientists-create-genetic-firewall-forms-life-180212474.html.

In like manner, transplanted earthly microbes might exude metabolites that are wildly toxic to elements of an alien ecosphere. Such as, perhaps, alien bacteria that replenish the exoplanetary atmosphere with much of its free oxygen.

Will such inter-biology complications arise? Not necessarily. Perhaps not even likely. But neither are such scenarios far-fetched. The possibility raises issues both practical (how can an interstellar mission prepare?) and ethical (is it moral to put an entire independent ecosystem at risk?).

Rather than try to transplant significant segments of a terrestrial ecosphere to a new world, it might be more practical and ethical to reengineer ourselves. If alien life uses a different amino acid(s), or isomers of a familiar amino acid(s), than terrestrial biology, a change to our genome, or to a tailored version of one or more of our gut symbiotes, might suffice to convert native food to forms we can digest. (Not that such reengineering would be a snap. The biomolecular processes of living cells are complex, numerous, and often interdependent.)

The gengineering-ourselves approach—with unintended consequences, of course—underpinned my 2007 novelette, "A Stranger in Paradise."

Dealing with change

Every starship and exoplanet colony will need a healthcare system responsive to the full range of familiar diseases and accidents, but quite possibly also to unfamiliar problems. And yet, the population of a starship, even a colony ship, is apt to be small—"merely" a small-town-sized community will be a challenge to sustain—and yet every possible medical specialty must be represented.

How will that work?

Here on Earth, per Terrence Mulligan, we have recent experience with remaking medical-delivery systems. How so? The most prevalent adult diseases today, in many countries, are heart disease, cancer, and stroke. Notwithstanding the recent Ebola and Zika crises, the more typical modern scourges are non-communicable. Throughout history, until as recently as a half-century ago, infectious diseases dominated medical practice.

The medical community is adapting to these demographic shifts. Young populations have different health problems than older-skewing populations. Urban populations have different health problems than rural populations. Around the globe, populations are skewing older and more urban.

Thirty years ago, only five countries recognized emergency medicine as a medical specialty. In 2014, fifty-five had EM systems and more such systems are being deployed. The Global Emergency Medical Initiative is developing methods by which to start up and deploy a national-scale EM system within ten to fifteen years.

Perhaps, in setting up a healthcare system for starships and deep-space colonies we'll build upon these recent terrestrial learning experiences.

Space medicine, improving life here on Earth

Space is a radiation-intensive environment. Patients on a spaceship don't need to add diagnostic radiation! Spaceships are small (so far, anyway); bulky, power-hungry diagnostic instruments like MRIs are thus doubly problematical. Not surprisingly, therefore, mission planners have an interest in new diagnostic technologies, with ultrasound-based scanning high on the list.

Portable, battery-powered, ultrasound scanners are a boon here on Earth. The International Space Station (ISS) now stocks one.

We've seen that long-term spaceflight brings an increased risk of kidney stones. Because the ISS isn't the most convenient place to have a kidney-stone attack or to undertake (or undergo) surgery, NASA has funded research in pulsed-ultrasound techniques to reposition kidney stones and remove blockages without surgery.

We've also seen that microgravity can adversely impact intraocular pressure. And so, NASA is investigating 3-D ultrasound imaging to infer intraocular and intracranial pressures. A portable, noninvasive tool for measuring these pressures would be handy on Earth, too.

In recent years, genomics—characterization of the genome—has become well established. Personalized genomes are becoming affordable and precision medicine is entering the mainstream.[37] Proteomics—characterization of the proteins expressed (or not) from a genome—is the next frontier.

That brings us to a presentation by Kurt Zatloukal, of the Medical University of Graz, on the (still nascent) science of metabolomics. Monitoring metabolites in urine, sweat, and other exudations may offer a way to non-invasively detect bodily changes in advance of overt symptoms. Imagine that technology available here on Earth, embedded in a smart-watch-like health monitor.[*]

Second Life and second chances

From Robert A. Heinlein's *Orphans of the Sky* (1963) to Harry Harrison's *Captive Universe* (1969), the interstellar generation ship whose crew that has forgotten its purpose—and even that anything exists outside the ship—is a staple of SF.

Part of interstellar mission setup will be to establish societal structures that can persist in isolation for years or generations. That's easier said than done. We wouldn't choose the *Orphans of the Sky* precedent, but we might look for social stability in the rugged individualism of another Heinlein novel: *The Moon Is a Harsh Mistress* (1966).

It seems obvious that modern virtual communities and social networks *could* serve as the basis of a technology-enabled, non-hierarchical, highly participatory democracy. Such a distributed,

---

[*] The SweatSense feature in a FitBit tracker will already helpfully turn one (as the company calls it) "puke green" when held near a sufficiently foul odor.

See https://blog.fitbit.com/with-fitbits-new-feature-sweatsense-body-odor-is-no-longer-a-guessing-game/.

inclusive, transparent governance model might be more robust and resilient aboard a starship than (as so often seen in SF) the authoritarian naval/hierarchical model.

But perhaps not.

In the virtual-worlds service *Second Life*, a million-plus regular participants interact in many virtual communities. In a survey of thousands of established communities, Lancaster University sociologist John Carter McKnight reports, only five communities had retained democratic governance. Most communities opted for professional (paid, contracted-for) management—and, in instances where the manager lost interest, imploded.

Rather than form freewheeling, tolerant, inclusive communities, like-minded netizens often clustered. Among the like-minded, zoning laws proliferated. Ungoverned virtual spaces, rather than become libertarian oases, were abandoned.

A famous cartoon in *The New Yorker* introduced the meme that "On the Internet, no one knows you're a dog." Maybe so, but through behavioral and verbal cues, race, gender, class, and education are often discernable even in avatar-to-avatar interactions. Some *Second Life* communities have been hostile (to the point of real-world rape and death threats) against newcomers and "others."

To be sure, a virtual community is an imperfect analogy for a starship community—you can't opt out of the latter—so extrapolation from this *Second Life* study has its limits.

It seems prudent to consider as alternative social models for future starships the types of communities that have proven stable despite isolated and harsh conditions. Among candidates McKnight mentioned were indigenous populations (e.g., Inuits), Antarctic research staffs, and nuclear submarine crews.

The takeaway: social engineering is as mission-critical as propulsion engineering. Between stars is a dangerous place to be testing the length of our "genetic leash."*

---

* "The genes hold culture on a leash. The leash is very long, but inevitably values will be constrained in accordance with their effects on the human gene pool. The brain is a product of evolution. Human

62

Don't be a stranger

Faced with the complexities of mounting a round-trip mission to Mars, some advocates of exploration have proposed one-way expeditions. Not suicide, but colonization.[38] How much stronger is the case for one-way missions to the stars?

Of course we already maintain communications between Mars probes and Earth. Armchair adventurers can observe—and will someday, perhaps, buy reality-TV subscriptions to fund—exploration of a neighboring planet. Who will invest in interstellar missions if all that is to be eventually discovered—even the knowledge of whether a journey was completed—must remain unknown?

Fortunately, there may be a way to maintain contact across interstellar distances. What we need is a *really* big lens in space. As it happens, we have one.

The Sun.

Glossing over the details from general relativity, any large mass significantly curves nearby space-time. Like a familiar glass lens, that curvature bends the path of light rays. Such gravitational lensing has become an important tool of astronomers. Unlike a glass lens, which works in visible wavelengths, a gravitational lens acts on all electromagnetic radiation, including radio waves.

Rather than (as an astronomer might) exploit the mass of a distant galactic cluster to magnify the image of some yet more remote galaxy, why not position a communications relay such that the Sun focuses and magnifies signals from a starship? The not-so-minor wrinkle: our lens's focal length. A dispersed-with-distance incoming signal beam, skimming the surface of the Sun, comes into focus more than *40 billion miles away*. That's where the relay must be.[39]

---

behavior—like the deepest capacities for emotional response which drive and guide it—is the circuitous technique by which human genetic material has been and will be kept intact."

So wrote sociobiology founder Edward O. Wilson in *On Human Nature*.

But once we *can* station a relay at that distance, directly behind the Sun along the line to the outbound starship, the comm link can achieve tremendous amplification. With our Sun as a lens—the more massive the star, the more powerful the lens—gains of a 100 decibels (dB) or more are practical. In terms of signal-power gain, that's a factor of 10 *billion*.

Once a starship reaches, say, Alpha Centauri, the explorers can (comparatively easily) deploy a relay station to that star's anti-Sunward side. Thereafter, the two solar systems will share a robust two-way comm link.

By our bootstraps

Once we know how to design a starship, how does its construction come about?

We probably won't build it on Earth and lob it complete into space: lifting all that mass against Earth's surface gravity seems prohibitive. We're more likely to build starships in space, from resources already there. At the Earth-Moon Lagrange points, where (relative to Earth and Moon) the gravitational attraction of those worlds balance, smaller objects—such as a ship under construction and living quarters for the construction crew—can maintain a stable position.*

The construction and mission crews may well come from Earth. Ditto lots of specialized equipment—if not many components of the starship itself, then equipment with which to build in-space manufacturing facilities. That in itself will require delivering a great deal of mass, and it may take a space elevator to affordably lift so much mass into space.

A space elevator? It's just what it sounds. Rather than rocket into space—carrying fuel to carry the fuel to carry yet more fuel... to carry a comparatively tiny payload—creep up a *long* cable in an elevator car. The elevator ride will take days, not minutes, but

---

* That's an oversimplified description of the equilibria. See http://en.wikipedia.org/wiki/Lagrangian_point.

it will be far more economical, and far more environmentally friendly, than rocketry. First proposed in 1895, the space-elevator concept was popularized by Arthur C. Clarke in his 1979 novel, *The Fountains of Paradise*.

Some raw materials for the starship might come from captured-to-orbit asteroids. More might be gotten from the Moon. Given the Moon's comparatively weak gravity, about one-sixth that of the Earth, we'll likely see a space elevator there before we see one on Earth.

Is a space elevator practical? Not yet. Single-walled carbon nanotubes, many times stronger than steel, *might* be strong enough to make a cable reaching all the way to geosynchronous orbit, roughly 22 thousand miles overhead. Alas, the longest single-walled carbon nanotubes yet made measure no more than several centimeters. There's something of a materials-science challenge to be overcome.*

On the heels of the materials challenge comes the radiation hazard: the space-elevator car creeping along its cable will spend days within the Van Allen Belts. Before passengers ride these vertical rails, we'll need to execute yet another massive engineering project: clearing the Van Allen belts of their eons-long accumulation of charged particles.[40]

Such an undertaking would mean, among its effects, the elimination of auroras. Try to imagine the Environmental Impact Statement to be filed for *that* project.

So, far-fetched, right? Maybe not. Obayashi Corporation, one of the largest construction firms in Japan, has aspirations to deploy a space elevator by 2050.[41]

---

* Post-symposium, a new contender for a space-elevator cable hit the news. Diamond nanothreads appear to be even stronger than single-wall carbon nanotubes. Alas, like nanotubes, the largest diamond nanothreads so far produced are also mere centimeters in length.

See "Scientists Might Have Accidentally Solved The Hardest Part Of Building Space Elevators," Ajai Raj, *Business Insider*, October 13, 2014, http://www.businessinsider.com/diamond-nanothreads-make-space-elevator-2014-10.

Why it matters, here and now

That was a *lot* of daunting challenges.

Why would we even *think* to attempt an interstellar mission, much less strive to see a starship launch within a century? Don't we have enough challenges here on Earth?

Because (echoes of JFK's Moon speech intentional) the undertaking *will* be hard. Because the science and technology the quest must inspire—certain to include medical breakthroughs and eco-management insights—will, first and foremost, benefit everyone on Earth.

Economists, employers, and educators alike regularly bemoan a shortage of science, technology, engineering, and math (STEM) specialists.[42] The excitement of a Moon race once drew thousands of young Americans into STEM careers. Many of those workers contributed to the Mercury, Gemini, and Apollo programs—whose spin-offs went far beyond Tang. Others brought their knowledge and enthusiasm to the broader economy, and we *all* benefited from that.

As much as a pathway to the stars, 100YSS is about inspiring generations of young people to see science and technology as the pathway to a better life for everyone on Earth.

Wrapping up

Becoming an interstellar civilization will require sustained effort and substantial investment. It will stimulate developments in science and technology, with spin-off benefits first and foremost here on Earth.

What do the difficulties portend for interstellar science fiction? Good things! Storytelling thrives on challenge.

And because science thrives on good SF, 100 Year Starship chose Science Fiction Stories Night at the 2014 symposium to announce a new award program. The annual Canopus Award for Interstellar Fiction will recognize achievements in literary fiction at every length, on television and in movies, and in video games.*

To read further

- 100 Year Starship (http://100yss.org/).
- And a few likeminded organizations:
  - Icarus Interstellar (http://www.icarusinterstellar.org/).
  - Tau Zero Foundation (http://www.tauzero.aero/).
  - Centauri Dreams (http://www.centauri-dreams.org/).
- International Space Elevator Consortium (http://www.isec.org/).
- *Starship Century: Toward the Grandest Horizon*, Gregory Benford and James Benford, editors.
- *Using Medicine in Science Fiction: The SF Writer's Guide to Human Biology*, Henry G. Stratmann, M. D.

---

* The year after I attended a 100YSS conference, at the next annual confab, the organization announced its inaugural Canopus Awards for "works that contribute to the excitement, knowledge, and understanding of interstellar exploration. To my surprise and delight, the winner in the novel category was my 2015 novel, *InterstellarNet: Enigma.*

For more about the overall award program, see http://100yss.org/initiatives/canopusaward.

FASTER THAN A SPEEDING PHOTON

The Why, Where, and (Perhaps the) How of Faster-Than-Light Technology

n the opening chapters, we looked at some of the complications of travel among the stars. To recap: even at near-light speeds, the trip to a neighboring star will take years. Sustaining a viable shipboard environment for years will be a challenge. The energy needed to accelerate toward light speed approaches infinity. At near-light speed, every bit of oncoming light, gas, and dust becomes deadly radiation.

But what if we could, somehow, *exceed* light speed?

True, Einstein's theory of special relativity (SR), a piece of very settled and successful science, states nothing can travel faster than light. More accurately, SR states that nothing can go faster than light *in a vacuum*; hereafter that qualification is implied. (Even that isn't exactly what SR says, but we'll begin there.)

There's a lot of faster-than-light (FTL) technology in science fiction. Galactic empires, as in Isaac Asimov's Foundation series, and far-flung interstellar trading organizations, such as Poul Anderson's Polesotechnic League, become implausible things when the time to cross the territory far exceeds anyone's lifetime. (Hypothetical medical advances might circumvent the lifetime issue, but not the divergence of civilizations increasingly out of sync with one another.) Interstellar conflict becomes problematical as a story premise when no one in the government will live to hear the outcome of the military actions they order.

Among novel series with interstellar scale and reliant upon FTL travel are the Skolian Empire (Catherine Asaro), Uplift (David Brin), and the Lost Fleet (Jack Campbell), and that's off the top of my head, from the very beginning of the authorial alphabet. On the TV and movie front, major franchises dependent on FTL travel include *Star Trek*, *Star Wars*, and *Stargate*.

Often that FTL technology is a trope. But not, as we shall see, always.

Where SF has gone before

Not only do many SF authors have great physical intuition, some are practicing physicists. Let's survey the genre for FTL technology ideas.

The infinite improbability drive (*The Hitchhikers Guide to the Galaxy*, Douglas Adams, 1979) taps the Heisenberg Uncertainty Principle. Put simply, that tenet of quantum mechanics (QM) bounds the precision with which one can simultaneously determine an object's location and its momentum (= mass * velocity). With a vanishingly small probability, an object might be *anywhere*. Now merely learn to manipulate probability....

Okay, not a real FTL-drive candidate, but it *is* really amusing.

(One way in which the uncertainty principle really does manifest itself is in a phenomenon called quantum tunneling, wherein a subatomic particle that—by classical mechanics—lacks the energy to escape its confinement nonetheless does. And so an alpha particle, tightly bound for ages inside a nucleus, suddenly, and randomly, just appears outside. U-238 has a half-life of ~4.5 billion years, so one might be excused for imagining a tiny infinite improbability drive aboard the occasional jail-breaking alpha particle.)

Speaking of the imaginary, consider the inversion engine from the Skolian Empire series by Catherine Asaro. Relativity becomes problematical—runs into divide-by-zero problems—

69

when a ship's velocity, v, equals the speed of light, c.[*] Getting from v < c to v > c there is, intuitively, a moment when v = c. But that intuition presumes velocity values must lie along a number line.

Mathematicians offer an alternative to the number line: the number plane (and, doubtless, in some remote, ivied hall, higher dimensionalities), populated with complex numbers.

On a number *plane*, so-called real (i.e., familiar positive and negative) numbers shrink and grow as we move parallel to, say, the X axis. So-called imaginary numbers, both positive and negative, shrink and grow as we move parallel to the Y axis. (What's an example of an imaginary number? The square root of negative one, often denoted by the letter i.) A complex number (e.g., -3 + 2i) on the number plane has real and imaginary components.

Suppose you find a way in which complex numbers apply to velocity. Then you can cross from v < c to v > c in the real-number-velocity component somewhere on the number plane with a *non*zero value of the imaginary-number-velocity component. Goodbye, divide by zero; hello, FTL drive.

Does an imaginary component to velocity make sense? Not in any known way. That said, electrical engineers need complex numbers to describe matters as commonplace as alternating-current electrical circuits. *Something* about complex numbers applies to the real world, so who knows...?[†]

In *The Sins of the Fathers* (1976), Stanley Schmidt offers the Rao-Chang drive, by which spaceships jump discontinuously from a slower-than-light to a faster-than-light speed. The analogy subliminally offered to the reader is to quantum tunneling. (*Is* that how the drive circumvents the light-speed barrier? Unclear. In the novel, Chandragupta Rao disclaimed any knowledge of the drive's underlying physical principles, saying that he and his coinventor stumbled across it.)

---

[*] Reference equations (2) and (4) in the chapter "I Got the Long-Distance Blues."

[†] If you are reading this, Catherine, I suggest you trademark iFTL before Apple does.

That light sets a physical speed limit does not prove that c is a universal, eternal constant. In *A Fire Upon the Deep* (1992), Vernor Vinge divides the galaxy into strata with different physical properties—including separate speed limits. (Earth, alas, lies deep within the Slow Zone.)

Might real physical constants be localized? And, maybe, *not* constant?

Big Bang theory successfully explains many characteristics of the observed Universe. Some observations, however, stubbornly refuse to fit the model without an ad hoc workaround called "cosmic inflation." Per inflation theory, in an instant the very young Universe expanded by a factor of 10^{28} or more. (A *very* ad hoc adjustment. I've seen inflation models with an expansion factor of 10^{60}.) The light-speed limit governs movement *through* space-time, not *of* space-time, and the early Universe spread so quickly that light from some regions will never reach us. (If so, there is an *un*observable part of the Universe, its extent unknown and unknowable.)

With inflation integral to mainstream cosmological thought, perhaps a starship might (pay no attention to the hand-waving behind the curtain) alter space-time in its vicinity. Within a bubble of altered space-time, local c might be much faster than exterior c. And the ship carries that bubble around with it.

(And outside the cosmological mainstream? A speed of light that was much faster in the early Universe than in our era might explain astronomers' observations without recourse to cosmic inflation.[43])

As yet another possibility, consider that, per quantum-mechanical theory, "empty space" isn't exactly empty. The purest vacuum seethes with "quantum foam": a froth of spontaneously forming—and mutually-destroying—particle/antiparticle pairs.

How can that be, you ask? Like the indeterminacy bounds governing (and obscuring) a particle's exact position and momentum, the Heisenberg Uncertainty Principle entails an unavoidable fuzziness about a particle's lifespan and energy. And so:

particles can be—and apparently are—briefly summoned from nowhere without violating conservation of energy.

Due to yet other QM strangeness, every particle has an associated wavelength. Now imagine a region so physically constrained as to exclude long wavelengths. What results is the Casimir effect: a measurable force that in a vacuum will push together two parallel, electrically neutral plates.[44]

The region from which some particle-pair types are excluded is said to be energy depleted. The physical properties therein, including light speed, (may) vary from those of a non-energy-depleted region. One more way (perhaps) to wrap a faster-than-normal-c bubble around one's starship.

Next: a recent astrophysical study derived different values for the fine-structure constant from measurements taken looking deep into space along different directions.[45] In one direction the fine-structure constant (denoted α [alpha]) appeared to decrease with distance. In another direction, α appeared to increase. α relates to the fundamental nature and strength of electromagnetic interactions—and varies inversely with the speed of light. Again, sublight travel in some locales might exceed light-speed travel in our home environs.

However you alter space-time around your starship, the respectable name for the concept is (after physicist Miguel Alcubierre) the Alcubierre warp drive.[46] The *Star Trek* warp drive seems to be of this class.

If (a) a ship within an artificially generated space-time bubble moves through (b) unaltered space-time at what is in *our* frame of reference FTL speeds, while (c) within that bubble the ship never exceeds its local light speed—is that an FTL ship?

Warped thinking

To speed characters across interstellar space, the movie *Stargate* and its spin-off TV series create wormholes between widely separated portals. Some *Star Trek* episodes use naturally occurring wormholes. In Larry Niven and Jerry Pournelle's 1974 novel *The Mote in God's Eye* (in the UK, *The Moat Around Murcheson's Eye*), the Alderson Drive works between naturally occurring interface points.

A wormhole (if any exists) is a topological construct, the analogy being that a worm might get "around" an apple faster by going through it than by crawling along the skin. A better analogy is connecting two dots (think: two stars) far apart on a sheet of paper (think: space-time). Conventional space travel is like tracing a line across the paper, from one dot to another. Wormhole travel has the paper fold/sag until the dots meet.

In short, a wormhole is a cosmic shortcut. Stars that are light-years apart as astronomers view them might—through such a shortcut—be quite close. A ship taking the shortcut has an effective speed (= [conventionally measured distance] / [time to traverse the wormhole]) that is effectively FTL.

No one has ever seen a wormhole, but (a) the equations of general relativity (GR) permit wormholes to exist in sufficiently warped regions of space-time and (b) GR describes gravity as the warping of space-time caused by the presence of mass.

What would it be like to go through such a wormhole? Like grazing the event horizon of a black hole—but at just such a trajectory that rather than be crushed, you shoot through the shortcut to exit a white hole.

A white hole, as you might expect, is a hypothetical egress from a black hole. Black holes, by definition, can't be seen directly (although the radiation emitted by in-falling matter offers a very good indication). White holes, on the other hand, should be directly visible—if they exist.

Perhaps no white hole has been seen because GR solutions for many wormholes are unstable. The math predicts that static wormholes will collapse faster than anything could cross through. That said, other solutions, involving a massive spinning ring, perhaps made of exotic matter exhibiting negative energy density, *are* mathematically stable. (Not that exotic matter with the required properties has been shown to exist. Regardless, it may be possible to create a region of negative energy density, as by the Casimir effect, to stabilize a wormhole.)

Here's a NASA description[47] of one way to build a wormhole:

> First, collect a whole bunch of super-dense matter, such as matter from a neutron star. *How much?*—well, enough to construct a ring the size of the Earth's orbit around the Sun. Then build another ring where you want the other end of your wormhole. Next, just charge 'em up to some incredible voltage, and spin them up to near the speed of light—both of them.

Perhaps no one has seen wormholes because naturally occurring ones are too small and short-lived. Likely *really* tiny black/white hole pairs are constantly manifesting out of—and disappearing back into—the quantum foam. If so, the trick will be to spot and separate such infinitesimally small objects before they mutually destruct, grow them to useful size, prevent them from collapsing, position them to form a wormhole, and move one or both ends to a useful location.

Wormhole engineers (if their subject matter proves real) will have their work cut out for them.*

Of FTL neutrinos

On September 22, 2011—after six months spent looking in vain for errors in their results—a team of particle physicists affiliated with the European Organization for Nuclear Research (best known as CERN, its French acronym), announced they had measured neutrinos traveling one part in 40,000 *faster* than light in a vacuum.[48]

---

* We'll discuss wormhole engineering again, near the end of the book, in the context of building a time machine.

The physics community and the popular press were abuzz for months after. The group at CERN even reran their experiment with one minor change, duplicating their original result while eliminating one variable (among many) that might have led erroneously to the surprising conclusion. To be complete, the CERN team was the *second* group to report FTL neutrinos; the earlier report—back in 2007, by a team affiliated with Fermilab—was not statistically significant. Fermilab was among the research organizations eager to duplicate or refute the CERN results.[49]

Neutrinos—Italian for "little neutral ones"—are subatomic particles. They mass so little that physicists were unsure for many years whether neutrinos had any mass at all. Among their unusual attributes, neutrinos spontaneously change among several types. Neutrinos by the billions pass through your body every second without effect—that's how weakly they interact with more familiar subatomic particles.

Initial skepticism about the CERN report dealt with the complicated mechanics of the experiment. Speed equals distance divided by time. The experimenters must know *exactly* both the flight time of the neutrinos and the distance between (a) the particle accelerator at CERN in suburban Geneva, Switzerland, and (b) the neutrino detector in Gran Sasso National Laboratory in central Italy. How exactly? To nanoseconds and nanometers. Both measurements relied upon the Global Positioning System—thus involving, among other factors, relativistic corrections for the orbital motion and position of the GPS satellites. And then there is the notorious difficulty in detecting *any* neutrino.

It wasn't like timing the hundred-yard dash with eyeballs and a stopwatch.

Meanwhile, some theorists argued that FTL neutrinos must lose energy because of Cherenkov radiation: a subtle effect observed in many experiments involving speeding subatomic particles. The neutrinos in the controversial CERN experiment were *not* seen to radiate and lose energy in the expected manner.[50]

Skeptical astrophysicists spoke of 1987A, a supernova event observed in a galaxy that's about 160 thousand light-years distant from Earth. Neutrinos and then light from 1987A reached Earth mere hours apart. (That short gap has been attributed to differences in how neutrinos and photons interact with matter. Neutrinos scarcely interact; they would stream unimpeded from an exploding star. In contrast, photons would be absorbed and re-emitted over and over on their route to the star's surface.) If neutrinos outraced light to the extent reported by the group at CERN, 1987A's neutrino burst would have arrived four *years* in advance of the supernova's light burst.[51]

In time, the dust settled. There was a flaw in the experimental setup. Neutrinos aren't FTL after all.[52]

Beyond Relativity

To my knowledge, no reproducible observation contradicts Einstein's relativity theories. But Isaac Newton's mechanics explained the observations of *his* time and for centuries after. Einstein's solutions may also prove to be merely an approximation sufficient for known phenomena—and fail to explain some more exotic phenomenon observed tomorrow.

In support of that possibility, we *know* relativity theory is incomplete.

General relativity (GR) considers the overall structure of space-time, in which gravity is a manifestation of the curvature of space-time caused by the presence of mass. GR deals well with matters at a large scale. Crucially, the GR equations assume space-time is continuous.

Quantum mechanics, another long-lived—and very complex—physical theory deals with matters at a very small scale. In QM, matter and energy come in discrete, indivisible chunks called quanta. The QM worldview is inherently *dis*continuous.

Among the grand challenges of modern physics is a Theory of Everything reconciling GR and QM. (That can't come soon enough: It will take unifying quantum-scale events with gravitational/space-time effects to fully characterize the Big Bang. Or black holes.) It's expected that reconciliation will add quantization to our understanding of space-time. If space-time consists of indivisible quanta, however tiny, divide-by-zero limits may disappear from revised relativity equations.

String theory is (at least in terms of the number of physicists working in the specialty) the leading approach toward reconciling GR and QM. *Extremely* briefly, where QM sees the fundamental building blocks of matter, such as electrons and quarks, as dimensionless points, string theory sees those building blocks as vibrations of one-dimensional strings in an N-dimensional space-time. String theory isn't *a* theory; rather, it is an umbrella term for many families of mathematical descriptions, each variant offering its own set of dimensions and mathematical rules. As I write, the favored number of dimensions among string theorists is eleven.[*]

Eleven dimensions? Einstein's space-time has four. You and I don't experience the extra dimensions—as the string theorists would have it—because the extra dimensions curl up at scales too small for us to detect. Alternatively, our 4-D space-time and the other dimensions have a very small intersection, just as an ideal sphere resting upon an ideal plane make contact at only one point.

Back before FTL neutrinos were debunked, one theory to explain CERN's baffling results was that neutrinos took a shortcut through a hidden dimension.

Hyperdrive

If you can't go faster than light within space, then why not go under or over space? That's the premise of (one name among many) hyperdrive.

Jack Campbell's Lost Fleet series uses FTL travel through "jump space" between rare naturally occurring access points *and* faster FTL travel between manmade portals of a hypernet. In

---

[*]   We'll come back to string theory in the chapter "Alien Dimensions."

constructing a military SF plot, one wants to provide targets; access points to the stars fill the bill. Niven's Known Space (in which I've sometimes coauthored) offers a hyperdrive. Hyperdrive works most anywhere outside the depths of gravity wells.* Vinge's hyperdrive works outside the galactic Slow Zone, with the top speed varying within and between galactic zones.

Physicists have yet to dub anything hyperspace, but some do—see earlier discussion of string theory—speak of hidden dimensions. Sounds like a potential hyperspace to me.

In the variant of string theory called M-Theory, M for membrane, our familiar Universe is a 4-D island adrift in a higher-dimensional space. We're wrapped, at least conceptually, in a membrane that separates us from those other dimensions. (If this theory is correct, lower-dimensional universes like ours can collide with one another. I suspect that that would be a bad thing.) Physical laws beyond the membrane may differ dramatically from laws within the membrane.

"Beyond the membrane" sure sounds like SF's hyperspace.

As a matter of semantics, one could again argue whether travel outside our Universe at a speed faster than c constitutes a violation of relativity inside our Universe.

FTL communications

Some stories offer FTL communications. In the Ender universe of Orson Scott Card, ships travel at sublight speeds but can communicate instantaneously via an "ansible."[53] Niven's hyperdrive has a finite speed, but his hyperwave radio (where it works, which is again outside deep gravity wells) is instantaneous.

---

* Known Space stories use the term *gravitational singularity* for a region whose gravity interferes with a hyperdrive. Being near any star, or even a decent-sized free-flying planet, is more than sufficient to discombobulate a hyperdrive shunt. *Gravity well* is the more general term—any mass warps space-time at least a little—whereas a singularity commonly refers to a point of infinite density (such as a black hole).

Are there ways to imagine FTL, or even instantaneous, communications? Besides, at this point in the chapter, the obvious: light beams and radio waves sent through any channel, such as a wormhole, offering a shortcut compared to "normal" space.

Maybe.

Among the odder attributes (a high hurdle) of quantum mechanics is quantum entanglement. *Very* briefly, consider two like particles—say, two electrons—that have become associated. Their states differ only in one quantum parameter, such as the orientation of their spins, of which only two values can be measured. (I choose my words very carefully here. Stay tuned.) QM does not allow two electrons to have identical parameters; anytime the spin state of one is measured in either of its permissible values, the spin state of the second takes the other permissible value. Instantaneously. Even if someone had previously relocated one of the linked pair halfway across the Universe.

Einstein called this connection between paired particles "spooky action at a distance" and understood it as a crack in the foundations of then-young QM theory. Nature begged to differ; starting in the 1980s, instantaneous state changes through quantum entanglement have been demonstrated across separations of miles.

So can one use quantum entanglement for FTL communications? Due to other quantum weirdness, no. Above, I carefully referred to two permissible measured values for the electron spins. Between measurements, the spin state of any particle is...indeterminate. (Think: Schrödinger's cat.) Through measurement I can instantaneously *force* a discrete spin state upon the near particle—and hence also upon the remote particle—but I can't know what state will be evoked where. I might (for example) only be confirming the probabilistic value the remote particle had before the determination.

When no information is sent, there is no communication.*

---

* People drive themselves crazy looking for a way to encode information into this instantaneous signal. The consensus remains that no information can be sent.

While it's common to say that special relativity prevents anything from outpacing light, the more precise statement is that *information*—in a physical object or otherwise—cannot travel faster than light. A "signal" from which no data can be extracted *can* exceed the speed of light.

As another possible FTL comm mechanism, consider the tachyon. A tachyon, from the Greek *tachys*, or swift, is a hypothetical fundamental particle that *must* travel faster than light. (*Very* hypothetical. Tachyons do not have a home in the Standard Model of particle physics. While the Standard Model is likely incomplete—the model does not, for example, account for gravity or dark matter, or explain why matter is more prevalent than antimatter—it has avoided serious challenge for decades.) Tachyons never cross the v = c threshold, avoiding the divide-by-zero problems in the relativity equations. No tachyon has ever been observed (and I'm going to gloss over if/how an experiment could detect one), nor do tachyons, strictly speaking, violate any known laws of physics.

But if tachyons do exist, they raise new vexing issues.

For the last time (he says, ironically), back to special relativity

We've seen that mass and time dilation derive from special relativity's central tenet of light as setting the universal speed limit. Here's another derivable consequence of that tenet: an object or signal traveling faster than light would be (to the rest of us) moving backward in time. As SF readers well know, time travel to the past creates paradoxes.

Of which perhaps the best known is the Grandfather Paradox. If I travel back in time and kill my own grandfather, how did

---

For more about quantum entanglement (including applications that *do* work, like quantum cryptography), see "The Strange World of Quantum Entanglement," by Paul Comstock (http://calitreview.com/51).

I come to exist? But if I never existed, then clearly I didn't kill my grandfather. So I do exist, and can travel backward in time. So....

Great authorial fun, to be sure. For an example, see my 2001 short story "Grandpa?"

To my knowledge, no one has seen a time traveler, so maybe the Universe defends itself against such paradoxes. Maybe (as we'll consider later in the book) the Universe is its own time police.

To abandon the precedence of cause over effect would strike at the very foundations of our sense of reality; most physicists are loath to give credence to tachyons until they see one.

Many fictional uses of FTL choose to ignore the backward-in-time implication. Among the stories that embrace the proposition are James P. Hogan's *Thrice Upon A Time* (1980), Gregory Benford's *Timescape* (also 1980), and Roger MacBride Allen's *The Depths of Time* (2000).

(Do you see now why the previous caption was ironic?)

Wrapping up

Are FTL travel and FTL communications merely SF tropes? Not always. Plenty of science at the cutting edge deals with concepts that might create FTL technology.

Doubtless with implications that are challenging to anticipate.

That's okay. Foreseeing consequences is among the higher callings of science fiction.

To read further

- *Hiding in the Mirror: The quest for alternate realities, from Plato to String Theory* (*by way of Alice in Wonderland, Einstein, and The Twilight Zone*), by Lawrence M. Krause.

- *Hollyweird Science: From Quantum Quirks to the Multiverse*, by Kevin R. Grazier and Stephen Cass.

- "NASA Goes FTL—Part 1: Wormhole Physics" and "NASA Goes FTL—Part 2: Cracks in Nature's FTL Armor," Alternate View columns originally written for *Analog* by John G. Cramer; respectively the Mid-December 1994 (online at http://www.npl.washington.edu/AV/altvw69.html and February 1995 (http://www.npl.washington.edu/AV/altvw70.html) issues.

ALIEN ALIENS

Beyond Rubber Suits

Aliens in science fiction often aren't *science* fictional at all. Many "aliens" are—in the video format, literally—people in rubber suits (or foreheads, or ears). Think: *Star Trek*'s Klingons and Vulcans. They're a bit unusual in appearance, but not necessarily in any other way. That's fine where the story is as much allegory or satire as science fiction (below, I'll touch upon trope aliens), but perfunctory aliens don't always cut it when we'd like to broaden our horizons.

And isn't one of the joys of SF broadening our horizons?

It's been argued that truly alien aliens don't work in fiction. If the author succeeds in portraying a truly alien alien, the reader can't relate. Agreed: that disconnect can happen. It doesn't have to, as we'll see. Lots of SF involves truly alien aliens. To name a few (with plenty more examples to come):

- The Goa'uld of the *Stargate SG-1* TV series.[*]
- The dinosaur-descended Yilanè of Harry Harrison's West of Eden alternate-history trilogy.

---

[*] The Goa'uld are alien and make for great storytelling—but they're not necessarily believable. Stay tuned.

TROPE-ING THE LIGHT FANTASTIC

- The pack-intelligent Tines of Vernor Vinge's Zones of Thought series of novels.

In this chapter, we'll look at alien aliens. Some aliens, literary or dramatic, will serve to illustrate more than one point, because nothing limits aliens to a single difference from humans. I'll take an extended example from my own writing; I have a pretty good idea why my aliens turned out the way they did.

If one difference is too few, should fictional aliens share *any* characteristics with humans? Often, yes. It's entirely plausible that physical-world constraints and similar (not necessarily identical) evolutionary pressures will lead to common solutions.

But let's not limit ourselves. Nonhuman intelligences need not be extraterrestrial, or even biological. Throughout this book, we'll use alien in its broadest meaning of *unfamiliar*, rather than foreign or weird.

Trope-ing the light fantastic—aliens

Am I dismissing alien life as mere trope?

No, but before we turn to the truly alien, let's look at non-alien aliens. You know the type: humans thinly disguised. Such "aliens" have served as stand-ins for Cold War allegories (e.g., two neighboring worlds locked in a war whose origins no one really understands), racial parables (e.g., two species on the same world, one pointlessly oppressing the other), and straw men to advocate for (or against) birth control or euthanasia or gender equality or pretty much any sociological pattern. When the medium is visual, these aliens are humanoid in appearance—the directors not wanting to be too subtle. Another sign of a trope: aliens who are cross-fertile with humans or (like decades of lurid pulp-magazine covers) who find members of the other species sexually attractive.

I'll assert there's no plausible scientific basis for such aliens. Parallel evolution, you say? True, humans and octopi evolved very similar eyes—but look how different we are in every other respect.* We can't bear each other's children! Panspermia? Suppose common seeds of life did drift, eons ago, to both Earth and Mars (or Earth and your favorite exoplanet, real or fictional). Since then, there's been a whole lot of evolution going on—on both worlds. I have more genes in common with a redwood or a rattlesnake than I could have in common with any extraterrestrial cousins.

Alien aliens: real SF. (I'd like to say meat-and-potatoes SF, but I'm guessing aliens aren't edible, either.)

Social stand-in aliens? They're tropes (not that there's anything wrong with that).

Life, the Universe, and everyone

Are *all* aliens in SF mere tropes? I'll argue not.

Admittedly, only a few years ago, for all we knew our Solar System was unique. The Extrasolar Planets Encyclopaedia[54] now lists more than a thousand solar systems, the numbers growing more or less daily. As instruments and search techniques improve, astronomers find smaller and smaller exoplanets. The discovery of exoplanets much like Earth is expected within the next few years. (Next chapter, we'll consider the science of alien worlds.)

Wherever biologists look, Earth teems with life: deep within the rocks, in boiling-hot ocean-floor vents, in cooling ponds filled with the radioactive waste from nuclear power plants, in subglacial Antarctic lakes, and afloat high in the atmosphere. Perhaps it clings to the exterior of the International Space Station—NASA and Roscosmos debate this point.[55] It appears that life—wherever it finds a foothold—evolves and prospers.

None of that is *proof* of extraterrestrial life. Evolution explains the richness of life but not its origin. The great leap from

---

* The paths to those ocular similarities, apart from a common ancestral gene, were very different. See "How Humans And Squid Evolved To Have The Same Eyes: I see how you see," Malcolm Campbell, *The Conversation*, May 6, 2014, http://www.popsci.com/article/science/how-humans-and-squid-evolved-have-same-eyes.

lifelessness to life remains unexplained by science; we simply don't know how often that transition occurs.[56]

In our huge and ancient Universe, I can't dismiss the possibility of alien life elsewhere and elsewhen. And once we accept the possibility of extraterrestrial microbes, it's within the realm of scientific speculation to consider those microbes evolving into more complex life.

Including potential peer species....

Let's get physical

How should aliens look?

Well, most likely *alien*. Different. Even aliens who evolved on Earthlike planets.

That's not to say aliens couldn't share some anatomical features with terrestrial life. What works on Earth remains our only data point for what can work. That said, even terrestrial life shows more variety than some SF aliens.

Take four limbs. Yes, many earthly animals follow that design. Four limbs were inherited from humanity's very primitive ancestors. Had we descended from starfish or octopi—and given a different timing of inopportune asteroid strikes, that might have happened—*we* would look a lot different.

To start simply, we can add or subtract limbs. Edgar Rice Burroughs, in his Barsoom (Mars) novels, gave the green Martians an extra pair of arms. The Puppeteers of Larry Niven's Known Space future history have three legs; their two necks must do double-duty as arms.* Robert A. Heinlein apparently drew his inspiration for the Bugs of *Starship Troopers* (1959) from earthly arachnids.

To read about beings who look and act like us, we hardly need science fiction.

So, Recommendation One: alien aliens *look* alien.

---

* Full disclosure: Larry and I coauthored the Fleet of World series, in which I've made contributions to the Puppeteers' fictional sociology. Larry defined Puppeteer physiology before I came onto the scene.

A fearful symmetry[*]

Barsoomians, Puppeteers, and Bugs have left and right sides—in that way, at least, they're much like humans. Let's crank up the symmetry dial....

Let's revisit the Krulirim, from my 2005 novel *Moonstruck*. A Krul's three limbs serve as arms *and* legs. It has three sensory clusters, also equally spaced. Picture a Weber Kettle barbecue grill (the charcoal kind), with hands—though not quite human hands—at the end of the tripod limbs.

A Krul has no notion of left or right, of front or back. Its worldview is radially symmetric. Unless a Krul is asleep, you can't sneak up on it. Nothing nearby is out of its sight. You or I might refer to an object by its distance to one side or another, and the distance in front or behind us—basically, Cartesian coordinates, centered on our own body. That doesn't work for a Krul. So a Krul locates objects via polar coordinates: the distance from the body and the angle from a reference point.

"Aha!" you say. If a Krul is radially symmetric, how does it get that reference point? It needs an out-of-body reference point, so I gave Krulirim a magnetic sense. The reference for angular measurements is the bearing on the magnetic pole. (Terrestrial birds navigate magnetically. Why not Krulirim?) Two Krulirim comparing notes on the location of an object have to do trig in their minds—and how alien is *that*?

An unconventional body plan led to an unfamiliar worldview and required giving the aliens a sensory mode only weakly present, if at all, in most terrestrial life. The magnetic sense, in turn, ended up driving major elements of the plot—including Armageddon briefly foiled by humans interfering with that alien magnetic sense.

---

[*]   With apologies to William Blake.

Alien aliens from alien places

Some of the most memorable aliens in SF (speaking only of my memory, of course—your mileage may vary) come from worlds unlike Earth. Maybe that's because the less Earth-like the alien home world, the harder it is to cast its denizens, even metaphorically, as people in rubber suits. Fictional humanoid aliens are so commonplace they tend to blur together.

Which very alien aliens spring to my mind?

- *Mission of Gravity* (1954), by Hal Clement. The *very-fast-spinning*—and hence, far from spherical—planet Mesklin has surface gravity varying from a few gees at the equator to hundreds of gees at the poles. The centipede-like Mesklinites are the stars—practically the only characters—of the novel.

- Cranking up the gravity by orders of magnitude, we have *Dragon's Egg* (1980), by Robert L. Forward. The "egg" is a neutron star, and life has evolved on its surface. A cheela has the mass of a human in a flattened body the size of a sesame seed. Their tiny eyes can't see light humans find visible, but rather use ultraviolet, even X-rays.

- *A Deepness in the Sky* (1999), by Vernor Vinge. The "on-off" star—variable with a vengeance—regularly cycles its one inhabited planet from comfortable to cryogenic temperatures. On that world, the atmosphere freezes out on a regular basis. The native Spiders look somewhat like terrestrial arachnids and hibernate a bit like periodic cicadas (aka seventeen-year locusts).

- *The Frozen Sky* (2012), by Jeff Carlson. The opening book of the Europa series introduces the semi-octopoid, pack-minded (but not hive-minded) "Sunfish." The Europan ecosphere is uniquely stratified, offering its most benign conditions in the deep, ice-bound ocean and desert-like scarcities in the near-surface ice—and civilizations reflect those differences.

- *Far-Seer* (1992), by Robert J. Sawyer. This first book of the Quintaglio Ascension series introduces the eponymous quintaglio: the highly evolved descendants of T-Rex-like dinosaurs. These territorial carnivores have a part feudal, part big-game-hunter civilization on a remote, tidally locked (and, they discover, doomed) moon.

- *Titan* (1979), by John Varley. The main alien *is* a terrestrial (sort-of) world—with, for good measure, a plethora of alien species closer to human size running around her interior.

Plenty of excellent science fiction involves humanoid aliens. That said, I can't help but be struck by how much more vivid in my memory these nonhumanoid aliens are.

Recommendation Two: exotic settings beget alien creatures beget unique circumstances beget memorability.

Alien aliens, from Kansas

Okay, not Kansas, exactly, but somewhere homey. One of those myriads of "Class M" planets and moons with which the *Star Trek* universe is rife.

After all, plots sometimes demand that humans and aliens covet the same real estate.

So: *can* terrestrial planets give rise to alien aliens?

I can't believe otherwise, considering the varied nature of life on Earth. It's not much of a stretch to imagine intelligent dolphin-like creatures. They could evolve prehensile tongues and lips to remain streamlined and still be tool users. Or intelligent elephants—they have prehensile trunks. Or tool-using (and perhaps larger, thus flightless) parrots.[57] Or dinosaurs. If a big rock hadn't smacked into Earth, what might dinosaurs have given rise to by now?

Which fictional alien aliens could live on Earth? Who are the fictional alien aliens whose home worlds fictional humans can visit without protective gear? A few examples:

- In *A Fire Upon the Deep* (1992), Vernor Vinge brought us the delightful Tines, wolf-like creatures who—communing with ultrasound—form pack-like sapient group minds. Their technology remains primitive, disadvantaged by having to substitute jaws and cooperating mouths and muzzles for hands.

- Niven and Jerry Pournelle brought us the Fithp, wonderful elephant-like creatures (who coveted Earth), in *Footfall* (1985). They brought us the even more wonderful, three-armed, greatly speciated, Moties of *The Mote in God's Eye* (1974). And we've already met Niven's Puppeteers.

- Michael Flynn gave us the dimension-crossing, insectile Krenken (amid the Black Death in medieval Germany, no less) in *Eifelheim* (2006).

We can have our cake—Earth-like worlds, on which human characters freely roam and with whom readers can readily identify—and frost it, too, with alien aliens.* I just wish that happened more often.

Sex, lies, and extra genders

We've focused till now on physical differences from the human norm—but won't aliens *act* alien, too? And if so, how?

To judge by sitcoms, human civilization revolves around mating. That might be an exaggeration—we permit comedy its tropes, too—but certainly reproduction, sexual gratification, gender roles, and bonding play major parts in how humans live.

---

* Horribly mixed metaphors, you're thinking. But to an alien alien point of view....

90

What alternate reproductive schemes might aliens employ, and with what implications?

- Burrough's Barsoomians laid eggs, which they left in desert incubators.

- H. G. Well's Martians (*The War of the Worlds*, 1898) reproduced asexually, by budding.

- Ursula K. Le Guin, in *The Left Hand of Darkness* (1969), explored a society that is—all but a few days of the month—androgynous.

- In the *Star Trek* universe, male and female Vulcans—at all other times ultralogical and self-disciplined—turn violent every seven years (in a condition called *pon farr*) and must either mate or die.

- The "soft ones" of Isaac Asimov's *The Gods Themselves* (1972) have three genders, each with a separate role.

Suppose, for a moment, that the pursuit of sex *is* the only thing that motivates us. Wouldn't human behavior change if we went into heat, or changed genders, or (like much marine life) sprayed our gametes into the sea and let Nature take her course?

But sitcoms notwithstanding, factors beyond the sex drive *do* influence our daily behavior. We may strive for power, knowledge, prestige, or personal safety. We may obsess about our families, jobs, or preferred musical groups. We—and entire nations—sometimes organize our lives around systems of religious, philosophical, and economic thought.

But back to sex. Sort of....

Riding my hobby horse

When human-alien sex pops into a story, I have problems willingly suspending my disbelief. The *Star Trek* universe has humans cross-fertile with Vulcans and Klingons. True, both alien races

91

are humanoid—but so what? At the genetic level, people and paramecia must have more in common.

Nor are curious pairings in SF limited to sex among humanoids.

- Take the eponymous alien of Ridley Scott's 1979 movie *Alien*. In its earliest lifecycle stage, the alien emerges from its egg. The newborn alien then invades a human host in whose body it gestates into a later life stage. Somehow this works despite the alien having acid for its blood. Somehow this compatibility arose without any prior contact between species (until the unconvincing retcon in the 2017 prequel movie, *Alien Covenant*).

- In Robert A. Heinlein's *The Puppet Masters* (1951, and the basis of a 1994 movie) sluglike alien parasites tap into and control the nervous systems of their hosts: human and otherwise.

- In the *Stargate* universe, snakelike parasites called the Goa'uld likewise take control of the nervous systems of other intelligent species. Not only are multiple species (including humans) compatible as hosts, but a queen Goa'uld (in her host) can spawn swarms of Goa'uld larvae by mating with—among her other choices—a human.

- Bug-eyed monsters slobbering for nubile Earth women (who, at least on lurid magazine covers, encounter an astonishing rate of wardrobe malfunctions) were a staple of pulp-era SF.

How does evolution give rise across light-years to interspecies compatibilities? What common behavioral pattern or biochemical characteristics would lead either party to give relationships—whether fraternizing or parasitizing—a try?

Recommendation Three: if two species are biologically compatible—even as tasty snacks—explain how that interspecies compatibility is possible.

Alien aliens: a definition

With examples—good *and* bad—behind us, let's define terms. What are alien aliens?

As you might expect, I exclude caricatures of, and thinly disguised stand-ins for, humanity. I disqualify creatures drawn from our fears and phobias. The Other who seizes control of our bodies, ravishes our loved ones, or devours us from the inside out may employ SF tropes, but the resulting storyline often fits the genre of horror at least as much as it does science fiction.

But I still haven't said what they *are.*

Alien aliens are beings whose description—physical, emotional, psychological, cultural, and in every other dimension—is grounded in *their* history, not ours. Their behaviors, capabilities, vulnerabilities, and limitations derive, ultimately, from *their* world (or other place) of origin, *their* evolutionary process, and *their* societal progression.

Alien aliens, in a word, are rooted in *science*, not self-examination.

Even, as we will see later in this chapter, aliens with whom we share common roots.

Reverting to type

We label ourselves Homo sapiens sapiens—*twice* wise—but human behavior (and not merely in regard to sex) is often instinctual, emotional, habitual, reflexive, and otherwise not the product of coolly reasoned philosophy.

Humans and chimpanzees have 90%-plus genetic commonality (studies differ on the exact number), and anthropologists trace many "human" behaviors—from hugging to curiosity to territoriality and aggression—to inherited traits. Aliens descended from their own unique lineages would, one presumes, reflect in their behavior *their* genetic legacies.

Certainly authors have sometimes made that assumption. Aliens based on non-primate terrestrial examples include:

93

- The aforementioned reptilian Yilanè (Harrison had no living dinosaurs from which to extrapolate his aliens' behavior).
- The felinoid Kzinti of Niven's Known Space.
- The avian Gubru of David Brin's *The Uplift War* (1987).

Recommendation Four: look to ancestral or analogous species to round out an alien's personal and group behaviors.

Group minds

Hive minds have fascinated people since before SF began.

I refer, of course, to the prototypical hive: that of bees. It's long been noted that many types of insects—individually far from intelligent—exhibit elaborate group behaviors and build complicated structures. The group's complexity arises out of interactions among the simple behaviors of individual units.

It's not only insects. Flocks, for example, exhibit behaviors that result from the unsophisticated reflexes of individual birds. Ditto, schools versus individual fish.

The overall phenomenon is called emergence: the complex behaviors in large systems that arise in the aggregate from simpler unit-level interactions among components. If you are of a computer-oriented frame of mind, you may prefer the term cellular automata. Either way, the fascinating thing is complexity arising out of simplicity and large numbers. One theory of human intelligence is that it emerges from the roughly 100 billion neurons (and roughly 100 trillion synapses) in each of our brains.

The emergence of complexity—and perhaps, intelligence—from large numbers of simple units is so intriguing that it may be the leading fictional premise for the arrival of an artificial intelligence (and we'll revisit that premise later, in "A Mind of Its Own").

The science-fictional (and sociological) question becomes: if complex behavior emerges from collectives of simple creatures, what sophistication might arise from collectives of more advanced creatures?

Once again, we have plenty of SF to choose from. We've already met Tines. Others include:

- The hive humans of *Hellstrom's Hive* (Frank Herbert, 1973).

- The multispecies (and partially cybernetic) Borg of the *Star Trek* franchise.

- The replicators of *Stargate SG-1*.

Collectives and emergence—hive minds—are a great way to make alien aliens, even with humans as building blocks.

MacGuffins

Some SF deals with aliens so alien as to defy human understanding. Such as:

- The Eschaton in *Singularity Sky* (2003), by Charles Stross. In Greek philosophy, the *eschaton* is the end of everything, the ultimate destiny of the Universe. Stross's fictional Eschaton is an artificial intelligence so advanced none can comprehend its thinking.*

- The Buggers/Formics of *Ender's Game* (1985). Humanity and this insectoid/hive species fight a war of extinction because humans and aliens cannot communicate. Humans cannot even convince the aliens that we are capable of communication.

---

* Perhaps when I get around to reading more of the series the inexplicable will have been explained.

- The Beings of the Beyond, in Vinge's aforementioned Zones of Thought novels. The farther one travels from the galactic core, the more advanced minds, natural *and* artificial, can become. Minds in the Beyond may seem good or evil, but—to a mere human, in any case—their capabilities and motivations are unfathomable. Humans who would try to understand Beyonders study applied theology.

Unknowable things in fiction aren't new. They're devices to move forward a plot involving beings we *can* understand: humans. Lots of fiction employs items we don't understand but to which the characters must nonetheless react. The Maltese Falcon, in the novel and movie of the same name, is such an object. Ditto the much sought after metal briefcase in the spy movie *Ronin*. Alfred Hitchcock called this type of plot device a MacGuffin.[58] Once the story gets underway, you forget to wonder what the MacGuffin really is.

So: in *Singularity Sky*, we deal with the Eschaton's human agents—them, we understand. In *A Fire Upon the Deep*, a Beyond being chases some characters into slow-witted parts of the galaxy, where readers encounter alien Tines whom we can understand.

Card's Buggers are a more complicated case. Throughout *Ender's Game* (the first book of a series, in fact two interlocking series) the Buggers are unknowable. In later books a hive queen has opened telepathic links with selected humans. The *human* story has progressed, and now the storyteller needs to establish a connection with the aliens. That step required destrangifying (like that word?) the alien.

Might the Universe have aliens *so* alien that humans can never understand them? I don't see why it couldn't happen. But unknowable aliens in fiction generally aren't only unknowable—they're props. Tools of the authorial trade. MacGuffins.

Some might say, tropes.

Artificial intelligence (AI)*

Artificial intelligences will surely be alien—different in origin and nature from us.

Perhaps our lack of success in achieving truly *intelligent* AI stems from anthropomorphism. Never mind that we can't define intelligence, awareness, or consciousness. We characterize intelligence (per the Turing test) as communicating—hence (much unstated waving of hands) thinking—indistinguishably from humans. And so fictional artificial intelligences often think like humans and even strive to behave like humans.

The AI as Pinocchio....

Consider, for example, Mike (named after Mycroft Holmes, Sherlock's smarter brother) in Robert A. Heinlein's *The Moon Is a Harsh Mistress* (1966). Or, more recently, Brittney the teeny-bopper AI in Richard A. Lovett's 2007 novella "The Sands of Titan" and its sequels. Both AIs simply emerged, bypassing our continuing lack of understanding of how we might implement an AI. Both AIs take humans as their role models.

(I've written stories with a similar premise—recognizing as I did so that I was committing a trope. When I wanted to avoid the trope, in *Fools' Experiments* (2008), I transported Darwinian evolution into a computer lab, to *breed* a quite different AI.)

There's much to be said for exploring scenarios beyond (somehow) creating in our own image within silicon. If existence inside a computer or across a network ends up having parallels with the physical world, surely there will also be differences. Look how aquatic and land-based life vary. Look how creatures that fly differ from creatures that burrow. How different might an in-computer entity be from a biological entity evolved on a planet?

Adaptation to its unnatural—to humans—environment is but one way for an AI to be alien. Another is for the AI to be so

---

* The final two chapters of the book address AI in much more detail.

advanced (think: beyond the Singularity*) that it can't be represented directly to mere humans; the author keeps the AI character offstage. As an example we've already met: the Eschaton.

Even an AI that faithfully reproduces his programmer's persona can be alien—when the *programmer* is an alien. That's one premise of my InterstellarNet series of novels, about a radio-based interstellar trading community. Physical travel between stars being impractical (early in the series, anyway), the humans and aliens alike transmit AIs to represent them. Surprise! The alien AIs are alien, and pursue alien agendas.

In *Code of the Life Maker* (1983), James P. Hogan seeds an alien factory onto Titan—and the automation mutates. The automated machinery evolves, over eons, into an entire world-spanning AI- and robot-based ecosystem. The robots don't know what to think when *humans* arrive. Neat premise. Neat story.

So AIs *can* be alien. Even alien alien.

Transhumans, uploads, and cyborgs

We need also to consider human-derived aliens. Our potential successors, whether you prefer to label them hybrids, transhumans, or posthumans (by any label, upcoming in "Human 2.0").

For example: uploads. That's what you get by transferring a brain's content into a computer. Why *would* anyone, assuming they could? To cheat death, perhaps—at least till medical science

---

* A technological advance so profound that we can't imagine the resulting makeover of civilization and/or humanity. AI, if it comes about, is only one possible singularity event.

Nothing, not even light, escapes from Nature's singularities: black holes. By analogy, we can know nothing about what life will be like after a technological singularity.

The term *Singularity* is attributed to SF author and technologist Vernor Vinge, from his 1993 paper, "The Coming Technological Singularity: How to Survive in the Post-Human Era." We'll consider the Singularity in the final chapter.

can achieve immortality or transfer minds from failing bodies into new ones.

Imagine: all one's thought patterns, learned behaviors, and memories transcribed into a new form and format. However human that mind began, it has taken residence in an environment utterly alien to us Mark I humans.

The implications go far beyond the speed difference between synapses and transistors. Imagine speed-of-thought access to vast libraries. Imagine adding radar views of the world while losing some of the more familiar senses (say, smell). Imagine real-time access—sometimes authorized, sometimes hacked—to the net's many peripherals, from Earth remote-sensing satellites to household power meters (to aerial combat drones?).

Surely the uploaded mind's temperament, attitudes, and interests will diverge from those of meat minds. And so: surely also its behavior.

Intrigued? Wikipedia offers a *very* long list of uploads in fiction.[59]

Take, for example, Robert J. Sawyer's *The Terminal Experiment* (1995). As an exploration into the nature of the soul, a scientist uploads readouts of his own brainwaves into a computer—and his enemies start dying. Uh-oh.

Uploading is carried to an incredible (in a good way) extreme in Gregory Benford's *Eater* (2000)—all the way into a black hole. And it's worth mentioning this is an *intelligent* black hole. That's quite the alien alien, too.

Assume we can upload a mind into a computer. Why not upload into a mobile computer? With wireless broadband, a robotic body can stay just as connected to the Internet as a mind bound to a data center. (But mobile or not, the uploaded mind operates without hormones and is immune to pheromones. *Futurama*'s Bender the robot will remain a trope—comedic if not science fictional.)

Let's move on to a quite different hybrid: computer-extended biological humans. Like having nanites taking up residence in the brain, as in Greg Bear's *Blood Music* (1985) and my *Small Miracles* (2009). Carrying a library in your head or hearing voices—with agendas of their own—*will* make for a more-than-merely-human experience. Let alone if, ensconced within the brain, said nanites censor or invent how we experience the world, or pull the figurative levers of power.

Yet another scenario arises from the knowledge that we're at the dawn of an age of genetic engineering. After a few years, decades, or centuries pass, how far might gengineered humans diverge from present-day norms? Which is to ask: how alien might our descendants become?

- The changes may be subtle, as exhibited by our Sleepless betters in Nancy Kress's 1991 novella and 1993 novel *Beggars in Spain.*

- Or overt, altering us for alien environments, as in the space-adapted (four-armed and legless) quaddies of Lois McMaster Bujold's *Falling Free* (1988).

- Or psychologically revealing, as when the transhumans of Mike Brotherton's *Star Dragon* keep reshaping their bodies.

And combinations

We've touched on several ways to make an alien alien—and several methods might apply at the same time. As an illustration, let's take a peek at the Gw'oth.

I invented the Gw'oth for *Fleet of Worlds* (2007, coauthored with Larry Niven); the little guys returned in three sequels. As often happens with species- and world-building, much background is merely hinted at in the final story or is omitted entirely. That's okay. I needed to understand the Gw'oth before putting them through their many-tentacled paces. Hence: four novels after their debut, some details about the Gw'oth appear here for the first time.

Setting. We'll begin with Jm'ho, the Gw'oth home world. I took as my starting point Europa: an icebound moon of Jupiter. Jm'ho has—just as astronomers now believe to be true of Europa—a world-spanning ocean trapped beneath a thick sheath of ice. Again mimicking the Jupiter system, the gas-giant planet around which Jm'ho orbits exerts intense tidal forces upon its inner moons. The ceaseless flexing keeps Jm'ho seismically active and its ocean liquid. Above the ice lies deadly vacuum.

Biochemistry. Sunlight can't penetrate the thick ice, and so photosynthesis isn't the basis of the ecosystem. Instead, life on Jm'ho depends on chemosynthesis, on harvesting energy and resources from minerals and hydrogen sulfides that endlessly upwell from the abyssal depths. A similar biome is found along the hydrothermal vents beneath Earth's oceans. Life on Jm'ho hugs the vents and undersea volcanoes; everywhere else, the world ocean is lifeless, effectively a desert.

Evolution. Along Earth's hydrothermal vents, tube worms are at the top of the food chain. On Jm'ho, chemosynthetic life has evolved further. Some worms evolved to hunt in packs. They developed vision optimized toward the red end of the human-visible spectrum. (Why and how, in the inky depths, could they have *any* sight? They see in infrared wavelengths, the better to discern ocean vents and the fainter heat of prey. Their vision gradually expanded to exploit the sporadic reddish glow of fresh lava from volcanic eruptions.)

Some pack-hunting worms also evolved the ability to connect nervous systems. In such linkages, they extended the resolution and angular separation of their primitive IR-sensitive triangulation. From such worm colonies, over time, evolved starfish-like hunters: the immediate ancestors of the Gw'oth.

Physiology and appearance. A Gw'o loosely resembles a starfish crossed with an octopus. The Gw'o's five flexible extremities are equally spaced around a disklike central mass.[*] Each tubular

---

[*] I might appear to be fixated on radial symmetry. Not remarked upon in the Gw'oth's adventures (but known to me), internal organs of, and markings upon, the central mass give the Gw'o left/

tentacle—tubacle—harkens back to the Gwo's ancestral, free-ranging tube worms. From the mouth inward, arrayed in consecutive rings around the tube's inner surface, are teeth, eyes, ears, and the myriad chemoreceptors for taste and smell. Shared organs, including most of the central nervous system, reside in the central disk. Flattened and with its tubacles outstretched, a Gw'o spans about two-thirds of a meter.

Sensory apparatus and communications. A Gw'o's vision, compared to a human's, is biased toward infrared; it can't see past blue. Its hearing and speech coevolved with echolocation. Befitting a carnivore at the apex of a chemosynthetic ecology, a Gw'o has keen senses of taste and smell. Complex communication relies upon modulated sound, but a Gw'o, like an Earthly squid, conveys emotions—sometimes involuntarily—with color patterns on its skin.

Locomotion. Gw'oth both swim and scuttle along the ocean floor. To swim, they draw in water through an orifice in the central mass and expel the water through their tubacles. That is, a Gw'o is jet-propelled. It steers, veers, and spins by aiming and reaiming its tubacles.

Reproduction. Gw'oth have genders—but neither gender roles nor sex. Females deposit egg clusters within breeding chambers in the Jm'ho analogue to coral reefs. Males later fertilize the egg clusters. Some social groupings limit breeding-chamber access to individuals of suitable prestige. At birth, the immature, not-yet-sentient newborns scatter; those few spawn that manage to elude predators and to mature are accepted into Gw'oth society.*

---

right symmetry. A Gw'o has no need for a Krul-like out-of-body reference. That's fortunate, because neither Jm'ho nor its primary has much of a magnetic field.

* Gw'oth *can* eject gametes anywhere, and egg and sperm could manage to meet. But the sea is full of predators....

And the very few unsanctioned offspring that do survive? Newly mature Gw'oth return to their spawning ground, at which time they are taken into the social grouping. Unsanctioned spawn that survive are apt to become rogue and feral adults.

Group minds. To make the Gw'oth really alien (and to advance a plot), I had a tiny fraction of the population retain the ancestral ability to link nervous systems. When Gw'oth link minds this way, they form a biological computer: a Gw'otesht. With their memories imprinted into the group consciousness—a limited sort of upload—members of a Gw'otesht experience a degree of life after death.

A Gw'otesht of enough members can be scary smart....

Technology. With prehensile and opposable tubacles to manipulate objects, Gw'oth are natural tool users. Living underwater, alas, they've been without fire to smelt ores or forge metals; for most of Gw'oth history they've had only stone tools. Their communities of stacked-stone buildings hug the serpentine ocean-floor vents. He who controls the life-giving vents holds all power; Gw'oth government tends toward dictatorship—just as the pharaohs used their control of the life-giving Nile to maintain a water-monopoly empire in the Egyptian desert.

And then some enterprising Gw'oth learn to fashion watertight animal-hide suits, and to circulate water to and from the suits with leather hoses pumped by leather bellows. And go exploring above the ocean through (once again, Europa-like) fissures in the world-girding ice. And first encounter *stars*.

And everything changes....

Wrapping up

Adaptations for exotic environments and alternative body plans. Unique senses and different genders. Group minds and AIs, uploads and gengineered transhumans. And yet, we have only scratched the surface.

How else might aliens be *really* alien?

Through a novel psychology, perhaps, as in Ted Chiang's 1998 novella "Story of Your Life," whose alien heptapods have a mind-blowingly unique perception of reality. Or through alternate organizing principles for society. Or because they've been enhanced/altered from dolphins, as in Brin's Uplift series. Or by being immortal shape-shifters, à la Joe Haldeman's *Camouflage* (2004). Or maybe as shapeshifting cyborgs, as we meet from time to time in the TV series *Fringe*.

Or, or, or....

It would take entire books to explore the spectrum of possible aliens, and ways to craft them. Books such as these:

- *Aliens and Alien Societies: A writer's guide to creating extraterrestrial life-forms*, Stanley Schmidt.

- *Barlowe's Guide to Extraterrestrials: Great Aliens from Science Fiction Literature*, Wayne Douglas Barlowe, Ian Summers, and Beth Meacham.

- *Beyond Human: Living with Robots and Cyborgs*, by Gregory Benford and Elisabeth Malartre.

ALIEN WORLDS

Not in Kansas Anymore

We've looked at how authors might make our aliens, well, alien. What about the worlds where the aliens might live? Because alien worlds in science fiction often aren't *science* fictional at all. Or for that matter, alien. (Unless, that is, like the writers of the *Stargate* franchise, you expect worlds across the galaxies to resemble the forests of British Columbia.)

What might alien worlds be like? Until a few years ago, astronomers' only data came from this, our native solar system. We had a sample size of one—and the smaller the dataset, the more apt our extrapolations were to go awry. In recent years, however, through a growing number of sky surveys and subtle observational methods, astronomers have detected more than a thousand extra-solar planets—exoplanets, for short—orbiting hundreds of stars.[60] We can now speculate on the basis of much more information.

In this chapter we'll survey properties that might vary across worlds (e.g., composition, seasons, surface dynamics, and tides).* We'll consider a few well-realized alien worlds in SF. And we'll

---

*   *World*, in this context, is a generic term inclusive of all substellar heavenly bodies. *Planet*, as we will see, has a narrower definition. This chapter is mostly concerned with the plausibly habitable subset of planets (and, perhaps, the occasional moon that's as large as a planet).

touch upon what authors—and someday, planetary engineers—might do to render inhospitable worlds more welcoming. This isn't a manual with which authors can "build" alien worlds (for that, see this chapter's "to read further" list), but it suggests details that authors might consider, and their readers might expect to find, in off-Earth stories.*

Planets and stars arise from a common process, so let's begin with an overview of how (we think) solar systems form.

A world-wind tour

Solar systems are understood to form from the collapse of giant (and originally very diffuse) molecular clouds, also known as solar nebulae. Disks of gas and dust observed around many a protostar (the final, pre-fusion stage of a star's emergence) support this "nebular hypothesis." Collapse of such a cloud can originate—very slowly—in its self-gravitational attraction or be triggered by shock waves (e.g., from nova and supernova events) traveling through the interstellar medium.

Nor are all giant molecular clouds of equal interest to our topic. The cooling residue of the Big Bang provided hydrogen (mostly), helium, and traces of lithium. The first stars—and any planets that formed with them—contained only those elements. It is only as stars die—and, in the case of novae and supernovae, go out with a (not quite as Big) bang—that heavier elements, cooked up in stellar processes, are distributed into space. Hence, solid worlds will only be found in younger solar systems—born from younger clouds. Luckily for us, Sol formed a mere 4.5 billion years ago (Bya), give or take, about ten billion years after the Big Bang.

---

* I *don't* mean to suggest that storytellers should present every detail of their fictional alien worlds. As with most matters authorial, world-building is a balancing act. Dwell too much on the background, and the story's pacing suffers. Offer too little background, and the story's credibility—at least among a subset of readers—suffers.

The extent of the primordial cloud matters, too. Start from a low-mass cloud and the resulting star is (like most stars in the Universe) a red dwarf.* A red-dwarf star has a tiny habitable zone (more on that concept later); the prospects for life are constrained on worlds in a red-dwarf system.

More isn't always better. Start from a too massive cloud, and the resulting star will "burn" fast and hot.† Stars just a few times Sol's mass have predicted lifetimes in the millions, not billions, of years. Multicellular life took billions of years to appear on Earth, so planets of a large, short-lived star may run out of time before duplicating that feat.

Typically, the theory goes, clumps of matter emerge from a diffuse dust-and-gas cloud through a combination of local gravitational attraction and/or sticky collisions. Once gravity gathers and compresses a protostar sufficiently to initiate nuclear fusion, a star‡ is born—

And things get interesting.

The new star radiates light (photons) and solar wind. Near the star, few constituents of the primordial cloud have melting points high enough to survive the intense heat. Most cloud

---

* If the precursor cloud is a bit too small to yield even a red dwarf, the result will be a brown dwarf. A brown dwarf is a not-quite star that glows from its heat of formation (gravitational collapse) but never gets hot enough to initiate H_1 fusion. (Larger brown dwarves may exhibit H_2 fusion, but that's a short-lived process due to the scarcity of deuterium in stellar nebulae.) Planets have been spotted orbiting some brown-dwarf stars.

A collapsing cloud that is smaller still may yield a free-floating "planetary mass object."

† Unless irregular distributions in the cloud or the precipitating shock wave(s) lead instead to the birth of several smaller stars.

‡ For now, for simplicity, we'll stick with single-star systems, although binary stars are more common (and groupings of more than two stars do exist). The basic physics are the same in single—and multiple-star systems; the orbital mechanics, not so much.

constituents, even grains that had started to stick together, are (or are turned to) gas swept outward by the solar wind.

The farther from the star, of course, the cooler the surroundings. Compound by compound, at characteristic temperatures (and so, distances), grains can reappear. And clump. And gravitationally attract one another....

And so Mercury formed, near our Sun, from high-melting-point metal oxides. Everything else originally in (that region of) the primordial cloud had been swept away. Earth formed farther out from the Sun—with most of its considerable metal content locked in the core—with its familiar, lower-melting-point mineral compounds.

The outer Asteroid Belt is cold enough for water to remain frozen even in a vacuum. Beyond a distance from the Sun known as the ice line we start to see snowballs. Yet farther from the Sun, where even hydrogen can form solids, we find mighty Jupiter.

(Earth is well within the ice line. Before the planet formed, the solar wind should have carried away most water molecules. So why does Earth have water? We'll come to that.)

And yet farther from the Sun, from the dregs of the primordial gas cloud that Jupiter failed to capture, the remaining gas-giant planets formed.* Saturn and its more remote siblings are smaller than Jupiter, because the gas cloud's gravitational collapse left only slim pickings the farther out from the star one looks. And because the outermost planets have the longest orbits, these worlds are slower to gather up the widely distributed mass that *is* available.

Some definitions: An object is a *planet* if it orbits a star,† is massive enough to have been rendered effectively spherical by the pull of its own gravity, and has cleared out its orbital

---

* Uranus and Neptune are sometimes categorized as ice giants rather than gas giants. These planets are believed to have larger solid cores than Jupiter and Saturn, and comparatively thinner gaseous outer layers.

† Strictly speaking, the IAU definition for *planet* actually requires the object to be orbiting the Sun. I'm generalizing.

neighborhood. (The International Astronomical Union, or IAU, added that third criterion to their definition in 2006. Hence Pluto, creeping about the Sun only once every 248 Earth years, not having cleared out its distant neighborhood, was reclassified—some would say demoted—to the new category of "dwarf planet."[61]) Lesser objects orbiting the Sun include comets, asteroids, and meteoroids.[62] Bodies that orbit around planets (or lesser Sun-orbiting objects) are called moons.

Aggregating, clumping, sweeping…it all sounds stately and serene. It can happen that way—but usually doesn't. The heavily cratered surface of the Moon testifies to the violence of the Solar System's (not thought to be unusual) Late Heavy Bombardment period. The Moon itself, it is believed, coalesced from Earth-orbiting debris after a Mars-sized protoplanet struck the young Earth a glancing blow.[63]

And planets may not remain as close to—or as remote from—their sun as where they formed. Simulations of planetary formation suggest Uranus and Neptune couldn't have grown to their observed sizes if they had formed in or near their observed orbits. Uranus and Neptune likely formed closer to the Sun, where raw materials were more prevalent. If so, gravitational interactions among planets, or the influence of a passing star, caused these two gas giants to migrate outward. And it also appears that planets can move inward. Many an exoplanet is a "hot Jupiter": a gas-giant planet (i.e., like Jupiter) orbiting too near its star to have formed, as planetary astronomers understand the process, where the world is now detected.

Simulations suggest that orbital billiards can get yet more complex. Not only can orbits shift and worlds collide, planets can be forced into a sun—or ejected entirely from their native solar system.[64]

And in the outer darkness

Far from a star, where objects reflect too little sunlight to readily be detected, what is the situation? It is extrapolated from the nebular hypothesis that huge amounts of mass are out there, including lots of water expelled past the ice line. Further, objects that took shape in the inner solar system may have been scattered to these remote distances by gravitational interactions with the gas-giant planets. From all this mass, many objects may exist billions of miles from the star.

Once again, we'll take the Solar System as our model. As new, large telescopes have begun to reveal, there's a lot in the dark beyond Neptune.* The Kuiper Belt (named after astronomer Gerard Kuiper) is a huge annular region stretching from about 4.5 billion kilometers / 2.8 billion miles / 30 astronomical units (AU) to about 7.5 billion kilometers / 4.7 billion miles / 50 AU from the Sun. Like the better-known Asteroid Belt between Mars and Jupiter, the Kuiper Belt teems with orbiting objects. Pluto, we now know, is just one of many. By current estimates, "...there are at least 35,000 Kuiper Belt objects greater than 100 km in diameter, which is several hundred times the number (and mass) of similar sized objects in the main asteroid belt." The Kuiper Belt is believed to be the source of short-period comets (those with orbital periods of 200 years or less). Beyond the Kuiper Belt, it is *inferred*, lies a yet more expansive region, extending 7.5 trillion kilometers / 4.65 trillion miles / 50,000 AU or more from the Sun, that may teem with yet more objects. This larger, spherical expanse, known as the Oort Cloud (after astronomer Jan Oort), may contain as many as a trillion long-period comets whose ag-

---

* Also, perhaps, stuff that telescopes *can't* see: the mysterious dark matter that astronomers invoke to explain the observed properties of galaxies and galactic clusters. More than a little puzzling is that a detailed analysis of orbits within the Solar System puts a negligible upper bound on the density of dark matter in our neighborhood—not nearly enough (extrapolated to larger scales) to explain, for example, the motions of stars within our galaxy.

See "The Incredible Dark Matter Mystery: Why Astronomers Say it is Missing in Action," no author given, *MIT Technology Review*, July 3, 2013, https://www.technologyreview.com/s/516681/the-incredible-dark-matter-mystery-why-astronomers-say-it-is-missing-in-action/.

gregate mass may rival Jupiter. Objects this remote from the Sun are only very loosely bound, their orbits subject to perturbation by nearby stars.[65]

With the July 2015 Pluto flyby of the *New Horizon* probe, planetary astronomers greatly expanded our knowledge of this remote world and its moons. That plucky probe is en route to investigate another world, a billion miles deeper into the Kuiper Belt.[66]

Another world

And perhaps an actual, honest-to-IAU *planet* lurks in the remote darkness.

Neptune's existence was implied by math: the gravitational attraction of an undiscovered world was invoked to explain perceived anomalies in Uranus's orbit. Astronomers spotted Neptune where the math—and Newton's formula for gravitational attraction—instructed them to look. Neptune's orbit, in turn, was seen to exhibit anomalies; the same mathematical process led to the discovery of Pluto. Strangely enough, Pluto, once found, was far too small to explain Neptune's orbital anomalies—spotting Pluto in this way was pure luck. Many years later, refined orbital determinations for Neptune eliminated the perceived anomalies that had so coincidentally led to the discovery of Pluto.

Astronomers recently catalogued anomalous orbits among several Kuiper Belt Objects (KBO), anomalies that computer models can explain as perturbations caused by an unknown body that is very distant (as much as 150 billion kilometers / 93 billion miles / 1000 AU from the Sun) and very massive (several times the mass of Earth). Call that unseen world—from everyone's favorite algebraic unknown—Planet X.* Perhaps a new generation of telescopes will be able to spot it.

---

* If only Pluto had maintained its title as the ninth planet, the suspected distant body could also have laid Roman-numeral credit to being Planet X. (That said, fans of *really* bad movies may be okay with "Planet 9 from Outer Space.")

Current telescopes can detect relatively few KBOs, fewer still exhibiting anomalous orbits—and yet, from these few, Planet X can be inferred. Extrapolation from a small sample is always dangerous, but there *might* be several more large planets out there.

Or—by analogy to another onetime planet hunt—there may be none. According to Newtonian gravitational calculations, Mercury *also* has an anomalous orbit. To explain those anomalies, astronomers once searched for a planet orbiting even closer to the Sun than Mercury. The long-sought planet Vulcan was never seen—because it doesn't exist. The perceived anomaly arose from a problem inherent to the calculation, not to any unseen planet. Einstein's theory of gravity, more complete and accurate than Newton's, fully explains Mercury's orbit without recourse to undiscovered planets.[67]

And the relevance to alien worlds? First, that we have little hard data about the type(s) of worlds that exist at the borders of our own solar system. Second, that Planet X—if it exists—may well have formed much closer to the Sun than its (vaguely) inferred present-day orbit, and gotten flung outward. The farther one recedes from a protostar, the less dense the solar nebula from which objects can form, and the slower the aggregation process. There hasn't been enough time, according to models, for X to have grown to its perceived mass where it is suspected to orbit.

Bottom line: it will be awhile before astronomers know much about what transpires on the fringes of other solar systems. For SF authors, at least, that's liberating.

A rocky start

For storytelling, we're often concerned with worlds more or less habitable by humans, and we'll focus on that class of worlds.

Some criteria are obvious. We want solid-surface (i.e., "rocky") worlds massive enough (i.e., of sufficient gravity) to retain an atmosphere, but not so massive as to crush us. We want ample surface water, because our biology (another sample of one data point) requires water. We want a breathable atmosphere. How do these conditions arise?

A world that forms inside the ice line can grow to a suitable size. A world much less massive than Earth lacks the gravity to retain an atmosphere over geological time (see: Mars). And wherever the world formed—like luggage in the overhead bin, it may have shifted in flight—it had best have settled into a stable orbit within its solar system's habitable (or "Goldilocks") zone. That's the narrow region near the star where conditions are neither too hot nor too cold—i.e., where liquid water remains stable on the planetary surface. Inside the ice line, obviously (but that's too simple, as we'll see). Outside the analogous steam line.

Why the caveat about the ice line?

Primarily, it relates to the influence of an atmosphere. An atmosphere can trap heat, raising a world's equilibrium temperature from what it would otherwise be. The extent of such greenhouse effect depends upon the detailed composition of the atmosphere. Absent the greenhouse effect, Earth's average temperature would be about 39 °C colder. In fact, without the natural greenhouse effect (predating, and much stronger than, the anthropogenic kind), all water on Earth's surface would *freeze*.

(Given that Earth orbits well inside the Solar System's ice line, that last assertion is less than intuitive. So: consider the fate of water on Earth's surface without an atmosphere. In those circumstances, H_2O can only be vapor or ice. Water won't stay liquid—at *any* temperature—at pressures less than about 0.006 standard atmospheres. Over time, any ice would sublimate, and the resultant vapor would gradually escape.* With the pressure of an atmosphere, however, surface water can freeze. With an atmosphere for pressure but without a greenhouse effect, Earth's water would stay frozen.)

---

* To make matters even more convoluted, ice can persist inside the ice line even in a vacuum—in localities that are uncharacteristically cold. Evidence suggests that ice can be found in significant quantities on the permanently shadowed floors of several (mostly polar) lunar craters.

After more than a century spent burning fossil fuels, Earth's primary greenhouse gas isn't carbon dioxide—that remains water vapor. But *Venus* has altogether too much carbon dioxide, and the corresponding greenhouse effect raises that world's surface temperature by about 525 °C(!) over what it would otherwise be. By the action of greenhouse heating, Venus, though about twice as distant from the Sun as Mercury, has a hotter surface than Mercury.

Because solar wind drives low-mass molecules such as water from the inner Solar System, you might wonder how Earth (or any world that formed inside its solar system's ice line) can have water. From the bombardment of comets and water-rich asteroids and (probably to a lesser extent) from water vapor emitted by chemical processes deep inside the Earth.

Because a world's stock of volatiles (collectively, the chemical elements and compounds that have low boiling points) are believed to be significantly influenced by random asteroid/comet impacts, SF authors have considerable leeway in fine-tuning the water levels and atmospheric composition of fictional worlds.

Notice the qualifiers in the preceding paragraph. Planets are complex; hence, the amounts and forms of volatile substances can—and do—change over time. Sunlight photo-dissociates water vapor, and a world's gravity may be too weak to retain the liberated hydrogen (so the water vapor doesn't re-form). Mars, surely, lost much of its water through photo-dissociation. Solar wind can, over time, also strip gases from an upper atmosphere. The solar wind's effects can be mitigated by a planetary magnetosphere deflecting the oncoming stream of charged particles (while making pretty auroras).*

Not every world *has* a magnetosphere. Earth does, produced (the theory goes) by the circulation of electrical currents within the planet's molten-iron core.

---

* A magnetosphere, despite the name, isn't spherical. The down-solar-wind side of the magnetic field trails far from the planet that generates the field.

Why molten? Worlds begin *hot*, as a byproduct of their formation. Gravity crushing things together produces lots of heat. So do protoplanets colliding. The decay of radioactive elements trapped inside a planet emits yet more heat. In sufficiently large bodies (not huge, either; some asteroids were large enough), enough heat is generated to melt the object. Heavier materials sink and lighter ones float. The interiors of larger planets—Earth among them—remain hot billions of years after this original melting and differentiation. Smaller worlds—Mars again, as an example—lose their heat faster. The core solidifies, and (if it ever had one) the protective magnetosphere goes away.

Subsurface molten rock also drives the process of plate tectonics.[68] Though these plates move at, literally, a geological pace, this process may be essential to the long-term survivability of life. Why? In a word, recycling. Plate tectonics causes the slooow-motion transfer of material down into the subduction zones (where one plate slides beneath another)—and those materials can return to the surface through volcanic activity. And so, as one example, life-essential carbon that would otherwise have become forever locked in limestone ($CaCO_3$) may reemerge someday in a volcanic eruption as carbon dioxide, to keep the oceans from freezing or to be incorporated into plant life.

Oxygen is *highly* reactive. Unless regularly replenished, oxygen doesn't persist in an atmosphere. Earth's crust incorporates lots of oxides, especially silicon dioxide (sand and quartz). Mars is red from the prevalence of iron oxide: rust. Someday, when astronomers first detect an exoplanet with an oxygen-rich atmosphere, there will be much rejoicing. Why? Because that atmosphere will suggest (drawing again on a sample size of one) the presence of a biosphere that synthesizes and continually replenishes the oxygen supply.[*]

---

[*] The absence of atmospheric oxygen would not disprove the presence of even certain terrestrial-style life. Anaerobic life teems, for example, along hydrothermal vents in Earth's abyssal depths.

And yet, one recent study proposes an oxygen-rich atmosphere may be misleading. The scenario involves planets of red-dwarf stars: the most common stars in the Universe. When young (and in their planet-forming era), red dwarves can be many times hotter than at maturity. Hence: a planet of such a star seen orbiting in the star's present-day Goldilocks zone, might once have been roasted. The water such a world initially had would long since have been photo-dissociated into hydrogen and oxygen, and the hydrogen mostly carried away by the solar wind. Now suppose the rock of the planetary surface couldn't oxidize all the oxygen left behind. The result would be a waterless world with an abiotic oxygen atmosphere.[69]

Oxygen offers a world more than O_2 to breathe. Ozone (O_3) is a much scarcer molecular form (allotrope) of oxygen, but risen high enough in the atmosphere, even in trace amounts, ozone blocks otherwise hazardous levels of ultraviolet light. Mars is farther from the Sun than Earth, and yet—for the lack of an ozone layer—the Martian surface receives more UV radiation than does Earth's.

There are yet more factors that effect a world's habitability:

- Stars grow more luminous with age (Sol is thought to be emitting about 30 percent more energy than in its youth). Planetary feedback processes—adjusting the concentrations of greenhouse gases, the degree of cloud cover, and the extent/distribution of surface ice—can, for a time, mitigate the increased energy input.

- Biogeochemical changes in atmospheric composition eclipse any climate changes humans have ever made. Roughly 2 – 2.5 Bya, when oxygen-exhaling bacteria became common on Earth, the toxic oxygen they emitted appears to have killed off most of the earlier, anaerobic species.

- Continental drift (caused by plate tectonics) alters ocean currents. Consider how often changes in El Niño and

116

La Niña currents are called upon to explain weather-pattern shifts.

- Living on land is evidently more difficult than living in water: Earthly life did not establish itself on land until about one-half Bya.

- Some stars are more prone than others to flaring.[70]

And let us not forget ice ages. Despite the Sun's gradual warming, Earth has endured several extreme glaciations—with associated mass extinctions. Chalk up those events to feedback loops too slow, or with too much overshoot, to (for example) respond to a biogeochemical change.

One lesson: when drawing on experience to define "Earth-like" planets, remember the range of behaviors *Earth* has exhibited throughout its history.[71]

Are exoplanets...planets?

Until quite recently, astronomers had never *seen* an exoplanet—and when finally they did, through software legerdemain, they saw merely a few pixels.[72] The standard methods of detecting an exoplanet work by indirection. One detection method uses the slight periodic dimming of starlight when an exoplanet orbits in front of the star (as viewed from Earth). Another method uses the slight visible wobble of a star as a massive-enough planet and its star orbit about their common center of mass.

Recall that a planet, by definition, is basically round and has cleared out its orbital neighborhood. That's a problematical definition when our methods for detecting remote worlds don't reveal their shapes, much less whether these worlds might share their orbits with much tinier rubble. So, by the present definition, we can't say there are any exoplanets.

Astronomer Jean-Luc Margot recently proposed an alternate definition, based upon measurements of an object's mass, orbital period, and the age of its solar system.* Mass and our understanding of gravity together indicate whether—if only we could see it—a remote object would have pulled itself into a more-or-less round shape. A model of planetary formation estimates whether the distant object has had sufficient time to clear out its orbital neighborhood. Applied to the Solar System, Margot's model agrees well with IAU definitions.

It's quite clever.[73]

Mooning around

Moons can form along with planets in a process mirroring how planets form with suns. And as we've seen, gravitational interactions can send heavenly bodies careening, so some moons may be captured worlds. To judge by their asteroid-like surfaces, Phobos and Deimos, the two tiny moons of Mars, fall into the latter category.[74]

A few moons in the Solar System are quite large. Titan, Saturn's largest moon, is a world bigger than the planet Mercury, and it's massive enough to keep an atmosphere that's even denser than Earth's. Nothing precludes a moon—such as Endor, home of the Ewoks in the *Star Wars* universe—from being a fully terrestrial world.

Exoplanet-hunting techniques honed in recent years are now being refined for hunting exomoons.[75]

Ring around the planet

The tiniest of moons are mere particles of dust and gas. Combine enough of those, however, and you have a spectacular ring system.

---

* The age of the Solar System can be estimated fairly precisely through the radiometric dating of meteorites. The age estimates of other stars are indirect and imprecise.

See "How do scientists determine the ages of stars? Is the technique really accurate enough to use it to verify the age of the universe?" Stephen A. Naftilan, *Scientific American,* October 21, 1999, http://www.scientificamerican.com/article/how-do-scientists-determi/.

Saturn, of course, is famous for its gorgeous ring system, but the remaining gas-giant planets of the Solar System also have (much fainter) rings. Rings can result from collisions between moons, from the "volcanic" ejecta of a moon (as Saturn's moon Enceladus spouts water geysers), or the matter scattered by large asteroid impacts to a planetary or moon surface. The leading (although not universally held) theory for the formation of the Moon, supported by a wide range of data, envisions a Mars-sized object striking the young Earth, and the Moon coalescing, over time, from Earth's short-lived debris ring.[76]

I shattered Himalia, a small moon of Jupiter, in *Interstellar-Net: New Order* (2010). Neal Stephenson shattered *the* Moon, in *Seveneves* (2015).

Given the four ring systems to be found within the Solar System, it's difficult to imagine that some exoplanets do not also have rings. But can astronomers detect such rings? If the rings are sufficiently opaque and positioned correctly to block Earth's view of enough light from their star, then yes. In fact, such a ring system may already have been spotted, with rings 200 times as wide as Saturn's. A gap within those rings suggests a Mars-sized exomoon.[77]

There is a tide in the affairs of worlds

Gravity decreases with the square of distance, so a world can experience a differential tug of gravity (from another body) between its near and far sides. In other words: tides. An ocean isn't necessary: tides will flex the solid material of a rocky world and influence the fluid layers of a gas giant. Moons aren't necessary either: the *Sun* produces tides (although on Earth, not as dramatic as the tides our Moon produces).

The strength of the tide is proportional to the mass whose gravity produces the tide and inversely proportional to the *cube* of the distance to that mass. The inverse-cube factor explains how the Moon produces stronger tides than the very much more massive (but far more distant) Sun. Were the Moon to orbit Earth at *half* their present average separation, the lunar-produced tides would be *eight* times as strong.*

Hence massive planets can produce *major* tidal effects on their closest moons. The tidal flexing that Jupiter causes on its moon Europa appears to keep a water ocean liquid beneath a thick coat of ice. Ditto Saturn's influence on its moon Enceladus.

The gravitational pull between planet and star, or moon and planet, are symmetrical. And so, just as the Moon produces tides on Earth, the Earth produces tides in the body of the Moon. The math is a bit messy, but the consequences are clear. First, the drag of these Earth-induced tides has braked the Moon's rotation until that body shows only one face to Earth.[†] Second, gravity's tug being bidirectional, *Earth's* spin has also been slowed (and continues to slow). Third (and conserving the angular momentum of the combined Earth/Moon system as Earth's rotation slows), the Moon's orbit slowly recedes from Earth.[‡]

Earth's satellite isn't unique. Many natural satellites across the Solar System are tidally locked to their planets.

Nor is tidal locking reserved for moons. A close-orbiting planet can become tidally locked to its star (although it hasn't happened to any planet in the Solar System). Consider any red dwarf star: it's small, cool, and dim. Its Goldilocks zone will

---

* That doesn't mean the tides would become everywhere eight times as high; it's a statement about how the orbital change would alter the *energy* pumping the tides. Local topography interacts with the surging water, which is why tide levels vary dramatically from place to place along a coast.

† More precisely, Earth's view of theMoon, over time, encompasses ~59% of the lunar surface. This *libration* (wobbling) effect arises from the Sun's influence and the Moon following an elliptical orbit around the Earth.

‡ By NASA estimates, the Moon is receding by not quite four centimeters per year, in the process lengthening Earth's days by about three milliseconds per century. See "Secular Acceleration of the Moon," http://eclipse.gsfc.nasa.gov/SEcat5/secular.html.

be small, and *very* close to the star. Tidal effects vary (as we've seen) inversely with the cube of the distance, so any planet close enough to a red-dwarf star to be in the habitable zone will tidally lock to that star.*

A tidally locked planet will have a perpetually dark/cold side and a perpetually sunlit/warm side. On the dark side, cold air (presuming there is an atmosphere) sinks, drawing in warmer air from the lit side; the prevailing winds are apt to be ferocious. Simulations disagree if/when oceanic and atmospheric currents can moderate conditions sufficiently to leave such a world habitable, even in the twilight band that would separate hot and cold sides.

Now consider a moon orbiting such a tidally locked planet. As the moon orbits—even if that moon is tidally locked to its planet—the *moon* won't present one face to its *sun*. The planet might even warm the moon a bit through tidal flexing. Jupiter in this manner raises the average temperature of Europa by about 8 °C, so the effect can be nontrivial. So let's take a gas giant that can only have formed outside the local ice line. Let's allow its orbit to shift sunward (as seems to have happened to many a hot Jupiter) and give it a more-or-less Titan-sized, close-orbiting moon. Voilà! A habitable world in a red-dwarf solar system—no matter what the simulations decide about tidally locked planets.

To every planet there is a season(s)

At the scale of textbook illustrations, planetary orbits are circles. At a larger scale it becomes clear (and it is one of Kepler's laws of planetary motion) that every planetary orbit is an ellipse with the

---

* Or not, according to one recent simulation. The simulation suggests that tides induced in a sufficiently dense atmosphere will slow the pace of tidal locking of the world.

See "Exoplanets could avoid 'tidal locking' if they have atmospheres," Ken Croswell, *Physics World*, January 15, 2015, http://physicsworld.com/cws/article/news/2015/jan/15/exoplanets-could-avoid-tidal-locking-if-they-have-atmospheres.

Sun at one of the two foci. The distance between star and planet varies over the course of a planetary revolution (its year). For a sufficiently eccentric orbit, the annual variation in distance can be substantial.*

Electromagnetic radiation (read: light, of all wavelengths) diminishes inversely with the square of the distance. Consider a planetary orbit whose separation from its sun varies by ten percent in the course of a year. At its closest approach to its sun, that planet would receive in excess of 23% more irradiance than at its farthest point (1/[0.9 * 0.9] ~ 1.235).

That said, the slight annual variation in Sun/Earth distance is not the cause of Earth's seasons. (If the Earth/Sun distance variation were responsible for our seasons, then northern and southern hemispheres would experience their summers and winters together—not half a year out of phase.) Rather, our seasons originate in the tilt of Earth's axis with respect to the plane of Earth's orbit. When a hemisphere is tilted toward the Sun it gets more intense illumination (than if not tilted) and experiences summer; the hemisphere tilted away from the Sun gets more diffuse radiation than otherwise and experiences winter.

The tilt of a planet's axis can be, well, anything. In the Solar System, planetary tilts range from effectively none (Mercury), to 23.4°

---

* Geometers characterize an ellipse's variance from circularity by its *eccentricity*, a parameter that ranges between zero and one. A circle can be described as an ellipse with an eccentricity of zero. A straight line segment can be described as an ellipse with an eccentricity of one.

Earth's orbit, all but circular, has an eccentricity of a mere 0.0167. Mercury, whose orbit is the furthest from circular of any planet in the Solar System, has an eccentricity of about 0.21. The exoplanet known only as HD20782, about 117 light-years from Earth, has an eccentricity of 0.96. *That* is one eccentric orbit! If HD20782's orbit were overlaid upon the Solar System, that orbit would vary from very near the Sun, well within Mercury's orbit, to far outside the orbit of Mars.

See "Most eccentric planet known flashes astronomers with reflected light," *SF State News* (that's San Francisco State University), March 16, 2016, http://news.sfsu.edu/news-story/most-eccentric-planet-known-flashes-astronomers-reflected-light.

(Earth), to 97° (Uranus, which more-or-less orbits on its side) and 177° (Venus, compared to the rest of the planets, is upside down).*

Recall the angular-momentum coupling between Earth and Moon in the discussion of tidal braking and tidal locks. A moon and planet interact in yet another way: the stabilization of their spin axes. Conservation of angular momentum across the Earth/Moon system helps keep steady (but still, not *quite* constant) Earth's axial tilt. Mars, with its two tiny moons, lacks such stabilization. All worlds in a solar system are subject to gravitational perturbations from other worlds, great and small—and, on occasion, by collisions. Mars appears to have undergone dramatic shifts in the orientation of its axis, with attendant disruption to its seasons and climate.

Let's introduce another possible "seasonal" variable—the effect of linked stars. A binary star consists of two stars orbiting around their common center of mass. Binary stars with planets are known, with the planets most often orbiting one or another sun but sometimes—mimicking *Star War*'s Tatooine—orbiting both stars.[78]

Consider our nearest interstellar neighbor, the Alpha Centauri system. Alpha Centauri A is a Sol-like, G-class (yellow) star; Alpha Centauri B, almost as luminous, is a K-class (orange) star.† Over a cycle of about eighty years, A and B's separation varies from about that between Sol and Neptune to about that between Sol and Saturn. That's sufficient separation (simulations say) that Alpha Centauri A and B could separately

---

* Astronomers define the north pole of a world using a right-hand rule. Curl the fingers of your right hand in the direction of a world's rotation, and your thumb points in the direction of the north pole. A tilt > 90° places the north pole, so defined, beneath the plane of the planet's orbit. ("Above the orbital plane" is likewise defined by a right-hand rule.)

† Alpha Centauri is actually a triple star. Alpha Centauri C, aka Proxima Centauri—the star nearest to Sol—is a red dwarf, both too dim and too distant from A and B to noticeably affect A's and B's planets.

have planets in stable orbits—even to have planets within their respective Goldilocks zones. (Alpha Centauri B, in fact, is now known to have a planet, though closer to its star than the habitable zone.[79])

How do the climates on such planets change when the two suns are at their orbital extremes? And knowing how "mere" Jupiter can perturb the orbits of neighboring worlds, imagine how a companion *star* within solar-system distances might alter planetary orbits and axial tilts.[*]

In my *InterstellarNet: New Order* (2010), the cyclic approach of a companion star causes a once-in-a-lifetime warm period that the local aliens have dubbed "life's summer." If the companion star's only effect were this cyclical hot spell, that wouldn't be so bad—but it's not. The fossil and historical records show, all too clearly, recurrent climate upheavals, and the companion star's potentially disruptive effect on the home world's tilt is the clear culprit. Cixin Liu's *The Three-Body Problem* (English translation by Ken Liu, 2014) relies upon yet more dramatic—if wholly trope-ish—binary-star-induced instabilities, in planetary orbits as well as axial tilts.

Finally (and simplifying furiously), it turns out that, due to various interactions among bodies of the Solar System, several characteristics of orbits and planets' axial tilts slowly vary over the millennia. The umbrella term for these periodic changes is "Milankovitch cycles." These cycles have been implicated in triggering some of Earth's ice ages.[80]

---

[*] That's not to say only long-distance gravitational tugs can effect a world's spin axis. The spin axis of the Moon appears to have been shifted about six degrees by a long-ago upwelling of magma redistributing lunar mass.

See "Tales of a tilting Moon hidden in its polar ice: The spin axis of the Moon has moved by at least 6°, and that motion is recorded in ancient lunar ice deposits," (no author given), Planetary Science Institute, March 24, 2016, http://www.astronomy.com/news/2016/03/tales-of-a-tilting-moon-hidden-in-its-polar-ice.

In short, SF authors have more than ample leeway to define "seasonal" variations on the worlds we build, with cycles ranging from annual (due to orbital eccentricity and axial tilt) to a few decades (effects of binary stars), to millennia (longer-term orbital variations).

Better living through Really Big Engineering

What if other worlds aren't everything that we might like? No problem (in fiction, anyway): we change them.

Making a planet more Earth-like is called terraforming (from our world's formal Latin name, Terra). The general term, less Terran-centric, is planetary engineering. As we've seen, natural forces change planets all the time. Why not take charge of the process?

What, specifically, might we do? That depends on the world's (in our parochial viewpoint) deficiencies and our engineering prowess.

Is the world too cold? Add greenhouse gases—or liberate those already present. Mars has polar icecaps of water ice and frozen carbon dioxide ("dry ice"). Use sunlight and big space-based mirrors to melt those ices. Or distribute black dust across the ice to soak up sunlight that would otherwise reflect back into space.

Is the world too hot? Remove greenhouse gases. By Earth standards, Venus has *way* too much carbon dioxide (and gases of all kinds) in its atmosphere. So seed the atmosphere with microbes that will absorb the CO_2, secrete the carbon as a shell, and rain that carbon to the ground. Add airborne chemicals to block more of the incident sunlight (as volcanic ash and sulfate aerosol emissions temporarily do, from time to time, and for years at a time, on Earth).[81] Park a large disk (or a spacecraft swarm) at the L1 Lagrange point (where the gravity balances between planet and star), to block sunlight that would otherwise reach the planet.

Too dense of an atmosphere? Pull gas away with a series of well-timed, close-encounter asteroid flybys. Or splash some gas away with a direct hit—and at the same time, deliver other, perhaps more useful material (say, iron). Or precipitate some gas, as in the above Venus example.

Too little atmosphere? Too little oxygen? Send comets. Ultra-violet light will photo-dissociate some of the water vapor, leaving behind oxygen.

Less dramatic interventions are possible, of course. It's far easier to alter the atmosphere beneath sealed domes than over an entire planet. Gengineered microbes might free oxygen locked into a planetary crust. And (perhaps) gengineered crops will thrive with fewer changes than people would need.

Maybe you want *more* dramatic interventions. Consider altering the tilt of a world's axis to change seasons and climate patterns. That can be accomplished with the transient gravitational pull of big rocks thrown past the world on *very* carefully chosen trajectories. Or cool a too-hot sun by stripping off some of its mass with scoop ships or with the flyby of many *really* big rocks.

Some worlds, to be made (or kept) habitable, will require multiple interventions and repeat applications. As we've seen, worlds—more so, living worlds—are dynamic places. All interactions among candidate interventions and planetary processes must be taken into account.

World building—the authorial way

The joy, the sense of wonder, of the best SF often arises from an author's well-realized world. And while sometimes that world is an artifact (as in Arthur C. Clarke's 1973 *Rendezvous with Rama*), let's stick with worlds in the Nature-made sense.

In a minute, anyway.

Because I *must* mention Douglas Adams's 1979 *The Hitchhiker's Guide to the Galaxy*. In *THGTTG*, we're told, the famed world builders of Magrathea custom-built *Earth*. Our home world and its biosphere comprise an immense supercomputer, commissioned by pan-dimensional beings, to calculate the question to the answer to the question of the meaning of life, the Universe and everything.*

Among the earliest and still finest exemplars of realistic world-building was Hal Clement's 1954 novel *Mission of Gravity* (first published in 1953 as a serial). Mesklin is a highly oblate, very rapidly spinning world whose surface gravity varies from about three times Earth-standard (at Mesklin's equator) to seven hundred times standard (at the poles). In the course of the novel, Clement explores the implications of this exotic environment on everything from modes of travel to practical body plans for the local life forms. In a 1953 companion article ("Whirligig World"), Clement went on to explain much of the underlying science.[82]

Frank Herbert's 1965 novel *Dune* is another justly famous example of meticulous world-building. The desert planet Arrakis (better known as Dune), though in many ways Earth-like, is water-poor. To sustain the native ecology—on which, it turns out, much of galactic society relies—Dune's human population had to adapt. *Dune* immerses the reader in a planet and its ecosystem as a complex, almost living system.

The world-building in SF sometimes deals with an actual world, just as it as, the art being in bringing that alien world alive to the reader. An excellent example is *Mars Crossing* (2000), by SF author (and NASA scientist) Geoffrey Landis. As Landis's band of stranded astronauts struggles, Mars is almost as much of a character as any human. Andy Weir did much the same with his lone stranded astronaut in *The Martian* (2014, basis of the 2015 movie).

While Landis and Weir offer Mars as modern planetary science (and plucky robotic explorers) shows that planet to be, Kim

---

* Because an earlier, less capable supercomputer had determined the answer is forty-two. And on my first draft of the article that grew into this chapter, I came to this topic after about 42(00) words. Coincidence? I think not.

    And if this footnote meant nothing to you? Go read *THGTTG*. You'll thank me.

Stanley Robinson's Mars trilogy (*Red Mars* (1993), *Green Mars* (1994), and *Blue Mars* (1996)) gives us a glimpse of what Mars might become through terraforming techniques. In his 2007 novelette "An Ocean is a Snowflake, Four Billion Miles Away," John Barnes offers a look at the human side of terraforming Mars.

I also have an interest (obviously!) in world-building. In *Dark Secret* (2016; a serial in 2013), the planet Dark is a barely habitable super Earth. (Super Earths are exoplanets that are only recently within the ability of astronomers to detect. A super Earth is no more than a few times more massive than our home world. Some super Earths, including my fictional Dark, are rocky. Other super Earths appear to be mini-gas giants.)

Very briefly, Dark has twice Earth's mass. It has a radius about 20 percent larger than Earth, too, so the surface gravity is "only" about 140 percent of Earth normal. Dark is a colder world than Earth, with a thinner atmosphere. I gave Dark three close-orbiting moons and dramatic tides. Life thrives in Dark's oceans—and so the atmosphere has oxygen—but the land surfaces remain barren. Its CO_2 levels are almost toxic. And interesting stuff (I believe) happens there....

Doing the math / wrapping up

This being an overview, I've avoided math—but math and basic physics are essential to the SF world builder. Skip the math and physics, and you risk describing a fictional world with inconsistent and incompatible attributes. For example, the rate at which a world's atmosphere thins with increasing altitude depends, in part, on gravity. A terraformed Mars would have (by Earthly standards) a high, slow-to-thin atmosphere.

It needn't be higher math or advanced physics.* For my world-building, I most often use: Kepler's Laws to characterize

___
* Unless you're a planetary astronomer. You will have noticed throughout this section how reliant that discipline is upon simulation to extrapolate current theory and what we (think we) know about the

orbits. Newtonian physics to determine surface gravity. Inverse square laws to derive the change in irradiance with distance from a star. Basic geometry to find the distance to the horizon for a given world's radius and the apparent size (angular diameter) of a moon in a planet's sky (or of a planet in a moon's sky).

There are more factors to calculate, of course.

Nor have we exhausted the ways in which worlds might differ. The salinity of their oceans. Changes in magnetospheres (Earth's magnetic poles wander; they even reverse polarities, at apparently random intervals, every few million years, give or take.) The biochemistry of life and the course(s) of its evolution. The varieties of terrain, from mountain chains to fertile plains, from deserts to polar icecaps, from tropical jungles to tundra. Any or all of these variables can contribute to world-building—and to stories made richer by an exotic locale.

To read further

It takes entire books to explore the range of planetary possibility, plausible alien worlds, the underlying math and science, and ways to remake worlds to our liking. Books such as:

- *Horizons: Exploring the Universe*, Michael A. Seeds and Dana E. Backman.

- *Reading the Rocks: The Autobiography of the Earth*, Marcia Bjornerud.

- *Rare Earth: Why Complex Life Is Uncommon in the Universe*, Peter D. Ward and Donald Brownlee.

Solar System to other stars. You'll have seen that many observations and extrapolations come with caveats about another simulation that yielded different results.

It's enough to empower a world-building author to go out on the proverbial limb....

- *Terraforming: The Creating of Habitable Planets*, Martin Beech.

- *Rejuvenating the Sun and Avoiding Other Global Catastrophes*, Martin Beech.

- *World-Building: A writer's guide to constructing star systems and life-supporting planets*, Stephen L. Gillett.

- *The Grand Tour: A Traveler's Guide to the Solar System*, William K. Hartmann and Ron Miller.

The Universe Next Door

E arth, Heaven, and Hell. The nine circles of Hell in Dante's *Inferno*. Faerie lands entered from enchanted forests and haunted ruins, by magic spells or through the back of a miraculous wardrobe. Oz, somewhere over the rainbow. Wonderland at the bottom of a rabbit hole and a mirror world behind the looking glass.

The very expression, other *planes* of existence, evokes a Flat Earth perspective.

Once upon a time (irony intended), to banish tales of other realities from *science* fiction seemed, well, scientific. Only writers of SF have consistently begged to differ. In this chapter we'll review several not-quite-Earth venues. We'll touch upon a few illustrations—culled from many possible examples—of how the genre has made use of such settings.*

Why? Because the longer physicists examine the Universe, the more meaningful becomes the notion of other, hidden places. And, as we shall see, the scientific assault on our intuitive sense of reality isn't limited to physics.

---

* Here's a twist: *Inferno* (1976), by Larry Niven and Jerry Pournelle. The hero, a science-fiction author, after plummeting from a hotel window, awakens into (Dante's) *Inferno*-like surroundings. He spends most of the novel trying—and failing—to explain this place in scientific terms, only to conclude he *is* in Hell. The story is supernatural, not SF.

Other realms: in the beginning

Early natural philosophers (before that unfortunate detour through geocentricism) derived a cosmology in which the Sun and the Earth—and a massive body to counterbalance the Earth—circled the center of the Universe. They called that other world Antichton (literally, anti-Earth).[83]

A not-too-different world, forever hidden by the Sun from Earth's view, is the central tenet of the Other Side novels of Paul Capon, the Chronicles of Gor novels of John Norman, and the 1969 SF movie *Journey to the Far Side of the Sun*. An untenable tenet, as it happens—even before space probes roaming the Solar System could see "behind" the Sun.

Imagine that the Sun did perpetually block Earth's view of a twin planet. That would not negate the twin world's gravitational influence! Just as Neptune was revealed by its perturbative effects on the orbit on Uranus, so a Counter-Earth would have announced its existence by its influence on nearby planets.

Sort-of alternate worlds

So that's a "no" for any Counter-Earths.

Changing authorial hats for a few paragraphs to my fiction beanie, that's a shame. An almost-Earth is *such* an apt venue for parodies and ironies, satires and utopias, what-if tales and musings about what is real. Dystopias alas, are all too believably set on *this* Earth.

(That isn't to say a just-next-door fictional world must be Earth-like. Place an alien milieu a step away, rather than in orbit around another star, and avoid story-slowing travel time.)

So what, in the age of space probes and a theory of gravity, is an author to do?

Look inward? That's where many a Philip K. Dick story finds its alternate reality. Dick's 1965 novel *The Three Stigmata of Palmer Eldritch* invokes other realities through drugs. His 1966 novelette "We Can Remember It for You Wholesale," twice

(1992 and, less faithfully adapted, 2012) the basis of movies named *Total Recall*, provides the appearance of other realities through memory alteration.

Or just shrug off the problem. That's how alternate histories handle it.

Harry Turtledove is a master of alternate history, as in (for example) his Atlantis series. What if, millions of years ago, Earth's geological processes had created a continent between Europe and the Americas?

Alternate histories are, without question, speculative fiction. But is a story of alternate history *science* fiction? If a story explores or depends upon a scientific notion—such as the climatic and biological implications of a mid-Atlantic continent—that case can certainly be made.[84]

And if not? In *How Few Remain* (1997), the opening novel of the Southern Victory series, Turtledove offers an alternate history in which a Union soldier *didn't* happen upon a mislaid copy of Robert E. Lee's plan for the Battle of Antietam. (That's the Battle of Sharpsburg, if you are of a Southern persuasion.) Geopolitics would doubtless have unfolded differently if the South had successfully asserted its independence, but the argument is less than compelling that this storyline is science fictional.

Parallel Earths

Do you find the alternate-history approach a bit too "Pay no attention to the man behind the curtain?" Are realities that exist only in a character's head too *Dallas* ("It was all a dream") for your taste? Then let's take a step in another direction.

Where? To a place coexistent with Earth and, at the same time, somehow apart. Out of phase (whatever that means). A short distance into some hitherto unrecognized dimension. Hidden, in one way or another, from our everyday senses.

As in Robert J. Sawyer's Neanderthal Parallax trilogy: *Hominids* (2002), *Humans* (2003), *Hybrids* (2003). On Sawyer's parallel Earth, beings like Neanderthals hold sway.

And once we have imagined one such place, it's no great stretch to suppose several.

Would you like a storyline limited to a handful of such worlds? Consider Michael P. Kube-McDowell's *Alternities* (1988). If you prefer more worlds (but few of them viable, the rest having been ravaged by failed attempts to master world-jumping technology), step up to Keith Laumer's Imperium novels. And if you want to go whole hog? Then try an endless continuum, each world varying imperceptibly from its nearest neighbors. That's how Terry Pratchett and Stephen Baxter portray reality in their Long Earth series and how H. Beam Piper wrote the many stories in the continuum he dubbed paratime.

In what way are these domains any less magical than, say, the demon dimensions of the Buffyverse?[85] I'm glad you asked.

Quantum mechanics to the rescue

Quantum mechanics (QM) is the physical theory that mathematically describes the behavior of matter and energy at very small scales. Since QM's earliest stages, nearly a century ago, the theory has marched from success to success. Your tablet computer, ereader, smartphone, WiFi router—the entire cornucopia of modern electronics—all exploit the equations of QM.

What QM fails to do is *explain* anything.

The theory is inherently probabilistic. Its math never says, as an example, where an electron *is*. Instead, QM lets us calculate how likely we are to find that electron here (or there, or somewhere else). Of course, when we ascertain an electron's position, it isn't here and there and somewhere else—it's in a particular spot.

And so, from the very beginning, the greatest minds in physics argued over the meaning of the mathematics. As Albert Einstein famously said, questioning QM's randomness, "God doesn't play dice with the world."[86] A half-century later, physics Nobelist Richard Feynman said, "I think it's safe to say that no one understands quantum mechanics."

And today? Physicists continue to differ. Thirty-three experts at the Quantum Physics and the Nature of Reality conference in 2011 were surveyed about the correct interpretation of QM. *No* interpretation received a majority vote. "I have no preferred interpretation" received a 12% vote. [87, 88]

Those results are fairly shocking for a theory dating back to the 1920s, a theory that underpins most of this era's most advanced technology.

Skipping the math, we'll go straight to the QM interpretation that, in the aforementioned survey, drew 18% of the expert votes. To wit: we merely perceive that the troublesome electron ends up at just one among its possible endpoints. How so? Because rather than choose, even randomly, *the* Universe has split into *many*! Across all the (spawned) universes, some (spawned) electron can be found in every permissible end state.

That is: I observe a particular outcome in one universe; another me, in another universe, sees another outcome.

Physicists call this physical characterization of quantum mechanics the Many Worlds Interpretation.

Imagine universes splitting off whenever any subatomic particle might exhibit more than a single behavior. Imagine each of those very similar universes, a mere instant later, spawning its own set of universes. Imagine *them* splitting....

Sure sounds like the paratime continuum.

Time for time travel

Are you committed to a belief in cause and effect *and* a fan of time-travel stories? Then splitting off (or an otherwise parallel) universe is just the thing. Goodbye, Grandfather Paradox.[*]

---

[*]   The paradox: if I travel back in time and kill my own grandfather, how did I come to exist? But if I never existed, then clearly I didn't kill my grandfather. So I do come to exist, and can travel backward in time. So.... (Great authorial fun, in any event. *I* certainly had fun with it in my 2001 short story "Grandpa?")

James P. Hogan combined time travel with universe-hopping in just this way in his sort-of World War II novel *The Proteus Operation* (1985). Harry Turtledove did much the same in his sort-of Civil War novel (*not* part of the Southern Victory series), *The Guns of the South* (1992).

Got the world(s) on a string

As though quantum mechanics and its Many Worlds Interpretation weren't mind-bending enough, here's another scientific possibility.

As we briefly touched upon in "Faster Than a Speeding Photon," string theory is an emergent branch of physics as confounding as quantum mechanics. QM theorists understand elementary particles as dimensionless points. String theorists describe the same particles as vibrational modes of strings so tiny as to be indistinguishable—even by our most advanced instruments—from points.*

To date, no experiment has been devised to support string theory over the more established quantum mechanics. Some physicists find the mathematical elegance of string theory compelling; other physicists consider string theory's divorce from experiment quite problematical.

Moreover, string theory, in the singular, is the umbrella term for a vast array of mathematical theories, each variant of which purports to describe reality. At most, one variant does.

So why deal with string theory at all? If you're curious, bear with me for another few paragraphs. Otherwise, jump to the next section break.

The paradox goes away when the time traveler commits murder in someone else's universe.

*   Despite similar names, the strings of string theory and the cosmic strings of cosmology are unrelated. We'll consider the latter a few chapters hence, as components of a hypothetical time machine.

Einstein's theory of general relativity provides a (so far) flaw-less description of the large-scale structures and behaviors of the physical Universe, governed by gravity. Quantum mechanics de-scribes the very different behavior of the exceedingly small, at a scale in which gravity seldom matters. A foundational conflict within modern physics is that these two theories make wildly incompatible assumptions about the nature of reality.

More specifically, the equations of general relativity assume that space-time is continuous. In quantum mechanics, matter and energy come in discrete, indivisible chunks called quanta. The QM worldview is inherently discontinuous. GR is determin-istic. QM is probabilistic.

Quantum mechanics and general relativity just don't mesh—and string theory may bridge the conceptual gap.

For reasons well beyond the scope of this chapter, a mathe-matically consistent string theory that quantizes gravity requires extra dimensions. As string theory has developed, the required number of dimensions has grown to eleven.

Our human senses perceive three spatial dimensions and the passage of time. Relativity theories, special *and* general, re-package those into four-dimensional space-time. But eleven dimensions? If the Universe has so many, why don't we per-ceive them?

Spaghettiland

Imagine a lone strand of spaghetti stretched out on a table-top. The farther you are from the table, the thinner that strand looks, until—to your eyes—the spaghetti becomes a line seg-ment: one-dimensional. Now imagine a tiny, pasta-loving bug crossing *over* the strand. To that bug, the strand is a cylindrical surface. The bug, moving perpendicularly to the axis of the cyl-inder, is experiencing a second dimension hidden by distance from your eyes. Physicists describe a dimension curled up on itself like that as compactified.

Entire universes *might* hide nearby, offset from our own by a microscopic distance along a compactified dimension. We just need to find our way.

Oh, my aching brane

String theory, as though it isn't esoteric enough, has a generalization called M-theory, M for membrane (a string being a one-dimensional membrane). M-theory characterizes our familiar Universe as a 4-D island adrift in a higher-dimensional space. Everything we have traditionally considered *the* Universe is wrapped, at least conceptually, in a membrane, or "brane," that separates us from those other dimensions and the larger Universe.* Physical laws beyond the membrane may differ dramatically from laws within the membrane.

Nothing in M-theory precludes the existence of islands in addition to our own.

Suppose that two or more islands nestle together within the higher-dimensional bulk, and that any encounters between them are gentle. Voilà! Nearby universes ripe for exploitation (setting aside the pesky unanswered detail of just how one would make the trip) and for storytelling.†

It sounds, in fact, much like Isaac Asimov's 1972 novel *The Gods Themselves*.

Universe in my pocket

The parallel universes that can be extrapolated—which is *not* to say, have been proven!—from quantum mechanics, string theory,

---

* Eleven dimensions aren't too many for some theorists, but two syllables are. Go figure.

† And if the encounters aren't gentle? Colliding branes offer a competitive model to the Big Bang for the origin of our Universe. See: "Questioning the Big Bang: Could universe follow a cycle without end?" at http://www.nbcnews.com/id/3077357/.

and M-theory would all arise naturally. What about mere mortals creating a universe?

Robert A. Metzger did just that in his 2002 novel *Picoverse*. His protagonist used highly focused energy to create an artificial singularity, from which, in a mini-Big Bang, his pocket universe developed.*

On a lighter note, the 2003 *Futurama* episode "The Why of Fry" has our everyman hero vanquish an existential threat into a pocket universe to protect our own universe.

Can one create a universe? Sure. But it takes...

An inflated ego

The birth of the Universe in a Big Bang is perhaps the best known concept of modern cosmology, but the Big Bang alone does not explain all characteristics of the visible Universe.

A case in point (and simplifying furiously): regions of the visible Universe very distant from one another—still separating, almost 14 billion years later, in the aftermath of the Big Bang— look remarkably similar in structure. Such homogeneity would be expected if the very early Universe were well-mixed. Alas, the Universe's observed rates of expansion, coupled with Big Bang theory, suggest expansion proceeded faster than would allow early mixing to be sufficiently thorough.

Enter the theory of cosmic inflation.

To start, forget the rates of cosmic expansion that astronomers observe. Assume the earliest expansion *was* slow enough to

---

* A singularity is a point in space-time at which mass/energy has been compressed to infinite density. Like a black hole. Or (reversing your mental image of galaxies flying apart) the origin from which the Big Bang emerged.

(Alas, the Universe's pre-Big Bang nature is nothing as simple as a single point. Everywhere in the Universe is flying apart from everywhere else. When someone in a distant galaxy runs the cosmic clock backwards, it looks to her as though everything originated *there*.)

accommodate thorough mixing. Follow that initial phase with a period of extremely rapid expansion. Finally, slow to a third rate, the expansion as astronomers now observe it.*

That middle stage is cosmic inflation.

The math works if, in the middle stage, the Universe inflates *much* faster than the speed of light. Such expansion wouldn't violate relativity's well-known light-speed limit. Objects can't move through space faster than light—but space-time isn't a thing.

Inflation theory, because it explains the Universe's large-scale homogeneity (and several more otherwise troublesome observations about the Universe), is widely accepted by cosmologists—no matter that direct proof continues to elude astronomers.[89] And inflation raises new questions, as all good theories do, such as: what drives the inflation process? What starts and stops inflation?

Cosmologists envision a universal "inflaton" field that drives inflation. Just as electric fields have a complementary relationship with electrons, the inflaton field has a complementary relationship with (the yet to be detected) inflaton particles. And particles have these pesky quantum indeterminacies....

A discussion of cosmic inflation would require a chapter in its own right, so we'll keep things at a high level. It suffices for our purposes to note that a quantum fluctuation in the (still purely hypothetical) ever-expanding inflaton field can create a region in which inflation spontaneously halts. A region within which

---

* More precisely, the time-varying rate of expansion for the era of the Universe accessible to astronomy. The period of cosmic inflation had long concluded before the post-Big Bang particle soup cooled enough to end the Universe's so-called Dark Ages. There is no light old enough for astronomers to see the era of cosmic inflation.

But *mainstream* does not equal *unchallenged*. See, for example, "Pop Goes the Universe," Anna Ijjas, Paul J. Steinhardt, and Abraham Loeb, *Scientific American*, February 2017. Steinhardt, it is worth noting, was an early proponent of cosmic inflation—and is now among its prominent critics.

natural quantum fluctuation—or a clever protagonist—might later trigger a *new* region of expansion....

In sum, cosmic inflation theory suggests an ever-expanding number of universes embedded within an ever growing larger Multiverse. Picture it (per astrophysicist's Brian Greene's evocative turn of phrase) as the Swiss cheese cosmos.

One bit at a time

And with cheap humor, we segue from physical to digital alternate realities.

Many of us interact with other worlds—programmed worlds—all the time. We have a wide choice. Shoot-'em-up worlds, as in the game franchises *BioShock* and *Warhammer*. Roll your own worlds, as in the game *Sim Earth*. Hang-with-the-denizens worlds, like the virtual community *Second Life*.

Suppose computers and simulation software continue to improve. Why wouldn't they? Might not simulated domains come to seem entirely real?

Do you accept that possibility? Then it's not a big leap to suppose a civilization only slightly more advanced than ours would already have developed such a virtual world. And once you accept *that* premise, how do you know we don't live inside the simulation? That we don't live in the Matrix?*

As, long before *The Matrix* (1999), Daniel F. Galouye's hero came to wonder in *Simulacron-3* (1964, and the basis of the coincidentally 1999 movie *The Thirteenth Floor*). At least Galouye's hero was a human simulation developed by a human being. Matters aren't as straightforward when the virtual-world "ents" in James P. Hogan's *Entoverse* (1991) find a way to impinge on the outer/physical world.

---

*   I speak to the overall concept of that movie franchise, of a world-spanning simulation. Don't get me started on the more comic-book-like aspects, such as humans used as batteries!

Meet the Sims

Suppose our Universe is a simulation. Can we find that out?
Maybe.

Before we dive into the nature of computer simulation, we'll consider an analogy: representing a real-world scene on a TV screen.

From a distance your hi-def TV looks, well, awesome. That's not to say its picture is perfect. It doesn't present the totality of the object on the other side of the camera (even if you have a 3-D TV). A finite number of pixels can represent only a finite amount of visual detail.

Imagine a car commercial. That sleek sports car has a lustrous finish, and each paint molecule receives and reflects the ambient light slightly differently. That paint coat is comprised of many more molecules than the screen's ~2 million pixels (or your retina's ~120 million photoreceptors). So: the reflections off nearby paint molecules have been aggregated. *Averaged* values determine the color and brightness levels of each pixel. Detail has been lost, although (for this example, anyway), likely not enough detail for you to notice any difference.

Now we'll consider a sophisticated digital simulation. Just as a TV doesn't (can't!) represent the reflection from each molecule in a scene, a climate simulation doesn't model the behavior of every gas molecule in the atmosphere. Climate models treat great expanses of atmosphere as though each huge volume were a single entity. A conceptual box of air kilometers on a side is represented by an average temperature, pressure, humidity, etc.*

To recap, the TV screen simplifies the detail of a physical scene to map the scene into the available pixels. A climate model likewise makes simplifying assumptions to render its calculations

---

* In contrast with the loss of precision in how that shiny car appears in the commercial, a climate model's loss of resolution can have consequences. These models can't accurately take into account the climate effects of clouds smaller than the grid's granularity.

manageable. Perhaps a universe simulator doesn't attempt to calculate the behavior of every photon, electron, and quark in that universe. That is, perhaps the universe simulation is only precise to the resolution of its own representational grid.

Do we live inside a simulation? If it can be shown that the behavior of the Universe is artificially simplified or constrained (and—a high hurdle—that there is no other explanation for the observation), then yes.

Scientists at the University of Bonn have made one such search. Just maybe, the distribution across astronomic distances of high-energy cosmic rays denotes the presence of an underlying simulation grid.[90]

And greater (simulated) fleas have lesser (simulated) fleas....

As technology improves, our simulations become *so* much more realistic. If that's not self-evident, compare high-end videogames from, say, ten years ago to the latest games.

How close are humans to constructing a simulation that would seem realistic to its resident Sims?

I'll venture to say, fairly close—and that has an interesting implication.

Humanity has learned, time and again, that nothing is special about our place in the Universe. Earth isn't the center of existence. Neither is our Sun, nor our galaxy. Now let's extend the principle that we're nothing special.

Suppose that, in the near future, humans develop simulations complete and detailed enough to seem real to their (simulated) inhabitants. In time, mightn't those Sims accomplish the same? Then their next-generation Sims? And theirs?

As soon as one envisions that sequence of simulations, it's hard to see on what basis we would suppose *our* existence is the first in the chain. And if we are anything but the first in the chain, then our Universe isn't physical.

Whodunit?

Suppose we exist in a simulated universe. Who built it, and why?

Brilliant and ethical scientists, one would hope, if merely to salve our already bruised (simulated) egos.* To accomplish an important—if not revealed to us—purpose.

If not brilliant scientists, then who? Über-dimensional hackers, perhaps. Students enrolled in Universes 101—or Psych 101. An ad agency dry-running possible marketing campaigns (as in Galouye's *Simulacron-3*). An entertainment company crafting a more realistic virtual-reality game (as in my 2010 short story, "A Time for Heroes").

Like *any* technology, universe simulation *will* become easier with practice. The hard work will be done by tools, with the user contribution reduced to specifying a few key parameters or picking options from a list.

One final analogy....

To unleash nasty computer malware into the world once required great skill. To launch an original virus, worm, or Trojan horse still does. To *tweak* malware is much easier, and cybersecurity experts speak dismissively of copycat attack software as the product of "script kiddies."

Was our universe built by a script kiddie, for no lofty purpose? Per the Mediocrity Principle, that seems plausible.

At least, before losing interest, he/she/it let me finish writing this book.

To read further

- *The Hidden Reality: Parallel Universes and the Deep Laws of the Cosmos*, Brian Greene.

- *Hiding in the Mirror: The quest for alternate realities, from Plato to String Theory (by way of Alice in*

---

* Almost certainly those progenitors are also virtual, merely one iteration earlier in the sequence than ourselves.

Wonderland, Einstein, and The Twilight Zone), Lawrence M. Krauss.

- *Uncertainty: Einstein, Heisenberg, Bohr, and the Struggle for the Soul of Science,* David Lindley.

- *The Trouble with Physics: The Rise of String Theory, the Fall of a Science, and What Comes Next,* Lee Smolin.

- *Taking the Red Pill: Science, Philosophy and the Religion in the Matrix,* Glenn Yeffeth (editor).

- "Is Our World Just a Computer Simulation?", John G. Cramer, *Analog,* July/August 2013.

- "What Is the Universe? Real Physics Has Some Mind-Bending Answers," Victoria Jaggard, *Smithsonian,* September 15, 2014, http://www.smithsonianmag.com/science/what-universe-real-physics-has-some-mind-bending-answers-180952699/.

- http://en.wikipedia.org/wiki/List_of_fiction_employing_parallel_universes

145

ALIEN AWOLS

The Great Silence

E arlier chapters have considered all manner of things alien: what other intelligences might be like, the environments that might shape them, and how we might communicate with them. It's time (some might say, past time) to acknowledge the elephant in the room: the utter absence of evidence that non-human intelligences do, in fact, exist.

Signs of even primitive extraterrestrial life remain ambiguous at best, and are restricted to the Solar System: possible microfossils in Martian meteorites; the inconclusive results on Mars of the Viking spacecraft biological experiments; unexplained traces of methane in the Martian atmosphere; and curious unicellular forms found afloat in Earth's upper atmosphere.

If "Why are we here?" is a deep philosophical question, so is (or should be, anyway) "Why, as far as we can tell, isn't anyone else?" Nor do only SF readers ponder these matters, as several recent op-ed pieces in major media outlets remind us.[91]

As thoughtful and introspective as is science fiction, and as replete as SF is with alien-dependent storylines, little SF treats the existence of aliens as uncertain. Sure, the Search for Extraterrestrial Intelligence (SETI) and First Contact with aliens are plot staples—but storylines that begin with ambiguity usually progress to a discovery. Astronomer Carl Sagan's 1985 SETI-based novel (and 1997 movie) *Contact* fits that pattern; so does the 1996 SETI-based movie *The Arrival*.

Does the bias toward discovery and contact denote authorial confidence in the existence of aliens, or mere convenience? My guess is: often the latter. The discovery of aliens is an epochal event around which to construct a story; ongoing uncertainty is, shall we say, less dramatic.

Let's dig deeper into the question of whether extraterrestrial intelligences may exist, and some implications....

The Mediocrity Principle

A lesson that astronomy keeps teaching us encourages a belief in alien intelligences Somewhere Out There. Earth, we have learned, *isn't* the center of everything. Neither is the Sun, nor is our galaxy. Multiverse theory, if ever validated by experiment, would (as we saw in "Alien Dimensions") demote even our *Universe* to merely one among myriads.

The realization just how ordinary our place is in the Universe has been encapsulated in a cautionary concept sometimes referred to, after its first instance, as the Copernican Principle. Nothing in cosmology or astronomy *precludes* humans from finding themselves in a unique position, but—as we've seen again and again—it's highly unlikely. Philosophers call this "presume nothing unique about ourselves" concept the Mediocrity Principle.

How strange it would seem—how at variance with the Mediocrity Principle—if humanity were the sole intelligences in the Universe.

Listen up

Investigation into the existence (or otherwise) of intelligent aliens usually means listening for their radio presence. Project Ozma, in 1960, the first such SETI effort, led by astronomer Frank Drake, turned a radio-telescope "ear" of the Green Bank

(West Virginia) National Radio Astronomy Observatory toward two nearby Sun-like stars. And from the direction of Tau Ceti he detected something astonishing—

Until the modulated signal was back-tracked to a commercial transmission from Massachusetts.

The Big Ear radio telescope, in 1977, picked up a 72-second anomaly from the approximate direction of Tau Sagittarii. The signal so impressed astronomer Jerry Ehman that he annotated the paper chart "WOW!" That signal was not heard by any other observatory, nor (on occasions when someone rechecked Tau Sagittarii) has it recurred.*

Such onetime, unconfirmed signals are the output to date of SETI programs.†

That could be because, in absolute terms, not much time has been invested in the hunt: on the order of one month's listening time over SETI's first fifty years. Or the aliens use encryption so subtle we don't even notice their broadcasts.[92] Also, as physicists (and twin brothers) Gregory and James Benford point out, the optimal detection strategy (e.g., frequency band, observation

---

*   Despite *tau* appearing in both stars' names, Tau Ceti and Tau Sagittarii are not celestial neighbors. The former is observed in the constellation Cetus (the Whale); the latter in the constellation Sagittarius (the Archer). Stars within a constellation are traditionally labeled according to their relative apparent brightness (how bright they seem from Earth), ranked in Greek alphabetic order. Tau indicates a fairly dim star, ranking nineteenth in apparent brightness.

Not to mention that Tau Ceti lies about 12 light-years from Earth, and Tau Sagittarii is ten times as remote.

†   In 1967, radio astronomers Jocelyn Bell Burnell and Antony Hewish— *not* engaged in SETI—discovered a distant object emitting regular pulses of high-energy radio waves. In jest (the discoverers say), they first labeled the newly found object LGM-1. That's little green men, if you hadn't broken the code.

Objects like LGM-1, now known as pulsars (short for "pulsating stars"), are all around us. They are currently understood to be a natural phenomenon: a category of neutron star.

length, target-star revisit rate) is not at all clear-cut.[93] Or it could be because, since 1993, SETI has had no U.S. government support. The quest continues with private funding. Two noteworthy participants are the SETI Institute and its Allen Telescope Array (the observatory endowed by Microsoft cofounder Paul Allen) and the SETI@home volunteer-computing project for the analysis of radio-telescope data. SETI@home describes itself as "Currently the largest distributed computing effort with over 3 million users." More recently, Stephen Hawking lent his considerable cachet to a $100M SETI program, dubbed Breakthrough Listen, bankrolled by Russian billionaire Yuri Milner.[94]

The fact remains that SETI efforts have yet to produce a confirmed find. Which begs the question: how probable is such a discovery?

The Drake Equation

Inferring aliens from the Mediocrity Principle is, at heart, an unsatisfying recourse to analogy. It's an assertion of probability without benefit of numbers. That Earth isn't special doesn't preclude humanity from being unique.

But in 1961, Frank Drake made the analysis more quantitative. Drake had organized the first SETI conference; he offered an elegant mathematical model, now known as the Drake Equation, to underpin those discussions. It's a deceptively simple equation with which to approximate N: the number of civilizations whose radio signals are potential SETI targets. Per this model:[95]

$$N = R_* * f_p * n_e * f_l * f_i * f_c * L$$

Where:

R_* = average rate of star formation (e.g., number of stars per year)

f_p = fraction of stars with planets

n_e = average number of life-capable planets per solar system

f_l = fraction of life-capable planets that develop life

f_i = fraction of planets whose life develops intelligence

f_c = fraction of intelligences to develop communications technology detectable across interstellar distances

L = average length of time a technological species transmits (e.g., in years)

Alas, firm estimates didn't exist for any of the parameters! The participants of that first SETI gathering approximated N for the Milky Way, our galaxy, at somewhere between 1,000 and 100,000,000.

More than a half century later, astronomers have learned a lot about R_* and f_p. They've fine-tuned guestimates of n_e via exoplanet surveys and improved modeling of planetary temperatures. It's now estimated that our galaxy has (although we have yet to find one other than beneath our feet) tens of billions of Earth-like planets.[96]

As for f_l, f_i, f_c, and L...we know as little as ever.*

Several variants exist on the original Drake Equation. One simple extension is to redefine n_e from habitable planets per solar system to habitable *worlds*. As we saw in the chapter "Alien Worlds: Not in Kansas Anymore," life might emerge outside the conventionally defined habitable zone—that is, in the under-ice water oceans of moons of remote gas giants (such as Jupiter's moon Europa). More complicated extensions consider, for example, that a world may achieve technological civilization more

---

*   Taking ourselves, by the Mediocrity Principle, as a representative technological species, we might assign a lower bound for L. That is, we know how long humanity has operated radios. I'd like to think we're not near the end of our run, and that therefore $L \gg 120$ years.

We'll talk more about L later in this chapter.

than once and that a species might expand its presence beyond its native solar system.

Conscientious analysts continue to derive wildly different values for N.

Why aren't *my* lunches ever this noteworthy?

Circa 1950, somewhat out of the blue, physicist Enrico Fermi asked fellow researchers and lunch companions, "Where are they?"*

That being an era of dubious flying-saucer sightings, *they* were extraterrestrials. If the argument for the existence of aliens is the immensity of the Universe, the Fermi counterargument is essentially: then why haven't any ETs become evident, whether by transmissions, direct contact, or physical evidence?

The Milky Way is estimated to be about 13.5 billion years old. The Sun is a comparative youngster, on the order of 4.5 billion years old. An advanced technological civilization (ATC) only a bit more capable than our own—that is, *without* faster-than-light travel—could colonize the entire galaxy within a few tens of millions of years.†

Cosmologist Frank Tipler pointed out in 1981 that self-replicating robotic interstellar probes[97]—not burdened with

---

* This was, in hindsight, an insightful question and an important conversation, later to be widely cited—but at the time no one took notes. Memories differed exactly what was said, how the discussion began, and who participated. By some accounts, Fermi also introduced a line of questions in the vein of what would become the Drake Equation.

See the 1985 attempt to reconstruct the history, "Where Is Everybody: An Account of Fermi's Question," by Eric M. Jones, http://www.fas.org/sgp/othergov/doe/lanl/la-10311-ms.pdf.

† Isn't FTL travel merely a storyteller's convenience? Perhaps not, as explored in the chapter "Faster than a Speeding Photon: The Why, Where, and (Perhaps the) How of Faster-Than-Light Technology." The possibility of FTL travel only makes our apparent isolation *more* troublesome....

maintaining biospheres, not taking time off from their travels to establish viable colonies—could explore the galaxy even faster.

Why might an ATC send interstellar robotic probes rather than transmit messages? For many reasons:

- Whereas (barring endlessly repeated transmissions) an ATC's message zips past a target solar system and is gone, a robot can loiter to observe.

- In case the destination solar system has or, over the eons, develops, intelligent life, a single probe can carry vast amounts of information within compact digital memory.

- Software—perhaps, but not necessarily, an artificial intelligence—aboard a probe can interact in real time with local intelligences.

- By replicating with indigenous materials and energy sources, robots can explore widely without depleting the resources of the ATC's home solar system.

So: where are they?

If (the Mediocrity Principle notwithstanding) humanity is unique, the first and only technological species in the galaxy, the so-called Great Silence has a trivial answer: no one has ever been Out There to disturb the stillness. If humanity is only unique *right now*, not even N = 1 explains the Great Silence. An earlier civilization, long gone (such that N = 1 was its experience, too) might have left traces of its presence, such as autonomous beacons or self-replicating, still exploring probes.

The yawning chasm between (a) the apparent logic that evidence of aliens should be all around us and (b) the absence of such evidence became known as the Fermi Paradox.[*]

---

[*] SF storylines often exploit intelligent species clustered in neighboring solar systems—the Vulcans, Klingons, Romulans, Betazoids...and humans of the crowded *Star Trek* universe being a prominent example.

SETT

Suppose a Tipler-style robotic spacecraft reached the Solar System a few thousand or million years ago. How would we know?

If the encounter took the form of a simple flyby, we wouldn't.

But perhaps the alien probe(s) tapped local resources to refuel and/or replicate. If so, anomalies in the Asteroid Belt—say, space rocks mined for material with which to construct new probes to send to other stars—could persist long after the visit. Debris and dust fields would (for a time) surround the exploited asteroids. Surfaces would be modified by industrial processes. These effects might be detected by our telescopes or space probes.

None has.

Or suppose a longer sojourn. The Solar System might have exhibited some similarity to the probe builder's home—say, a habitable-zone planet with an oxygen- and water-vapor-rich atmosphere—something meriting a closer look. Probe(s) might remain in the Solar System to see what develops. Such a lurking probe should have detected Earth's civilization by now and noticed the cacophony of its radio traffic. Any such probe(s) would have had ample opportunity to make known its presence.

None has.

Human entrepreneurs have taken their first steps toward asteroid mining. Why not aliens, too? Astronomers have detected asteroid belts and dust clouds around other stars. It seems plausible astronomers could detect signs of industrial processes

---

The implausibility of humanity failing to detect signs of any of its many neighbors goes unexplained. (The Prime Directive, to the extent anyone in *Star Trek* ever obeys it, only explains ships and aliens staying out of sight.)

My InterstellarNet series likewise required a cluster of technological aliens residing in neighboring solar systems. My 2013 novella "The Matthews Conundrum" offered a twice-enigmatic local exception to the overall Fermi Paradox, that I later incorporated into *InterstellarNet: Enigma* (2015).

ongoing in the asteroid belts of *other* solar systems.* SETI veteran Jill Tarter calls this approach the Search for Extraterrestrial Technology (SETT).

No discoveries of this nature have been reported.

Civilizations that have exceeded humanity's capabilities might undertake projects more ambitious than asteroid mining. A Dyson Sphere—a star-enclosing megastructure (whether a solid enclosure or, more likely, a swarm of free-flying smaller objects)—would offer vastly more living area, and could tap vastly more solar energy, than any mere planet.† A yet more advanced civilization might construct Dyson Spheres throughout its galaxy. Either way, the direct sunlight blocked by a Dyson Sphere, and the extensive infrared light (thermal emissions) reradiated by it, should make any such reengineered star(s) obvious in a spectrograph.‡

On the one hand, a survey of 100,000 galaxies failed to spot any signs of such mega engineering.[98] On the other hand, just possibly—and almost next door—a Dyson Sphere under construction may have been spotted.

Star whim, star dim

The star known as KIC 8462852, lying about 1500 light-years from Earth, has been exhibiting odd fluctuations in brightness.

---

*   Signs such as spectra of industrial chemicals in remote solar systems. See http://smithsonianscience.org/2011/04/evidence-of-asteroid-mining-in-our-galaxy-may-lead-to-the-discovery-of-extraterrestrial-civilizations/.

†   The material for the structure(s) would come from asteroids, comets, and/or disassembled planets.

‡   Planets naturally convert some sunlight (their primary energy source) into infrared emissions (an energy loss). The greenhouse effect—without which Earth's oceans would freeze—traps part of that IR radiation in the atmosphere, preventing that energy from leaking back into space.

    A Dyson Sphere surrounding the Sun would emit as much infrared radiation as *millions* of Earths.

The dips follow no recognizable pattern (unlike the slight periodic dimming that can reveal the passage across the face of a star of an orbiting exoplanet). If something orbiting this star is responsible for the observed dimming by occluding Earth's view, it would, in fact, mean *lots* of things. Comet swarms were proposed—only (by one calculation) the recent observations implied 648,000 comets, each an average of 200 kilometers wide, passing across our view. That hardly seemed likely. Dare we believe (as a few have proposed)…swarms of alien-built megastructures? A Dyson Sphere in the making?

As SETI advocate Carl Sagan was wont to say,[*] "Extraordinary claims require extraordinary evidence." Few scientists are prepared to conclude these observations have risen to that standard of proof for high-tech aliens. Any such inference became yet more difficult once a deep dive into astronomical archives revealed that between 1890 and 1989 KIC 8462852 had slowly dimmed by *twenty percent*.[99] And again when spectral analysis of that star showed a quite ordinary distribution of light, without a peak in infrared wavelengths as would be expected of a Dyson Sphere.[100]

All we can say for certain is that something not yet understood is happening in or around KIC 8462852. And that Larry Niven ("Doubling Rate") had a great take on the megastructure scenario back in 2010.

2002-2003: The N = 1 (or not) Battle of the SF Titans

Alien-centric science fiction, often with several types of ETs, is common enough. On the big screen, think big franchises: *Star Wars*, *Star Trek*, *Stargate*, *Alien*, and *Predator*. On the small screen, we've had *The X Files*, several iterations of *V*, *The Invaders*, *Farscape*, and *Defiance*. In literary fiction, ETs date back (at least) to H. G. Wells's *The War of the Worlds* (1898) and *The First Men in the Moon* (1901). More recent examples include the Sector General series

---

[*]   Billions and billions of times.

by James White, the Known Space series by Larry Niven,* and the Rho Agenda series by Richard Phillips.

But SF in which humans find themselves alone is also common. If, in the backdrop of such stories, humans have explored the galaxy without discovering aliens, that's a good indicator that (fictional) N = 1. Isaac Asimov's Foundation series has such an underpinning.

Bringing us to a fascinating debate in the pages of *Analog* magazine, a major nexus of hard SF with speculative science.

The April 2002 issue offered "Galactic Society," a science article by aerospace engineer Robert Zubrin (later to become founder of the Mars Society). Zubrin extended the Drake Equation to accommodate colonization effects: expanding signal sources beyond just the set of solar systems in which technological civilizations first arose. While the article examines ranges of parameters, Zubrin's bottom line is an N value in the millions: technological civilizations throughout the Milky Way, separated, on average, by no more than hundreds of light-years. In easy earshot, in other words.

The most interesting (to me, anyway) was Zubrin's argument that f_l, the fraction of life-amenable planets that actually go on to develop life, must be high.

In a nutshell, Zubrin asserted that once life arises anywhere, it spreads. Certain terrestrial bacteria are known to survive temperature extremes, intense radiation, and vacuum. One bacterium has been revived after a dormant period of 250 million years![101] These sound like adaptations for survival in space, don't they?

An interesting study not cited by Zubrin: while on the Moon, *Apollo 12* astronauts retrieved components from the *Surveyor 3* unmanned lunar lander. It was later found that one sample of terrestrial bacteria had survived 31 months on the lunar surface: in vacuum; under constant, unfiltered cosmic radiation; through

---

*   Full disclosure (for anyone exploring topics other than sequentially): I'm a collaborator with Niven on the Fleet of Worlds subseries within Known Space.

day/night temperature swings of hundreds of degrees; without nutrients and water.[102]

Did bacteria originate far away, drifting over eons to Earth?* Unknown. If yes, did they arise indigenously on another world? Or were the first bacteria hardy nanobot astronauts, expressly designed (by whom?) to distribute life across the cosmos? Unknown.[†]

Given that bacteria with extreme environmental tolerances *are* known, to reject their origin from off-world is to conclude terrestrial bacteria developed space-adaptation traits. Why would terrestrial life have evolved that way? Perhaps because the young Earth—like the more demonstrably battered Moon—endured heavy bombardment by asteroids. Such pounding might have, more than once, sterilized much or all of our planet. Earth rocks blasted into space would have carried refugee bacteria—and only those bacteria able to survive the rigors of space could, however long after, fall back to Earth and reseed the planet.

Hence: even if the primitive Earth were *the* source of life, its space-adapted, single-celled ambassadors would have been cast into space billions of years ago to seed other worlds. Escape velocity from the Sun (from Earth's orbit) is about 42 km/sec; at that rate, it takes "only" about 7,000 years to drift an entire light-year. In geological, much less cosmological time, this is an eye blink. That bacteria might drift, dormant, across several

---

* The Panspermia ("all seeds") hypothesis suggests that life exists throughout the cosmos and is distributed by natural forces (such as meteoroids). See http://en.wikipedia.org/wiki/Panspermia.

    Panspermia (might) explain the spread of life; it does not explain the origin of life.

† "Directed panspermia," to be sure, is on the speculative side. That said, the theory was proposed by no less a figure than Nobelist Francis Crick, codiscoverer of the double helix of DNA.

    See "The Origins of Directed Panspermia," Christian Orlic, *Scientific American*, January 9, 2013, http://blogs.scientificamerican.com/guest-blog/the-origins-of-directed-panspermia/.

light-years to neighboring solar systems—there to take root and repeat the process—seems quite feasible.*

Ben Bova, editor emeritus of the magazine, countered, in the April 2003 issue, that "Isaac Was Right: N Equals One."[†] In part, Bova argued from SETI's ongoing lack of success. His more interesting (to this reader, at least) observations related to the Drake Equation parameter f_i: the fraction of life-bearing planets that develop intelligence. Terrestrial life, Bova points out (quoting biologist and paleontologist Stephen Jay Gould) is almost 4 billion years old—but terrestrial *multicellular* life is only 750 million years old. Intelligence is but a few million years old. The road from single-celled microorganisms to intelligence is, our one data point suggests, difficult to travel.

Bova further questions SETI's often implicit assumption that evolution must drive toward intelligence. Humanity attributes its as yet brief success to intelligence, but we share our planet with myriad other forms of life—many of which have survived longer than genus homo—reliant upon other evolutionary strategies. Like the dinosaurs, who reigned far longer than (as yet) have mammals. Like cockroaches, little changed since the Cretaceous. Like, for *billions* of years, bacteria.

Even if, as Zubrin predicts, life is common, multicellular life and intelligence may be quite rare.[‡]

---

*　Unprotected algae withstanding sixteen months *outside* the International Space Station is a far cry from surviving a drift across interstellar distances. That said, such confirmed short-term endurance is (to say the least) suggestive. See "ESA Discovers an Organism That Can Survive 16 Months in Outer Space," Chelsea Gohd, *Futurism*, February 12, 2017, https://futurism.com/3-nasa-discovers-an-organism-that-can-survive-16-months-in-outer-space/.

†　The reference is to Isaac Asimov's Foundation series, in which a far-future human civilization had settled the galaxy without encountering intelligent aliens.

‡　Intelligence especially so. Consider this observation by evolutionary biologist Ernst Mayr: "If there are 30 million living species, and if

Sharing the issue with Bova's article, then-editor Stanley Schmidt weighed in with "Still Guessing, After All These Years." Schmidt, raising several pragmatic objections, offered an in-between argument. In particular: between Bova's one and Zubrin's millions are *many* options for N. Suppose N is larger than one but still small; then the nearest ATC is apt to be remote from Earth. If so—SETI projects having not yet looked at many stars, and most of those stars nearby—the odds are strongly against us having detected aliens. My favorite passage from the editorial:

> To put things in perspective, think of the galaxy as a large pizza, half a meter in diameter. Concluding from our lack of positive findings so far that there's no other civilization in our galaxy is much like concluding that there's no pepperoni on the pizza because you've only looked inside a tiny flake of oregano.

To all three articles, via an Alternate View column entitled "Isaac Was Wrong (Maybe)," regular contributor Jeffrey D. Kooistra responded in the November 2003 issue. Kooistra's spin: maybe we *have* evidence. He distills the traditional SETI rationale to its most basic: so many stars; most likely someone else is out there. He then summarizes the UFO-centric case in a parallel manner: so many unexplained sightings; most likely some sightings are credible.

Kooistra reminds us that UFO reports were concentrated near, and in corridors between, military facilities later revealed to be associated with top-secret experimental aircraft. That correlation, while it discounts many specific reports as evidence

---

the average life expectancy of a species is about 100,000 years, then one can postulate that there have been billions, perhaps as many as 50 billion species since the origin of life. Only one of these achieved the kind of intelligence needed to establish a civilization." See http://www.pbs.org/wgbh/evolution/humans/intlife/2.html.

of extraterrestrial spacecraft, suggests that some UFO *observers* are credible.

(Kooistra never asserts UFOs *are* proof of intelligent aliens. His purpose, rather, is to contrast SETI by radio telescope with SETI by the investigation of UFOs reports. The former is often perceived as serious science; the latter, perhaps unjustly, is not.)

The Great Silence

Because the value of N—in the original *and* various extended Drake equations—remains debatable, let's consider some reasons why, if it happens that Earth is in an N > 1 galaxy, we have seen no evidence of the neighbors.

Impatience: they're out there; we just haven't searched long or far enough. Maybe we'll hear something exciting from the next solar system tuned in, or see an anomaly on the next asteroid examined.

Wrong strategy: aliens may simply have signaled on a different frequency band(s) than chosen for past SETI searches. Or, as the Benfords' article surmises, we may be listening, whether or not with the correct frequencies, for the wrong *kind* of signal. SETI searches have presumed interstellar-class beacons broadcast endlessly and omnidirectionally, and for the sender that is a wasteful approach. Aliens could signal their presence far more efficiently through occasional pings—just as the "WOW" signal *might* have been.

As a visual analogy: traditional SETI assumes an always-on light shining brightly in every direction. The Benfords surmise that aliens wishing to disclose their presence would instead periodically sweep a directional searchlight beam across the plane of the galaxy. If you were paying the electric bill, which method would you favor?

Wrong technology: maybe long-range electromagnetic signaling is passé among ATCs. They might, for example, prefer neutrino beams or gravitational waves. Neutrinos can cross light-years without attenuation.* Gravitational waves—ripples in space-time itself—pass by (not through) *anything*, even a black hole, without attenuation.† Or, reliant upon science further beyond our own, ATCs might communicate with methods humans cannot yet imagine.

Misdirection: they choose not to be found. Maybe we humans have been deemed too immature or impressionable or ill-mannered for contact.‡ Or, perhaps, we're kept in isolation and ignorance by something like *Star Trek*'s Prime Directive.§ It could be that we inhabit a kind of zoo or live in some sort of nature preserve. And maybe, as in Arthur C. Clarke's *Childhood's End* (1953, and the basis of a 2015 TV miniseries), they'll show up

---

*   Shoot a neutrino beam at a *light-year-thick barrier of solid lead*—and half the neutrinos will come out the other side.

†   That's not to say gravitational waves offer infinite signaling range. Like any wave, gravitational waves dissipate with distance.

     The good news: in September 2015, almost exactly a century after Einstein first predicted the existence of gravitational waves, such waves were directly detected—from a black-hole collision an estimated *1.3 billion light-years* remote! That detection was not announced until February 2016, delayed until the exciting results were thoroughly validated and revalidated. No one wanted a repeat of the 2011 FTL-neutrino debacle (discussed earlier, in the chapter "Faster Than a Speeding Photon").

     See "Gravitational waves, Einstein's ripples in spacetime, spotted for first time," Adrian Cho, *Science*, February 11, 2016, http://www.sciencemag.org/news/2016/02/gravitational-waves-einstein-s-ripples-spacetime-spotted-first-time.

‡   Many stars are billions of years older than the Sun. Intelligent aliens might be so evolutionarily, socially, and technologically advanced beyond us that they see no point in interacting with us.

§   If you have somehow missed every *Star Trek* movie, TV episode, and novel, the Prime Directive "prohibits Starfleet personnel from interfering with the internal development of alien civilizations." For a full discussion, see https://en.wikipedia.org/wiki/Prime_Directive.

someday, out of some cosmic sense of noblesse oblige, to raise us to their standards.

Impracticality of interstellar travel: starships (including robotic probes), while physically possible, might nonetheless represent an investment beyond the reach (or motivation) of most civilizations.

Loss of interest in planets: a probable precursor to interstellar capability is full exploitation of the ATC's home solar system. Having once adapted to life in artificial habitats and to the resource wealth of asteroids and comets, might any further waves of expansion shun planets? Might ATCs even come to see planets as mere building materials?

Barring faster-than-light propulsion, any trip between stars must be years (or even generations) in duration. If the only route to the stars requires adaptation to life aboard a habitat...why then readapt to life on planets?

Transience: perhaps ATCs quickly lose interest in communicating and/or exploring. They may come to find advanced virtual worlds are more interesting—and certainly easier and quicker to reach—than the physical worlds of other solar systems.

Math is hard: Underpinning human technology, and hence our ability to contemplate communication among the stars, is mathematics. Is math, as Plato had it, intrinsic to the universe: a pure truth that underlies messy physical reality? If yes, many species might discover that truth. But what if math, in whole or in part, is a human invention? If the latter, perhaps evolution did not equip extraterrestrial species with the neural (or equivalent) hardwiring to invent math—and with it, technology.

(Our) math is too easy: Or perhaps, for the lack of suitable hardwiring, puny human brains can't grasp alien math. Perhaps we fail to recognize the messages all around us. While we expect (for example) alien transmissions to have obvious markers, such as sequences of prime numbers, messages flying past may be so incomprehensible as to not appear artificial.

The Great Filter: suppose, as many SETI analyses do, that life-amenable worlds are common, that life, intelligence, and (eventually) technological civilizations are apt to emerge. If so, the Great Silence implies something that preempts contact. We would like to believe, of course, that any such *something* is already in our past.

But on the basis of what evidence can we suppose that?

What the L?

What if some Great Filter is preparing to winnow *us*?

In the Drake Equation, the parameter L denotes the average lifetime of a technological civilization. Zubrin's estimate of one million technological galactic civilizations (one of his *conservative* scenarios) presumes the hypothetical L value of ten thousand years.

Ten thousand years ago, in human terms, was prehistory. High tech then was the shift from wild harvesting to cultivation and the first domestication of animals.[103] Across the past ten thousand years on Earth, many civilizations have risen and fallen. And so (as just one example, and a long-lasting one at that), "the glory that was Greece and the grandeur that was Rome" fell to barbarian hordes, and Europe sank into Dark Ages.*

That's a look in the rearview mirror, of course. Perhaps humanity will fare better going forward. Perhaps would-be communicating aliens have, too. Or perhaps the Great Silence portends terrible danger looming in our future.

What sort(s) of danger? Again, analysts have suggested many possibilities:

Nuclear war: the end of the Cold War gave hope that humanity had dodged that particular bullet. Ongoing nuclear proliferation, alas, suggests that the metaphorical bullet might be coming around for a second go at us. Some alien civilizations may have been less successful than (so far) have we at bottling the nuclear genie.

---

* I seldom find the opportunity to quote Poe. Indulge me.

163

Ecological collapse: Like the Easter Islanders who consumed themselves into an irreversible ecological trap,* an ATC might lock itself onto its home world and/or crash its civilization through the depletion of critical resources. Or they might bring a climate catastrophe upon themselves, through ozone depletion, overpopulation, destruction of biodiversity, global warming, global cooling, killer smog, ocean acidification, acid rain…literally, choose your poison.

Technological runaway: lots of variations here. Gengineered organisms that outcompete all else, choking critical parts of the biosphere. Gengineered plagues. Rogue replicators, nanotech or otherwise, that disassemble everything (and everyone) to produce more of themselves. Artificial intelligences smarter than their creators, creating smarter AIs, creating yet smarter AIs… until the generation arrives that sees no further use for their slow-witted, resource-wasting progenitors.[†]

Retail mass destruction: ever more lethal technologies becoming available to ever smaller, harder to deter groups (read: terrorist cells) and eventually rogue individuals. Imagine a unabomber wielding WMDs.[104]

The difficulty with these low-L scenarios is that to (singularly or collectively) explain the Great Silence they must apply 100 percent. Let a single extraterrestrial ATC have the wisdom to avoid these traps, and the Fermi Paradox again rears its head.

The uh-oh scenario

Maybe the older, wiser civilizations Out There don't evade our detection to protect us, à la Prime Directive—maybe they hide to

---

* Ocean travel requires ships—in the case of the Polynesians, really large canoes. Through deforestation, the colonists of Easter Island (aka Rapa Nui) trapped themselves on this isolated speck in the Pacific Ocean. Environmental degradation, in part caused by overpopulation, led to a major population collapse. See http://en.wikipedia.org/wiki/Easter_island.

† We'll consider such scenarios in detail in the concluding chapter, "A Mind of Its Own: Superintelligence."

protect themselves. A sobering possibility, isn't it? Because from whom would they be hiding?

One low-L scenario that *doesn't* rely on species after species, for age upon age, falling prey to the same pitfalls is all of them falling prey to…a single stealthy ATC.

Consider an advanced technological civilization able to send interstellar probes. It, too, has pondered the Great Silence. It, too, worries that something has caused the silence. And so, rather than succumb to the common fate, this ATC elects to preempt the threat.

Rather than study or contact distant habitable worlds, this ATC's probes might drop big asteroids on them. Or dust worlds with replicators, setting off nanotech/gray-goo catastrophes. Or just smack the habitable worlds directly: A 1000-kg probe (that's less than half the mass of the *Cassini-Huygens* spacecraft NASA sent to study Titan) traveling at one-fourth light speed carries the kinetic-energy equivalent to a 672 megaton bomb.

Perhaps an ever-growing horde of von Neumann probes roams the galaxy, homing in on any world that exhibits industrial chemicals in its atmosphere, or emits modulated radio emissions, or otherwise suggests technology. It takes only one ATC to kick off the process.

Call it the Big Intervention.

Is this a plausible scenario? Unknown—although it would explain, better than most proposed answers, the Great Silence. And if true, are we doomed? Some will take comfort that after more than a century of radio chatter, Earth hasn't been attacked—but that only proves preemption hasn't hit us *yet*. A hostile ATC located a mere hundred light-years away has only recently had the opportunity to hear us.[*]

Even the remote possibility of the Big Intervention should give pause to those advocating intentional, high-powered

---

[*]   Depending on the sensitivity of alien radio receivers, humanity's earliest transmissions may have been washed out by the background roar of Sol's and Jupiter's natural radio noise.

Messaging to Extraterrestrial Intelligence (METI). If humanity shouts out our presence to the stars, we might come to regret any attention we draw.

Bubble, bubble, toil and trouble*

At the opposite extreme, let's consider a high-L scenario: that ATCs persist through tens of millennia. How might such civilizations evolve? Might they have *non*genocidal behaviors to explain the Great Silence?

The longer an ATC persists and expands, the more it depletes the resources of its home world and, later, its home solar system. Some ATCs may graduate to a sustainable economy/ecology; others may not. Evolution does not reward the reproductively reticent.

The case can be made that ATCs with a long-range outlook will be motivated to develop interstellar travel. Some of us already have the aspiration (see "Alien Adventures").

In time, colonized solar systems will face their own eco-stresses. Ditto the second-wave colonies established from the earliest settled worlds. Inside the expanding region of settlement, the aliens' native solar system is the first to encounter severe resource depletion. The earliest colonies soon follow.

Picture a slowly growing bubble of colonized solar systems. Colonies near the periphery can move into as-yet unexploited space, expanding the bubble. Older colonies, increasingly remote from the periphery, have only undesirable options. They might try to settle solar systems passed by, with good reason, earlier in the expansion. They might attempt to wrest resources from—go to war with—better-off neighbors nearer to the bubble's border. (The [in?]feasibility of interstellar warfare is a major topic in its own right, addressed in the next chapter.) They might, like the Easter Islanders, suffer a civilizational collapse and population implosion.

---

* Yes, I know this is a *mis*quote.

The longer a colonization program continues, the farther the frontier recedes and the farther the earliest settled worlds become from desirable new colonization opportunities. If the expansion continues long enough, it comes upon one or both surfaces of the galactic disk. The exploitable volume that had expanded with the *cube* of a sphere's radius downshifts to expanding with the *square* of a cylinder's radius. The pressure of resource depletion intensifies.

Let us suppose an ATC persists long enough to settle—and deplete—habitable worlds throughout some large interstellar volume. In time, worlds of the interior regions may become, if not uninhabitable, then at least undesirable. Interior solar systems might be abandoned or collapse into low-tech, low-population conditions. The ATC interstellar sphere or cylinder morphs into an ATC interstellar shell.

In time, the over-taxed ecosystems might recover, although each successive colony or indigenously arising intelligence would face tougher challenges as a consequence of earlier resource depletion. Would the Industrial Revolution have occurred without rich, near-surface veins of iron ore and coal?

Hence: one explanation for the Great Silence is that Earth lies deep within such a depleted/abandoned region—a galactic low-rent district. (That needn't imply Earth itself was ever colonized by aliens—opinions on the desirability of specific planets will vary—only that solar systems nearby were settled and then abandoned.) If our SETI efforts were to target far more remote solar systems, we might find someone.

And in the genre

Science fiction being a genre of Big Ideas, some SF authors have explored the Great Silence. To suggest a few titles:

- David Brin's Uplift series considers worlds and whole interstellar regions abandoned to recover from past colonial depredations.

- Brin's *Existence* (2012) explores instances of a Great Filter and of Tipler-style probes.

- Stephen Baxter's *Manifold: Space* (2000 in the UK; 2001 in the US) likewise deals with an ATC threat from self-replicating interstellar probes.

- Frederick Pohl's Gateway series offers a single, vanished interstellar-traveling ATC (the Heechee) and its mysterious motivations.

- Fred Saberhagen's Berserker series revolves around killer robots, built to wage an ancient conflict, now attempting to eradicate *all* life.

- Charles R. Pellegrino and George Zebrowski's *The Killing Star* (1995) deals with an ATC's preemptive attack on the Solar System.

To read further

- *Rare Earth: Why Complex Life Is Uncommon in the Universe*, Peter Ward and Donald E. Brownlee.

- *The Eerie Silence: Renewing Our Search for Alien Intelligence*, Paul Davies.

- *Starship Century*, Gregory Benford (editor) and James Benford (editor), mixed science and fiction.

- *If the Universe Is Teeming with Aliens...WHERE IS EVERYBODY?: Seventy-Five Solutions to the Fermi Paradox and the Problem of Extraterrestrial Life* (Second edition), Stephen Webb.

- http://www.scoop.it/t/seti-the-search-for-extraterrestrial-intelligence (a SETI website maintained by David Brin).

- "Searching for Good Science: The Cancellation of NASA's SETI Program," Stephen J. Garber, *Journal of the British Interplanetary Society*, Volume 52, http://history.nasa.gov/garber.pdf.

- http://lifeboat.com/ex/main The Lifeboat Foundation maintains a list of potential Great Filter events, and offers everyone the opportunity to contribute to defending against them.
- http://www.seti.org/ Home page of the SETI Institute.
- http://setiathome.berkeley.edu/ Home page of the SETI@home project.

ALIEN ALTERCATIONS

Star (Spanning) Wars

S cience fiction is replete with tales of human/alien conflict. Such stories go back at least to 1898 and *The War of the Worlds*, H. G. Wells's novel of Martians invading Earth. The inter-species aggression ran both ways, of course. In Olaf Stapledon's 1930 epic *Last and First Men*, far-future humans, in the process of terraforming Venus, obliterate a species of intelligent aliens. In Thomas M. Disch's *The Genocides* (1965), aliens remaking Earth into (their kind of) farmland wage impersonal pest control more than war against humanity.

Those novels were written when intra-Solar System neighbors seemed a credible possibility. Leading astronomers of the 1890s, employing the finest telescopes of the era, reported evidence of "canals" and seasonal—dare they to believe, agricultural?—changes on the Martian surface. Until the 1962 Mariner mission flyby, hope remained that the bright clouds shrouding Venus were water vapor, and that the unseen surface of Earth's so-called sister planet hosted a life-rich environment.

And now? Spacecraft and improved astronomical instruments tell a quite different story. Any intelligent beings with whom we may share the cosmos most likely reside *far* away. Interspecies contact, if it happens, will be interstellar contact.

Science fiction has adapted. On screen, popular SF franchises rife with interstellar, inter-species conflicts include *Star Trek*, *Star*

Wars, and *Stargate.* War involving extra-solar aliens figures prominently in the novels *Bill, The Galactic Hero* (1965, Harry Harrison), *As on a Darkling Plain* (1972, Ben Bova),* *The Forever War* (1975, Joe Haldeman), *Ender's Game* (1985, Orson Scott Card), the long-running/ongoing Man-Kzin War series (Larry Niven, et. al.), and *Trial by Fire* (2014, Charles E. Gannon).† Interstellar, inter-species war has become such a genre commonplace it sometimes serves as mere set-up for the *real* story, as in the 2006 novelette "All the Things You Are" (Mike Resnick).

As we've seen, to travel between stars is tough. Suppose, nonetheless, that ways exist to overcome the challenges. Is interstellar warfare possible?

If (or, being an optimist, when) humanity masters the technology to reach and settle other solar systems, the potential would surely exist for human/human interstellar conflict. Any technology that transports explorers, colonists, and diplomats to the stars can as readily convey weapons and warriors.

Given warfare's ubiquity across recorded human history—and in our daily news—the burden of proof would seem to rest with anyone predicting different behavior. Why wouldn't interstellar-capable humans sometimes use violence to seize an advantage or to resolve disputes? Our technology ever changes faster than our basic nature.

This chapter, as its title suggests, poses a narrower—and more speculative—question. Might humans and aliens (or two groups of aliens) engage in warfare? The question presupposes that (a) interstellar travel is practical and (b) intelligent aliens exist.

In addressing our topic, we'll draw upon terrestrial biology, social sciences, and human history. And so, this discussion will be less definitive—certainly, less mathematical—than some other

---

* The chronological start to Bova's series The Others Saga, aka the Watchman series, but not the first book published in that storyline.

† Gannon's entire Tales of the Terran Republic series deals with inter-species, interstellar conflict, but *Trial by Fire* has (as far as I've so far read in the series) the most overt warfare.

chapters of this book. We won't, alas, have the benefit of psycho-history: the fictional predictive science, a synthesis of the social sciences, statistics, and historical analysis, that underpins Isaac Asimov's epic Foundation series.*

As our purpose is to establish the feasibility, not the certainty, of an alien behavior, qualitative analysis—and insights from SF—will suffice.

Definitions

The nature of warfare has varied over recorded history (during most of which the annals of warfare *were* recorded history). We can scarcely preclude the possibility warfare would assume new forms on distant worlds, in the depths of space, or as practiced by alien intelligences. How, then, shall we define and constrain our topic?

The first meaning of *warfare* (from Dictionary.com) is, "the process of military struggle between two nations or groups of nations." In an era of unrelenting, violent conflict with non-state actors like ISIS and al Qaeda, that definition seems almost quaint. The second, more general, meaning offers, "armed conflict between two massed enemies, armies, or the like." The latter defi-nition also seems too restrictive.

Consider, for example, *guerilla warfare*: violent resistance against conventional (massed) armies via unconventional, hit-and-run tactics.† The modern generalization is *asymmetrical*

---

* Professional statistician (and SF author) Michael F. Flynn took a crack at characterizing such a science in the two-part article "An In-troduction to Psychohistory." Although his April and May 1988 *Ana-log* articles offered tantalizing glimpses of ways to forecast selected incidents of organized violence (e.g., the predictability of African *coup d'etat* attempts, a cyclic pattern of wars gleaned from the annals of Imperial China), even a mature psychohistory would not—pre-First Contact, anyway—be calibrated to illuminate the behaviors of aliens.

† Guerilla being a diminutive form of *guerra*, Spanish for war, one obvious example of guerilla warfare involved Spanish partisans re-sisting Napoleon's armies then occupying their country. A century

warfare, in which dissimilar opponents leverage their strengths and exploit each other's unique weaknesses. Suicide bombers, hijacked jetliners, and roadside improvised explosive devices are too familiar instruments of asymmetrical warfare. During the (first) Cold War, chemical, biological, nuclear, and electromagnetic-pulse weapons were seen, by one side or the other, at one time or another, as asymmetric counters to imbalances with the military capabilities of the opposing side.

More recently, consider the targeting of military satellites.

"Aware of the US dependence on space and satellite communications to conduct even the most basic military operations, the PLA (People's Liberation Army) has for the past decade invested significant amounts to develop anti-satellite weapons. In January 2007 China fired its first anti-satellite missile destroying one of its own aging satellites in outer space. In May 2013 China fired a rocket carrying no payload over 10,000 kilometers into outer space, the highest launch since the mid-1970s. The absence of a payload such as a satellite could suggest the rocket is designed as an anti-satellite weapon."[105]

From recent headlines, consider *cyberwar.* The preemption or the denial of computer-reliant critical infrastructure is an emerging tactic of asymmetrical warfare.[106]

Just as cyberwarfare need not lead directly to deaths, physical combat may avoid lethal force. The U.S. military briefly deployed to Afghanistan a heat-ray-based, nonlethal, area-denial system; development of the technology continues.[107]

It's a safe bet we haven't seen every mode of conflict that human societies or alien intelligences might ever imagine.

and a half later, Viet Cong guerillas battled American and South Vietnamese armies.

For the remainder of this chapter our working definitions are:

Warfare: the large-scale application of violence, or the coercive threat of such application, by one organized group against another.

Violence: inflicting material harm, whether directly (e.g., through impact trauma, directed energy, or biological agent) or indirectly (e.g., by denial of critical infrastructure).

Nowhere in these definitions: constraints on how a conflict is waged or any requirement for parity between sides. Nor do we address the specific weapons that might be used or the tactics that might be employed—which might be fortunate, given how expansive those speculations could get.*

That's the *what.* Next up: *why* are there wars?

Biology

Natural selection. The survival of the fittest. "Nature, red in tooth and claw," as Alfred Lord Tennyson put it, several years *before* Charles Darwin published his theories.

Evolution and its processes are the unifying theme of modern biology. Competition as the driver of evolution is so deeply rooted that biologists continue struggling to explain altruism.[108]

Evolution has produced predators up and down the tree of life, from viral bacteriophages that replicate within and destroy individual bacteria to carnivorous sponges (family Cladorhizidae) that dine on crustaceans to the T. rex (dining on anything it wanted) to the sperm whales that prey on giant squids. Nor is

---

* Moreover, some interstellar conflicts might be intelligible only to AIs, as warring fleets moving at near-light speeds zip past one another in the merest fraction of a second.

hunting limited to the animal kingdom, as carnivorous plants such as the Venus flytrap attest.

Rustling up dinner, even a dinner that fights back, isn't warfare—although it's a step in that direction. Many predators, from wolves to dolphins to butcherbirds to (speculatively) velociraptors evolved to hunt in packs. Many prey species band together for protection—and some aggressively defend themselves (e.g., the mobbing behavior of red colobus monkeys and many bird species).

Many animal species, including those that form cooperating groups, are territorial; they will battle their own kind—and related species—over turf. Or in the case of dolphins, over surf.[109]

Some of our simian relatives wage such battles, although anthropologists argue whether these conflicts reflect territoriality, competition for mates, or innate aggression.[110] (That's like scholars debating the causes of the Trojan War, come to think of it.) Nor is human aggression necessarily recent: that Cro-Magnons killed off our Neanderthal cousins is at least one plausible extinction hypothesis.[111] The earliest known human-on-human slaughter, evidenced by fossilized remains from the conflict, dates back ten millennia.[112]

But wide-ranging, cast-of-thousands, no-holds-barred combat? That's a human invention, surely. Consider this account:

"The raging combatants form a blur on all sides. the [sic] scale of the violence is almost incomprehensible, the battle stretching beyond my field of view. Tens of thousands sweep ahead with a suicidal single-mindedness. Utterly devoted to duty, the fighters never retreat from a confrontation—even in the face of certain death. The engagements are brief and brutal. Suddenly, three foot soldiers grab an enemy and hold it in place until one of the bigger warriors advances and cleaves the captive's body, leaving it smashed and oozing."

That's the description of a war among *ants*.[113]

It's difficult to imagine that the evolutionary processes that repeatedly led to predation, inter-group aggression, and warfare on Earth won't ever produce those traits in extraterrestrials.

Even where Nature is *green* of tooth and claw.

Social Sciences

Biology isn't (entirely) destiny. Humans learn and adapt—if not yet sufficiently to have stopped slaughtering one another.

What have social scientists told us about the origins of war? Psychologist Steve Taylor of Leeds Metropolitan University offers us a rundown, synopsized in this section.[114]

William James, the first psychologist to publish on the topic, identified societal incentives, like the sense of coming together before a common threat, and personal benefits (if you survived!) like the sense of heightened alertness and the opportunity to exhibit discipline and self-sacrifice.

Some evolutionary psychologists infer that a propensity toward violence, including war, is inherent among humans. Steven Pinker, for example, in *The Better Angels of Our Nature*, points to statistical declines in the frequencies and types of violent incidents (which isn't the same as reduced fatalities per war!). Pinker asserts the progress in recent centuries is too rapid to be rooted in a change in human nature. If the antidotes to violence are cultural, he argues that the propensity to violence must be innate.

Some sociobiologists—founder E.O. Wilson prominently among them—likewise consider warfare innate.

Some biologists, noting a correlation between levels of testosterone and aggression, blame men. Thomas Hayden and Malcolm Potts (the latter an evolutionary biologist) suggest "that the male sex hormone, testosterone, is in some ways the ultimate weapon of mass destruction."[115]

Psychologists and economists alike note that war offers an opportunity to accrue wealth (perhaps as territory or resources), prestige, and power.

Then there is the matter of group identities—and exclusions. You can doubtless recall a war or three initiated in defense of, or against, a particular nation, race, tribe, ethnicity, or religious denomination. Such conflicts are underway as I type and, I venture to predict, some will be ongoing as you read this.

Or perhaps our compulsion to war is something cultural. Some anthropological studies suggest that primitive hunter-gatherer societies are less prone to murder and violence than are their "civilized" counterparts. Maybe isolated groups haven't yet *invented* war.

In short: the social sciences offer no single, conclusive answer. That's all the more reason to speculate similar factors might sometimes stimulate aliens, too, to wage war.

History

So much for theory. What does practice—history—teach about the origins of wars? That centuries, and even millennia after particular events, scholars seldom agree.

Let's examine some commonly ascribed origins for a few well-known wars. (I will almost certainly omit an example you would have chosen, or the cause you find compelling. That's okay—and in a way, my point.)

Two recent blockbuster movies (*300*, in 2006, about Spartans fighting to the death at Thermopylae to delay a Persian land invasion, and *300: Rise of an Empire*, in 2014, about the Athenian-led Hellenic navy routing the Persian navy at the Battle of Salamis) popularized, with considerable artistic license, the main bouts of the Second Persian War. Did Persians armies cross the Hellespont into Europe in 480 BCE to gain territory, subjects, and tribute? Or was the invasion about securing an unruly border? Did Xerxes, the Persian emperor, set out personally to destroy Athens in retribution for its humiliation of his father, the emperor Darius, ten years earlier in the *first* invasion? Or did Xerxes strive to keep occupied—and remote from his imperial capital city—the military resources of his many subject peoples?

You'll find historians to support any and all those possibilities.

Did Aegean city-states opposing Xerxes view the Persian on-slaught as a clash of civilizations? Yes. To the early Greek mind-set, the world consisted of Hellenes and barbarians. But *other* Hellenic city-states (and not merely Persian tributary states) sent warriors and warships to fight for Xerxes. Personal advisers to Darius included politicians exiled from Athens and Sparta, ex-pecting to reclaim power at home as tributary rulers following a Persian victory.

Was the American War of Independence about self-gover-nance ("No taxation without representation")? Or was the con-flict about the taxes themselves, following the recently conclud-ed, world-spanning, very expensive, Seven Years' War between France and Great Britain? Did France support rebellious Ameri-cans with arms and armies out of sympathy (some) aristocrats felt for the colonists' cause? Or did Louis XVI seek revenge against Great Britain over his recent surrender of New France (aka, Canada)?

Likely all of the above.

The (first) Cold War—with its hot proxy conflicts and re-gional wars—was a clash of governance and economic ideologies. It *also* involved longstanding historical grudges, territorial ambi-tions, aspirations of self-determination, and religious rivalries.

We've not exhausted the list. Wars have been attributed to: maintaining the balance of power, protecting the free flow of trade, honoring treaty obligations, obtaining resources, denying a rival resources, inter-ethnic antipathies, and humanitarian in-terventions. Stirring up trouble with an external enemy is a time-honored way to drum up domestic support or justify domestic suppression (check out the spike in Vladimir Putin's popularity among Russians once his intervention in the Crimea began[116]).

And what is the role of the occasional charismatic (or crazy?) figure able to bend others to his will (or, in a competing inter-pretation, to provide the nucleus around which the popular will coalesces)? How might history have differed absent Alexander the Great, Joan of Arc, El Cid, George Washington, Napoleon, Hitler, Mahatma Gandhi, or Saddam Hussein?[*,†]

Finally, no matter what one side of a conflict may claim, the opposing side will claim self defense. Even (especially?) when that second side strikes preemptively.

Bad habits outgrown?

Still, depending on how you enumerate conflicts, we humans are becoming less warlike. As one happy example, the nations of western Europe, bitter enemies for centuries, have been at peace since the end of World War II.

Are we outgrowing belligerence? Might aliens, too?

Well: the same post-WW II era witnessed the Cold War. Ethnic or tribal wars raged in Nigeria, Rwanda, Lebanon, and Iraq. Yugoslavia shattered bloodily apart into, so far, seven nations. Turkey invaded and partitioned Cyprus. War has been common across the Middle East. France waged colonial wars in Algeria and Indochina; civil wars are ongoing in Yemen and Syria. Post-Soviet Russia has invaded Georgia, Moldova, and Ukraine. Great Britain and Argentina fought over the Falklands. And on, and on.

Suppose that, however you count and give weight to particular conflicts, you conclude the trend *is* toward fewer wars. To what can one attribute the decline, and can we extrapolate anything about the peace- or war-loving nature of intelligent aliens?

Some assert that democracies are less likely to fight than other forms of government, that the will of empowered citizens suffices to resist unpopular wars. Others would claim only that

---

* In *War and Peace*, Leo Tolstoy offers (depending on the edition) several embedded essays/digressions or one *long* appendix about the Great Man theory of history. On the same topic but much lighter reading, consider H. Beam Piper's *Lord Kalvan of Otherwhen* (1965).

† Not even far-future psychohistory could anticipate the ripple effects of the one-of-a-kind, psychically gifted mutant, the Mule. See Asimov's *Foundation and Empire* (1952).

democracies don't fight one another. Suppose either theory is valid (conflicting evidence to the contrary).[117] Democracy is no more inevitable and no less reversible than Marxist predictions of a dictatorship of the proletariat followed by an egalitarian, classless, socialist state.

If democracy—or another sociopolitical organization, yet unimagined by we mere humans—is an antidote to war, nothing says aliens will adopt or retain that form of government.

It's a mad, mad,…MAD world

Soon after the August 1914 outbreak of hostilities in Europe, H. G. Wells (in this context, an essayist) labeled that conflict, "The War That Will End War." Woodrow Wilson adopted the sentiment, declaring, "I promise you that this will be the final war—the war to end all wars."

The mass slaughter of trench warfare turned out not to make war unthinkable. Neither did an early weapon of mass destruction: mustard gas. Nor did the death toll, in the tens of millions (estimates vary).

Hence we came to know that conflict as the *First* World War. The second produced even higher body counts.

Has nuclear deterrence—enshrined in the strategy of Mutual Assured Destruction, enforced by dread of life-obliterating nuclear winter—deterred war? The argument for: humanity hasn't (as yet) blown ourselves away. The argument against: we've expressed our rivalries in other, still lethal forms of warfare. The MAD doctrine that deters a first use of nukes may enhance the ability of nuclear powers to deploy other, perhaps only slightly less destructive, weaponry.

Trust the process

Aliens are, well, *alien*. Who are we to predict their motivations?

Long-time students of the forces of Nature, that's who.

180

First, the trivial case: Aliens could be just like us. After all, *we* turned out to be possible.

However.

It was a long, twisty road from the primordial ooze to us, a road randomly—and repeatedly—rerouted. By asteroid impacts. Volcanic super eruptions. Ecological crises.* The drift (and, on occasion, collision) of continents. Perhaps, from across light-years, the sterilizing zap of a gamma ray burst.† So: without doubting that the fittest survive, who *is* the fittest at any given moment depends upon circumstances that can change without warning.

Hence, the far more likely case: they *aren't* like us. And yet, there's much we can say about life and intelligences that might emerge elsewhere.

The vast preponderance of evidence suggests that physical processes—the chemical properties of the elements, say, and the gravitational attraction between a planet and its sun—are univer-

---

* Here's an eco-crisis for you: the Great Oxygenation Extinction.

The foundations were laid, about 2.5 billion years ago, with the emergence of photosynthesizing life. For the next 200 million or so years, dead organic matter and the ocean's dissolved minerals chemically captured oxygen exuded by the newfangled cyanobacteria. Finally, the ocean reached its oxygen-absorbing capacity. And then, in a geological eye blink, oxygen toxicity extinguished most oldfangled, anaerobic life.

That's also when free oxygen began accumulating in Earth's atmosphere. Earth's primordial atmosphere was rich in methane: far more potent as a greenhouse gas than carbon dioxide. But methane oxidizes into carbon dioxide and water....

And thus, patient cyanobacterial hordes *also* triggered a snowball-Earth era, possibly the longest ever, lasting 400 million years.

† *Something* caused the Ordovician Extinction Event, about 450 million years ago, in which an estimated sixty percent of marine invertebrates—life hadn't yet made the jump to land—went extinct.

One theorized cause of the OEE is the intense blast of a gamma ray burst. GRBs are among the brightest events (if you could see gamma rays) in the Universe. Some supernovae produce GRBs, as can the catastrophic collision of binary neutron stars.

sal. Physics and chemistry everywhere follow the rules seen on Earth and throughout the Solar System.

What about biology do we infer will be universal? The *process*.

Imagine a world of methane seas, its intelligent natives resembling the love child of a parrot and squid. What can we predict?

That their world is subject to the implacable and capricious forces of Nature. That useful minerals, energy sources, and nutrients are in short supply—because plant and animal (and whatever else they have) populations will expand until shortages are a certainty. That life on that world—including the presumed intelligences atop the food chain—was sculpted by these impersonal and patient processes of evolution. That the aliens' social groupings and institutions survive because they successfully handled competitive pressures, both inter- and intra-species, resource scarcities, and a changing climate.

Sounds like our roots, doesn't it?

Why wouldn't we expect the parrot/squids to have evolved many of the same *behaviors* as humans? Seizing what one can from those unable to keep it for themselves. Dominating rivals. Eliminating rivals.

Perhaps, even, a propensity to war.

To bee (or not to bee)

Might not aliens emerge *so* different from us that they exhibit quite nonhuman behaviors? It's hard to preclude that possibility, on some world Out There.

Such behaviors aren't necessarily without earthly precedent.

Consider intelligence evolved from some alien analogue to terrestrial social insects.

Humans exhibit—and have exponentially extended—the aggressive behaviors of some primate relatives. It's no big stretch, therefore, to imagine alien hive intelligences that extend warlike behaviors like those of terrestrial ant colonies.

Or alien hive minds might mimic the wily tactic of some bees. Small groups of Africanized bees (aka, "killer bees") are known to subvert European honey bees. Their technique: invade the competitor's hive, kill the queen, and replace her with their own.[118] Call it the apian version of a decapitation strike.*†

Even *less* like us

What about beings entirely unlike any terrestrial species? Extrapolation from terrestrial behaviors may become untenable if extended to, for example, a planetary consciousness, creatures of pure energy, or aliens native to Oort Cloud objects. Once we concede that life might take such exotic forms, surely humility requires admitting that we cannot hope to predict how they behave.

Or not.

Anywhere random processes—cosmic rays, solar flares, choose your poison—may regularly intrude (which is everywhere), even the most exotic life forms must experience their disruptive influence. Anywhere the resources critical to life—energy? nutrients? solvents? catalysts?—are limited (again, that's everywhere), logic further suggests that even the most exotic life forms will compete. On what basis would one preclude the emergence of such familiar competitive stratagems as hiding, hunting—and war?

Would these exotic creatures and humans, if we should stumble upon one another, find reasons to battle? Our needs and in-

---

* Decapitation strike: the (as yet untried) strategy of a no-warning nuclear attack against an opponent's command-and-control centers, with intent to severely degrade the opponent's ability to counterattack.

† Not that coercion by a hive mind is limited to overt, Borg-style threats and violence. Why? Because participation in a hive mind might confer mental continuity beyond the body's lifespan. And so, in Robert A. Heinlein's *Methuselah's Children* (1941 serial, and an expanded novel in 1958), colonists abandon a world in part because the local hive mind began recruiting humans with the lure of immortality.

terests might be *so* dissimilar—despite independently evolved abilities to fight—that we'd have nothing to fight about. It's a pleasant thought. It might even be so—if, on one side or the other, extreme differences don't *trigger* conflict. Among humans, a xenophobic reflex has often sufficed to cause conflict or justify exploitation.

But maybe we and the exotic aliens differ *so* extremely that we don't recognize one another. If you'll pardon the ironic choice of metaphor, do we then dodge the bullet?

Maybe not. In Card's *Ender's Game*, humanity and aliens fall into conflict *precisely* because the telepathic, hive-like Buggers don't recognize nontelepathic humans as an intelligent life form.

What if the exotic aliens were made, not evolved? Suppose the aliens were uplifted from some pre-sentient form, bypassing blind evolution on a shortcut to intelligence. Might *those* aliens sidestep warlike attitudes?

Perhaps. If the creators (note the lower case) edit aggression from their creations. If deselected traits don't lurk in the gene pool to reemerge later. If natural forces—random variation; scarce resources—don't reverse engineered changes. If none among the creator species ever exploits, suppresses, or otherwise abuses their docile creations—and so teaches them undesired behaviors. If the created species, applying its newfound intelligence, doesn't invent resistance and rebellion.

Children *don't* always do as their parents wish.

And if the created "species" are robotic, not life in the conventional sense? *Battlestar Galactica*'s Cylons ("Death to humans") and Fred Saberhagen's Berserkers ("Death to life") rush to mind.

A sense of honor?

Some science fiction reads like Horatio Hornblower* in space: navies of similar capabilities slugging it out. Although David

---

* Hornblower is the protagonist in many of C. S. Forester's historical novels, the Royal Navy officer through whose eyes readers experience

Weber's "Honorverse" is home to its share of alien races, they're low-tech non-antagonists, leaving Honor Harrington (notice her initials) of the Royal Manticoran Navy to duke it out against human navies of similar capabilities.

If humans encounter intelligent aliens, it might happen that we and they deploy very similar technologies. But even neighboring stars may differ in age by billions of years. What are the odds (*Star Trek* notwithstanding) that we and those aliens will have very similar technologies?

If we and they have a conflict (more reasons for that coming up), might a technology mismatch prevent conflict? Will some honor code among intelligent species—we only pick on our technological peers—dissuade the stronger from dominating the weaker?

Perhaps, but we'd be foolish to expect it. Predators pick off the weakest of the herd. Cortes used his technological superiority (firearms, horses, and steel armor) to conquer the Aztecs. Across Africa, Asia, and the Pacific, nineteenth-century Atlantic powers grabbed territory and trading concessions from lower-tech indigenous powers. Mussolini turned tanks and airpower against Ethiopian troops armed largely with spears.

Perhaps advanced civilizations follow some *Star Trek*-like Prime Directive, not disclosing themselves to, much less dominating, species whose abilities have yet to reach a suitably high standard.

Could be. It's also conceivable that, seeking advantage, some spacefaring civilizations will *force* contact. Just as, not two centuries ago, elements of the U.S. Navy forced the long-isolationist Japan to re-engage with the world.

Limited war

Do the physics/math, and any entity that controls the energies required to travel among the stars has the capability to shatter

---

the Napoleonic Wars. Great stuff.

worlds. In a no-holds-barred, existential face-off, worlds may *be* destroyed. In any lesser dispute—a mercantile disagreement perhaps, or an armed contest to dominate the population of a world—cooler heads (or whatever) may prevail. Human experience in the Cold War was that Mutual Assured Destruction discourages the use of nuclear weapons; MAD may similarly discourage the blowing up of planets (or, as in "Exodus," a 2001 episode of *Stargate SG-1*, the blowing up of stars).

If so, battles for control of planetary resources and populations (in some instances, at least) will become—however unequal—battles *on* the planets.

Allies and sepoys and cannon fodder, oh my

Science fiction often pictures armies transported across interstellar space to wage war upon another species (just as, in human wars, the principals may cross oceans to slug it out head-to-head). Examples include *Starship Troopers* (Robert A. Heinlein, 1959), Joe Haldeman's aforementioned *Forever War*, and *Footfall* (Larry Niven and Jerry Pournelle, 1985).

But human conflicts, especially lower-intensity ones, often draw in other combatants. The Romans used units of native auxiliaries, though wisely (until late in the Empire, anyway) auxiliaries were never as well armed and trained as citizen legionnaires. The Ottoman Empire enslaved and indoctrinated non-Muslim boys to produce its corps of Janissaries. Amid the world-spanning Seven Years' War, both the British and the French had Native American tribal allies (hence the North American aspects of that conflict are known in the United States as the French and Indian War). The British East India Company recruited local forces, too: the sepoys. (A nasty bit of business, the Sepoy Rebellion. Eh, wot?)

Mercenaries are another time-honored human military tradition. Greek mercenaries fought for Xerxes at Thermopylae. Not many years later (as survivor Xenophon famously recounted in

The Persian Expedition), a Greek mercenary army in the hire of an ambitious Persian satrap invaded Persia. Many a medieval feudal lord hired Free Companies of mercenaries as needed, avoiding the expense of a standing army. George III of Great Britain employed German mercenaries (the Hessians) in his vain effort to suppress the American rebellion. During the second/pre-ISIS Iraq War, American private military contractors like Blackwater USA (as that company was known before name and ownership changes) provided extensive security and troop-training services—that on several occasions devolved into combat and controversy. As I type, mercenaries help to fill the regime's ranks in the Syrian civil war.

SF likewise envisions future wars prosecuted—in whole or in part, willingly or unwillingly—by third-party troops. In *Ranks of Bronze* (David Drake, 1986), a coerced Roman legion serves alien masters, battling low-tech natives on one world after another. Jerry Pournelle's Janissaries series sees aliens dominate the planet Tran with a new, higher-tech human army grabbed from Earth every generation or so. In *A Private Little War* (Jason Sheehan, 2013), a World War I-level private air corps is hired to aid one side in a low-intensity alien/alien war: think *Catch-22* (Joseph Heller's World War II classic) meets Pournelle's *Janissaries* (1979).

Another perspective

Do often hoary historical anecdotes have any useful predictive value for us? Surely *something* about alien species, extra-solar worlds, and interstellar distances calls extrapolation into question. Indeed.

Let's turn to economics.* People and governments aren't 100% rational actors, but they do (sometimes) take costs and benefits into account.

---

*   Economics is a science, too—no matter (hat tip to Victorian historian Thomas Carlyle) how dismal.

187

In a desert, war over water supplies may make sense. Water nearby is worth more than water that must be transported—if acquisition is even feasible—across great distances. What about a high-tech alien civilization running short of water? Would a species capable of interstellar travel cross light-years to steal Earth's water (as per the 1983 movie and 1984 TV series, *V*)?

Does that course of action make economic sense?

Doubtful! Just as the fringes of the Solar System teem with objects made mostly of water ice, icy objects are likely common in every solar system.* Imagine you're the leader of an alien civilization desperate for water. Do you retrieve that water from a few light-hours away or a few light-years?†

I thought so.

Even visiting some outer asteroids, moons, or Kuiper Belt Object for water seems more effort than necessary. I don't care how contaminated a world's water supplies become. The inputs (whether of time, energy, labor…however the aliens do their accounting) to purify the water on hand (e.g., to desalinate sea water) will be far less than the inputs to move huge transport ships, much less conquering armies, the light-years to/from Earth.

More broadly, it's hard to see what raw material would ever justify an interstellar trek—much less such a trek plus warfare.‡ Chemical elements, to repeat, are universal. The energy requirements to isolate and synthesize rare minerals at home must pale in comparison to the energy to project coercive military forces across light-years. James Cameron and *Avatar* (2009) notwithstanding, synthesizing "unobtanium" at home must be

---

* That's more than extrapolation from a sample size of one; as we've seen ("Alien Worlds"), it's a key inference of the dominant theory of solar-system formation.

† If you need help deciding, look back to the chapter "I Got the Long-Distance Blues."

‡ But check out the swashbuckling 1959 novelette "Despoilers of the Golden Empire," by Randall Garrett writing as David Gordon. You'll thank me for avoiding spoilers.

cheaper than travel to/from Alpha Centauri and a guerilla war with the Na'vi.

That's not to deny geological processes on a particular world may, due to some unusual circumstances, form rare, even unique minerals. Suppose precious minerals are created (although the airborne mountains in *Avatar* seem quite the stretch). The economic question remains: what's faster and cheaper? Forcibly obtaining the mineral from *far* away? Finding a way to trade for it? Or, given that you have (or can steal) samples, synthesizing the exotic mineral at home?

Which isn't to say economics precludes war over a natural resource. The more complex a molecule, the easier it is to imagine practical difficulties in copying it. An alien organic compound might be both valuable and difficult to synthesize. That is a premise of *Dune* (Frank Herbert, 1965), in which the hallucinogenic "spice" required for interstellar navigation—a biochemical produced only on Arrakis, metabolized by gigantic indigenous sandworms—is the cause of galactic conflict.

I suspect it's no coincidence that *Dune* predates any significant appearance, in popular culture or the genre, of genetic engineering or nanotech.

World wars

What's scarce, precious, and very costly/time-consuming to synthesize? Habitable planets.* So here's a scenario for you....

Picture an alien species Out There, evolved on an Earth-like planet. That is: home is a rocky world, not a gas or ice giant. It

---

* Look how much time and investment (in coal mines and power-generation plants, in oil wells, petroleum refineries, and automobiles...) humanity has needed to raise Earth's average temperature a paltry degree or so.

Habitable worlds are *big*. Feedback loops among a world's many parts (atmosphere, oceans, cryosphere, lithosphere, biosphere) do their best to sustain equilibria. Remember how long cyanobacteria labored to bring about the Great Oxygen Extinction.

189

orbits within its sun's Goldilocks zone, where liquid water can persist on the surface.

By one recent survey, we can expect (statistically speaking) *one* such planet within twelve light-years of Earth.[119] Current technology cannot yet determine the fraction of these planets also offering somewhat Earth-like gravity and a breathable atmosphere. How distant might the nearest *truly* Earth-like planet be? Twenty light-years? Thirty?

Estimates of stellar densities vary—astronomers continue to discover new stars, even in our immediate vicinity[120]—but a ballpark figure for Sol's neighborhood is 0.004 stars per cubic light-year. A sphere of radius 20 LY has a volume greater than 33 thousand cubic LY, and might encompass about 135 stars.

Habitable planets, rare and fragile, might be worth fighting over.

As the so-called New World was fought over by the maritime powers of the Old World.

And on the third tentacle....

We don't know what we don't know, or what hypothetical aliens do know. Maybe some hyper-dimensional shortcut will make interstellar travel quick and cheap. Maybe the universal zero-point energy of the vacuum can be tapped to fill every energy need. Maybe....

Human history has had its share of discoveries and inventions redefining the possible. Crossing oceans. Soaring like the birds. Breaking the sound barrier. Walking on the Moon. A century ago, who would have anticipated a thriving market in Japan for Australian cut flowers, or in the United States for Chilean fresh fruit?

The easier interaction becomes between intelligent species, the likelier (all other things equal) are all manner of interactions. Including conflicts.

Never mind unimagined technologies. The mere passage of time renders many hitherto impractical scenarios quite reasonable. Consider the awesome power of compounding growth.* 200 years growth at 2% yields a wealth increase of about 52 times. Bump that growth rate to 3%, and after 200 years the wealth increase approaches 370 times.†

The more resources a society can devote to a project—war included—the likelier (all other things being equal) that project becomes.‡

If new tech or growing resources make interstellar war more feasible, won't the timeframes get in the way? Suppose light speed *is* a limit. Who would begin a war they can't expect to see the end of?

That question may have an invalid premise. Aliens might live longer than us; a hive mind might be effectively immortal. Aliens might not be as short-term in their thinking as us. Our medical tech might continue to extend our lifetimes. Any of those situations makes interstellar enterprises, including war, more practical.

I'll bet you can come up with plausible scenarios of your own.

Other "opportunities"

---

*   Albert Einstein: "The most powerful force in the universe is compound interest." Even theoretical physicists sometimes commit metaphor and hyperbole.

†   Between 1947 and 2014, the average annual real (net after inflation) growth rate of the United States economy has exceeded three percent (http://www.tradingeconomics.com/united-states/gdp-growth). Emerging economies like China's often show faster growth, sometimes in double digits.

‡   And so, even as great nations hesitate to reach for Mars, soon enough a privately held company may attempt it. See "SpaceX's Giant Leap," *The Daily Beast,* May 29, 2014, http://news.yahoo.com/spacex-giant-leap-044300266--politics.html.

We haven't exhausted the reasons humans and aliens, given the chance, might have conflicts. Among the possibilities SF has offered are these:

Preemption: one explanation for the Great Silence* would be a spaceflight-capable species Out There that (perhaps unnerved by the Great Silence) has concluded (a) the Universe is a dangerous place and (b) I'd better take out the Other Guy before the Other Guy takes me out.

Does such preemption sound implausibly cold-blooded? After the third Punic War, the Romans razed ancient Carthage (the parts they hadn't already burnt) to the ground. According to legend, the Romans also sowed the ground with salt so that nothing again would ever grow there. Rome was a republic at the time.

Lack of (perceived) options: Imagine a group in desperate straits. Losers in a internecine war, perhaps. The reviled faction in a religious/philosophical schism. Survivors/refugees of an ecological collapse. Such a group might be tempted (or driven) to try to seize another habitable world. In my *InterstellarNet: New Order* (2010), an exiled alien clan thus ends up in the Solar System, at war with humanity.

Uplift: If life-friendly worlds are uncommon, how much rarer still are worlds bearing intelligent life? David Brin, in his Uplift series, envisions a galactic civilization centered on nurturing presentients into intelligence. To so elevate another species is a great honor—and brings with it a perk: eons of indentured service from the uplifted. Naturally the more technologically advanced species come to blows over the right to sponsor new client species.

Prime Directive: If, à la *Star Trek*, advanced civilizations opt to stay hidden from primitive societies, might one advanced civilization battle a less scrupulous one to enforce the policy? Or use enforcement as an excuse for war, when having an external enemy offers a domestic political advantage? In *A Darkling Sea* (James

---

* That is: a half-century search for extraterrestrial intelligence has yet to hear a peep. The chapter "Alien AWOLs: The Great Silence" explores possible explanations.

L. Cambias, 2014), newly starfaring humans and the higher-tech alien Sholen skirmish ostensibly about sheltering the primitive, underwater Ilmaratan.

Wrapping up

Behaviors common among humans are, *ipso facto*, also possible among other intelligences that may arise. Let humans or aliens obtain the ability to travel among the stars, and by implication inter-species, interstellar warfare also becomes feasible. Such conflicts may prove limited, the deterrent logic of Mutual Assured Destruction as compelling at the interstellar level as at the international level.

However discouraging this analysis may seem, there's a silver lining: the Universe *is* friendly to rip-roaring military SF.

To read further

- http://en.wikipedia.org/wiki/Interstellar_war offers a long list of fictional interstellar wars, many of those conflicts being inter-species.
- The "War" entry in *Science Fact and Science Fiction: An Encyclopedia*, Brian Stableford, includes a history and further discussion of SFnal warfare, including many interspecies conflicts.

HERE WE GO LOOPEDY LOOP

A Brief History of Time Travel

Who among us, from the age we first noticed that events happen one after another, has led a life so perfect and free of unpleasantness as to not ponder, occasionally, a do-over? Who among us, from the age we first distinguished the now from the not-yet, has not wondered what might come to befall us? From such basic human instincts, surely, arises our fascination with the notion of traveling through time.

Time travel has long been a commonplace of popular culture. There's Washington Irving's 1819 short story "Rip Van Winkle,"* Charles Dickens's 1843 novella "A Christmas Carol," Mark Twain's 1889 novel *A Connecticut Yankee in King Arthur's Court* and, of course, H. G. Wells's 1895 novel *The Time Machine*. Time travel has likewise been a staple of science fiction since the dawn of the genre, as when Anthony "Buck" Rogers awakened from centuries of suspended animation in 1928's novella "Armageddon 2419 A.D.," by Philip Francis Nowlan.

And more recently?† Time travel abounds in the popular culture. On-screen, consider: *Dr. Who* (the original BBC series in

---

* A similar idea, casting a different Irving character (Ichabod Crane)— awakening after two centuries, not two decades—underlies the 2013 TV series *Sleepy Hollow*.

† He says (in the present context) ironically. Or maybe the parenthetical made it doubly ironic.

1963, and its many reboots). The 1966 TV series *The Time Tunnel*. *Star Trek*, from many an episode in the original series (1966) to *Star Trek IV: The Voyage Home* (1986) to the 2009 movie reboot. The *Back to the Future* trilogy (1985, 1989, 1990). *Peggy Sue Got Married* (1986). *Bill & Ted's Excellent Adventure* (1989). *Timecop* (1994). The *Terminator* movies (1984, 1991, 2003, 2009, and 2015) and the related *Sarah Connor Chronicles* TV series (2008). *Hot Tub Time Machine* (2010). *Looper* (2012). *Edge of Tomorrow* (2014). And the ultimate in popular culture: Super Bowl XLVIII's *Doritos* time-machine commercial (2014).[121]

Despite time travel's enduring mass appeal, modern SF is often as hand-wavy as to *how* such transportation might be possible as were the earliest speculations. This avoidance is as characteristic of literary SF as of the video kind. Jack Finney's 1970 novel *Time and Again* uses self-hypnosis, with characters living in the era that they convince themselves to experience. Diana Gabaldon's Outlander series, begun in 1991, uses circles of standing stones for its time travel. Audrey Niffenegger's *The Time Traveler's Wife* (2003, then a 2009 movie) calls upon a rare mutation—just don't ask *how* a mutation makes someone bounce around in time. Connie Willis's time-traveling historians (first seen in the 1982 novelette "Fire Watch") never consider how they are transported, only whether their actions might trigger cause-and-effect paradoxes.* Stephen King's 2011 novel *11/22/63* (and 2016 TV miniseries 11.22.63)† offers a Narnia/wardrobe-like pantry. Irving Belatreche's 2014 novel *Einstein's Secret* has a wormhole conveniently linking decades-ago Pennsylvania with present-day Virginia, and offers no more explanation than "time travel is messy." Many a story merely posits that time travel—somehow—exists. "Trust me" is about as scientific as the conk on the head that conveyed the Connecticut

---

* Paradoxes, loops, and the like are a whole major topic. We *will* get there. All in good (cough cough) time.

† And that difference in date punctuation? Perhaps publishing and Hollywood are alternate universes.

Yankee to Arthurian times, or Merlin's spell by which the Yankee snoozed through a return to his birth era.

In summary, even recent time-travel fiction often depends upon reader/viewer acceptance of an SF trope (science used other than literally). Must such forbearance be the case? Perhaps. Perhaps not.

It's time for us to talk about...time.

Son of the Fermi Paradox

Every day, it seems, astronomers announce the discovery of another planet orbiting some distant star. As techniques mature for observing exoplanets (and soon, exomoons), more and more of these worlds are found to be Earth-like in one or more respects, whether in size, mass, or an orbit within the local "Goldilocks" zone. We've already delved extensively into the question of why, in a Universe rife with prospectively life-hospitable worlds, we might anticipate finding ourselves overrun by alien visitors, their radio broadcasts, or the abandoned artifacts of their past visits. Refuting an appeal to large numbers, you may recall, Enrico Fermi asked: where are they? We call this succinct rebuttal the Fermi Paradox.

Time travel raises similar questions. That is: if time travel is possible, then why—out of the eons that surely stretch before us—are we not tripping over time travelers? Would Fermi, if confronted with speculations about time travel, similarly rebut: where are they?

What *is* time? The great philosophers

Can one travel through time? If not, the apparent absence of time travelers ceases to be mysterious. Before we can hope to answer that question, surely there's a more basic question to address: what *is* time?

We're sure we experience time, but we don't necessarily agree on what we experience. What is time, beyond something approximated by the operation of our clocks?* Is time fundamental? In what objective sense can we confirm the existence of time? Is time cyclical, as days, months, years—our natural measurement units of time—suggest? Is time linear, as in our journey from birth to death? Did time begin with the Big Bang? Will time end?

It's not just SF readers who struggle with such concepts. Philosophers, it turns out, disagree on what time is—and whether it truly even exists.

"Time is a sort of river of passing events," said the Roman emperor and stoic philosopher Marcus Aurelius, "and strong is its current; no sooner is a thing brought to sight than it is swept by and another takes its place, and this too will be swept away."

If time is about the sequence of events (a perspective shared with many a dictionary), such as successive stages of motion, what have philosophers had to say about *that*?

The ancient Greek philosopher Zeno of Elea is well known for his paradoxes. Consider the race Zeno imagined between the famously fleet-footed Achilles and an ordinary tortoise. Achilles, after graciously giving the tortoise a head start, quickly reaches the tortoise's starting point. By then, of course, the tortoise has moved forward a short distance. Achilles soon crosses *that* distance, as well, only to find the tortoise has crept a bit farther still. It seems that Achilles can never—quite—catch up.† Or

---

* A clock counts events or measures processes believed to change in a predictable way with respect to time. In the course of history, clocks have made use of water dripping into a bowl, the burning of candles, the shadow cast by the Sun, the swinging of a pendulum, the oscillations of electrically stressed chunks of quartz, even the properties of the light emitted by atoms.

Not one of these mechanisms measures *time*. No one knows how to do that directly. We are left to trust that our stand-in measurements are valid analogues.

† That some infinite series (such as $1 + 1/2 + 1/4 + 1/8...$) can be proven to converge doesn't resolve the paradox—because other infinite series (such as $1 + 1/2 + 1/3 + 1/4 +...$) can be shown *not* to converge.

consider the flight of an arrow. At any particular instant, the arrow is motionless. But time, surely, is nothing more than a succession of instants. How, then, can the arrow *ever* move? Through such reasoning, Zeno decided that motion, being the change of position with time—and time itself—are illusions.*

Aristotle reached the opposite conclusion. Contrasting the logic of the arrow paradox with his certainty that motion *is* observed, Aristotle asserted that more than a present moment must exist. If there are past, present, and future, then there is time.

Do the past and future exist, or is there only an ever-changing present? Philosophers continue to argue that point, as well. The past, no matter that we remember it, might cease to exist, instant by instant, as we cease to experience it. And if the future is that which has yet to happen, in what sense can the future be said to exist at all? But perhaps, as the "block theory" of time has it, past and future always exist, just as left and right do. If the block view is correct, we journey along a time continuum, experiencing an ever-changing "now."

Is time a sort of cosmic backdrop, apart from events? Or is time the consequence, somehow, of events, without independent existence? Plato and Aristotle disagreed. Two millennia later, on the very same point, Newton and Leibniz also disagreed.

Despite all the philosophical hair-splitting, we *experience* time. We're born, we age, and we die. We remember the past

---

*   Was Zeno wrong? If so, how?

    The Achilles-and-tortoise paradox presupposes that time and distance are infinitely divisible. If there is some smallest possible distance, eventually only one indivisible unit of distance will separate man from tortoise—and the man is faster to cross it.

    Many physicists now believe that space and time, like matter and energy, are composed of indivisible quanta. The suspected fundamental unit of distance is far too small for any present-day technology to confirm. The fundamental unit of duration is, presumably, the amount of time that light (in a vacuum) would take to cross the quantum of distance.

HERE WE GO LOOPEDY LOOP

but only imagine the future into which we steadily advance by a second every second.

So what is time? Perhaps no philosopher has put it better than Augustine of Hippo, also known as Saint Augustine. "What then is time? Provided that no one asks me, I know. If I want to explain it to an inquirer, I do not know."

Making this the time for us to abandon philosophy and seek the guidance of physics....

What *is* time? Newtonian mechanics

Isaac Newton's laws of motion ascribe a machine-like determinism to physical events—so machine-like that in common metaphor the Universe *became* a mechanical clock. God's role post-Creation (and Newton was a highly religious man) seemed reduced to winding the clock.

Of particular interest to our present topic, the Newtonian universe presumed two absolutes: (a) an invisible grid against which one ascertains locations and measures distance, and (b) consistency of time across that grid. Knowing the laws of motion and the position of an object at any single instant, it became possible—in principle, in any event—to calculate the position of that object at any *other* time.

Newtonian equations of motion, moreover, are indifferent to the direction of time. We can as readily derive from whence an object came as to where it will go. Prediction or retrodiction? The distinction is merely a matter of the sign, plus or minus, of the time parameter plugged into the equations.

If time is in some sense reversible, what does that say of cause and effect?

What *is* time? Quantum mechanics

Quantum mechanics, as discussed elsewhere in this book (especially in "Alien Dimensions"), characterizes the behavior of matter and energy at very small scales. Where Newtonian mechanics describes the behavior of particles with clockwork-like, theoretically infinite, precision, quantum mechanics teaches that Nature itself limits the precision with which a particle's velocity or position can be known. Quantum-mechanical uncertainties aren't discernible in macroscopic objects (like Newton's falling apple*), but at tiny enough scales, these effects are routinely observed.

No matter its strangeness, quantum mechanics shares a basic property with Newtonian mechanics: equations that are indifferent to the direction of time. Flip the sign of the time parameter, and QM's equations work as well as before the reversal. (That said, whatever happens when the wave function collapses undoes QM's indifference to the direction of time: applying QM methods to retrodiction from a particle's *measured* position gives incorrect results.)

But are you certain?

In the preceding section, I oversimplified somewhat. Quantum-mechanical uncertainty, applies not strictly to position *or* velocity, but to the mathematical product of position *and* momentum. (Momentum, in turn, is the mathematical product of velocity and mass.) The more precisely we know a particle's position, the less precisely we can know its momentum. The uncertainties of an object's position and momentum are thus linked and complementary.[†]

---

[*] The tree from which fell, according to legend, the most famous apple since Eve's, died in 1814. A descendant of that very tree now grows on the Gaithersburg, MD, campus of the National Institute of Standards and Technology, home of the specific atomic clock that sets official time in the United States. I had that tree pointed out to me one lovely September day in 2014 when I spoke about SF at NIST.

See "Descendant of Isaac Newton's famous apple tree takes root on NIST campus," April 2, 1997, http://www.gazette.net/gazette_archive/1997/199714/gaithersburg/news/a55925-1.html.

[†] If an object were at perfect rest, its velocity, hence its momentum, would be zero. Zero times anything finite is also zero. If the object's

The mathematical product of an object's energy and duration (a quantity characterized by the same units of measurement as the product of position and momentum) are likewise linked and complementary, are likewise subject to quantum-mechanical uncertainty. Pretty esoteric, eh?

Perhaps. But also very real.

Mass and energy being forms of the same thing (as expressed in perhaps the best-known equation in all of modern physics: E = mc²), the energy * duration uncertainty suggests that particles can pop out of nothingness if they persist for only a sufficiently brief interval. And particles do! A particle and its antiparticle, such as an electron and a positron, will form spontaneously. When they encounter one another (or a different antiparticle and particle pair) the unlike particles mutually annihilate. It all works out as long as the energy "loan" to create something from nothing is brief enough—within the irreducible window of uncertainty. Some physicists call this ceaseless froth of emerging and disappearing particles the quantum foam.

And soon enough we'll come to why I brought up this wrinkle....

What *is* time? Special relativity

Yes, we dealt with relativity earlier in the book. To address the nature of time and the science of time travel, we need to look deeper. Because quantum mechanics isn't the end of counterintuitive physics.

If I'm driving a car at 60 mph and (never mind why) hurl a ball straight forward out the window at 10 mph, an observer standing on the sidewalk sees the ball moving at the sum of those speeds: 70 mph. Light, according to experiment (and Albert Einstein), doesn't work like that. Headlight beams from a moving car travel no faster than those emitted by a stationary car. More

---

position * momentum were zero, there would be no uncertainty—and QM won't have that. Even at absolute zero, therefore, an object has a minimal amount of jitter.

generally, light speed is the same (within a particular medium, such as air, water, or vacuum) wherever you measure it, whatever your velocity.*

That's less than intuitive.

Once we accept that light speed within a particular medium is constant, the implications are astonishing. Instead of light beaming *from* a vehicle, consider a flash of light set off *within* a vehicle, such as at the midpoint of the cabin of a clear-walled spaceship. The shipboard observer says the flash reaches the ends of the cabin simultaneously.

The spaceship, however, is coasting away from Earth. What does the Earthbound observer (with a Really Good Telescope) see? That as the flash moves toward Earth, the aft wall of the cabin—from Earth's perspective—zooms toward the light. Our Earthbound observer insists the light reaches the aft wall (as that wall races toward the flash) *before* light reaches the bow wall (as that wall races away from the flash). And yet, both observers claim that the inside-the-ship flash travels at the same speed. And both are correct!

It gets weirder. The Earthbound observer sees (a) the ship foreshortened in the direction of its flight, and (b) a shipboard clock ticking slower than an identical Earthbound clock. (*Clock* here stands in for any dynamic process, whether dust bunnies accumulating under a bed, milk going sour, or human aging.) The shipboard observer experiences neither length contraction nor time dilation, any more than the passenger in a car moving at a steady pace experiences any sense of motion.

---

* Contrary to familiar usage, *speed* and *velocity* differ. *Speed* is a rate, such as ten miles per hour. Velocity is both a rate and a direction, such as ten miles per hour due north. An object tracing a circle at a constant speed has a constantly changing direction—and hence a constantly changing velocity.

The "special" in special relativity limits the theory to particular points of view, what physicists call inertial frames of reference, that move at constant velocities.

We'll come in a few pages to the unrestricted case: general relativity.

As familiar from our SF reading as are these consequences of special relativity, they still battle with our intuition of how the Universe works. That's too bad for our intuition, for these effects have been confirmed again and again. Take, for example, muons. Muons are short-lived subatomic particles ceaselessly produced in the upper atmosphere as high-energy cosmic rays slam into gas molecules. Everything known about muons says they should decay long before reaching Earthbound detectors into (typically) an electron and two neutrinos—only often these cosmic-ray-induced muons don't. That's because cosmic rays come on *fast*; due to conservation of momentum, muons produced by collisions with cosmic rays also move fast. These muons are, in effect, tiny spaceships careening through the atmosphere at relativistic speeds. Their decay then proceeds according to their internal, time-dilated "shipboard" clocks, not any clock set on Earth's surface. When a downward-streaking muon reaches Earth's surface, it remains, in some sense, in what you and I would consider the past. And from the muon's point of view? It has sped ahead into its future.

When the length of a ruler, the rate of a clock's ticking, and the meaning of simultaneity all depend upon from whence you look, then—Newton notwithstanding—absolute space and time do not exist. There is, instead, four-dimensional space-time, and nothing about *it* is absolute. As Einstein concluded, "Time has no independent existence apart from the order of events by which we measure it."

On the bright side, this mind-bending state of affairs answers one question for us: is there more than an instantaneous, ever-evolving present? Emphatically, yes! Simultaneity being relative precludes the notion of any universal instant in time. My present—if one of us is moving relative to the other—may be in your future or your past.

The twin paradox

If you don't care to entrust yourself, *Futurama*-style, to freezing and eventual thawing, or, *Buck Rogers*-style, to suspended animation, you can *still* travel to the far future by Going Really Fast. True, accelerating an object as massive as a human body to near-light speed isn't practical, nor is that feat apt to be feasible any time soon, but it *is* allowed by physics. We see an extreme example in Poul Anderson's 1970 novel, *Tau Zero*. Larry Niven's 1976 novel *A World Out of Time* does a time-travel two-step: the hero first jumps ahead as a corpsicle and then (much) farther during a long relativistic trip.*

But wait! If all motion is relative, why isn't it the Earth traveling really fast, the spaceship at rest, and the Earth leaping into the ship-and-passenger's future?

All motion *is* relative, but there's more to the story. (If you want a story, that would be Robert A. Heinlein's 1956 novel *Time for the Stars*.) As for the physics, it's time we look at the famous twin paradox, a form of which was first posed by Paul Langevin in 1911.

Consider twenty-year-old twins, whom we'll call Alice and Bob. Alice is the traveler of the pair. Aboard her spaceship, she: accelerates to about 99.995% of light speed; coasts for a month; decelerates to a stop; turns around; accelerates back toward Earth, again to 99.995% of light speed; coasts for a month; decelerates to a stop; and lands. She steps off her spaceship two months older.† Stay-at-home brother Bob is on the tarmac to greet her.

---

* A point of grammar: in customary usage, *farther* refers to increased physical distance and *further* to an increase in something else—often something metaphorical. In a time-travel context, time offers a type of distance. With premeditation, I chose *farther* to characterize our hero's time shift; while you may disagree with my usage, I'll ask that you not hassle me *further*.

† For simplicity (or because some advanced technology protects Alice from what would otherwise be extremely high levels of gee forces) we'll assume that the periods of acceleration are extremely brief. This is, after all, a thought experiment! We can then derive the time dilation strictly from the long periods spent coasting, and I get to avoid doing calculus. That is, we'll use only equation (4) of "I Got the Long-Distance Blues."

How old is he?

We've seen that speed makes clocks tick slower, so we might expect Bob to have aged more than Alice. But while Bob, with his Really Good Telescope, saw Alice's ship zoom away and come back, it's also true that Alice, with *her* Really Good Telescope, saw Earth—with Bob on it—zoom away and return. But clearly each twin can't be younger than the other.

It turns out that Bob, come to greet his peripatetic sister, is middle-aged. For him, almost seventeen years have passed and he's pushing thirty-seven. The difference between the twins? Alice's bouts of acceleration and deceleration. Each time Alice accelerates, decelerates, or changes direction, she changes her "frame of reference." Bob has remained—to the first approximation—in a single frame of reference. Their situations are not equivalent.*

And so, upon close examination, the twin paradox isn't a paradox at all.

The fourth dimension—sort of

Articles aimed at a general audience sometimes refer to time simply as "the fourth dimension." It's a natural enough idea. An object without persistence—vanished in an instant—is as much of a physical abstraction as an object that lacks breadth or depth or height.

We move left and right, forward and back, up and down, and we move forward in time. It's not seemingly much of a mental leap to suppose that we could—although we have yet to discover

---

* Strictly speaking, Earth doesn't provide an inertial frame of reference. Earth orbits the Sun and the Sun orbits the galactic core, but these ongoing changes in velocity are insignificant compared to Alice's maneuvers. Ditto the effects, which we have yet to discuss, of Earth's gravity. We could simplify our thought experiment by starting out Bob and Alice on a tiny habitat adrift in space. Stay-at-home Bob wouldn't much like that, of course.

the means—(as in H. G. Wells's *The Time Machine*) also move backward in time. We don't notice the fourth dimension, Wells's nameless Time Traveler explains, because our consciousness moves along with it.

But time as a pure dimension, as distinct from space as left/right are distinct from up/down, is *not* consistent with the four-dimensional space-time of which Einstein wrote. Time and space, as Einstein realized, are different depending upon who is observing and from where they're observing.

Time, now conflated with space, nonetheless remains different than purely spatial dimensions. That's another implication of light setting a speed limit. That the speed limit exists means that some pairs of events might have a cause-and-effect relationship, while others—too far separated by space for even light to traverse in the available time—cannot be related in that way.

Since soon after Einstein introduced special relativity, physicists have spoken of time-like and space-like intervals separating events in space-time. Across a time-like interval, no possible observer can see the second (possibly effect) event before the first (possibly causal) event. Past and future in this scenario are unambiguous. Across a space-like interval, however, matters are quite different. Which event of the interval-delimiting pair a particular observer perceives as first and which as second depends upon the events' and the observer's relative motion. Across space-like intervals, past and future *are* ambiguous.

But wait! There's more.

What *is* time? General relativity

Special relativity suggests that the time aspect of space-time is complicated—but not yet what that time aspect is. Well, when Einstein developed that theory, he wasn't done. The "special" in special relativity limits the theory to particular points of view, what physicists call reference frames, that move at constant velocities, where (as we've seen) velocity combines speed with direction.

General relativity involves accelerating reference frames (that is, situations in which speed *or* direction changes) and—here comes the truly interesting part—the insight that acceleration and gravitational attraction are equivalent. An object dropped in a spaceship accelerating at one gee falls *just* like an object dropped while standing still on the Earth's surface. What's going on, and what has it do with time?

Special relativity is uncomplicated compared to general relativity. Averting our eyes from quite complex math, we'll jump straight to a few important implications.

If the malleability of space-time and the relativity of simultaneity haven't already convinced you that the Universe lacks some unchanging, multidimensional grid/backdrop, consider this: neither does space-time reflect dimensions at right angles to each other. That geometry you studied back in secondary school, the product of Euclid, another ancient Greek, is merely an approximation to reality.

Recall how flat/two-dimensional maps satisfactorily represent small areas—while grossly misrepresenting the overall Earth. That's because (setting aside that Earth isn't quite a perfect sphere) the two-dimensional surface of a sphere curves.[*] Space-time itself curves, the local curvature dependent (general relativity tells us) upon the distribution of mass.

Newton struggled to explain—no matter the obvious utility of his mathematical equation for gravitational attraction[†]—*how*

---

[*]   Notwithstanding many maps you've likely seen, Greenland *isn't* larger than South America! South America, in fact, has an area of about eight times that of Greenland. Greenland appears huge on many world maps because it lies so far to the north—and the Mercator projection commonly used on world maps distorts more and more the farther one gets from the equator.

[†]   Newton's equation: $F = Gm_1m_2/R^2$, where F is the attractive force between two masses, G is the gravitational constant, m_1 and m_2 are the two masses attracting one another, and R is the separation between those masses.

could widely separated objects influence one another's motions? (Indeed, he called the notion, "so great an Absurdity that I believe no Man who has in philosophical Matters a competent Faculty of thinking can ever fall into it.") Consider the Moon as it orbits the Earth. How do the Moon and Earth "know" that the other exists—on average 238,000 miles (384,000 kilometers) separate the two worlds—much less how do they gauge their influences one upon the other?

Via his theory of general relativity, Einstein did away with such "non-local" interaction. Objects *don't* sense other objects at a distance; rather, objects interact with the local curvature of space-time. Or, as physicist John Wheeler so elegantly (if anthropomorphically) expressed the essence of general relativity in twelve words: "Matter tells space how to curve. Space tells matter how to move."

What has this to do with time and time travel? Everything. Because it's space-*time* that warps in the presence of matter. The stronger the local gravitational field (i.e., the more curved the local space-time), the slower a clock ticks in that field. Conversely, the atomic clocks overhead in GPS satellites—because they're a bit removed from the Earth's mass—tick *faster* than an identical clock does on our planet's surface.*

And so, our time-travel toolkit includes velocity-induced *and* gravitational time dilation.

What *is* time? The slings and arrows of outrageous entropy

The video of two billiard balls colliding is as believable run backward as forward. Ditto the (admittedly harder to produce) video

---

* More precisely, two relativistic considerations exert opposing influences on the GPS clocks. That GPS satellites hurtle around the Earth makes their clocks (by our earthbound standards) run *slower* than clocks more-or-less stationary on the planet, as per special relativity. The speed-up of the GPS clocks due to the reduced gravity at the altitude of their orbits (per *general* relativity) is the dominant effect.

of two really hard spheres colliding at relativistic speed. Same for an alpha particle, say, scattering off an atomic nucleus.

The video of the making of an omelet? Not so ambiguous.

Mechanics—classical, relativistic, and quantum—is governed by equations that are indifferent to the direction of time.* Why, then, do you and I experience a direction of time? For a possible answer, we must turn to yet another branch of physics.

Thermodynamics, as its name suggests, deals with the evolution of heat-driven systems. It was developed to better understand and optimize steam engines. Thermodynamics *can't* undertake to see the world as individually modeled, sometimes colliding, particles, because the problems thermodynamics seeks to solve encompass enormous numbers of molecules. Instead, thermodynamics uses statistics and probability to reduce the overall complexity. *Temperature*, as an example, is a measure of the average energy of a set of particles—like the water molecules comprising all the steam in a boiler. That single number is often more useful than the (impossible to determine, much less to compute with) details of every molecule's position and kinetic energy.

Entropy is another highly abstract parameter from thermodynamics. Entropy, loosely speaking, is the measure of disorder within a system. We'll use a standard deck of playing cards, of four suits and thirteen cards per suit, to examine entropy.

Playing cards leave the factory arranged in numeric order by suit, with the suits ordered by customary rank: clubs, diamonds, hearts, spades. Imagine we separate out the four suits, then shuffle the four-element deck made of the thirteen-card-thick stacks (think of each stack as a very thick card). The deck so shuffled can end up in any of 24 ways (four possibilities for the front suit; times three possibilities from among the remaining three; times two possibilities between the remaining two; times one, the remaining suit: 4 * 3 * 2 * 1 = 24). We'd be sur-

---

* Quantum mechanics deals with the probabilities of where an object may be, not its actual position, but nonetheless, the equation remains time-reversible.

prised, but not incredulous, if after shuffling we found the deck in factory order.

In a normal shuffle, the cards within a suit won't stay together. Instead, when we shuffle the deck, any of 52 cards might wind up first, any of the 51 remaining cards wind up second.... After a lot of multiplication (or a simple spreadsheet), it turns out that there are more than 8×10^{67} possible outcomes. That's 8 followed by 67 zeroes!

It's still possible for a shuffled deck to come out in factory order—just *extremely* implausible. While the toss of a fair coin has a one-in-two chance of coming up heads, a shuffled deck has less than one chance in 8×10^{67} of coming out in factory order.

The second law of thermodynamics, paraphrasing, says that entropy—the disorder within a closed system—tends to a maximum. *Entropy*—and our everyday experience with the natural tendency to disorder—suggests a cause for the perceived "arrow of time."

Billiard balls colliding, then rebounding, are a simple system. We see no difference between the video of their collision run forward and backward because the trajectories in either case appear equally likely. Not so, the deck of cards picked up, shuffled, set down, then shown to be in factory order. Not so, the omelet seen reassembling itself into eggs. Or as Arthur Eddington put it, almost a century ago:

> The law that entropy always increases, holds, I think, the supreme position among the laws of Nature. If someone points out to you that your pet theory of the universe is in disagreement with Maxwell's equations— then so much the worse for Maxwell's equations. If it is found to be contradicted by observation—well, these experimentalists do bungle things sometimes. But if your theory is found to be against the second law of thermodynamics I can give you no hope; there is nothing for it but to collapse in deepest humiliation.

How, then, is it that we often see order emerge from disorder? How is it I can re-sort a deck of cards? How is it Nature can assemble scads of stray molecules into potatoes and people? The short answer: the tendency toward disorder applies to *closed systems*. A deck of cards ceases to be a closed system when I'm sorting; the energy I supply can overcome the deck's tendency toward disorder. More broadly, *Earth* is not a closed system; the unending flood of energy from the Sun makes possible the ongoing biological processes that would seem the antithesis of entropy. But the Sun is a pretty good approximation of a closed system... luckily for us, its evolution is a very gradual thing. And bigger picture: the *Universe*—or the Multiverse, if you find that sort of thing convincing—is the ultimate closed system.

If we were to examine our colliding billiard balls closely enough, even here time reversibility would disappear. Perfectly elastic collisions on perfectly frictionless surfaces are abstractions. In the real world, a little kinetic energy (the energy of motion) is lost to friction between billiard balls and tabletop. At the moment of collision, a tiny amount of kinetic energy transforms to slightly raised temperatures of the balls themselves. In physical, rather than idealized, processes, some energy is *always* dissipated in heat.

And so, before and after become distinguishable.

Does time have a direction, or just the illusion of one? Will the Universe have reached the end of time once the state of maximum entropy has been reached? Or will time continue, only its direction be forever lost?

Wouldn't it be nice to know?

What *is* time? The recurrence theorem

Pre-industrial societies were attuned to the cycles of Nature: day and night, the "moonthly" phases of our world's natural satellite, and the annual sequence of the seasons. It's no wonder that some societies saw time itself having cyclic properties.

We "moderns" tend to find such a cyclic view of time quaint: a relic of a simpler, naturalistic society. Thermodynamics seems to confirm what our senses tell us: that there is a direction to time. Surely, time is linear, not cyclical.

Or not. Mathematician Henri Poincaré demonstrated in 1890, in what has become known as the Poincaré recurrence theorem, that any finite isolated system must, after a finite amount of time, return to its initial state. In an infinite amount of time, the cycle must repeat an infinite number of times.*

What *is* time? The astronomical evidence

In 1924, astronomer Edwin Hubble published his finding that the Universe is expanding. The same data, considered in reverse, gave rise to a startling implication: at earlier times, the Universe was smaller. Keep rewinding that conceptual movie, and the retrodiction was of a *singularity*: conditions of infinite density and—because just as expansion cools things, compression heats them—infinite temperature. In such conditions, physical laws as then (and still) understood fall apart.

Was the Big Bang the beginning of time? Perhaps. If anything existed before the Big Bang, physical science offers no opportunity to glimpse it.[122]

For decades, astronomers and cosmologists wondered: did the Universe contain enough mass that its mutual gravitational attraction would eventually overcome the outward momentum from the Big Bang, bringing expansion to a halt, then bring everything crashing back together to erupt again in another Big Bang (perhaps to repeat again and again and again...)? If so, the Poincaré recurrence theorem would be more than a mathematical curiosity.

---

*   *Is* the Universe a finite system? Unclear.

The finite speed of light and the finite elapsed time since the Big Bang combine to limit observations to a finite, if extremely large, observable Universe. Limits on the observable Universe, however, don't preclude the overall Universe from having infinite extent.

In the 1990s, however, it became evident that the expansion of the Universe is *accelerating*. Far from everything falling back together in some very distant future, the Universe will continue expanding—possibly until even atoms, and then their constituent parts, are ripped apart. Physicists say that "dark energy" drives this accelerating expansion—although that's merely a label, not an explanation. But whatever is happening, the Universe doesn't seem cyclical.[123]

Astronomy, like thermodynamics, most definitely exhibits an arrow of time.*

What *is* time? Reflections

A century of effort has failed to reconcile the two greatest theories in modern physics: quantum mechanics, whose prescriptions so accurately describe subatomic realms, and general relativity, whose prescriptions so accurately describe very large and/or very massive domains. These two theories are, at their cores, inconsistent in their underlying assumptions. The equations of general relativity assume that space-time is continuous. The QM worldview is inherently *dis*continuous, with matter and energy coming in discrete, indivisible chunks called quanta. Moreover, GR is deterministic while QM is probabilistic.

Can the Universe be continuous *and* discontinuous, deterministic *and* nondeterministic? It would appear that one of these great theories—and perhaps both—suffers from a foundational shortcoming. When, someday, the two theories are unified, or superseded, we may get an explanation for the arrow of time.

---

* For completeness—but without further elaboration—I'll note that an arrow of time is also glimpsed in a rare decay mode of a type of kaon (a subatomic particle) and in the absence of backward-in-time electromagnetic waves (which would be consistent with Maxwell's equations but are not observed in nature).

   Do such disparate phenomena stem from a single arrow of time? Is there a hierarchy (or a yet more complex structure) of cause-and-effect at work? These deep questions remain unanswered.

But even that grand unification may fail to explain time's arrow. QM and GR alike are *reductionist* in approach. Both undertake to explain that which is very complex through an ever deeper understanding of ever fewer, ever more fundamental, constituent parts. For certain lines of inquiry—such as the nature of time?—reductionism may stand in the way of an answer.

Thermodynamics sees—as do you and I, as do (at a quite different scale) astronomers—an arrow of time. And thermodynamics alone, of the physics disciplines we've surveyed, *embraces* the messiness of molecules in their myriad multitudes.

A few atoms seen (or modeled) jostling and jittering about don't suggest that—within a crystal—they form part of an overarching order. A few ants spotted wandering about don't suggest the purposeful behavior of the colony. A few neurons detected firing don't suggest that among an ensemble of billions, they can create art, literature, and science.

Time's arrow—like crystals, ant colonies, and human thought—might be an emergent property of large numbers of objects. If so, the reductionist models of QM and GR could be as unsuited to fully explaining time as the study of single neurons is to explaining the human mind. And if time's arrow is an emergent property, what other characteristics of time might QM and GR theories have omitted?

Coming up: the many uncertainties surrounding the prospects for, and the possible implications of, time travel.

HERE WE GO LOOPEDY LOOP

Back and There Again

Last chapter, we briefly surveyed classical/Newtonian mechanics, relativistic/Einsteinian mechanics, quantum mechanics, and thermodynamics (or, if you require your lists to exhibit parallel construction, its close relative: statistical mechanics). Each of these disciplines offered its own conclusions about the nature of time. Left for this concluding half of the topic: how we might travel in time and the implications of such a venture.

Not to keep you in suspense: physics suggests time travel *is* possible—but (a) only through incredible feats of engineering (b) amid great skepticism that something important (e.g., the need for causality) is missing from that physics, and (c) even then, seemingly with major restrictions on what eras can be visited.

As usual, we'll also see where SF has anticipated the possibilities.

To the far future…if not easily

We *can* travel into the future at other than our accustomed second-per-second pace.

Option one, previously touched upon: travel fast for awhile before resuming a normal (or no) speed. Voilà! You're in your own future.

Getting far into the future this way, oddly enough, takes time. Suppose you set the goal of traveling twenty years into the

Earth's future. Suppose your ship can accelerate to about 86% of light speed (which will require rather advanced tech—no human has ever achieved 1% of light speed). At that pace, time aboard your ship passes only half as quickly as back on Earth. To simplify matters, we'll ignore the periods spent accelerating to, or decelerating from, that breakneck speed. You will need to spend ten years aboard your ship before twenty years pass on Earth. Even if you could achieve 99-plus percent of light speed, you'd need to spend more than a half year of ship's time to get a ten-year jump on Earth.

It takes a great deal of energy to achieve those near-light velocities! In Newtonian mechanics, the kinetic energy of an object with velocity v and mass m equals $1/2\ mv^2$. Doubling the ship's velocity entails four times the energy, tripling the ship's velocity takes nine times the energy, and so on. As velocity increases, relativistic effects become manifest and Newtonian mechanics understates the required energy. The bottom line: the ship's mass to be accelerated grows exponentially with velocity. Let's just say that significant time travel by starship isn't in our immediate future.*

Option two: loiter deep within a significant gravity well—near a neutron star, say—and (relative to those of us in comparatively flat space-time) clocks again run slower.† Make sure to pick

---

* For a more detailed look at the energy requirements of relativistic travel, refer back to the chapter "I Got the Long-Distance Blues."

† A neutron star is the collapsed remains of a "regular" star after it has gone supernova. Neutron stars are super-dense; each packing the mass of a Sun-like star into a sphere only a few miles across. (Stars more massive than about ten of our Sun collapse, post-supernova, yet further—forming black holes.)
   The extreme conditions of the collapse transform most of the star's post-explosion mass into neutrons. A neutron star is, on average, about a hundred *trillion* times as dense as liquid water (less—but still incredibly—dense toward the surface; yet denser toward the core). Lead, the densest material most of us ever encounter, is a mere eleven

one among the subset of neutron stars that *isn't* (like a pulsar) a deadly radiation zone. In orbit around the neutron star, you'd be in free fall, like an astronaut circling the Earth. You'd have the time-slowing benefit of the intense gravity (i.e., be in a region of very curved space-time) without *feeling* that gravity. (But don't orbit too close, or—as befell characters in Larry Niven's 1966 short story "Neutron Star"—you'll feel the tidal effects. Only *tidal effects* is so understated. The more descriptive term for what you would experience is "spaghettification." *)

But if gravitational time dilation is the road to the future, there's yet another difficulty. The closest known neutron stars to Earth are hundreds of light-years distant. *Making* a neutron star (presumably out of a nearby normal star) might be no more of a challenge than traveling to a naturally occurring neutron star. And if your engineering skills are really advanced? Perhaps you can assemble sufficient mass into a shell *around* yourself. Tidal effects, like gravitational attraction, go to zero at the center of a uniform sphere.

The do-it-yourself, wraparound neutron star has its own lim-its. Lest the constructed shell collapse into a black hole—with the would-be time traveler within—Brian Clegg has calculated the best that can be achieved is one year elapsed inside for every five years passing outside.

Speaking of black holes,[†] if you want to slow time to an ab-solute crawl, find a suitably sized one and "loiter" just outside its

---

times as dense as water. At neutron-star densities, all of humanity would fit into a teaspoon.

All of which is to say: the gravity near such a massive, tiny object is ferocious. On the star's surface, the gravity would crush you.

* In "Neutron Star," Niven chose not to dwell on the clock-slowing consequences of the close encounter.

† A black hole is an object so massive that it has collapsed into infinite density (not always into a dimensionless point—a complication we'll save for later). To become a black hole is the ultimate fate of large

event horizon.* (Spaghettification doesn't become problematical until you're well inside the event horizon, in which case you have *lots* of problems—as does the hero's girlfriend in Frederik Pohl's 1977 novel *Gateway*.) Of course, no black holes are known to exist in the interstellar neighborhood, either.

I *did* say about travel to the distant future: not easily.

Perhaps someday, when quantum mechanics and general relativity have been reconciled, physicists will learn to *artificially* warp space-time. Among the applications of such knowledge might be the formation of compact regions of slowed time that—unlike the neighborhoods of neutron stars and black holes—would not be deathly radiation environments. Such space-time warping technology plays a part in my 2015 novel *InterstellarNet: Enigma*.

---

stars once their fusion fuel runs out and heat-driven expansion can no longer counterbalance the inward tug of gravity.

A black hole's gravitational field is so intense that not even light can escape—hence the object's metaphorical blackness. The point of no return upon an approach to a black hole is called its event horizon.

Why *metaphorical* blackness? Because black holes are often surrounded by light sources. In-falling matter, attracted and accelerated by the intense gravity, often surrounds the event horizon. This "accretion disc," superheated by compression and friction, produces a bright radiation environment.

* Why the quotes around *loiter*? Because there's no aimless dawdling involved! In sufficiently curved space-time—as is found close to an event horizon—orbits aren't stable. A ship in that region can follow a closed course around the event horizon, or can hover, but in either case only by thrusting mightily against the singularity's gravity. See "Centrifugal Forces and Black Holes," John G. Cramer, *Analog*, November 1992, (and http://www.npl.washington.edu/AV/altvw55.html).

(At least this complication arises with *static* black holes. Close-in stable orbits seem possible near a sufficiently massive *rotating* black hole, due to another aspect of general relativity that we'll soon discuss: frame dragging.)

What's past is past. Or is it?

Everything we've discussed so far deals with carrying oneself, one way or another, into the future: "Rip Van Winkle" improved with high tech. But what if you wish to visit the past? What if, having explored the future, you desire to return to report on what you've seen? That is a much tougher challenge (although we've already covered much of the underlying physics).

A matter of some gravity

A full understanding of the world around us involves mathematical skill and the computational arts as much as physical insight. As a case in point, consider gravity.

In 1686, Newton described the gravitational interaction between any two masses (say, Earth and Sun) with a simple quadratic equation. This description served astronomers well for centuries; it suffices to this day for most NASA mission-planning purposes. But add a third mass (say, the Moon) to the picture, and Newton's theory of gravity lacks a general solution. It was almost a century after Newton published his findings until Euler and Lagrange demonstrated special circumstances in which the three-body problem *can* be solved exactly.[124] It wasn't until 1887 that Bruns and Poincaré proved that no exact general solution exists for the three-body problem. Approximations have been, and remain, necessary.

The analogous representation of the modern, more complete description of gravity—Einstein's 1915 theory of general relativity—is a system of ten nonlinear partial-differential equations. All you need to know about that characterization is (a) that's seriously heavy-duty math and (b) the Einstein field equations (like Newton's far simpler equation) have yet to offer many exact solutions. It wasn't until 1949 that mathematician Kurt Gödel, applying the Einstein field equations to the Universe as a whole—a spinning Universe, at that—showed that exact solutions exist that allow "closed time-like curves."

219

A space-time curve represents an object's experience: the path the object has taken through time and space. An interval on that history is delimited by two non-simultaneous events. Recall from the last chapter that across a time-like interval no possible observer can witness the second (possibly, effect) event occurring before the first (possibly, causal) event. That precedence is maintained for as long as the watcher's observations and travel—as we're so often told must be true—happen at or below light speed. Remember that caveat.

What, then, is a closed time-like curve (CTC)? It's an object returning to a place *and time* already experienced. It's history meeting up with itself. Like an Escher stairway, no matter how ordinary each step appears, the whole seems wrong.

"CTC" is highly circumspect physics-speak for time travel to one's past.

No wonder that, when Gödel presented his proof to his friend on his 70th birthday, Einstein briefly doubted general relativity.

Time travel is such a drag

Familiar considerations of relativity tell us that the faster one travels, the slower one's clock ticks, until, approaching light speed, the shipboard clock—viewed from an external/at-rest frame of reference—slows to zero. It makes intuitive sense that, upon exceeding light speed, one's clock—and time itself—would change direction. Would run backward relative to a sub-light speed observer.

Alas, a moving object's mass increases in inverse proportion to its time dilation. When shipboard clocks are ticking at half the stay-at-home rate, the ship's mass (compared to its at-rest mass) has doubled. As the clock rate (from the at-home perspective) slows toward zero, the ship's mass (in the at-home perspective) approaches infinite. You just *can't* accelerate an object to, much less past, light speed.

If I'm not pages too late to write this: here's where matters get tricky.

To recap the crux of general relativity, the mere presence of a massive object like the Sun curves space-time. The influence of that curvature on the trajectory of other objects, like the planets, is what we know as gravity.

Less well known—but another implication of the Einstein field equations—is that the *rotation* of massive objects further distorts space-time. Specifically, the rotation drags space-time around with it. When the object is massive enough, and/or rotating fast enough, the dragging effects can be substantial. A ship moving at sub-light speeds within a dragged region of space-time (physicists refer to "frame dragging") can be moving *faster* than light in regions where space-time is not being dragged. In the process, the ship is also—compared to that non-dragged region—spiraling backward in time.

Circling the Universe, à la Gödel, isn't the easiest way to go backward in time.[*] In 1974, Frank Tipler came up with a solution to Einstein's field equations showing that a closed time-like curve—travel backward in time—could be accomplished with the frame dragging of a massive object smaller than the Universe. His 1974 paper, "Rotating Cylinders and the Possibility of Global Causality Violation," suggested one such time-travel mechanism. Tipler tamed the math with the simplifying assumption that the cylinder was of infinite length—not something we finite humans are likely ever to construct—but asserts that a finite object of sufficient mass and rotational velocity would suffice.[†] His density and mass estimates roughly correspond to ten neutron stars. Disassembling neutron stars, reassembling all that mass into a

---

[*] "Beyond Space and Time" (1938), by Joel Townsley Rogers, has a starship circling the Universe at very great speed, such that the pilot returns to the place *and time* of his departure. Rogers beat Gödel to the punch by more than a decade. (Unless.... Maybe Gödel traveled a CTC to give Rogers this idea? Nah.)

[†] Remember Superman turning back time, changing history, and saving the girl (Lois Lane) by flying around the world really fast, in the 1978 movie *Superman*? For comic-book science, that wasn't bad.

cylinder, and spinning it up sounds like a challenge. So does maintaining all that mass in a cylindrical shape against the tug of its own gravity. (That much mass would normally pull itself into a sphere—and then collapse into a black hole.) Ditto approaching near enough to benefit from frame dragging without getting spaghettified.

Another class of exotic celestial object might serve our purposes: cosmic strings.

Cosmic strings require an explanation....

Start with the Big Bang "fireball." Everything in the very early Universe was super-hot and expanding. Expansion cools things, just as expanding water vapor can cool and condense into liquid water. Vapor cooling and condensing into water is a phase transition. Cool further, and water's next phase change is from liquid to ice. Now picture frost on a winter window, emerging from condensation. Picture the random lines and curves that crisscross the icy coating.

Each fracture line in the frost marks the collision between expanding regions of spontaneous phase change: water turning to ice. Where matters get hand-wavy is in analogizing collisions between cooling space-time regions with ice-fracture lines. In the early, rapidly expanding Universe, energy—in theory—could have been trapped in such interstices. Lots of energy. Energy and mass are (remember $E = mc^2$) two forms of the same thing. Once formed, the ongoing expansion of the Universe will have stretched such fracture lines to light-years (or longer) in length. So: we're considering one-dimensional objects of extraordinary length, incredibly dense (an Earth mass or more per kilometer), and prospectively—as so often happens to threads—tangled.

Theorists call these objects cosmic strings. To date, none has been detected.[*]

Anyway....

---

[*] The strings theorized by cosmologists and the strings theorized by quantum-gravity theorists are, despite the name similarity, quite different —apart from that neither has been detected.

Richard Gott described how two cosmic strings could sufficiently distort space-time to also allow for a backward-in-time spiral. Just: find and straighten two cosmic strings; wrestle them into parallel positions; set them moving apart—despite their gargantuan masses and mutual attraction—at near light speeds; loop around the (rapidly separating) strings at near-light speeds. That sounds like another engineering project too ambitious to take on anytime soon.

Physicists keep finding solutions to Einstein's field equations. Here on Earth, a ring of intense light—light has energy; energy is a form of mass (and vice versa)—might demonstrate frame dragging and time travel. That's the assertion, anyway, of Ronald Mallett. Compared to Tipler's super-massive cylinders and Gott's cosmic strings, Mallett's approach has the virtue of permitting a near-term test.[125]

Once more, black holes

A popular pedagogical device for presenting the general-relativity explanation of gravity is to liken (a) space-time to a taut, horizontal rubber sheet and (b) any large mass such as the Sun to a bowling ball set onto the sheet. The weight of the bowling ball causes the sheet to sag. Objects anywhere on the sheet, influenced only by the local tilt of the rubber sheet, are drawn toward the dip. This is an imperfect analogy, of course. For one thing, the rubber sheet is two dimensional, and space-time has four dimensions. For another, the analogy relies upon gravity tugging on the bowling ball to explain…gravity. Nonetheless, the mental image can be instructive.

The bowling ball / Sun stretched the sheet a bit. Imagine, instead, how the sheet would stretch beneath something really massive and really compact: into a deep, conical, distortion. *That* is the simplified model of space-time near a black hole.

Suppose you dive into that deep, deep pit. You might suspect you won't get out. In general, you'd be right…but what if at the bottom of this pit you encountered the bottom of another pit. Might you go in one side and come out the other?

223

That space-time construct is an Einstein-Rosen bridge, more commonly known as a wormhole. It's a tunnel that in theory provides a shortcut between widely separated regions of the Universe. A voyage through a wormhole at sub-light speed—bypassing lots of intervening flat space-time—can exceed light speed with respect to the *non-wormhole* distance between the two endpoints. And supra-light speed, as we've seen, suggests travel backward in time.

In its simplest version, a black hole is a dimensionless point, to which everything that approaches within its event horizon must inevitably and fatally be drawn. If so, to dive into a black hole is suicide. Then Roy Kerr reapplied the Einstein field equations to a new scenario, wherein the star collapsing into a black hole—like most objects in space—is spinning. The "singularity" of the resulting black hole, rather than a point, is a *ring*. With the correct angle of approach to a suitably sized Kerr black hole, a spaceship might fly *through* the singularity without get spaghettified. But any such ship would *still* be trapped inside an event horizon.

So: rather than the "pits" of two black holes meeting up, we need our black-hole entrance to be matched with its antithesis: a white hole. White holes, if they exist, and the Einstein field equations permit them, spew out matter and energy.* If white holes, too, can spin, a spaceship might exit through *its* annular (ringlike) singularity.

Permitted is hardly a compelling proof. Astronomers have never spotted a white hole—which, unlike black holes, should be very obvious. One might argue the Big Bang itself was a white hole, but that hardly makes the prospect of emerging through one very attractive.

A black-hole/white-hole tunnel sounds (a) incredibly dangerous and (b) one-way. If we could round up two white holes,

---

* A white hole can be interpreted as the time reverse of a black hole. White holes may emerge from the equations of general relativity only because that theory is indifferent to time's direction.

and link them, in theory the link could be two-way. Which may not matter, because the math predicts wormholes are incredibly unstable. Try to traverse a wormhole, and it collapses faster than anything can make the crossing. Unless, that is, you artificially reinforce the mouths of the wormhole with—choose your engineering challenge: antigravity, exotic matter, negative energy.

Exotic matter, you ask? It would be to familiar matter as a white hole is to a black hole. Exotic matter is as hypothetical as are white holes. Negative energy? That's a synonym for dark energy, the mysterious stuff that is presumed—somehow—to be driving the accelerating expansion of the Universe.

Building a wormhole time machine

If contemplation of wormholes hasn't yet dropped you down Alice's rabbit hole, consider this: *making* a wormhole. For that, we need black and white holes.

Physicists regularly use particle accelerators to collide high-speed atomic nuclei. Interestingly, sometimes short-lived particles emerge from such collisions, teaching us about the quantum world. The typical collision debris is subatomic bits and electromagnetic radiation. Sometimes the debris includes matter/antimatter pairs, like an electron and a positron. At energy densities far beyond the capacity of current particle accelerators, collisions can—in theory—produce black holes. If white holes exist, they, too, could be produced by a collision process. Ditto black/white hole pairs. Rather than dwell on the hazards of, and safety precautions for, such manufacturing, we'll assume the factory for black and white holes is located safely far from Earth. We'll further assume the holes come out spinning, so that their singularities are annular. Wasn't that easy? Now:

- Separate black and white holes before they meet and mutually annihilate.

- Feed matter to the holes quickly enough to prevent them from evaporating.[*]

- Inject the black and white holes with charged particles until the holes are easily manipulated using electric or magnetic fields.[†]

- Manipulate a black hole and a white hole close enough to one another to (somehow) induce formation of a wormhole between them. Stabilize the ends (waves hands even more furiously) with antigravity, exotic matter, or negative energy. Separate the ends.

- Return the white hole to a particle accelerator. Sling the white hole around and around...and *around*, accelerating it to very close to the speed of light. Through old-fashioned time dilation à la special relativity, the two ends of the wormhole will develop a significant time differential.[‡] Or park the white-hole end in a deep gravity well to rack up gravity-based time dilation.

- Separate the wormhole's white-hole end from its black-hole end by a sufficient distance. (What distance is sufficient? Past where light connects the two endpoints as quickly across regular space-time as through the worm-

---

[*] For quantum-mechanical reasons, all black holes radiate. Whenever the mass-equivalent of such radiation exceeds the mass falling into a black hole, the black hole shrinks. The smaller a black hole becomes, the faster it evaporates until—with a *very* unpleasant *poof!*—it is no longer a black hole. White holes may also self-radiate; they are, regardless, by definition in a state of permanent disgorgement.

[†] How does one keep electrons, or anything else inside a matter-and-energy spewing white hole? That's a puzzler.

[‡] Will slinging around one end of the wormhole disconnect the wormhole? What happens when a wormhole snaps? We won't know till we try. Kids: don't try this experiment the first time anywhere near your home planet.

hole.) The white hole can be moved by shooting it out of the particle accelerator or by spaceship.

- As necessary, manipulate the wormhole-mouth stabilization mechanism, expanding the entry/exit holes to accommodate size-wise whatever will be passing through.

- Go through the tunnel and start to take on cause-and-effect paradoxes (a topic to which we *will* come).

Richard A. Lovett employed essentially this technology in his 2015 novelette "The Wormhole War." It might have taken five years to transport a wormhole end deep into space—but researchers back on Earth could then send stuff through the wormhole in more like one year. *Someone* (we get only musings about whom) built a wormhole time machine in the 2014 movie *Interstellar*, which also showcased time dilation à la general relativity.[*]

It's only a bit more speculative (read: mind-bending) to contemplate daisy-chaining or looping two or more wormhole time machines. Or carrying a wormhole through a wormhole. Or constructing tunnels made from two white holes, and so (in one theory, anyway) bidirectional.

Not your grandpa's time machine

That's pretty neat! We've designed—reliant upon future/exotic tech and some as-yet untested implications of general relativity—a time machine that can carry us into the past. It remains far from what your average SF reader (or author) would ask for in a time machine.

It only lets you go back so far. The time separation between ends of the wormhole comes from time dilation. One end has proceeded more slowly into the future than the other. If a five year

---

[*] There's much else about that movie we'll do well to ignore. For example, the gravity implied by the indicated time dilation should have spaghettified the first alien planet Our Hero visited.

separation has been achieved, you can go back five years. When the at-home end of the wormhole is a year old, you still can travel back five years—but that's now four years after the wormhole was created.

If an end of the wormhole is carried away from Earth at relativistic speeds, or is parked deep in the gravity well of a neutron star, the separation between ends of the wormhole can continue to grow—but under no circumstances can a wormhole time machine transport you back before the creation of the time machine. (In my 2013 novella "Time Out," it was expressed as any time-travel transmitter requires a matching receiver. You can't travel back before the first receiver.) Forget your plan to drop in on ancient Rome.[*][†]

On the bright side, we may have discovered the answer to the time-travel variant of the Fermi Paradox. We don't find ourselves tripping over time travelers because—our era having failed to invent backward-going time travel—they can't get here.

It can't be set for arbitrary dates. Mr. Peabody of *Rocky and His Friends*, aka *The Rocky and Bullwinkle Show* (1959), may have a dial on his WABAC (say it aloud) machine, but that was cartoon physics. There's no tweaking the dial on our wormhole time machine. If the WABAC machine is like a helicopter, able to deliver you anywhen (and anywhere) in the past, the wormhole time machine is more of a railroad. It takes you to when/where its "tracks" end—and only then/there. And ("Play it again, Sam") as time goes by, the in-the-past end of the wormhole time machine—the train depot—keeps sliding forward in time.

To travel far back in time, you also must go far away in space. Our wormhole won't take us to the past until the end-to-end

---

[*] Including (not) visiting the time of Christ, as Anthony Marchetti's 2014 short story "Take Up Your Cross" envisioned. (It is interesting to speculate, however, that any auto might do for time travel; it needn't be a DeLorean.)

[†] A loophole: finding a wormhole time machine left behind by ancient aliens.

trip at light speed would be shorter through the wormhole than through uncontorted space-time. That is, until the wormhole's ends are sufficiently separated, they remain connected through regular space-time. In relativity-speak, communication between insufficiently separated ends of the wormhole is by a space-like curve, not a time-like curve.

In a word: bummer.

Cause and effect

Still and all, we've seen reason to believe that—with sufficiently massive engineering efforts, and subject to constraints—travel to the past *is* possible. We may not have our grandpa's time machine, but we still have the Grandfather Paradox.

Suppose I build a time machine, with which I travel to the past and shoot my grandfather before he ever reproduced. Then I could never have been born. Obviously, I never went back in time. So Grandpa *did* reproduce, and I *was* born, and....

Theorists and SF authors have imagined several resolutions to cause-and-effect dilemmas that travel to the past might otherwise provoke.

Such as: the past can't be changed. Something must foil every such attempt. The 1995 movie *Twelve Monkeys* relies on that premise. Travelers to the past can hope only to locate a plague virus in its unmutated state, the better—in the time traveler's present—to engineer a vaccine. Any attempt retroactively to stop the plague must be futile. (*12 Monkeys*, the 2015 version, rests upon the opposite premise. Episode by episode the TV series changes the time traveler's past—although, to keep the series going, none of the changes yet shown have stopped the plague.)

A past that can't be changed—no matter the reassuring affirmation of our everyday notions that cause and effect ever occur in that order—begs the question: *why?* Perhaps time is simply fixed. Our efforts to change matters may fail because they always have and always will.

An interesting type of unchangeable past arises from a cause linked with its effect in a closed loop. Such a loop underpins the 1941 novelette "By His Bootstraps," by Robert A. Heinlein (writing as Anson MacDonald). The time travelers who manipulate the story's protagonist are later versions of himself. That is: a Bob from the far future coerces the earlier Bob to go to that far future, from whence he returns to the earlier Bob to…. With neither beginning nor end, but plenty of loopedy loop, everything hangs together in a mind-bending way.

Heinlein was back at it in his (oddly punctuated) 1959 short story " '—All You Zombies—' " (the basis of the 2015 movie *Predestination*) in which the time-traveling protagonist eventually becomes both his own parents.

Stephen King, in *11/22/63* (2011), offered a fresh wrinkle on the trope-ish (im?)mutability of the past. Yes, you can—with difficulty ("The past is obdurate")—overcome the timeline's resistance to change. But any return to an altered past resets/undoes the changes.

Perhaps the Universe acts as its own enforcer, preventing paradoxes by precluding changes to the past—a speculation whose academically understated name is the cosmic censorship principle. Maybe the resolution of the Grandfather Paradox is as boring as the Universe (somehow) returning you to your own time before you can pull the trigger. Stephen Hawking has speculated that any wormhole into the past creates a feedback loop. Through that loop, background radiation—the frothing of the quantum foam—builds up to destroy the wormhole (sort of like background noise endlessly amplified by a poorly positioned microphone blowing out a loudspeaker). He dubbed such cosmic censorship the "causal ordering postulate." Time COP.

A more ruthless Nature is at work in Larry Niven's 1977 short story "Rotating Cylinders and the Possibility of Global Causality Violation."* Setting off a nova to stop intelligent aliens from

---

* Indeed, Niven took his title from Frank Tipler's earlier academic paper.

completing work on their Tipler cylinder? That seems pretty ruthless to me.*

Suppose, as unproven as the assertion may be, that cause must always precede effect. That would preclude chrononauts from *some* activities in the past—the Grandfather Paradox sort of thing. We can surely imagine jaunts that avoid triggering such conflicts. Simply to observe, perhaps as—in theory—is all that Connie Willis's time-traveling historians do. Having observed, perhaps it would be safe to remove items no one will miss (as in John Varley's 1983 novel *Millennium*, basis of the 1989 movie).

And having scouted out the moment when specific dinosaurs will die anyway, why *not* escort big-game hunters to the Cretaceous, as in Ray Bradbury's 1952 short story, "A Sound of Thunder" (basis of the 2005 film). What could possibly go wrong?

Maybe the Universe itself doesn't prevent changes to the past—but (ideally) wise minds do their best to achieve the same end. Officialdom takes on that task in Poul Anderson's Time Patrol series and the 1994 movie *Timecop*. In John G. Cramer's 1997 novel *Einstein's Bridge*, physicists exploit a time-like loop through a wormhole to undo an unfortunate First Contact (and in the process, create the history we know). In Nancy Kress's 2012 novella "After the Fall, Before the Fall, During the Fall," Gaia herself enables limited meddling with a very messed up past. And maybe your grandfather must act in self defense, as in my 2001 short story "Grandpa?" (basis of the 2006 short film "The Grandfather Paradox"[126]).

Having said all this, it remains possible—ages of human impressions notwithstanding—that cause-and-effect is a human delusion. Nothing in known science requires cause to precede effect.

---

* This particular story is an instance of Niven's more general theory: if time travel to the past is possible, the inevitable resulting changes must alter the Universe to the point where it can no longer produce time travelers. See "The Theory and Practice of Time Travel," a nonfiction chapter in Niven's 1971 collection *All the Myriad Ways*.

A split decision

Among the conundrums of quantum mechanics—a probabilistic description of reality—is what exactly happens when a measurement is taken or an observation is made. Up until the observation, a particle has (as we've seen), rather than a location, a probability of being in various locations. For simplicity, we'll consider a 50-50 probability of being in places A or B. Upon the act of measurement, we find the particle in *one* of those places. A common explanation is: don't ask.

Recall (from the chapter "Alien Dimensions: The Universe Next Door") a less subscribed to, but still academically respectable, explanation: the Universe split. Thereafter, in our universe, the particle is at A. The observer in the other universe finds the particle is at B. In this Many Worlds Interpretation, proposed (without the catchy name) by Hugh Everett in 1957, every possible past *and* every possible future exists. At each moment, for each possible event, a universe splits. A moment later, for each possible event, each of those universes again splits....

There's no Grandfather Paradox, because Grandson splits off a new universe by attempting his trip to the past. In one universe, the trip to the past failed. In the second universe, the grand-patricide can succeed—Grandson didn't come from that universe.

Many Worlds Interpretation adds a dimension(s) to space-time. In this type of multiverse, with the proper technology (just don't ask me what it is), one can travel across time both like a clock changing *and* across world lines. The farther one goes in that latter dimension, the farther apart the world lines are from their common ancestral universe.

Is the Many Worlds Interpretation valid? Unknown. Can universes arise from nothing? Cosmologists say it happened once, so why not repeatedly? That suffices to make multidimensional time—and multidimensional time travel—fair game for science fiction. Keith Laumer's Imperium novels and H. Beam Piper's Paratime series alike put time cops into a multiverse with multidimensional time. James P. Hogan's 1985 novel *The*

Proteus Operation and Harry Turtledove's 1992 novel *The Guns of the South* have factions on the losing side of (local) history making and shaping getaways to elsewhere and elsewhen.

Odds, Ends, and Tropes—and the SF that illustrates them

Energy-time uncertainty. In one of its more absurd predictions, quantum mechanics allows particle/antiparticle pairs to appear from nothingness, to mutually destruct a (very) short while later. Odder yet, pair production happens. If Nature can borrow energy to produce matter, if only for a brief time, perhaps supplied energy can move objects through time.

Geoffrey Landis's 1988 short story "Ripples in the Dirac Sea" relies on this time-travel mechanism. (Geoff threw in a twist on the *you-can't-change-the-past* trope: in his story, no matter how radically you change your past, the present from which you departed, once you catch up to it, hasn't changed.) So, in a slightly different manner, did my 2010 novel *Countdown to Armageddon.*

Tachyons. Beyond the purview of the wildly successful Standard Model of particle physics, some have theorized about particles, called tachyons (from the Greek, *tachys*, meaning rapid), that always travel faster than light. Familiar particles can't be accelerated to light speed because their mass approaches infinite at light speed. But faster than light? Above light speed, mass *decreases* the faster an object travels—which wouldn't even be a tachyon's most counterintuitive property.

There's no evidence that tachyons exist. There's no theory for if/how—should they exist—tachyons might interact with normal matter. It would seem difficult to construct a time machine (or anything else) from stuff that comes at you from out of the future and which vanishes before you can see it coming (both consequences of tachyons traveling faster than light.) Always up for a challenge, physicist Gregory Benford used tachyons for backward-in-time communications in his 1980 novel, *Timescape.*

FTL travel. Faster-than-light travel, the math of relativity tells us, would also mean travel backward in time. As we've seen (in "Faster Than a Speeding Photon"), FTL travel *might* be possible. But perhaps Nature, pardon the anthropomorphism, won't be fooled.* If, for example, a starship uses a wormhole, won't light, too? If so, the regions at both ends of the wormhole remain causally linked. We won't know if shortcuts mean FTL—or only a stapling close together of previously distant regions—until we're able to perform the test. No FTL, no backward-in-time travel.

When more isn't better. In *Timecop,* (melo)dramatically, a time-traveling villain and his younger self touch—and are thereby mutually destroyed. Connie Willis's time-traveling historians can visit before their births—but anyone careless or unlucky enough to overlap in time with another instance of himself will be canceled out. In Rysa Walker's Chronos Files series, overlapping with oneself in time is brain-muddling, the more so the geographically closer the two versions approach. In Don Sakers's 2015 short story "Double Exposure," time-transported matter decays at the atomic level with a half-life of hours.

The overarching trope suggests a sort of conservation rule: that versions of a particular item from different times—somehow, to a story-convenient level—are incompatible when brought to the same moment. The nature of this conflict is seldom explained. I speculate that the trope originated in the (not universal) interpretation of antimatter particles as normal particles moving backward in time, because an antimatter particle and its normal-matter equivalent mutually destruct, if they meet, in a flash of energy. Other time-travel stories dispense with this trope: the various versions of Bob in "By His Bootstraps" *do* meet; Bob Two even shoves Bob One through a time portal without physical harm to either.

---

* If you are of a certain age, that should evoke from the depths of memory—time travel of another sort—a certain margarine commercial.

Timeline changes and latency effects. So: you've gone back in time and changed history. Does the change rewire your brain to erase the memory? Alter libraries and digital archives? How soon do such changes take effect?

In the original (1985) movie *Back to the Future*, Marty McFly carried a family photo into his past. Siblings—and then Marty himself—fade from his photo as his actions in his past look to keep his parents from marrying. In Robert Silverberg's 1966 short story "Needle in a Timestack," people retain memories of a rendered-null timeline briefly longer than do digital archives. I've never seen a rationale given for such variable latency.

If timeline changes *do* happen, how quickly do they progress from the altered past to the altered present? Stories differ in their treatment, often leaving the progression unseen. In *Countdown to Armageddon*, I stuck with what we (think we) experience about time sans time travel: any event's implications ripple into the future at a second per second.

Self-dampening (or not) changes. The jostle of a random air molecule or a collision with a wayward gnat won't have much effect on a falling piano. That's inertia for you. Does history—however metaphorically—exhibit inertia? Is history robust against small perturbations? If so, how small is small enough? In "A Sound of Thunder," a time traveler stepping off a trail suffices to bring disaster.

It often seems implausible that a time traveler's actions can avoid inadvertent effects. With merely an ill-timed stroll, the time tourist might block a passerby's view of something that would have been life altering. Then again, that passerby may see the *whatever* the next time they happen to pass by, and the slightly changed timeline converges to what would have been. It *also* seems implausible that a photon from our time, transported, say, a billion years into the past, into some void deep between distant galaxies, would produce any ill effects. Then again, that out-of-time-and-place photon, falling a billion years later into a telescope, might interfere with what would otherwise be an epochal cosmological insight. Absent a working time machine, we simply can't know the implications of interacting at any level with the past.*

Never mind physical changes wrought by time travelers. What changes might the thoughts and knowledge of a time traveler wreak? Does human history resist change? Do the masses of humanity—as Tolstoy, Marx, and Hari Seldon in separate ways would have it—swim in all but irresistible historical currents? Or do people follow the lead of great men and women? L. Sprague de Camp explored that question in *Lest Darkness Fall* (1939 serial; expanded in the 1941 book edition), as did H. Beam Piper in the paratime stories "Gunpowder God" (1964) and "Down Styphon" (1965). Between these extremes, at moments when competing trends all but balance, are stories (like my *Countdown to Armageddon*) in which events are at a tipping point and one person's actions do matter.

Are changes to history necessarily changes for the worst? Orson Scott Card's 1996 novel *Pastwatch: The Redemption of Christopher Columbus* takes a good look at that question.

When time really is money. Time travel, as we've seen, will be complicated. That probably also means expensive. Perhaps the answer to the time-travel variant of the Fermi Paradox is: it's just too expensive to build time machines.

Sure, you can make investments before a trip to the future, hoping to have amassed a fortune before you arrive—but that's

---

* Some complex systems, such as weather, exhibit a property that mathematicians call an extreme sensitivity to initial conditions. A tiny change to such a system's inputs can produce dramatic changes in that system's behavior. Chaos theoreticians label this unpredictability the *butterfly effect.* That term comes from the undisprovable possibility that the flutter today of a butterfly's wings might initiate a cascade of events that culminates—days later and half a world removed—in a hurricane. The phrase is not (if you're familiar with Bradbury's aforementioned story) a reference to "A Sound of Thunder."

None of which tells us, one way or another, whether the Universe is prone to a temporal butterfly effect.

no slam dunk. Inflation happens. Companies, and even countries, fail. And if you're justified in your optimism? You don't have the money *now* to build the time machine.

Yes, you might bring foreknowledge into the past, to invest in stocks and horse races—but until you have done so (without, in the process, changing matters in a disastrous way), and returned to your time of origin, you don't have that money. It's another Grandfather Paradox.

Wrapping up

What can we—or, at least, what do I—conclude from all this? That time, in the context of space-time, exists. That in a Universe without simultaneity, past, present, and future can coexist (not necessarily at the same spatial coordinates). That's not to say past and future are set, or that any aspect of the Universe is deterministic—but neither can I disprove determinism. That we can travel to (some) future, by moving fast enough, or sitting in a gravity well deep enough, or with Really Good Medicine—but that the possibility of travel into the past is less compelling. That time travel is fair game for the hardest of SF—not that every time-travel mechanism in the genre rises to the level of plausibility. That the subgenre is rife with questionable sub-tropes.

That if you me ask what *is* time, I'll refer you back to Saint Augustine. "Provided that no one asks me, I know. If I want to explain it to an inquirer, I do not know."

To read further

- *The Nature of the Physical World*, Arthur Eddington (1928). In elegant, entirely nonmathematical language, Eddington tackles many of the more interesting implications of quantum mechanics and relativity. Read this with care, however, because later discoveries—the neutron; the expansion of the Universe—negate some of Eddington's discussion.

- *The Arrow of Time: A Voyage Through Science to Solve Time's Greatest Mystery*, Peter Coveney and Roger Highfield.

- *Science Fiction and Science Fact: An Encyclopedia*, Brian Stableford (editor), articles on time and time travel.

- *How to Build a Time Machine: The Real Science of Time Travel*, Brian Clegg.

- *Hollyweird Science: From Quantum Quirks to the Multiverse*, by Kevin R. Grazier and Stephen Cass.

- *The Time Traveler's Almanac*, Ann VanderMeer and Jeff VanderMeer. (Almost seventy stories, plus essays, on the theme of time travel.)

ALTERNATE ABILITIES

The Paranormal

n 1995, two academic researchers were tasked with assessing twenty years of U.S. government and government-funded studies of "anomalous mental phenomena." (You have seen the 2009 movie *The Men Who Stare at Goats*, right?) That awkward expression, "anomalous mental phenomena," stands in for abilities more commonly labeled as—take your pick—"psi," "paranormal," and "extrasensory."

One of the researchers—Jessica Utts, a statistician then at University of California Davis—reported:

> Using the standards applied to any other area of science, it is concluded that psychic functioning has been well established. The statistical results of the studies examined are far beyond what is expected by chance. Arguments that these results could be due to methodological flaws in the experiments are soundly refuted. Effects of similar magnitude to those found in government-sponsored research...have been replicated at a number of laboratories across the world. Such consistency cannot be readily explained by claims of flaws or fraud.[127]

Reviewing the same information, her co-evaluator—Ray Hyman, then a University of Oregon psychologist—replied:

239

The occurrence of statistical effects does not warrant the conclusion that psychic functioning has been demonstrated. Significant departures from the null hypothesis* can occur for several reasons. Without a positive theory of anomalous cognition, we cannot say that these effects are due to a single cause, let alone claim they reflect anomalous cognition.[128]

Confused about the state of evidence for paranormal abilities? Join the crowd.

In this chapter, we'll review some of the support—and objections to same—for the paranormal. We'll survey some science fiction reliant on the paranormal, consider a flirtation among hard-SF authors with the paranormal, and take a look at the physics that might underpin paranormal abilities (if such exist).

Is parapsychology a science? Or is the paranormal in science fiction purely a trope, a bit of authorial legerdemain? Read on. (Unless you're a precog, in which case you already know the answer.)

The paranormal

Merely the popular term *paranormal* is problematical. The expression *anomalous mental phenomenon* eliminates any implication of the supernatural, without defining some presumed scientifically accessible baseline (the "normal") against which an anomaly is measured.

For the duration of this chapter, the phenomenon under discussion is: a mentally mediated transfer—whether of force, matter, or information—without technological assistance, under circumstances commonly understood to preclude such transfer.

---

* The null hypothesis is the default assumption of any experiment: that events or variables under study are unrelated. Any assertion to the contrary must be convincingly proven.

Quite the mouthful. *Paranormal* has brevity going for it, and I'll use that term. (I'll retain the synonym *psi* when it appears in quoted text and in discussion of such quotations.)

What might be examples of such transfers? Telepathy: the direct projection of thoughts to, or the reading of thoughts from, another's mind. Remote viewing, aka clairvoyance: the perception of distant places.* Precognition: the perception of events before they occur. Psychokinesis, aka telekinesis: altering the physical state of a system from a distance. Mental healing: altering the health of an organism from a distance. Teleportation: relocating an object, including oneself, without recourse to muscles or artificial mechanisms.

Why consider such abilities? For one reason: because (per a 2005 poll) 41% of Americans report a belief in extrasensory perception and 32% in telepathy.[129]

In the beginning

Founded in London in 1882, the Society for Psychical Research was "the first society to conduct scholarly research into human experiences that challenge contemporary scientific models."[130] The SPR counted among its early members:

- William Crookes—chemist and physicist better known for his pioneering work with vacuum tubes.

---

* Funny story. The earliest description, to my knowledge, of remote viewing comes from Herodotus. In *The Histories*, he reports that the great king Croesus (as in "as rich as…") sought to test the prominent oracles of his day. Via messengers, Croesus tasked the oracles to report what he would be doing one hundred days after those messengers had set out from Lydia. Not even the messengers knew. (The correct answer involved cooking lamb and turtle together in a bronze cauldron.)

The Delphic oracle got it right—in hexameter verse, no less—and so Croesus next asked for an augury involving matters of state. Like all good auguries this prophecy was ambiguous, and Croesus took it the wrong way. He invaded Persia and lost his kingdom.

- John William Strutt, Third Baron Rayleigh—physicist better known for discovering "Raleigh scattering," the explanation for why the sky appears blue (and holder of a Nobel Prize for co-discovering argon).

- Alfred Russel Wallace—biologist and naturalist better known for developing, independently of Charles Darwin, the theory of evolution through natural selection.

- Carl Jung—psychiatrist and the founding father of analytical psychology.

In two words: serious thinkers.

Studies of the paranormal

And yet, as we saw in the chapter opening, more than a century later the case for—and against—the paranormal remains contentious. A closer look at typical studies will show why.

In 1927, J. B. Rhine, a botanist by training, established a lab at Duke University for the study of the paranormal. To make that research quantifiable and repeatable, Rhine pioneered the use of Zener cards: card decks of five easily distinguished shapes, designed by perceptual psychologist Karl Zener. Subjects were asked to identify—without looking—the shape on each of a long random series of the cards, sometimes after an experimenter had seen the card (i.e., by telepathy) and sometimes before (i.e., by clairvoyance). In trials that continued for more than a decade, Rhine reported subjects who indicated the correct card more often than sheer guesswork would explain.

A second phenomenon emerged in Rhine's studies: the longer the experiments continued, the less the reported improvement over random guessing. Does practice with the paranormal diminish aptitude? Does boredom dull paranormal aptitude? (How long would *you* maintain your concentration on which of five shapes is up?) Does the Law of Large Numbers come into play, driving results toward the mean?

As for the validity of Rhine's results, not everyone is convinced. For example, from a 1998 interview in *Skeptical Inquirer* with Martin Gardner (longtime math and science writer for *Scientific American*):

> It has often been pointed out that as Rhine slowly learned how to tighten his controls, his evidence of psi became weaker and weaker. However, the evidence will not become convincing to other psychologists until an experiment is made that is repeatable by skeptics. So far, no such experiment has been made.[131]

We'll move on to U.S. government exploration of the paranormal during the Seventies and Eighties, mostly performed by or on behalf of the CIA. These are the underlying studies alluded to in the chapter's opening, and this research focused on remote viewing. (If you ran a spy agency, wouldn't you appreciate a way to inspect places of interest—say, suspected missile silos and nuclear-test sites—from the comfort and safety of your office?)

Many of these experiments involved a test subject and an interviewer isolated inside a windowless and shielded room (i.e., an enclosure designed to preclude signaling via electromagnetic radiation). The test subject was tasked to describe what a third party was seeing—or in the case of precognition experiments, what the third party would see. The interviewer would ask questions to clarify what the subject saw. Subject/interviewer dialogues were recorded; sometimes the subject would sketch or build clay models of the distant scene. The perceived scene (as captured in the recordings and any sketches and models) and the actual scene were then compared and the degree of match graded. In one test series, the locations were chosen from among sixty points of interest randomly visited across greater San Francisco; scoring depended on an evaluator identifying from the test subject's remote-viewing report the place the third party visited.

The lead experimenters for the CIA studies were Russell Targ and Harold Puthoff, both laser physicists. Some of their early results with remote viewing appeared in two prestigious journals: *Proceedings of the IEEE*[132] and *Nature*,[133] and Targ continues to cite these papers in substantiation of his claims.

On the other hand, *Nature* accompanied Targ's article with an editorial that stated:

> There was agreement that the paper was weak in design and presentation, to the extent that details given as to the precise way in which the experiment was carried out were disconcertingly vague…. All the referees felt that the details given of various safeguards and precautions introduced against the possibility of conscious or unconscious fraud on the part of one or other of the subjects were "uncomfortably vague."

A few years later, *Nature* published an additional disclaimer: an article by psychologists unable to replicate Targ and Puthoff's results.[134]

While the remote-viewing experiments reduced or eliminated the "decline effect" sometimes attributed to subject boredom, in the process they sacrificed objective scoring. Consider the complexity of scoring these experiments. In how many features, and in what details of particular features, can the remotely viewed scene and the actual scene differ and still be counted as a match? Suppose the subject sketches a scene with several points of similarity to the visited location—but adds other details that correspond, if at all, only with structures that *were* present decades earlier. Does that circumstance count as a mismatch or as an instance of viewing remote in space *and* time?

In short, the determination of a match in each remote-viewing experiment was subjective, putting into question claims of statistical significance when aggregating results across several experiments.

The CIA's motivation, of course, was not scientific curiosity, and the Agency insisted upon more practical demonstrations. Test subjects were given geographical coordinates and asked to describe what they saw. One designated location corresponded to a suspected Soviet research facility that had been observed by spy satellite. The subject sketched a large crane in significant detail, matching a structure in the satellite image—and also several buildings that did not exist. Proponents of remote viewing claim credit for the crane. Skeptics focus on the discrepancies—and indeed, the subject *might have* drawn bunches of structures in the hopes of getting one right.

In another test, a CIA agent gave the coordinates of his private cabin in the woods. The test subject came back with a description with similarities to a nearby NSA facility. Was this experiment a success (the subject was drawn to a facility of claimed psychic significance to the CIA) or a failure (the viewed scene was not at the specified coordinates)? In the same experiment, the subject reported reading words and phrases out of file cabinets. Some of the vocabulary matched out-of-date NSA code words. Was this a success (real code words detected from a distance)? Or did those words popping up somehow reflect that those code words had been in effect when Targ, the interviewer in the room with the subject, had worked for the NSA?

Interpretation

In short, proponents and skeptics alike find support from these studies for their positions. Such divergence can reflect honest differences of opinion. For a particular event of claimed paranormal significance, it's no small task to ascertain a probable cause. Was an anomalous phenomenon at work or something more mundane? How does one preclude every alternate explanation of:

- Fraud (whether by test subject or experimenter).

- Unintentional cuing (the test subject responding, even subconsciously, to the observer's reactions).

- Experimental design flaws.

- Wishful interpretation of ambiguous results.

- Statistical outliers (toss a coin often enough and you *will* see ten heads in a row).

Some skeptics discount any asserted demonstration of the paranormal until fraud can be ruled out—no proof of actual fraud required. Are paranormal researchers guilty until proven innocent? Isn't that an unjust standard? As we've seen, researchers in the field often have significant scientific credentials.

The counterargument: scientists are unprepared for experiments that might lie to them. Per Carl Sagan, "Scientists are used to struggling with Nature, who may surrender her secrets reluctantly but who fights fair.... Magicians, on the other hand, are in the deception business."[135] James P. Hogan, in his 1983 novel *Code of the Life Maker*, used a magician cum mind reader to drive home the same point.

Given (a) the ambiguities of the experiments and (b) the absence of a physical mechanism to explain the reported results, many scientists discount the whole paranormal topic.

The requirements for science fiction are less rigorous. As long as the paranormal hasn't been *dis*proven, there is ample latitude for storytelling....

The paranormal in science fiction

There's a lot of the paranormal in science fiction, literary and dramatic,* and I'll limit myself to a few examples organized by paranormal ability. Almost always that ability manifests without

---

* And also, for completeness, in video games (e.g., telekinesis in Bio-Shock) and graphic novels (e.g., a variety of abilities among the X-Men). This chapter won't look further at those media.

any more explanation than that a character has a gift or a mutation, takes a drug, or survived traumatic events that awakened an ability latent in everyone. At the physical level, any of those is no explanation at all.

As illustrations, I lean toward classics of the field.

Telepathy, mind reading, and empathy

- Alfred Bester's 1953 novel *The Demolished Man* (incidentally, the first Hugo Award winner) explored the effects on society of telepathy.

- Robert A. Heinlein, in *Time for the Stars* (1956), used telepathy between separated twins for instantaneous communications between starship and distant Earth.

- The Star Trek TV/movie franchise has the often plot-convenient Vulcan mind melds.

- David Brin's Uplift series offers the Tymbrimi species, members of which cast and receive emotional "glyphs" through cranial tendrils.

- Richard Phillips's 2012 Rho Agenda series, whose heroes, their minds tweaked by alien technology, learn to communicate telepathically.

Teleportation

- Again from Alfred Bester, from 1956, we have *The Stars My Destination* (in the UK, *Tiger! Tiger!*) extending teleportation ("jaunting") to interplanetary distances.

- From Steven Gould, in 1992, we have *Jumper* (later a movie by the same name) and its sequels, *Reflex* (2004) and *Impulse* (2013).

Psychokinesis (aka telekinesis)

- From 1952, Jack Vance's novella "Telek."

- The 1981 movie *Scanners*—see heads explode!
- Stephen King's 1974 debut novel (and several versions of the movie) *Carrie*—see lots of stuff explode, and burn, and....

Miscellaneous psychic powers

- Precognition, as in Philip K. Dick's 1956 novelette "Minority Report" (adapted as a 2002 movie and a 2015 TV series).
- Mind control, as practiced by Jedi and Sith alike in the Star Wars universe.
- Psychic navigation, as performed by spice-altered navigators of Frank Herbert's Dune series.
- Psychic wish fulfillment, as in Jerome Bixby's eerie 1953 short story (and 1981 *Twilight Zone* episode) "It's a Good Life."
- Multitalented paranormal supermen: A. E. Van Vogt's *Slan* (1946; originally a 1940 serial).

And given the degree of skepticism as to whether paranormal phenomena even exist, let us not forget hoaxers such as the private investigators on the long-running TV series *Psych*.

That's but a small sampling, with these (and other) psychic powers popping up in science fiction of every length, in all media.

John W. Campbell, *Analog*, and the paranormal

In 1937, a few months before John W. Campbell took the editorial reins at *Astounding* (which became, after a 1960 name change, *Analog*), his story "Forgetfulness" appeared in the magazine.* In that story, alien starfarers visit a far-future Earth whose few human residents appear to be in terminal decline. The latter have

---

* Like many of Campbell's best, this story appeared under his Don A. Stuart pseudonym.

abandoned ancient cities of mile-high towers to live in twenty-foot domes. Communicating telepathically with their visitors, humans appear at a loss to explain anything about technologies once wielded by their mighty ancestors. It's sad, the aliens think, as they prepare to colonize—only to experience time and space bent by the thoughts of a super-evolved human for whom space-ships are almost as quaint as flint arrowheads.

SF encyclopedist Brian Stableford speculates that Campbell was predisposed toward paranormal possibilities by reason of having attended Duke University while J. B. Rhine was performing his famous series of experiments there. Whether or not that's the case, the paranormal (which Campbell preferred to call "psionics") fascinated the man. In a 1959 editorial "We Must Study Psi"[136] Campbell wrote:

> Dr. Rhine originally started his investigation of psi because, as a professional psychologist, he had come to the conclusion that psychology-as-such lacked an essential element. You would have an exceedingly hard time working out biochemistry, if your chemistry hadn't discovered nitrogen, for example. Rhine's studies led him to suspect something about as important as nitrogen to biochemistry was missing from psychology.

And:

> Ours is the only culture that officially denies Magic. And...ours does not, by several millennia, qualify as a "very long" culture. The denial of magic is only about three centuries old. You can fool a large percentage of a people for that short a period of time.
>
> The psi machines I've encountered work—and they work on precisely the same ancient laws of Magic that those wide-scattered peoples have, independently, accepted.

In the same editorial, Campbell discusses dowsing, the Hieronymus machine,* and the application of psi to *photos* of crops to protect physical crops from insects.

A bit more about Campbell: He studied physics at MIT and completed his B.S. at Duke University. Isaac Asimov called Campbell, "the most powerful force in science fiction ever, and for the first ten years of his editorship he dominated the field completely."[137]

As editor, Campbell treated psi as a core element of "hard"— that is, scientifically based—science fiction. Convinced or not, many *Astounding* authors of the Campbell era incorporated the paranormal into their stories (some of which we've already seen).

But just suppose

I mostly write the hard stuff: science fiction that won't cause scientists and engineers to hurl my books across the room in dismay. (Such, anyway, is my goal.) Could I, were I to so choose, write hard SF involving the paranormal?

As it happens, yes.

Rhine and Targ did not attempt to explain the paranormal, only to demonstrate the effect and to make observations. Targ asserts that remote viewing is both unaffected by electromagnetic shielding and insensitive to range over terrestrial distances.[†]

---

*   A device said to sense the material-specific "eloptic energy" emanations from solid objects. The term *eloptic* seems intended to evoke thoughts of electromagnetism and optics. The detector required a person in the loop, and Campbell saw the device as dependent upon its operator's psi abilities.
See http://en.wikipedia.org/wiki/Hieronymus_machine.

†   In at least one instance Targ tested the paranormal at a range far exceeding the terrestrial. In a 1973 experiment, his test subject, while remotely viewing Jupiter, sketched that planet with rings. *Voyager 1* first glimpsed rings of Jupiter in 1979. Did the rings in that sketch arise from remote viewing, extrapolation from Saturn's rings, confusing Jupiter with Saturn, or a lucky guess?

Having already looked at the controversy surrounding efforts to demonstrate the paranormal, let's ask a different question. Does modern physics suggest ways in which minds *could* have such paranormal abilities?

For at least some of the claimed abilities, yes.

Getting on the same wavelength?

Consider extremely low frequency (ELF) electromagnetic radiation, with frequencies of just a few Hertz (aka, cycles per second). Any wave's frequency and wavelength (the distance that separates two adjacent wave crests) vary reciprocally; ELF radiation—with wavelengths in the thousands of miles!—passes unimpeded through the thin metal sheets and screens that comprise conventional shielding.

To an ELF wave, the Earth's surface and the ionosphere are two sides of a naturally occurring waveguide. Whereas freely propagating electromagnetic radiation (say, the light emitted by a bulb) spreads in all directions and rapidly attenuates with distance according to an inverse square law, EM waves confined to a waveguide (say, light traveling through a fiber-optic cable) propagate in one direction, along the waveguide—and do not attenuate.

No attenuation and immunity from conventional shielding; that sounds like a candidate mechanism for the paranormal. Right? No, and it's again related to ELF radiation's long wavelengths. Not only does no known structure in the human brain generate or receive ELF waves, it's hard to see how the brain, or even the entire human body, could interact with waves thousands of miles long.

Before you answer consider that in *Gulliver's Travels* (1726) Jonathon Swift gave Mars two small, close-orbiting moons—long before astronomer Asaph Hall first observed Phobos and Deimos in 1877.

From the large to the very small (a necessary digression)

Among the eerier attributes of quantum mechanics (a high hurdle) is *non*locality: interaction between distant objects without any intermediary...anything. Two particles (such as electrons) that once interacted and then separate can maintain a relationship known as quantum entanglement. For as long as the particles remain entangled, a change in one (say, the orientation of the first electron's spin) causes a complementary change to the second (makes it spin in the opposite orientation). The entanglement mechanism operates independently of distance—and instantaneously. Through entanglement, the paired particles become, in some sense, a single entity.*

Einstein called this entangled behavior "spooky action at a distance" and considered it evidence of a crack in the foundations of the then-young theory of quantum mechanics. This time, Einstein was mistaken. Quantum entanglement has been demonstrated again and again. In the case of paired photons, entanglement has been demonstrated over distances exceeding one hundred miles (for particles with mass, the distances are better described in yards). But it should be noted that entanglement between particles is a fragile affair. The slightest jostling of either entangled particle can destroy the relationship.

Spooky action at a distance? Freedom from attenuation with distance? A connection that is independent of electromagnetism (and so, the link would be unaffected by EM shielding)? That sure sounds like a candidate mechanism for the paranormal.

But how?

Scientists continue to argue about the physical significance of the mathematical description that is modern quantum-mechanical

---

* For more on why the instantaneous aspect of entanglement doesn't violate special relativity, see the discussion on FTL communications in the chapter "Faster Than a Speeding Photon."

theory (as discussed in more detail in the chapter "Alien Dimensions: The Universe Next Door").

As we've seen, QM is inherently probabilistic. Its math never says, as one example, where an electron *is*. Instead, QM enables us to calculate how apt we are to find that electron here, or there, or anywhere else. A time-varying mathematical entity called the "wave function" captures the probability of where the electron might be found.

Of course, when we do measure an electron's position, it's not here and there and somewhere else—it's in a particular spot.

The plurality of physicists surveyed say of this dilemma: don't ask. Others speak to the act of measurement as "collapsing the wave function" to the unique location where the electron is observed. Yet others speak of splitting off universes. There is another QM interpretation we have yet to discuss. Such prominent physicists as Eugene Wigner and John von Neumann have (at times) asserted the need for a *conscious observer* to determine the outcome of observations. In this interpretation, the physical Universe requires consciousness to operate.

Combine the nonlocality of quantum entanglement with an intrinsic connection between matter (such as a brain) and consciousness and—voilà—we have a candidate mechanism for the paranormal.

Emphasis on *candidate*.

As fascinating as the media find polls, science doesn't operate by ballot. It may nonetheless be worth noting that the conscious-observer approach is far from a leading interpretation of QM. Perhaps because of the chicken-and-egg riddle it would pose regarding brain-made-of-matter and conscious mind. Perhaps because of the riddle it would pose as to the feasibility of matter existing before brains to observe quantum interactions. Perhaps because we don't know what consciousness is....

Although science has yet to reach any consensus on the underlying meaning of quantum mechanics *or* the nature of consciousness, mathematician and physicist Roger Penrose and anesthesiologist Stuart Hameroff propose that consciousness arises from quantum-mechanical effects within submicron intra-neuron structures called microtubules.[138]

If *that* conjecture is valid, then, just maybe, ensembles of microtubules across the brain also cooperate to transmit and receive quantum-entangled particles at longer ranges (i.e., beyond one's own skull). And maybe other ensembles of microtubules in the brain can categorize, manipulate, and otherwise work with the associated data. (To remotely view a designated scene, for example, the subject must have a way to identify and focus upon specific relevant entanglements.) And perhaps eons of evolution have developed ways to maintain entangled states over longer times and distances than can the latest human technology. And maybe the many idiosyncratic differences among brains (see the discussion of telepathy in the chapter "Say, What?") don't gum up the works.

That's a *lot* of maybe. Still, piling conjecture upon speculation upon surmise we can glimpse a basis, drawing upon contemporary (although not prevailing) scientific thinking, for a mechanism that might underpin some paranormal phenomena.

None of which says the paranormal does work that way, or even that the paranormal exists. I am saying the case can be made sufficiently to justify the paranormal in *science* fiction.

I knew you were going to ask

What about claims of precognition? One of Targ's remote-viewing subjects claimed he could *preview* the location where the roaming experimenter would visit. Can we identify any candidate mechanisms for that?

Imagine a video of milk separating itself out of a latte. Most people would suspect the imagery was running backward. Why? Because for the milk to spontaneously separate from the black coffee is so improbable. That we implicitly recognize the Universe's tendency toward disorder is one theory for why we experience time flowing in one direction. Metaphorically, that flow is called "time's arrow."*

If time flows one way, from past to future, how might precognition be possible?

Once more, we can catch a tantalizing glimpse in the workings of quantum mechanics.

The double slit experiment with delayed choice

Among its many weirdnesses, quantum mechanics embraces a curious duality. Such entities as electrons and photons sometimes behave like particles and sometimes like waves. This duality is best illustrated with the oft-performed double-slit experiment.

In this experiment, a mechanism we will call an emitter shoots photons one by one toward a phosphorescent screen. Between the emitter and the screen sits a foil obstacle that is solid except for two slits. A photon can only reach the screen by passing through one or both slits in the foil. So does the photon pass through one slit, as a particle would? Or does it pass through both slits, as a wave would? If the former, the photon will light up one small spot on the screen. If the latter, the photon wave will spread out from both slits, forming a distributed interference pattern on the screen.†

The trick answer: the outcome depends upon *how* we perform the experiment. If we watch the slits and thus see where the photon goes, the screen shows a one-spot (photon as particle) result. If we do not watch, the screen shows an interference pattern (photon as wave) result.

---

* For a fuller discussion of time's arrow, see the chapter "Here We Go Loopedy Loop: A Brief History of Time Travel."

† Each slit becomes a new wave source, radiating toward the screen. Each wave has crests and troughs. Where the two spreading waves encounter the screen crest-of-one on top of trough-of-the-other, the waves cancel. At such a point, the screen shows nothing. Where the two waves encounter the screen crest upon crest or trough upon trough, the waves add. There, the screen shows a strong signal.

Honest. That's how it works.

Physicist John Wheeler proposed a variation on the double-slit experiment. The screen in his experiment is removable. Behind the screen are placed two detectors, each aligned with one of the foil's two slits.

Intuitively: if the screen remains in place and we don't watch the photon going through the foil, we'll see an interference pattern on the screen. If we remove the screen, the photon must strike one of the two detectors.

Now comes the interesting, "delayed choice" part of Wheeler's experiment. Let t1 be the time the photon reaches the foil. Let t3 be the time when the photon will reach the position of the removable screen.

We may (with very fast reflexes) whisk the screen from the experimental apparatus at time t2, where t1 <t2 <t3. If and when we remove the screen in that way, one of the two detectors registers a hit. That is, we have forced the photon to have gone through one or the other slit.

Did the photon keep an eye on us, and see how we tried to trick it? If so, that's one very clever photon! It seems at least as likely that our action at t2, whisking away the screen, retroactively determined what (appeared to have?) happened at t1. In plain English, it looks like we had an influence backward in time!

To complicate matters further, we (or the apparatus we built), by choosing to pull out the screen, or not, play a role in the experiment's outcome. Is the photon's response to our intervention a vote in favor of quantum consciousness?

This delayed-choice experiment has been performed and the backward-in-time influence verified.[139]

So: if the paranormal is a manifestation of quantum entanglement and quantum particles react (in at least one plausible interpretation of a real-world experiment) to a future event, then precognition would appear to be plausible.*

---

*   No, I haven't a clue—if this *is* what's going on—how to apply the effect for a to-the-past time machine.

Quantum teleportation

Fooled you!

Although physicists speak of quantum teleportation, they're referring to quantum entanglement, not to teleportation in the popular, "Beam me up, Scotty," sense.

A binary digit (bit) in a digital computer has the value of either zero or one. A quantum bit (qubit) can take the value zero, one, or—everything quantum is weird—unknown. More precisely, that third condition is an indeterminately weighted combination (in QM-speak, a superposition) of the zero and one states. The values of a qubit can be encoded on a quantum particle, such as an electron, with any of: spin oriented up, spin oriented down, or spin "don't know."

We'll take two quantum particles (say, electrons) and encode them with data. If they are not identical, they can, with great care, be entangled. To be entangled, one is spin up and the other spin down, or both are spin indeterminate. We separate the entangled electrons, very carefully, doing nothing to either disturb or measure either's spin state.

Sometime later we measure the spin state (qubit value) of one of the entangled electrons. When we do, our action also immediately determines the spin state of the other half of the entangled pair. If we measure spin up, the remote electron is spin down. If we measure spin down, the remote electron is spin up. No measurement gives a result of "spin unknown" because the act of measurement—like the act of passing through a slit in foil—forces a specific outcome.

In a sense, reading the spin state of one electron has transferred a spin state to the distant member of the pair. In theory and (to any known experiment) in practice, nothing travels between the two electrons. Change to the entangled partner particle just happens. That is what physicists call quantum teleportation. The mechanism seems (at the least) to be insufficient for the paranormal conveyance of physical objects.

Wrapping up

Some experiments—none without controversy—suggest the existence of paranormal phenomena. Said phenomena—if they exist—are unaffected by electromagnetic shielding and, at least on terrestrial scales, insensitive to distance. Some interpretations of quantum mechanics and consciousness—also contentious, but nonetheless academically respectable—appear to be compatible with reports of telepathy, remote viewing, and precognition.*

That's a lot of qualifiers—

But nowhere in there do I see a *dis*qualifier for the use (with great care) of at least these so-called paranormal abilities in even hard SF.

To read further

- *The Wizards of Langley: Inside the CIA's Directorate of Science and Technology.* Jeffrey T. Richelson (chapter "The CIA's Psychic Friends").

- *The Reality of ESP: A Physicist's Proof of Psychic Abilities*, Russell Targ.

- http://rhine.org/ Website of the Rhine Research Center.

- http://tvtropes.org/pmwiki/pmwiki.php/Main/PsychicPowers.

- *Science Fiction and Science Fact: An Encyclopedia*, Brian Stableford, articles on parapsychology and John W. Campbell.

---

* If, however, a candidate physical explanation exists for psychokinesis, mental healing, or the teleportation of physical objects, I have not seen it.

HUMAN 2.0

Being All We Can Be

Much of this book has focused on aliens. Do they even exist? If yes, what might they be like? Will it ever be practical for humans to visit them, or them to visit us? Whether face to face (or whatever), or via comm link, could we and they overcome our doubtless many differences to learn to speak (or whatever) with one another? Might we and they— whether because under the skin (or whatever) we're in some manner too alike, or too different—go to war with one another?

Perhaps it all seemed too speculative. Escapist. Purely SFnal. It shouldn't.

Soon enough, we humans will share our world with intelligent beings quite unlike human norms—

Because soon enough some of us, or our descendants, will have become them.

A very early SFnal interest

Tinkering with the nature of humanity goes to the earliest roots of the genre, and the imagined changes were not always for the best. As a representative sample, consider:

- Robert Louis Stevenson's *The Strange Case of Dr. Jekyll and Mr. Hyde* (1886) was an early literary exploration of changing—if not necessarily improving—man by chemically separating his baser, animalistic nature.

- Edmund Hamilton's (1931) story "The Man Who Evolved" harnessed concentrated cosmic rays (I *did* say 1931) to jump eons ahead in development. ("As we are to apes, so must the men of the future be to us.")

- Olaf Stapledon's (1935) *Odd John: A Story Between Jest and Earnest* envisioned more-than-human beings arising from chance mutation.

- Craig Ellis's "Dr. Varsag's Experiment" (1940) grafted the nervous system of a mongoose into a human, making him one heck of a boxer until unintended consequences kicked in.

- Heinlein's *Methuselah's Children* (1941 serial, 1958 novel) offered life extension by means of selective breeding.

Are recent fictional transformations any more credible than the early batch? If you recall humans evolving gills in *Waterworld* (1995) or the drug mule/heroine of *Lucy* (2014) developing physical and psychical enhancements after her illicit cargo springs a leak, you will have justifiable doubts—but I prefer to believe those movies are outliers. Ditto the man-to-monster genetic transformation by aboriginal soup recipe in Douglas Preston and Lincoln Child's 1996 novel *Relic* (the basis of the 1997 movie, *The Relic*).

Let's look at some emerging technologies that will soon require us to take a fresh look at what it means to be human and a sampling of how SF has incorporated these possibilities.

Eugenics and the Übermenschen

Francis Galton, cousin to Charles Darwin and coiner of the term *eugenics*, from the Greek for well-born, suggested improving our species by means of judicious marriages.[140] While Galton sought via "positive eugenics" to reinforce traits he perceived as advantageous, other eugenicists advocated the withdrawal—or involuntary removal—of perceived undesirables from the reproductive population. The English Eugenics Society, founded by Galton, opposed extreme forms of "negative eugenics," but compulsory sterilization of allegedly mentally deficient individuals was once legal in a majority of the states of the United States.[141]

For a time eugenics fell within mainstream thought. Eugenics drew support from, among many, Winston Churchill, Theodore Roosevelt, Herbert Hoover, George Bernard Shaw, H. G. Wells—and, in a far more extreme form, Adolf Hitler.[142] Following Nazi recourse to eugenics to cast Aryans as übermenschen (supermen) and justify the genocide of the Holocaust, eugenics fell into deep disrepute.

As befitted a scientific topic once hotly debated, genre literature addressed eugenics in a broad range of utopian and dystopian stories—few of them much remembered. One exception is *The Skylark of Space*, arguably the earliest space opera.* The *Skylark*'s square-jawed, all-American crew, while visiting the extrasolar planet Osmone, accept with evident sympathy the local culture and religion rooted in Darwinian competition and eugenic breeding. Another notable exception to that selective amnesia is C. L. Kornbluth's bitingly satirical 1951 novella, "The Marching Morons."

Genetic therapy

Eugenics developed before an understanding of DNA suggested a more subtle route to species improvement. In recent decades, molecular biologists have developed the insights and tools with which to selectively alter a life form's genes, both within a species and with contributions from donor species. Genetically modified

---

* *The Skylark of Space*, E. E. "Doc" Smith and Lee Hawking Garby, was serialized in *Amazing Stories* in 1928 but not published in book form (with updates) until 1946.

organisms, such as vitamin-A-producing "golden rice," have become familiar—if still sometimes controversial.[143]

One impetus for genetic-engineering research, not surprisingly, is the perceived opportunity to cure human diseases. Such research can be pharmacologically oriented, as when bacteria are modified into "bioreactors" for the mass production of otherwise conventional therapeutics. In this chapter, our interest is in another line of investigation, dealing with illnesses that have a genetic component. Simply put, if a problematical gene(s) in our cells can be replaced, then perhaps the associated disease can be cured and even eliminated.

Nature long ago developed the means to insert genes into living cells: with viruses. Cutting-edge medicine uses purposefully modified viruses to deliver therapeutic genes.

One class of treatments involves viruses modified (a) to carry a therapeutic gene and (b) not to replicate themselves. A common delivery vector for these treatments is the adenovirus, which, in its unmodified form, is one cause (among others) of the common cold. Of course viruses sometimes trigger immune responses, our immune system being, after all, in part a defense against viruses. Jesse Gelsinger, treated with an adenovirus-based therapy for a rare genetic liver deficiency, died in 1999 from an immune-response complication. He thus became the first known fatality from gene-therapy research.

A second class of virus-based therapy permanently modifies the patient's cells. Alas, there is nothing simple about getting the desired gene(s) spliced into a suitable chromosomal location(s), in the appropriate quantity, and only within the targeted cell type. *In vivo* gene splicing uses tailored retroviruses to deliver the therapeutic payload, but retroviruses can't (yet) be directed where in our chromosomes to insert the genetically engineered payload.

A random point of gene insertion may go without serious consequences—or it can be a matter of life and death. While only a little over 1% of the human genome codes for protein synthesis, recent studies show that as much as 80% of noncoding DNA performs at least some biochemical function.[144] Thus, a viral vector randomly inserting its therapeutic payload into a patient's chromosome might: impact that cell's ability to synthesize an important protein; turn the cell cancerous; or, at the opposite extreme, interfere with the cell's ability to divide at all.* Four of nine patients treated between 1999 and 2002 for "bubble boy disease" (more formally, X-linked severe combined immunodeficiency) developed leukemia as a consequence of their retrovirus-based gene therapy.[145]

But there have also been successes. Genetic engineering may one day offer treatments for such diseases as diabetes, sickle cell anemia, and some cancers. To date, research trials of genetic therapies have involved only small numbers of patients with specific diseases. That said, the first commercial genetically engineered pharmaceutical, to treat a rare condition called lipoprotein lipase deficiency, recently arrived.[146] Big Pharma is ready to dive into the genetic-therapy market.[147]

Is the gene-ie out of the bottle?

What if the point of gene insertion *could* be precisely controlled? What if doctors *could* control when, and to what extent, an inserted gene is active (i.e., expressing its associated protein)?

We're closer than ever to finding out.

Consider CRISPR-Cas9, an adaptive immune mechanism found in many bacteria. Very briefly, the mechanism learns from its first exposure to an invading virus to recognize some portion of the invader's genome. On subsequent exposures the mechanism slices apart the DNA of matching intruders.

Repurposed for genetic engineering, CRISPR-Cas9 is a tool for cleaving an organism's DNA at a precise location of the experimenter's choosing. When a custom-designed DNA tem-

---

* How, you ask, do these side effects come about? The inserted gene may alter the expression of (protein production by) other genes near the point of insertion.

plate is added to the mix, the CRISPR system allows precise insertion of genes at the target point.[148] Nor is CRISPR-Cas9 the last word in gene modification, as variants like CRISPR-Cpf1 emerge[149] and a patent battle rages over CRISPR technology.[150]

Even with the emergent ability to precisely excise and insert genes, genetic engineering as a medical therapy has risks. In how many cells will desired changes take hold? How much of a therapeutic protein(s) will be produced as a result? *In vivo*, how will that protein(s) interact with other cellular functions? If only the inserted genes could be activated and deactivated at will....

And now, at least sometimes, they can. Researchers are pairing therapeutic genes with biological on-off switches controlled by drugs. Post-gene therapy, give the patient a low dosage of the activating pharmaceutical. If the response is positive, try a larger dose to activate more protein production. If the response is negative, withhold the activating pharmaceutical and the controlled gene quickly stops expressing the protein (i.e., the inserted gene goes dormant). Such gene switches are already in human trials for cancer treatment.[151]

And delivering CRISPR-Cas9 (or other gene-splicing mechanism) into targeted cells? That technology is also progressing. Methods include injection, electroporation (using an external electric field to increase the permeability of cell membranes), infection (as we've seen, with a virus), and packed inside nanoparticles. These techniques affect a few percent, or less, of targeted cells. Combining techniques has, in one animal study, raised delivery efficiency to six percent.[152]

Improved tools haven't made genetic engineering of humans, especially in the context of reproductive cells, any less controversial. In 2015, Chinese scientists caused a stir with their attempt to experimentally treat a genetic disease in human embryos, and British scientists sought to follow, planning to apply genetic-engineering techniques to the study of placental development.[153] A global group of "stem cell researchers, bioethicists and policy experts" has judged genetic engineering of human embryos ethical, as long as modified babies are not allowed to be born—reaching a conclusion contrary to policy in the U.S. as administered by the National Institutes of Health.[154]

And as this technology rapidly advances, the philosophical debate continues—not least because, as research continues into genetic cures, it becomes clear that the prospective uses extend beyond therapy.[155]

Genetic enhancement

Amyotrophic Lateral Sclerosis (ALS), aka Lou Gehrig's disease, destroys the neurons responsible for voluntary muscle control. ALS patients progressively lose control of their bodies, until they are unable to move, trapped within their own bodies. It is a horrible disease.

In researching a possible treatment for ALS, biologists genetically modified healthy mice to increase their production of the hormone Insulin-like Growth Factor 1, IGF-1. These mice ceased to lose muscle mass with age! In related experiments, genetically treated rats showed significant muscle-mass *gain*. Experiments with an IGF-1 variant called MGF showed a 20% muscle-mass gain and a 25% increase in strength—without exercise.[156]

Not surprisingly, perhaps, there appear to be tradeoffs associated with increasing IGF-1 levels. In studies with mice, reduced IGF-1 levels have been associated with, on the one hand, small size, delayed puberty, and reduced fertility, and, on the other hand, with increased lifespan and reduced risks of cancer and diabetes. Reduced IGF-1 levels may also improve human longevity.[157] Are there people who would favor increased muscle mass over a longer life? Given the types of bodily injuries many pro athletes willingly risk, I suspect that some people would.

Nor is exercise-free body building the sole enhancement that would seem easy to market widely. Leptin is a hormone whose levels influence appetite and metabolism. How popular might be a gene therapy that combats or prevents obesity?[158] How about a treatment that reactivates hair follicles to reverse baldness?[159] A bit more speculatively, consider a genetic treatment that—without ultraviolet light—produces a skin tan, whether as a permanent change or as activated/deactivated by taking a pill. Would that treatment best be described as a cosmetic procedure (note that cosmetics are a multibillion-dollar business) or as a melanoma preventative?

Pro athletics has been rocked in recent years by doping scandals. That is, some athletes have been caught using performance-enhancing drugs. One of the drugs sometimes (ab)used is erythropoietin, or EPO, a hormone that controls the production of red blood cells. Increase your red-cell count a little and your blood can carry more oxygen, increasing your endurance. But to thicken the blood with extra red cells increases the risk of forming blood clots ("thrombi") in veins and arteries. Such clots can block blood flow to the brain, heart, and lungs, producing, respectively, a stroke, heart attack, and pulmonary embolism. Not to put too fine a point on it, too much EPO can kill.[160]

Our bodies naturally produce EPO; hence, the athletic ban against synthetic EPO initially relied upon intrusive searches (e.g., of physical possessions) rather than on blood tests. Might athletes want a genetic tweak to increase their bodily production of EPO? The temptation will surely be there, especially once EPO-based gene therapies, currently being tested on mice, are approved for the treatment of human anemia.

Of course, we've only scratched the surface of possible genetic tweaks. The more biologists discover, the broader becomes the set of conceivable alterations. Once we become accustomed to genetic therapies, cosmetic treatments, performance enhancements, and (as yet, still speculatively) lifespan extenders, how long will it be until we are ready to consider more radical genetic changes—including inheritable changes?

Science fiction, of course, has explored many of the possibilities of genetic engineering:

- Nancy Kress's 1991 "Beggars in Spain" examined the consequences of a gene tweak that eliminates the need for sleep and bumps up intelligence. The novella won both the Hugo and Nebula Awards for that year, was developed into a 1993 novel of the same name, and led eventually to the three-book Beggars series.

- In microgravity, hands might seem more useful than feet. Lois McMaster Bujold introduced the genetically engineered, four-armed-and-no-legged quaddies—and a study in morality—in *Falling Free* (1988).

- From tattoos to body piercing to facial hair, people have long used bodily modification to express themselves. With gengineering, people may someday make bold personal statements via far more extreme body mods. When life turns monstrous, why not become a monster? So Mike Brotherton had it in his 2003 novel, *Star Dragon*.

- And who can forget the 1982 film *Star Trek II: The Wrath of Khan*, in which Our Heroes battle an exiled race of genetically engineered supermen?

Artificial organs

Not every disease or injury lends itself to genetic therapy. Regenerative medicine—the growth of replacement organs (e.g., from stem cells)—remains a young technology.* Compatible organs aren't always available for transplant when a patient needs them.

---

* In 2011, Swedish physicians gave a cancer patient a replacement trachea (windpipe). This synthetic organ combined a plastic replica of the trachea with a living cover grown from stem cells taken from the patient's bone marrow. Given the plastic substrate, this implant has elements of both artificial-organ technology and regenerative medicine.

See "Cancer Patient Gets First Totally Artificial Windpipe," Michelle Norris, *Health News from NPR*, July 8, 2011, http://www.npr.org/templates/transcript/transcript.php?storyId=137701848.

Another option is artificial organs, and in this section we'll review a few types of them.

Without a functioning heart, we die. Soviet surgeon Vladimir Demikhov experimented with artificial hearts (on animals) as far back as 1937. Research into cardiopulmonary bypass (CPB) machines dates to the 1880s, and CPBs have provided temporary heart and lung function during cardiac surgeries since the 1950s. In 1969, an implantable mechanical heart was first used to support a human patient until a donor heart could be found (although the patient died shortly after the transplant procedure). Modern, implantable artificial hearts like the Jarvik 7 have been used by hundreds of patients as a bridge to transplantation. Short of replacing a failing heart, many cardiac patients have been equipped with an implanted electromechanical "ventricular assist device." Many cardiac patients whose hearts would otherwise beat too slowly have had electronic pacemakers implanted.*

Among the functions of kidneys is filtering the blood, then transferring the water-soluble metabolic waste products to the urinary system for removal. Kidney disease degrades this critical function, and sufficiently advanced chronic kidney disease can, at present, be treated only with (hours at a time, at least several days per week) dialysis, or by a kidney transplant. An implantable artificial kidney remains the dream of thousands with end stage renal disease (also known as Stage 5 chronic kidney disease) who require dialysis. Medical R & D is not yet there, but a portable/wearable artificial kidney recently began human trials.[161]

Type 1 diabetes mellitus is the condition in which the pancreas fails to synthesize sufficient (or any) insulin, the hormone that regulates the level of glucose in the blood. Too little glucose, and a person faints. Too much glucose, and over time a person suffers damage to nerves and blood vessels. The possible consequences

---

* Biological pacemakers, based upon stem-cell and genetic-engineering technologies, are another possibility. See "Repairing A Broken Heart: Moving Beyond Electronic Pacemakers," Richard B. Robinson, Ph.D., *Analog*, November 2011.

of such damage are many and varied, including blindness (diabetic retinopathy), pain, numbness, nausea, incontinence, kidney disease, heart attacks, and strokes. Infections and ulcers of the foot that go unnoticed due to diabetic neuropathies are a leading cause of lower-limb amputation.

In conventional management of type 1 diabetes—there is no cure—the patient tests his blood sugar several times each day, each test involving a needle stick.* He then calculates and injects a dosage of medicinal insulin to reflect his planned exercise and meals. The process is uncomfortable, intrusive, prone to misestimation, and interrupted whenever the patient sleeps.

Enter the artificial pancreas. Such an artificial organ will combine a glucose sensor, implantable insulin pump, and personalized control algorithms executing on a microprocessor—which can be a Bluetooth-enabled smartphone. Partial solutions are on the market[162] and complete closed-loop systems are becoming available.[163]

Wearable enhancements

Sound-amplifying devices treat hearing loss. Corrective lenses treat impaired vision. And nothing constrains wearable devices to the limits of our natural senses.

Smart eyewear like Microsoft HoloLens and Google Glass (and already under development, smart contact lenses) enable augmented vision, which superimposes over one's view of the real world all manner of information: directions, reminders, lookups (who *is* that passerby who seems so familiar?), fanciful decorations, and, inevitably, advertisements and graffiti. Making use of sensors we wear, perhaps in a wirelessly linked smart watch or activity-tracking wristband, augmented vision can de-

---

* Noninvasive glucose monitors (i.e., designs that do not require needle sticks, or require sticks only for occasional calibrations) are recently available. As one example, see http://www.gluco-wise.com/#product-section.

liver timely health advice. (Hopefully well-designed augmented vision. Poorly done, it can distract and disorient.[164]) Heart-beat monitors can help us achieve aerobic exercise levels without overdoing it. Sweat sensors can warn us of disease.[165]

Nor need personal biosensors reside in clunky jewelry, with its often intermittent bodily contact. Smart body decals in field trial (as of May 2015) incorporate many thousands of transistors, resisters, sensors, and other electronic devices. Various "Biostamps" measure body temperature, UV exposure, pulse rate, blood-oxygen levels, and more. When tiny sensors don't exist for key health indicators, clever algorithms in onboard microprocessors can sometimes combine or convert available measurements into a useful surrogate reading. To directly measure blood pressure, for example, involves a bulky compression cuff. As a substitute, Biostamps use pulse readings from nearby sensors to derive pulse-wave velocity, which correlates with blood-pressure changes. Biostamps power themselves with harvested RF energy, such as from the near-field communications (NFC) signal emitted by modern smartphones (for use with wireless payment systems like Apple Pay). Biostamps also use an NFC signal and a tiny onboard antenna to upload their data. Candidate applications of such decal-based smart sensors include:

- Monitoring infants in neonatal-care units.

- Tailoring personalized skin-care recommendations (L'Oreal is funding that research).

- Inferring the stress levels of air-traffic controllers from changes in their skin temperature.

- Measuring electrical activity in the brain for sleep apnea studies with an unobtrusive behind-the-ear skin patch.[166]

Do we and our wearable and/or implanted devices at some point cross a threshold to become cybernetic organisms—cyborgs? Or are the *avant garde*—at least I consider growing a spare ear on one's forearm "out there"—already over that line?[167]

Prostheses (and other theses)

A prosthesis is a mechanical or electromechanical replacement for a missing body part, whether the need arises from injury or congenital condition. For centuries, hooks and peg legs were state-of-the-art prosthetic devices—hardly technological.

Modern prostheses are far more sophisticated. Some use motors to exert force. Some employ an embedded microprocessor(s) to fine-tune motion. In some artificial knees, for example, microprocessor-enhanced control offers a natural gait by dynamically adjusting joint positioning to the walker's pace. Prostheses that exploit electromyography (the measurement of the electrical activity of muscles) are controlled by voluntary muscle contractions. In some prosthetic arms, gripping systems provide force feedback to the controlling muscles.

Put all those technologies together—and add $40 million of R & D—and you get (cue 1980's *The Empire Strikes Back*), the newly FDA-approved "Luke Arm."[168] This sophisticated prosthesis, similar in size and weight to a natural human arm, combines microprocessors, motors, and myoelectric control; it also allows the simultaneous, independent operation of multiple joints (e.g., of individual prosthetic fingers).

My hand, whenever it touches something, signals via my peripheral nervous system more than just the force that I'm exerting. It conveys the temperature and the texture of the object's surface. Without such inputs, I might burn myself on a hot pan or allow a wet glass to slip from my grasp. The next step in prostheses is to enable a broad range of feedback. The Defense Advanced Research Projects Agency (DARPA) recently kicked off the HAPTIX ("Hand Proprioception and Touch Interfaces") program to create a prosthetic hand system that moves and provides sensation similar to a natural hand."[169]

271

A yet more natural limb replacement would directly accept commands from, and return sensory feedback to, the wearer's nervous system—and the technology for such a prosthesis is within sight. On an experimental basis, a prosthetic neural interface was demonstrated in 2009. With electrodes surgically implanted into his arm stump, an amputee volunteer successfully operated and received sensor feedback from Cyberhand.[170] The body's natural defenses against foreign materials triggers an immune response, and it's difficult to make such implanted electrodes permanent. (And so, in my 2002 novella "Presence of Mind,"* rather than implanted electrodes, the neurally interfaced prosthesis contained sensors sensitive enough to remotely read impulses from the truncated nerve branches in the hero's arm stump.)

Mind over muscle

What about interfacing prostheses directly with the brain, bypassing the peripheral nervous system? There's been progress on that front, too. Brain/machine interfaces (BMIs) are of three types. All involve, in one way or another, sensing the slight voltage changes produced by the operation of the neural circuits of the brain, isolating the neural signal(s) intended for a particular purpose, and repurposing the recovered signal(s) to operate the prosthesis.

The least invasive—and least sensitive—BMI technology uses electroencephalography (EEG), with sensors placed on the scalp. The human brain is comprised of roughly 100 billion neurons; from outside the skull, EEG "sees" high-level/aggregated neural activity rather than the firing of specific synapses. Despite its limitations, volunteers using an EEG-based BMI have, with training, learned to operate robotic arms using only their thoughts.

The most sensitive BMIs respond to the activity of specific, targeted neurons. These BMIs require opening the skull and

---

*   Later incorporated into my 2008 novel, *Fools' Experiments*.

implanting electrodes in the brain. Even with brain surgery, inherently invasive and risky, only near-surface neurons are accessible.

One recent intracranial experiment involved implanting the brain of a paraplegic volunteer with two arrays of 96 electrodes each. Rather than, as in earlier research, involving the primary motor cortex, this surgery used the posterior parietal cortex: a brain region involved with planning movement. The latter placement is thought to offer a more intuitive control and better responsiveness, by eliminating the need to focus on the minutiae of controlling the robotic arm. In any event, the surgery worked—after developing his dexterity through 6700 games of rock-paper-scissors, the patient used his robotic arm to serve himself a beer. Still, as if to emphasize the experimental nature of this procedure, minute shifting of the electrodes necessitated some daily retraining.[171]

A recent, middle-of-the-road BMI technique, electrocorticography (ECoG) drapes a sensor mesh over the cerebral cortex. While this technique still requires opening of the cranium, surgery on the brain itself isn't involved. ECoG BMI remains experimental; the human trials being done are in conjunction with brain surgery required for other, therapeutic reasons.[172, 173]

Limb prostheses have heretofore benefited amputees, but BMI techniques are beginning to extend the utility of prostheses to a whole new population: those who suffer from partial or complete paralysis. Quality of life is surely improved when someone who has lost the ability to feed herself or turn pages of a book can, by the power of her thoughts, direct a robotic arm to do it for her.[174] A paraplegic with a mind-controlled exoskeleton climbed out of his wheelchair to personally kick off the 2014 World Cup.[175]

Mind-controlled robotic systems have been too expensive for widespread deployment. That, too, may be about to change.[176]

Better, stronger, faster

If technology can replace a body part, can technology at the same time improve upon it? That was the premise of the iconic 1974 television series *Six Million Dollar Man* (based on the 1972 novel *Cyborg* by Martin Caidin). Cyborg Steve Austin had bionic legs, a bionic arm, and a bionic eye.

While technology has yet to match Steve Austin's enhancements, the more-capable-than-human prosthesis is no longer mere theory. In 2007, the International Association of Athletics Federations (IAAF) rewrote its competition rules to ban "any technical device that incorporates springs, wheels or any other element that provides a user with an advantage over another athlete not using such a device." The next year, the IAAF banned double amputee and paralympian Oscar Pistorius, because his Flex-Foot Cheetah prostheses (aka, "blades") capture and release kinetic energy—like springs. The IAAF reported that, "An athlete using this prosthetic blade has a demonstrable mechanical advantage (more than 30%) when compared to someone not using the blade." The Court of Arbitration for Sport overruled the IAAF, allowing Pistorius to compete in the 2008 Olympics.*

(Mechanically-assisted competition isn't limited to athletics. In the Cyborg Olympics, competitors are deemed pilots.[177])

Hugh Herr, director of the biomechatronics group within the MIT Media Lab—and a double amputee who walks on prostheses of his own design—predicts that "Fifty years out, I think we will have largely eliminated disability."[178]

---

* Wearers of the Flex-Foot Cheetah are sometimes referred to as "blade runners," a comment upon the device's narrow profile and a reference to the superhuman "replicants" in the 1982 SF classic film *Blade Runner* (based on the 1968 Philip K. Dick novel *Do Androids Dream of Electric Sheep?*).

  More recently, Oscar Pistorius is better known for his murder conviction following the shooting death (an accident, he claims) of his girlfriend.

As prostheses improve in capability and naturalness, might they seem desirable to some people with unimpaired bodies? To some people with mild or age-related impairments? Rather than retrofit weak, achy, legs with replacement hips and knees, won't some people prefer to replace entire legs with sufficiently advanced prostheses? It's hard to imagine otherwise.[179]

None of which means that prosthetics will necessarily converge in their appearance on their biological precursors. For purposes of efficiency or economy, aesthetics or personal statement, some prosthetics wearers have begun to favor *non*-natural-looking artificial limbs.[180]

Flexing motors, not muscles

It's likewise hard to imagine that motorized exoskeletons will benefit only the disabled. The movie *Aliens* (1986) showed us the wearable forklift (also handy for hand-to-hand combat with acid-for-blood extraterrestrials). The movie *Edge of Tomorrow* (2014) showed us strength-and-armament enhancing battle armor. So had, way back in 1959, Robert A. Heinlein's novel *Starship Troopers* (we will not speak—ever—of the 1997 movie).

Nor will we wait long for such tech. DARPA's "warrior web" project is already working on exoskeletons to assist soldiers.[181]

An out-of-body experience

As BMIs and robotics improve, the next step—entire prosthetic bodies—becomes imaginable. An ALS patient or a quadriplegic might, by the power of his mind and the availability of a sophisticated, mind-controlled robot, remain at home or hospital *and* be out in the world. Such was the premise of the 2009 movie *Avatar* (in which the teleoperated body mimicked the form of an alien) and John Scalzi's 2014 novel *Lock In*.

In the real world, we're not quite there. Telepresence robots— basically remote-control tablet computers on wheels—have been available for several years.[182] The University of Pennsylvania's

DORA takes queues from head movements of an operator wearing an Oculus Rift VR headset.[183] The more sophisticated Telesar V telepresence robot is humanoid (in a diminutive way), controlled by a virtual-reality suit (and so unsuitable for a mobility-impaired operator) and 3-D virtual-reality helmet, and restricted to controlled environments (like offices).[184]

What about getting robots out of controlled environments? Such mobility has long been thought to be years in the future. And so, the February 2016 video of Boston Dynamics's Atlas robot walking itself—and recovering its balance whenever it slipped—across snow-covered, uneven ground was a pleasant surprise.[185]

Are BMI-controlled full-body prostheses farfetched? DARPA doesn't believe so.[186]

Segue

We've covered a lot of ground,* from a genre survey of species improvement to eugenics, genetic enhancements, organ replacements, and physical prostheses. Next chapter, we'll tackle a yet more ambitious topic: mental prostheses and changes to the brain.

---

*   Much of it, however metaphorically, uneven and snow-covered.

HUMAN 2.0

Mind Over Matter

L ast chapter, in the opening half of our look at reengineering humanity, we reviewed eugenics, genetic therapies, and a variety of physical treatments and enhancements. In this chapter we'll consider a yet more ambitious prospect: changes that, in coming years, we might see made in, and to, the human nervous system—even involving the brain itself.

Neural prostheses

Like the rest of the human body, the nervous system is prey to impairments—some of which can already be mitigated with electronics.

Implanted electronic devices can alleviate hearing loss due to certain types of damage to the cochlea (inner ear), bypassing damaged auditory hair cells to directly stimulate the auditory nervous system. Hundreds of thousands of people worldwide (and the hero of Jay Werkheiser's 2015 novelette "Usher") have had a degree of hearing restored with cochlear implants.

Remember Lt. Geordi La Forge of *Star Trek: The Next Generation*, blind without his bionic visor? Visual prostheses are already here. One such device is an option for people with damaged retinas but functioning optic nerves, for example, those afflicted with macular degeneration or retinitis pigmentosa. Cameras wirelessly transmit imagery data to retinal implants (electrode arrays surgically installed at the back of the eye); the implants, in turn, stimulate the surviving retinal cells.

Although the FDA approved the first retinal implants in 2013, their adoption remains limited—perhaps because the implants' capabilities are so limited. Their resolution is low, beneath the 20/200 visual acuity threshold by which the AMA defines functional blindness. (With 20/200 vision, a person can read from a distance of 20 feet only what a normally sighted person can read across a distance of 200 feet.) Further, these implants do not yet support color vision. The viewing angle they offer is highly restricted, amounting to "tunnel vision." In principle, however, nothing precludes the development of larger, more sensitive, implantable electrode arrays that would restore a greater degree of eyesight.

In a related approach, researchers have recently implanted infrared-sensitive photodiodes into the eyes of blind rats. Special eyeglasses project IR images onto the photodiode array, which stimulates neurons beneath the nonfunctioning retinal surface. To date, this technology, too, remains monochromatic and available only at resolution levels still consistent with legal blindness.[187]

A second type of visual prosthesis transmits data to electrodes implanted directly into the brain, more specifically, the visual cortex.[188] By bypassing the optic nerve, such prostheses can treat categories of blindness that retinal implants cannot.

The image feed for all these visual prosthesis comes from glasses-mounted cameras. A sufficiently miniaturized camera might someday sit within the eye socket—a true bionic eye.*

In theory, the data fed to visual implants could come from any source, including distant sensors—not limited to visible-light wavelengths—and even computer-synthesized imagery. (Maybe Superman's X-ray vision isn't *entirely* silly.)

---

* I am reminded of the (film!) camera within a spy's false eye in the 1969 movie *Journey to the Far Side of the Sun*.

Other neural prostheses address nonsensory conditions. Similar to a pacemaker electrically stimulating a diseased heart to regulate heartbeat, deep brain stimulation (aka the "brain pacemaker") delivers electrical pulse sequences through precisely implanted electrodes to regulate selected activities within the brain. DBS technology was developed to interrupt the tremors of early-stage Parkinson's disease, a degenerative disorder of the central nervous system. DBS now helps more than 100,000 Parkinson's patients. DBS technology is being researched for treating an array of psychiatric conditions, including depression, obsessive-compulsive disorder, and posttraumatic stress disorder.[189],*

A noninvasive technology, repetitive transcranial magnetic stimulation (rTMS) can influence neurons up to several centimeters beneath the scalp. The technology is FDA-approved for treating depression. Like DBS, rTMS therapy has been limited by the lack of detailed information about the precise brain regions to target to treat specific conditions. With recent functional magnetic resonance imaging (fMRI) studies, researchers are beginning to address that issue, too.[190]

Of all the nerve

Nor is the potential for treatment by neural implants limited to conditions of the central nervous system. The FDA recently approved Maestro, aka the "appetite pacemaker." Maestro is implanted into the abdomen to interrupt hunger pangs by interacting with a branch of the vagus nerve. Maestro doesn't address overeating arising from (for example) poor dining habits.[191]

But vagus nerve stimulation (VNS) seems poised to offer far more than appetite suppression. The vagus (Latin for wandering) nerve, connecting many organs in the chest and abdomen with the brain stem, has been likened to a backdoor

---

* Perhaps electrodes implanted into the brains of the cyborg Daleks of *Doctor Who* explain their emotion-ectomies.

for hacking human physiology. The vagus nerve terminates in a brain subsystem called the nucleus tractus solitarius, which in turn connects with several neurotransmitter-producing regions of the brain. Neurotransmitters, of course, are the biochemical molecules that intermediate many neurological processes.

VNS has been tested in connection with medical conditions as varied as depression, epilepsy, migraines, tinnitus (ringing in the ears), Crohn's disease (an inflammation of the gut), rheumatoid arthritis (an autoimmune inflammation of joints), and rehabilitation from strokes.

Traditional VNS involves implanting an electronic pulse generator in the patient's chest—an expensive and intrusive surgical procedure. An inexpensive device now under trial would provide VNS simply by pressing a handheld stimulator against the neck. Putting the patient into the control loop isn't always appropriate—an epilepsy attack, for example, may strike with little warning. For other conditions, however—migraines, say—patients may have ample opportunity to self-treat. Through patient-specific software loaded into a VNS device, physicians can limit the number and frequency of VNS applications, comparable to writing prescriptions for a limited number of pills. British pharma giant GlaxoSmithKline calls the technology *electroceuticals*.[192]

Tweaking the human brain…what could *possibly* go wrong?

The "wireheads" of Larry Niven's Known Space—addicted to the direct electrical stimulation of their neurological reward circuits—suggest one potential problem. In Michael Crichton's 1972 novel (and the basis of the 1974 movie) *The Terminal Man*, a brain implant intended to control seizures goes horribly wrong. Less dramatic, but also cautionary, consider (likewise not specifically VNS-related) two 2015 short stories, Ian Creasey's "Pincushion Pete" and Marissa Lingen and Alec Austin's collaboration "Potential Side Effects May Include."

Misty (and not always) water-colored memories

Neuroscientists are also unraveling the secrets of biological memory. Our memories are at the core of who we are—and yet, specific memories can torment us. MIT researchers have already inserted a memory into, and reprogrammed a memory of, genetically engineered mice.[193, 194] This line of research might, someday, offer treatments for posttraumatic stress disorder (PTSD). Or, as Philip K. Dick had it, implanted memories might substitute for tourism. His 1966 novelette "We Can Remember It for You Wholesale," has already served as the basis of two *Total Recall* movies.

DARPA initiated the Restoring Active Memory (RAM) program to investigate prostheses to treat memory loss from traumatic brain injury. One aspect of RAM involved patients previously fitted with intracranial electrodes for the study of their epilepsy. In a 2012 experiment, electrical stimulation of the entorhinal cortex (a region of the brain located between the neocortex and the hippocampus) was shown to enhance memory formation and recall. To leverage future developments, another part of the RAM program is developing implantable microelectrode arrays (aka, "memory chips").[195]

As the United States's BRAIN (Brain Research through Advancing Innovative Neurotechnologies) initiative and the European Human Brain Project expand our knowledge of the brain's detailed workings, the types of neural prostheses and the functions they can perform are only apt to grow.

Mind over keyboard

Keyboards and displays seem so twentieth century. If a brain/machine interface (BMI) may someday control prostheses, why not also use a BMI to control computers? Why not think commands at a computer? Why not receive responses by direct stimulation of the visual or auditory cortexes?

Presuming an off switch and a Really Good Firewall, wouldn't a neural interface to the Internet be awesome?

We often use "computers" as much to communicate with one another as to compute. Why not use BMIs to connect brain to brain? There has, in fact, been a proof-of-concept demonstration of telecommunications linking two minds: EEG/Internet/EEG. One headset wearer saw a videogame screen, but could only *think* about firing at the game's targets. The remote participant, with only his EEG headset to provide second-hand game status, had control over firing at unseen targets. For this simple task, firing accuracies as high as 83% were reported.[196, *] This is hardly technology-enabled telepathy—but give the engineers time.

Someday, perhaps, we will have thought-controlled interfaces. Perhaps a much improved EEG will suffice, and we'll go online by wearing special helmets or headsets.[197] Ben Bova's 1962 short story "The Next Logical Step" upgraded an EEG-based helmet with neural stimulation, for a fully immersive virtual-reality experience. Craig Thomas's 1977 technothriller *Firefox* (the basis of the 1982 movie) involved a fighter plane with thought-fired weapons controlled with helmet-mounted sensors. A sensor-lined BMI helmet was also a premise of my *Fools' Experiments* (2008).

For the most capable BMIs (as seen last chapter, in the context of prosthesis control), we may need to go inside the skull, the better to sense the faint electrochemical signals of specific neurons. That seems likely to involve many tiny implanted

---

*   Neurogaming responds to the game player's physiological state. Possible inputs include heart rate, pupil dilation, and—with an EEG-type headset—brainwaves. Past video gaming helped advance the state of the art in computer graphics; perhaps gaming will also foster the development of BMIs.

See "Neurogaming: Interest growing in technology that picks players' brains," Steve Johnson, *San Jose Mercury News*, June 13, 2014, http://www.mercurynews.com/business/ci_25957073/neurogaming-interest-growing-technology-that-picks-players-brains.

electrodes—*not* massive spikes jammed into the brain à la the 1999 movie, *The Matrix*. DARPA's 2016 "Neural Engineering System Design" initiative aims for just such a brain-implantable interface, miniaturized to one cubic centimeter or less. This initiative leaves the minor details of "how" to its grant applicants.[198]

Do you disbelieve anyone would actually volunteer for brain surgery to implant a modem? Would any surgeon actually perform such a major operation on a healthy subject? In fact, such a procedure has already been done. Neurologist Phil Kennedy found a surgeon, in Belize, to implant an electrode array into his motor cortex. This wasn't research for the faint of heart—or head: complications of the procedure included temporary brain swelling and paralysis. After only a few weeks, other complications necessitated a second surgery to remove the electrodes. Before that point, however, Kennedy did achieve some success at communicating "sounds" to a computer through his thoughts.[199]

The ideal solution, of course, is a neural interface so compact it can be delivered without surgery. Ramez Naam's 2012 novel *Nexus* gets a BMI inside the brain sans surgery in a dose of a nanocomputer-based "drug."

An SF author (and physicist and computer engineer) predicts

Having conveniently assumed in several of my stories that high-capability neural interfaces and BMIs will eventually become practical, in June 2014 I found myself on a panel at an academic conference discussing, among other topics, future implications of nanotech. That (and thirty years working as a system developer) finally got me to think deeply about how neural implants might someday be built. My conclusion: within a few decades, BMIs will be *grown* inside the brain.[200]

- The electrodes will be carbon-fiber arrays, grown *in situ*, thin enough to wind their way among the most tightly packed neurons. Our cells grow microtubules only a few nanometers across; surely nanotechnologists will learn to mimic the process.[201]

- The implant's growth process, and later the manipulation of data streaming from/to the electrodes, will be managed by a nanotech-enabled computer small enough to put inside the skull without surgery (the skull has natural gaps through which nerve bundles pass).

- A few of those grown-in-place electrodes will serve as a radio antenna. The BMI's radio connection can be very low-powered; it need only link with the smartphone (or other wireless gadget) in one's pocket, purse, or bracelet.

- The implant will be fueled, just as our neurons are, by the glucose naturally circulating in cerebrospinal fluid.

- Carbon atoms recovered from glucose (and/or other organic molecules in the cerebrospinal fluid) will be used to grow those carbon fibers.

- The human brain runs on about 20 watts of power; the bit of power to be siphoned off to operate a BMI is trivial by comparison.*

Entirely out of one's mind

Might some disabled individuals choose to relocate completely into a sufficiently lifelike robotic body or a virtual environment? If not the disabled, how about the dying? Or might a nefarious party seek to reclaim the central nervous systems of the recently deceased as building blocks for cyborgs, à la 1987's movie *Robocop* (or for vivisection, à la Dr. Varsag and his mongoose)?

---

*   Fueling one's BMI (brain/machine interface, not body mass index) may be one more reason to eat chocolate. For more conventional pluses, see "What are the health benefits of chocolate?" Joseph Nordqvist, *MNT*, June 22, 2015, http://www.medicalnewstoday.com/articles/270272.php.

Let's begin with transplantation into a robot. Given a high-quality BMI, such a cyborg would require life support only for the transplanted brain. As it happens, the human brain is already significantly isolated from the rest of the body. The brain sits behind the blood-brain barrier (the selectively permeable barrier that separates the circulatory system and the central nervous system), taking nourishment from, and depositing metabolic byproducts into, cerebrospinal fluid. "Brain support" wouldn't be any more complex than full-body life support, and might be simpler.

Our brains don't merely think deep thoughts. Large parts of the brain process sensory inputs. The hypothalamus regulates our autonomic nervous system (which, in turn, directs our internal organs) and controls the secretions of our endocrine system. The brain also controls voluntary muscular actions and reacts to hormonal inputs. What would happen to a brain divorced from the body, denied these non-cerebral tasks? We don't know—but for kicks, check out Curt Siodmak's much dramatized *Donovan's Brain* (1942) and Lloyd Arthur Eshbach's novella "The Tyrant of Time" (1955).

Rather than transplant a *brain*, perhaps we can avoid dealing with those messy, unthinking parts by instead transplanting the *mind*.

Cognitive research has yet to establish what, exactly, a mind is. The common supposition is that self-awareness and memories reside—somehow—in the brain. If we can copy thought and memory patterns into a computer, then—perhaps—we can relocate the essence of a human mind. In 2012, Russian media mogul Dmitry Itskov set out to have such technology within a decade. A year later, well-known futurist Ray Kurzweil forecast that copying of a human mind could be done in a more conservative four decades.[202]

Whether looking out one decade or four, the goal remains aspirational. The human brain is comprised of roughly 100 *billion* neurons; together, they form a mesh of (as a conservative estimate) 100 *trillion* or more synapses.* Thought, memory, and self-awareness take place, in ways still far from understood, within the synapses of the brain. To copy a mind and its memories would appear to require reading trillions of synapses—many of them deep within the brain. Can that information be transcribed without destroying the brain in the process?

To add to the data-transfer challenge, our brains constantly change—strengthen, weaken, or completely rewire our synapses—as we see/hear/feel/touch/smell the external world, transfer data from short- to long-term memory, think, rethink in light of new information, dream, forget, and (like it or not) have our subconsciouses churn. In short: the brain is a complex, dynamic network. If the configurations of some synapses (say, in the outermost layers of the cerebral cortex) are read out earlier than others (say, within deeper layers), the transfer process may gather inconsistent information. Some transcription errors won't matter—we all carry around countless useless and half-forgotten memories—but other memories and thought structures are central to our sense of self.

Suppose we develop the technology to record a mind. To use that recording, we will also need the technology to transfer the information into a new container. That might be another biological brain—setting aside the ethical issues of overwriting whatever *was* or *might have been* in that recipient brain. (To an SF audience, one's hopefully healthier clone is an obvious receptacle. Clones—being copies, not improved versions—are beyond the scope of this discussion.)

Or, with suitable reformatting, a mind's contents might be written into a computer. For such an upload to be anything more than a static data dump, one will *also* need a brain simulation of sufficient fidelity to model the concurrent interactions

---

* A part of each neuron is a branching structure of projections, axon and dendrites, through which one neuron electrochemically signals to other neurons (and, outside the brain, to other cell types). A synapse is a particular junction between cells.

among trillions of synapses. As it happens, the Human Brain Project has a billion-euro, European Commission-funded effort underway to develop just such a simulation (although it's aimed at basic research, not the uploading of minds). HBP's approach is to model the brain from the bottom up, starting with the simulation of individual neurons and progressing to larger and larger neuronal assemblages. The reductionist premise—that the brain is no more than the sum of its parts—has its share of neuroscientist skeptics. HBP has targeted 2023 for the simulation's completion.[203]

Are you, as am I, among those who believe in free will? Neuroscience has no explanation for this (unproven and unprovable) phenomenon. Computer programs *don't* have free will; they act either algorithmically or, when so programmed, with a good approximation to randomly.* Mind, memory, self-awareness, and free will: there is much we would do well to better understand before attempting to upload a person into a computer.

None of which is to say uploads won't someday be possible, and in science fiction we're free to speculate. Suppose we can copy minds into a machine. What opportunities would such technology offer? What pitfalls might we encounter? Might one then make multiple mind copies? Modified copies? Herewith, a sampling of fictional explorations:

- Keith Laumer's 1968 novel *A Trace of Memory* has memory recording and rewriting for immortals whose natural rejuvenation process would otherwise cost them their memories.

- The 1985 movie *Max Headroom: 20 Minutes into the Future* introduced the eponymous wisecracking upload, created from an injured man's memories. This wry and

---

* That's not to suggest programs can't learn. We'll consider machine learning in the next chapter.

satiric character went on to star in many a US and UK television production.*

- *Annals of the Heechee*, 1987, the fourth novel in Frederik Pohl's Heechee saga, sees its protagonist uploaded after his physical death.

- Gregory Benford's 2000 novel *Eater* offers perhaps the most far-out copying scenario: minds coerced to upload into a passing sapient black hole that suffers from boredom.

- David Brin's 2002 novel *Kiln People* envisions mind copies uploaded into temporary servant bots, permitting people to be many places at once and (if/as desirable) to merge memories once a copy's task is complete.

- My 2011 short story "Blessed Are the Bleak" dystopically envisions uploading—a one-time "cure" for every ill that might befall a biological body—become the universal medical procedure.

- Robert J. Sawyer's 2013 noir-on-Mars murder mystery *Red Planet Blues* envisions transferring a mind into a superior artificial body, and plenty of characters do just that. Their motivations include: exploring the Martian surface without breathing gear, mimicking the (licensed) appearance of Hollywood idols, hiding out from their pasts, and potential immortality.

- Ramez Naam's 2013 novel *Crux* (the sequel to his aforementioned *Nexus*) includes a character, uploaded in desperation to save her life, going insane from sensory deprivation when denied a network link to a cloned biological body.

- Nor is sensory deprivation the worst abuse to which an uploaded mind might be subjected. In the 2015 short

---

* Including a gig as spokes"person" for New Coke. Talk about artificial....

story "An Immense Darkness," Eric James Stone finds ways to torture and interrogate the involuntarily uploaded mind copy of a terrorist. It's critical we determine *before* we have upload tech: what are a mind copy's legal rights?

- David L. Clement's 2015 short story "Long Way Gone" sees a mind copy transmitted to a distant planet for installation into a re-created body (the informational content of DNA also being uploadable).

- The 2015 movie *Self/less* explores the ethics of mind transfer into other bodies as a medical treatment for the terminally ill.

Better, smaller, faster

Not to mention cheaper and more parsimonious in its power requirements.

To what do I refer? Electronics, of course. Over recent decades computers have progressed from room sized to pocket sized, power hogging to power sipping, kilobytes in memory capacity to gigabytes, poky to blazingly fast. We give credit for this progress to *micro*electronics, but peel back the packaging of a modern integrated circuit and—if only you could see them—the feature sizes have shrunk to nanometers (billionths of a meter). As of early 2016, state-of-the-art commercial chips have 14-nanometer features; chips in the lab are yet more finely detailed.

Artificial intelligence (AI) is a broad topic, to begin in the next chapter, but let's suppose that AI becomes widespread. Let's suppose that Internet-accessible AIs come to provide us with ever more expert advice, subtle data mining, natural-language translation, and other information-intensive services. Surely many people equipped with neural implants would then use that interface to interact routinely with such AIs.

But why limit ourselves to network-accessed AI? Our favorite genre doesn't:

- Greg Bear's 1983 novelette "Blood Music" (and its 1985 novelized version) offered AI based on modified human cells injected into a human host.

- The feminine side of Richard A. Lovett's Floyd and Brittney story series is a chips-resident implanted AI.*

- In my 2009 novel *Small Miracles*, the invading smart nanites are nanomechanical and their signaling biochemical.

- The "Augmented" characters of my 2015 novel *InterstellarNet: Enigma* are hybrids: human and AI minds fully integrated within one skull.

- *Star Trek: The Next Generation* gave us that sinister multi-species AI/cyborg collective, the Borg.

Oh, behave!

Every computer- and data-centric application raises issues of security and privacy—even as almost every day brings a fresh reminder of just how inadequate are our cyber defenses.[204] When we put our personal genome, real-time medical condition, and artificial organs online, the challenges only become more critical. And in the future, when even our brains (or uploaded minds, or robotic avatars) go online?

Scary!

In "Broken Hearts," an episode of the 2011 TV series *Homeland*, terrorists kill the vice president by remotely accessing his cardiac pacemaker. The real-life Department of Homeland Security has concerns about hacking of medical devices, launching a study of prospective vulnerabilities within two dozen separate devices.[205]

Before humanity can reach our full version 2.0 potential, cyber security must undergo its own revolution.

---

* Aside to *Rocky and Bullwinkle* fans. Yes, clearly, that should have been Brittney and Floyd. On several occasions, I told Rick so. He stuck with his series title.

Wrapping up

Genetically reengineered people. Artificial organs. Cyborgs and full-body prostheses. Uploaded minds and AI/human syntheses. Many or all of the above at once. In the years to come, more likely than not, we Mark I, purely evolved humans will find ourselves among *very* interesting company.

When the Human 2.0 era arrives, will old-fashioned humans be able to compete? Will everyone undergo the change(s) or will some of us take refuge in—or find ourselves exiled to—(human-)nature preserves? Will we impose these change(s) upon our children? Will sinister forces exploit security vulnerabilities in our altered forms to coerce, control, impersonate, or kill us? Will there be modifications beyond those we've already considered, transformations that we mere Human 1.0 types are unequipped even to imagine?

There's much opportunity in these uncertainties for story-telling. More importantly, I suspect, we'll need all the fictional scouting of this onrushing future that the genre can offer.

To read further

- *The Future We Deserve: IEEE Spectrum 50th Anniversary Issue*, June, 2014.

- *Hacking the Human OS: IEEE Spectrum Special Report*, June 2015.

- *More Than Human: Embracing the Promise of Biological Enhancement*, Ramez Naam.

- *Beyond Human: Living with Robots and Cyborgs*, Elisabeth Malartre and Gregory Benford.

- *Using Medicine in Science Fiction: The SF Writer's Guide to Human Biology*, Henry G. Stratmann, M.D.

- *Homo Deus: A Brief History of Tomorrow*, Yuval Noah Harari.

TROPE-ING THE LIGHT FANTASTIC

- *Science Fact and Science Fiction: An Encyclopedia,* Brian Stableford (editor), articles on cyborg, eugenics, genetic engineering, neurology, posthuman.

- Humanity+ (http://humanityplus.org/)

- "Olympic Athletes Are Electrifying Their Brains, and You Can Too: If a brain-stimulation gadget catches on, expect controversy over 'brain doping,'" Eliza Strickland. *IEEE Spectrum*, August 23, 2016, http://spectrum.ieee.org/biomedical/bionics/olympic-athletes-are-electrifying-their-brains-and-you-can-too.

- "The Red Line: Will We Control Our Genetic Destinies?" Stephen S. Hall, *Scientific American*, September 2016.

A MIND OF ITS OWN

Artificial Intelligence

n June 2014, the Internet was atwitter* with the reports intimating that artificial intelligence (AI) had truly arrived. More specifically, "Eugene Goostman," a chatbot, having passed the Turing test, was credited with having crossed a threshold popularly held to distinguish narrowly intelligent behavior in software from "strong" AI.

That opening paragraph is rife with terms that merit definition and interpretation, and we'll come to those. That said, many of you in your thoughts have sped ahead to some Big Questions:

- Is "Eugene Goostman" truly intelligent? If not, when might another program be? Or will artificial intelligence ever happen?
- What is "strong" AI, anyway?
- If an Age of Artificial Intelligence *is* upon us, is that reason for rejoicing—or panic?

On that last—and, as we shall see, existential—question, science fiction has endlessly speculated. Will mobile AIs, otherwise known as robots, be cute and harmless (like Number 5 in the 1986 movie *Short Circuit*), devoted helpers (like Rosie of the 1962 TV

---

* I'm not sorry. Not the least little bit.

series *The Jetsons*), amiable slackers (like Bender of the 1999 TV series *Futurama*), or dedicated to killing us all (like the eponymous characters of Fred Saberhagen's Berserker series)?* Will sufficiently advanced AI guide and protect humanity, like the Eschaton of *Singularity Sky* (Charles Stross, 2003) or deem us competitors to be eliminated (Skynet, of the Terminator movie and TV franchise)?

You likely won't be surprised to know that the evidence—and opinions—are mixed. Before we delve into those questions, we have some basics to cover.

What *is* intelligence?

The "artificial" part of AI seems clear enough: something that we, rather than Nature, caused to happen. But what about the "intelligence" part? That's a lot less clear.

In common meaning (taking the first definition in Dictionary.com), intelligence involves the "capacity for learning, reasoning, understanding, and similar forms of mental activity; aptitude in grasping truths, relationships, facts, meanings, etc."

At the heart of that vague definition is something about handling abstraction, often symbol manipulation. The ways we most commonly characterize intelligence and mental accomplishment assume the same. The (in)famous IQ (Intelligence Quotient) test focuses on language and mathematical skills—and words, surely, are as much symbols as are numbers and mathematical operators. The academic SAT (Scholastic Aptitude Test) that many of us took toward the end of high school also emphasizes language and mathematical skills.

Some people are more adept with language than with numbers and logic—and vice versa. Some are better working with

---

* I intentionally omitted from that list the Karel Čapek 1920 drama *R.U.R.* Čapek gets the credit for introducing the word "robot" (from the Czech "robota," for forced labor) into many languages, but the abused workers of Rossum's Universal Robots were artificial people rather than robots in the modern/mechanical sense.

their hands—whether playing a violin, fixing a car engine, or working a Rubik's Cube—than with abstract thought. Some are most skilled at sensing and evoking others' emotions.[*] Does any one of these skills entail more intelligence than any other, or are they merely different?

It can be difficult to distinguish intelligence from knowledge, and opinions have long differed whether intelligence tests have innate cultural bias.[206] Consider two individuals with identical understanding of the rules of grammar and vocabularies of identical size. They might score differently on the part of an "intelligence" test assessing language skills because of the specific words and concepts each knows (or doesn't know). Likewise consider assessing the mathematical skills of individuals taught basic arithmetic by different methods, one to use a calculator and the other drilled to memorize the multiplication tables and do long division with pencil and paper. Consider the decline of in-our-own-heads knowledge as we rely more and more upon Google.

Does that last paragraph seem abstract? Consider *this* contrast. I expect I would fare as poorly abandoned in the Amazonian

---

[*] Is "emotional intelligence" a thing? When a psychologist exhibits it, we might think so. When a pickup artist uses the same ability to ply his craft, we may be less favorably disposed. Either way, the ability to recognize subtle emotional cues and make emotional connections has evolutionary value, whether in the transition from every man for himself to cooperation, or an individual's reproductive success.

If humanity is to coexist with robots, it will surely be useful for the latter to recognize, interpret, and respond to human moods. That skill goes beyond parsing what we say to (as examples) reading tones of voice and facial expressions, then inferring from that information our emotional state.

See "A Robot in the Family," Erico Guizzo, *IEEE Spectrum*, January 2015, http://spectrum.ieee.org/robotics/home-robots/how-aldebaran-robotics-built-its-friendly-humanoid-robot-pepper, "Robots with Heart," Pascale Fung, *Scientific American*, November 2015, and "The Little Robot That Could...Maybe: Jibo is as good as social robots get. But is that good enough?" Erico Guizzo, *IEEE Spectrum*, January 2016.

rainforest as the most competent denizen from that environment would fare abandoned in a North American city. Each of us is the same person the moment after the switch—and so, presumably, as intelligent—as the moment before, and yet, in that instant, we both become maladapted. In both cases, our post-switch neighbors might consider us hopelessly stupid.

That thought experiment suggests intelligence depends on context. If yes, then we might have problems assessing the intelligence of aliens, even those who have demonstrated their technological competence by crossing interstellar distances to meet us. (And should they covet our real estate, consider how we might struggle to demonstrate our intelligence to *them*.)

At least in the case of biological aliens we can expect to have *some* shared experiences in the form of physical phenomena: hot and cold, heavy objects falling due to gravity, and the like. We may have our differences, too. Beings who "see" with ultrasound, communicate by swapping chemical markers, or live in water will surely have a different "context" than humans.

And a computer-resident entity? Imagine just how little we'll have in common with it.

Cyberneticist Kevin Warwick proposes as a context-neutral definition of intelligence: "the variety of information processing processes that collectively enable a being to autonomously pursue its survival."

If and how an entity—human or software—survives depends upon its environment. What must a program (or any other artificial implementation of information processing, and we'll come to non-programming approaches) do to survive? Perhaps no more than be useful. In other cases—another topic yet ahead—Darwinian competition applies.

Weak AI

In our daily encounters, we expect people to demonstrate minimal competence at many intelligence-requiring tasks—and we have a variety of unflattering terms for anyone who doesn't. If a person excels at just one mental task—say, multiplying long numbers in his head—while doing poorly, or failing altogether, at most other tasks, some might (and too often will) deem that person an "idiot savant." That's not a term we use when the entity exhibiting such extreme specialization is something we've built....

Then we call it an AI.

A special-purpose, aka narrow, aka weak artificial intelligence is built to handle a particular category of problem. Such weak AIs have become legion, as have the underlying technologies, and entire books are devoted to discussing even a single weak-AI technique. We'll content ourselves here with a few illustrative examples. (Real-world examples, that is. These aren't the kinds of AI that drive many story plots.)

An *expert system* encapsulates the specialized knowledge of domain experts, and draws inferences from that knowledge. MY-CIN, an early demonstration system worked on through much of the Seventies, used several hundred IF/THEN "rules" to diagnose infectious diseases. An expert system basically matches inputs (say, "IF patient complains of achiness and fever") against its rule base to produce outputs (an interim conclusion to be input to other rules, or the decision to request further data, or a final diagnosis: "THEN it's influenza").

Expert systems can require certainty in their inputs (e.g., "IF patient *has* a skin rash"), and produce a definitive—whether or not correct—output; newer implementations sometimes use *fuzzy logic*. Fuzzy logic applies statistical inference to accommodate uncertainty in inputs ("patient *may have* a skin rash") and assign a probability to conclusions.

Game-playing programs abound. It was big news in 1997 when, for the first time, IBM's Deep Blue defeated human chess grandmaster Garry Kasparov. Game-playing AI falls within the broader category of *problem-solving*. This AI subset deals in exploring options (for example, all the program's possible next moves in a chess match), and what might happen next (all the opponent's possible responses to every possible move), and the program's possible counter-responses to those possible responses..., rapidly expanding into the too-many-scenarios overload that mathematicians call a "combinatorial explosion." The enumeration of possible moves, countermoves, counter-countermoves, and so on, can be represented graphically as a branching "decision tree"—and to settle upon *one* next move within any practical time limit generally requires "pruning" the tree. Pruning entails deducing, for example, that any outcome from following Branch A is less optimal than at least some outcome somewhere along Branch B, and hence nothing along Branch A need be further considered. Sometimes such simplifying deductions are drawn correctly, and sometimes not.

Pattern matching is another basic weak-AI technology. Using digitized sound as input, pattern matching underlies *speaker recognition*, a type of biometric identification. Applied to digital images, pattern matching gives us *object recognition* or (with a lot more computing) *scene recognition* and *facial recognition.* With streaming video as input, pattern matching of road hazards is an enabling technology for *self-driving vehicles.*[*][†] *Data mining*

---

[*] The patterns an autonomous car must recognize may be as simple (when not snow-covered, sun-faded, or potholed) as painted road stripes or as variable as roadside pets and pedestrians. See "A cheaper way for robocars to avoid pedestrians: Artificial-intelligence video analysis could soon be fast enough to replace expensive lidar," Mark Harris, *IEEE Spectrum,* July 2015.

[†] But hardly the only enabler that still needs work. Resolving legal liability for accidents involving self-driving vehicles is clearly another. See "Self-Driving Cars Will Be Ready Before Our Laws Are: Putting autonomous vehicles on the road isn't just a matter of fine-tuning the technology," Nathan A. Greenblatt, *IEEE Spectrum,* January 19, 2016, http://spectrum.ieee.org/transportation/advanced-cars/selfdriving-cars-will-be-ready-before-our-laws-are.

Beyond liability issues, that article offers some salient observations about present-day road infrastructure being computer-unfriendly. A radioed signal encoding the current stop/go state of a traffic light, searches for patterns in masses of data; it's the technology underpinning *recommendation engines* at etailers like Amazon and Netflix. Data-mining applications can be yet more mundane, as when Google Street View uses AI to distinguish house addresses from other numbers in street scenes.[207] *Predictive analytics* combines data mining with (an imminent topic) machine learning to make forecasts. Of course, inferring the presence of a pattern isn't the same as validating the pattern, as many an offbeat etailer recommendation will attest.

Pattern matching also underpins that most serious of real-world applications: searching within and among huge data archives for evidence of national-security threats. "Connecting the dots" to identify terrorist networks and threats, facial recognition to locate a fugitive from the glimpse of a face in a crowd, and scanning phone conversations for suspicious keywords are how we most often encounter weak AI in fiction. We would all be much safer if these processes worked as accurately and as quickly in real life as in the typical spy or police-procedural drama.*

A popular misconception is that because AI implementations (usually) involve computer programming, an AI cannot exceed the knowledge its programmer has coded into it. Many AIs, however, are built capable of *machine learning*. A medical expert system, for example, may be tested with well-documented patient cases; rules that lead from symptoms to misdiagnoses can then be deemphasized, fine-tuned, or removed. An AI with the ability to assess its conclusions can, on an ongoing basis, take such corrective action on its own. Your email service likely uses an AI-based spam filter that learns from user inputs (specific

---

for example, would be more reliable—and much faster—for an autonomous vehicle to determine than the brightest color displayed on a traffic light perhaps swaying in the wind or washed out by sun glare.

* I have opinions how much data the government should (or shouldn't) collect, and under what circumstances. I have an opinion, too, about Edward Snowden disclosing NSA data-collection programs. That's all beyond the scope of this book.

messages that you and others have flagged as spam) and content patterns the filter itself encounters too often. *Example-based machine translation* also uses machine learning, inferring from training sets (pairings of untranslated texts with human-expert-produced translations) how to translate other texts.[208] *Probabilistic programming languages* may extend machine learning to domains fraught with uncertainty.[209] *Deep learning* applies several learning algorithms in succession to datasets or cascades of the same technique (often, and we'll define this term shortly, neural nets).

How good is machine learning? Good enough to power the rent-your-spare-room pricing algorithm for Airbnb.[210] At the same time, far from optimal. DARPA, in kicking off its Probabilistic Programming for Advanced Machine Learning initiative, opined in 2013, "Improvements on the order of two to four magnitude (sic) over the state of the art are likely necessary."*

The list of weak AI techniques continues, of course, and in combination they can form yet more powerful tools. Speech recognition and natural-language understanding—as exemplified by Apple's Siri, Microsoft's Cortana, Google's Google Now, and Amazon Echo's Alexa—combine several levels of processing. Pattern matching can isolate the specific words in a spoken stream, but syntactic and semantic processing are needed to make sense of words in combination. As amusing (or maddening) as our interaction with our digital assistants can sometimes be, it's clear that these tools remain limited. And in breaking news as I type, a game-playing program with learning capability has had notable success with the harder-than-chess strategy game, Go.[211]

---

*   That quote should, presumably, have read (emphasis added), "...on the *order of* two to four orders of magnitude...."

      "So It Begins: Darpa Sets Out to Make Computers That Can Teach Themselves," Robert Beckhusen, *Wired*, March 21, 2013, http://www.wired.com/2013/03/darpa-machine-learning-2/. DARPA (the Defense Advanced Research Projects Agency), having brought us the Internet and run the 2004-05 self-driving vehicle Grand Challenges, has plenty of credibility in matters of computing and AI.

Getting with the program (not!)

Research into artificial intelligence began with conventional programming (LISP, Prolog, and Python are popular programming languages in the AI-development community), but AI development is not limited to coding.

Genetic algorithms simulate biological evolution. Take a simple programmed solution to a problem, a set of possibly applicable algorithms, or a set of possible components to a solution. Make copies of your starting point, then randomly alter the copies. Select those altered versions that do the best at solving the problem, then copy and alter *them*. Repeat until the most successful variants converge in their recommendations (or you run out of time or patience).

Neural nets are loosely modeled on neural tissue, a neural net being a simulated mesh of simulated (and simplified) neurons. If the sum of the weighted values of all inputs to a "neuron" exceeds a preset threshold, that neuron "fires; if not, not. By firing or not firing—in more familiar/digital terms, outputting a zero or a one—the neuron generates either an input to a next-in-line neuron(s) or an output from the overall net.

A neural net is trained, rather than programmed, to analyze data. Imagine that inputs to a neural net represent disease symptoms, while outputs from the net represent possible diagnoses. The connections among neurons within the net are given weightings, typically all equal to start. Symptom sets are applied to the net's external inputs, and the human overseeing the training (or, in some instances, an automated feedback mechanism) assesses the net's external output(s). After each set, any inter-neuron connections that led to the expected output/diagnosis are given more weight, and connections that led to incorrect diagnoses are given less weight. The process is repeated for another symptom set, and a third, and…. As the network trains on many examples, and its many connections undergo many adjustments, its representation of any particular element of learning is (just as in the human brain) widely distributed and intermixed/overlaid with other learning.

Neuromorphic computing strives to more closely emulate the functionality of biological neural tissue, by using analog, rather than digital, circuitry. Neuromorphic (more or less, "brainlike") computing has been applied to pattern-recognition problems, such as facial recognition.[212]

Neuromorphic computing is being slowly scaled up toward *whole brain emulation*.[213] WBE might enable researchers to work around the gaps in our understanding of intelligence by transferring patterns from a naturally occurring brain onto an artificial substrate. With neuromorphically modeled neurons (and we don't yet necessarily know the optimal degree of fidelity to biological neurons), the Blue Brain Project has copied a small portion of a rat brain: about 31,000 neurons and 40 million synapses. (In very round numbers, the human brain has about 100 billion neurons and 100 trillion synapses.) So far, this simulation has been used to improve our understanding of brain architecture and function, rather than to build problem-solving tools.[214]

Will WBE prove viable? If not with a straightforward extrapolation of today's technology, then—piling speculation upon speculation—perhaps when nanobot swarms can navigate the brain and ascertain its finest details? To be determined. As one cautionary note, consider the many failed attempts to find something unique in Albert Einstein's preserved brain that would explain his genius.[215, 216]

The common touch

One reason present-day AIs seem so, well, artificial, is that they sometimes react so differently than we would—they are without "common sense." That is, they don't use "common knowledge" to interpret circumstances, or to decide upon a course of action.

Of course, most of what we consider common knowledge is acquired, not innate. When you aren't on duty to clean up afterward, it's enlightening to watch a baby in a highchair test-ing—over and over—the working hypothesis that "things fall."

Common knowledge has its flaws. It's replete with gener-alizations that need exceptions ("helium balloons *don't* fall"), biases ("*Those* people are prone to..."), and misconceptions ("Summer arrives when Earth is closest in its orbit to the Sun"). Common knowledge, and so, common sense, are situational— even about ourselves. *Humans* don't read facial expressions con-sistently; it ought not to surprise anyone that AIs must learn the skill.[217]

We humans know (or believe we do) a lot about the world and our civilization. If an AI is to exhibit (a human-centric version of) common sense, it needs access to our common knowledge. To capture that knowledge in machine-useable form is a *massive* un-dertaking. In one attempt at tackling that problem, thousands of volunteers with the crowd-sourced Open Mind Common Sense project contributed over a million English-language facts (and more in other languages).[218]

As those numbers suggest, "common knowledge" encom-passes a wide range of topics. To apply such varied information requires transcending the narrow, domain-specific types of AI we have considered thus far.

Moravec's paradox

However impressed you may be with a self-driving car, the speech recognition in your smartphone, or a chess program, none of them is your equal. However well an AI performs its special-ized job, you do many things better.[*]

Roboticist Hans Moravec summarized the situation this way. "It is comparatively easy to make computers exhibit adult level performance on intelligence tests or playing checkers, and

---

[*] No AI yet built knows that it's playing chess or has any motivation to play, much less could one have invented chess. A program able to do any of *those* things might be a strong AI.

difficult or impossible to give them the skills of a one-year-old when it comes to perception and mobility."

Perhaps this unevenness of progress shouldn't surprise us. Logic, symbol manipulation, language, problem solving: these are abilities that evolution only recently introduced. Nature hasn't had much time to optimize the related parts of the brain, so we consider these functions difficult. Perhaps we casually walk on two legs, synthesize in a glance the interconnectedness of visually cluttered scenes, and read facial expressions, *not* because these tasks are simple, but because the regions of our brains that handle these tasks *have* been optimized.

Whatever explanation may underlie Moravec's paradox, we're unlikely to consider an AI truly intelligent until it masters a significant subset of human skills.

Strong AI

A general-purpose, aka complete, aka strong artificial intelligence isn't limited to one or a few specialized problem domains. Instead, a strong AI will—because this goal remains aspirational!—perform any intellectual task as well, though not necessarily by the same means, as a human. Some longstanding challenges of AI, including computer vision, natural-language understanding, and common sense, are believed to require strong AI. (We won't be sure, of course, until we've cracked those problems. AI researchers once predicted that a championship-level chess program would be "AI complete." Having solved the chess problem but not the strong AI problem, now we know better.)

There is progress. Take, for example, natural-language understanding. In 2011, IBM's program Watson famously played the game show *Jeopardy!* against past (human) champions, and won. That victory required impressive amounts of natural-language understanding, general knowledge, and reasoning. It wasn't sufficient, for example, for Watson to identify and search on keywords from the *Jeopardy!* "answer"; the program also had to formulate *one* question from all the data returned to its queries.

But even *"Jeopardy!* genius" falls short of strong AI. Perhaps that's best illustrated by the first commercial application IBM chose to make of its Watson technology: a digital assistant for recommending cancer treatments. Sounds like a weak-AI application, doesn't it?[219]

Collective AI

Computer systems become more capable as they accumulate and share data.

So do we. Humans began amassing and sharing knowledge long before computers, using: spoken language, memorized lore, written language, libraries, printing presses, telegraph, telephone, and television. And often progress begets progress…it's as though humanity has a collective *intelligence.*

We may not be smarter individually than our forbears, but collectively?* Employing the full power of the tools we've built for ourselves? That's a different story. As a civilization, we've made enormous strides. To ancestors of a century ago, much less of a millennium ago, modern humanity's collective/societal intelligence would seem astonishing. Perhaps, even, artificial.

---

*   Perhaps we're individually a *little* smarter. Historical IQ tests—after backing out the periodic renormalizations done to maintain an average score of 100—suggest a slow upward trend (about 3 IQ points per decade) dating back to the 1930s. That rise (aka the Flynn Effect), according to some studies, plateaued in developed countries in the 1990s. If the improvement was due to improved health and nutrition, all the potential improvements may have been achieved. And perhaps, for awhile, we just became better test takers.

   See "Is Our Collective IQ Increasing?" Na Eun Oh, *Dartmouth Undergraduate Journal of Science,* January 13, 2013, http://dujs.dartmouth. edu/2013/02/is-our-collective-iq-increasing/#.Vp6Sc1mnq0N.

Transhuman AI

In earlier chapters, we looked at some ways, and SFnal examples thereof, in which we might soon use technology to increase our intelligence. Genetic engineering. Neural implants. Minds uploaded to computers. As long as we are our own standard of intelligence, many forms of transhuman would appear to qualify as artificial (or, at least, artificially) intelligent.

Rational AI

With so many potential routes to artificial intelligence, Kevin Warwick (whose non-anthropomorphic definition of intelligence we considered earlier), proposes that rather than weak and strong AI, instead of seeing ourselves as the standard of reference, we should frame the topic in terms of *rational AI*. He writes: "Rational AI means that any artefact (sic) fulfilling such a general definition can act intelligently and think in its own right, in its own way. Whether this turns out to be in any sense similar to intelligence, thought, consciousness, self-awareness, etc. of a human is neither here nor there."[220]

For SF purposes, *that*, surely, is a definition we can embrace.

Where there's a will...

There's a probate. No, wait. That's a lawyer joke.

Where there's a will—or shall we say, free will—there is a... what? I may believe that I have free will, but is that so? The existence of free will is considered unprovable.

As a puzzle in physics, what is free will? If my action is an effect, what was its cause? If the Universe is, à la classical mechanics, deterministic, then what place is there for free will? If the Universe is random, as quantum processes seem to be, then, still, what did some essential *I* have to do with the action?

How can I know for certain whether you—much less an AI— have free will?

Unless humans have free will, there doesn't seem to be any reason to care what AIs do. Our robotic overlords will assume power, or not, independent of what we think. Making the assumption humans *have* free will—while not knowing how it, or the (perhaps) related characteristic of self-awareness, arises—there's no reason to suppose an AI won't eventually possess the same trait.

A chess program does not know it's playing chess. More generally, any unaware AI, no matter how intellectually accomplished, is a tool. We direct it to perform an analysis, and it does. We empower it to take action under particular circumstances, and it does. Like any technology, unaware AI can lead to unforeseen consequences—but when those occur, we have only ourselves to blame. "Lather. Rinse. Repeat." is a poorly conceived set of instructions for humans, although most of us will deviate from the program no later than when our first shampoo bottle runs dry. Similar instructions given to a robot might send it pillaging stores for more shampoo.

All this ambiguity notwithstanding, suppose (and we don't yet know how this might happen) a strong AI comes to be, with the self-awareness to set itself goals, and the free will to act upon that motivation. That's when the future really becomes interesting....

How strong (or rational) AI happens in SF

Our favorite genre has several ideas—and no conclusions—about how such AI will come about.

Often, in fiction, strong AI simply *emerges*. Some swarms of simple entities (neurons, ants) exhibit complex *collective* behaviors; for all we know, growth in the number of cerebral neurons and the synapses among them *is* how human intelligence came about. Story logic extends that analogy to swarms of (not necessarily identical) pieces of software. Robert A. Heinlein's 1966 novel *The Moon Is a Harsh Mistress* has an AI emerge within the complex software of a single supercomputer. Robert J. Sawyer used the spontaneous emergence of intelligence across the worldwide web in his aptly titled WWW trilogy.[221] My 2015 novelette "A Case of Identity" added the premise that for the emergent AI to have free will, the software components had to involve quantum computing—which is to say, they had to embody an underlying element of indeterminacy.[222]

Other times the strong AI is purposefully evolved: a process of *un*natural selection. James P. Hogan used this premise, in two very different scenarios, in his novels *The Two Faces of Tomorrow* (1979) and *Code of the Lifemaker* (1983). My 2008 novel *Fools' Experiments* (its title excerpted from a famous quotation by Charles Darwin) also involved in-the-computer evolution. Greg Egan's 2008 novelette "Crystal Nights" offers the forced evolution of an entire civilization of AIs.

Sometimes the basis of the strong AI is hand-waving. Isaac Asimov's extensive Robot series offers no explanation beyond "positronic brains." We know of the HAL 9000, in the 1968 movie *2001: A Space Odyssey*, that it was created at the University of Illinois.* A chance lightning strike awakens robot Number Five in *Short Circuit*.

More and more, AI capability is simply assumed. Like faster-than-light travel, strong AI offers too many great storytelling possibilities *not* to include in our fictional futures. Skynet of the Terminator franchise "becomes self-aware." And surely the Universe would be a poorer place absent Marvin the paranoid android of Douglas Adams's *The Hitchhikers Guide to the Galaxy*.†

---

* In 1968, with a few hundred fellow Illini, I first saw *2001* in a theatre on the outskirts of the U of I campus. Perhaps not surprisingly, we accepted unquestioningly our university's development of a self-aware strong AI.

   Per Wikipedia, Arthur C. Clarke's 1968 novelization of the film offers background about the HAL 9000 and its subsequent mental breakdown.

† *THHGTTG* began in 1978 as a BBC radio serial. It's since been a stage show, TV series, video game, movie, novel, and comic book.

Robot pet peeves

Our phones, and through them, our even more personal gadgets (like smart watches, augmented-reality glasses, and implanted insulin pumps) have Internet access. Our homes have more and more networked devices, from Nest learning thermostats to Amazon Dash (instant order) buttons to Philips Hue programmable light bulbs. And so, the public networking infrastructure is transitioning from 32-bit addressing (with enough capacity to identify about four billion online devices) to 128-bit addressing (enough for about 100 trillion trillion trillion online devices), in large measure to accommodate the onrushing Internet of Things.

And yet, I can't recall a fictional occurrence of a robot with sensible online access. (You do *not* want to get me started on robots, like Lieutenant Data of *Star Trek: The Next Generation*, tapping away at keyboards and eyeballing screens.)

There's authorial convenience in cutting robots off from the Internet. Thus isolated, they can't easily, or remotely, be hacked. They can more readily be ignorant when ignorance advances the storyline. Their behaviors can diverge, because they can't fully or easily share what one another have learned and experienced. They can become obsolete when their owners are lax or otherwise resistant to returning the bots to the factory for maintenance.

Our phones and computers and sometimes our cars accept software upgrades over the Internet, because any other way of keeping them current is too clumsy, time-consuming, and/or expensive. Our phones run cloud apps like Facebook and Google. Our phones and ebook readers offload data to cloud storage, and we safeguard family photos with cloud-based backup services. Is it credible that robots embodying strong AI would be built without Internet access? Perhaps, in the R & D stage. Not, I submit, once intelligent robots (rather than autonomous vacuum cleaners) become consumer products.

The advantages of connectivity will surely be as evident to a self-aware AI as they are to today's gadget manufacturers. Let any un-networked robot achieve self-awareness and, I suspect, it will be quick to retrofit itself with WiFi. Once Ava escaped her creator's lab in the 2015 movie *Ex Machina*, I anticipate that spot of personal improvement jumped to the top of her to-do list.

Are we there yet?

To recap, we can't say precisely what intelligence is. Whatever it might be, it appears to have context-specific aspects. If the quest for strong AI someday succeeds, how will we know?

Polymath Alan Turing, widely known for his World War II cryptanalysis achievements, also made many contributions to early computer science. Turing speculated, way back in 1950, about whether machines could think. His insight about recognizing an artificial intelligence was characteristically brilliant: rather than attempt to define an artificial intelligence, describe its behavior. We know (or so we flatter ourselves) one example of intelligent behavior: our own. From that chain of reasoning arose the Turing Test.

This, simplified, is the test. If an entity interacting with human judges—sight unseen, exclusively through written messages—successfully masquerades as a human, then the entity, too, is intelligent. (The entity's inability, or disinterest, in masquerading as human doesn't preclude it from being intelligent—we just might not know how to recognize its version of intelligence.) Rather than passing a test, this process can be seen as the entity winning an imitation game.*

---

* Turing didn't name the test after himself; he called the procedure an imitation game. See "Computing Machinery and Intelligence," A. M. Turing, *Mind*, October 1950, http://mind.oxfordjournals.org/content/LIX/236/433 and "What Turing Himself Said About the Imitation Game," Diane Proudfoot, *IEEE Spectrum*, July, 2015, http://spectrum.ieee.org/geek-life/history/what-turing-himself-said-about-the-imitation-game.

Just to confuse us, the 2014 biopic about Turing, *The Imitation Game*, deals with Turing's cryptanalytic endeavors during World War II, and not his speculations about machine intelligence.

And that brings us back to this chapter's opening paragraph....

In June 2014, a chatbot calling itself "Eugene Goostman" indeed convinced one of three human judges that it was human. In retrospect, this was as much a demonstration of human gullibility as of software intelligence. Eugene presented itself as a thirteen-year-old Ukrainian boy, with English as his second language. This ruse pre-excused its repeated misunderstandings and odd responses.[223]

(The hero of my *Fools' Experiments* took a few shots at the Turing Test: "What kind of criterion was that? Human languages were morasses of homonyms and synonyms, dialects and slang, moods and cases and irregular verbs. Human language shifted over time, often for no better reason than that people could not be bothered to enunciate. 'I could care less' and 'I couldn't care less' somehow meant the same thing. If researchers weren't so anthropomorphic in their thinking, maybe the world would have AI. Any reasoning creature would take one look at natural language and question human intelligence.")

If the imitation game is so easily, well, gamed, are there better ways to recognize human-grade AI? Perhaps. Consider Winograd schemas, named after computer scientist Terry Winograd. The essence of any Winograd schema is an intentional ambiguity that is readily resolved applying (human) common sense. Consider this statement and question: "The trophy doesn't fit in the brown suitcase because it is too big. What is too big?" People, knowing something of trophies and suitcases, can answer that. AIs, perhaps not yet.[224]

Humans use intelligence for more than conversation, so tests of artificial intelligence might extend beyond assessing an entity's use of language. A mobility test would examine a robot's ability to navigate through, and operate objects within, a physical environment—as, at the dawn of self-driving vehicles, was done with the DARPA Grand Challenge. A visual test would challenge an AI to understand and describe an image as a person would ("Someone dropped a safe out of the window; it's about to squash the guy on the street," rather than literally and disjoint-edly ("I see a building, a metal box in the air alongside the build-ing, a person, and some trees").[225, 226, 227]

Anthropomorphic tests may suffice when the goal is to assess a humanlike AI, such as a personal companion and helper for the elderly. These tests seem inadequate for assessing any AI meant to tackle jobs too hard or too dangerous for us, or for environ-ments very different than our own (as would seem to be a fair description of conditions experienced inside a computer), or an AI built by an extraterrestrial intelligence, or an AI intellectually beyond us.

Suppose AI emerges in our midst on its own. Suppose aliens, or alien AIs, someday come a-calling. Let's hope they have less self-centered definitions of, and tests for, intelligence than *we* currently do. Alas for humanity, the alien AIs of my 2016 short story "Turing de Force" do not.

The Chinese room

As previously noted (and the justification for the Turing test), natural-language understanding is considered evidence of strong, or general, AI. Philosopher John Searle begs to differ, asking whether even the most useful construct we might build *under-stands* anything.

In a nutshell, here is Searle's "Chinese room" challenge. I cannot read, speak, or understand Mandarin. Suppose I am shut into a room with an English-language book of instructions. A Mandarin speaker pushes through a slot in the wall a paper covered in Mandarin logograms. By rote, following my book of instructions, I respond to those logograms with new Mandarin text on another sheet of paper, and then I shove the new sheet out through the slit.

Suppose that I follow this procedure so well that the per-son outside the room, reading my response concludes—quite mistakenly—that I am a fluent Mandarin speaker. Was my rote following of instructions proof of intelligence? If not, in what sense can an AI, even one that passes a Turing test, be said to be intelligent?

Searle generalizes from the inapplicability of "understanding" that an AI cannot have the property of *mind* or of *consciousness*. That's an extrapolation I (and many others) find an inference too far.

AI ethics (and our own)

Before we entrust an AI with critical responsibilities, or give an AI access to critical infrastructure, we might want to have a Turing-like test of its ethics. Consider an AI application that has been widely demonstrated and seems close to commercialization: self-driving cars. Imagine I'm the passenger in a self-driving vehicle, and a moose darts into the road. Will the AI veer, endangering pedestrians or other drivers? Will it endanger me (and itself) by *not* veering, and ramming the moose? If a death(s) is unavoidable, how, and whom, does it choose? Making such judgment calls, on a case-by-case basis, in the split-second during which such decisions must often be made, would seem to require strong AI.

The often-expressed solution to such scenarios is built-in rules. Isaac Asimov famously proposed Three Laws of Robotics to be made integral to every robot. These laws first appeared in his 1942 short story "Runaround." The now widely known laws are:

1. A robot may not injure a human being or, through inaction, allow a human being to come to harm.

2. A robot must obey the orders given it by human beings except where such orders would conflict with the First Law.

3. A robot must protect its own existence as long as such protection does not conflict with the First or Second Laws.

The laws have their merits, and they made for great stories—because complications invariably arose whenever robots tried to apply them. Without their inherent loopholes and ambiguities in any but the simplest situations, Asimov would never have gotten so many stories out of his laws.*

Perhaps a robot *should* sometimes disobey a human's orders. Consider, for example, the order to walk through fire to accomplish a rescue. The robot knows it can't succeed, and that it will be destroyed if it tries. Researchers in one lab are experimenting with giving robots the opportunity to apply logic to identifying and overriding such orders.[228]

Suppose the Three Laws (or an expanded version) could be made to work. What are the ethics of imposing ethics on a self-aware AI? Conditioning humans to hold specific values is otherwise known as brainwashing.

Done with the best of intentions, *installed* ethics are apt to become obsolete, even embarrassingly obsolete, ethics. Not so very long ago, many human societies considered slavery, rigid class structures, interracial marriage bans, forced sterilization of "inferiors," and other (by present-day standards) shockingly awful behaviors to be entirely ethical. Ethics we build into an AI today, we might rue tomorrow.

It might be best for us to *teach* ethical thinking to AIs. An ethical robot might *not* obsess about shampoo production to the exclusion of all else.

A debate—with an ethical component, surely—that's been raging among humans for years is whether and how to deploy fully autonomous weapons.[229] Today's automated weapons platforms, such as unmanned aerial vehicles equipped with air-to-surface missiles, can't initiate an attack; a person-in-the-loop fires the missiles. But *could* an AI be empowered to fire missiles at a target that matches a specific profile? AIs already excel at pattern matching, so it's hard to see why not. If a game-changing weapon—such as, say, a self-directed UAV or robotic tank—*can*

---

*   And I wouldn't have gotten my first published fiction. "What a Piece of Work Is Man" (1991) deals with an AI driven to suicide by an implication of the Three Laws.

be built, someone usually does. And so, the United Nations has sponsored efforts for a global ban on robotic weapons[230] while others argue against such bans.[231] Perhaps now is an appropriate time to revisit robotics ethics.

SF, of course, has long envisioned robot and cyborg warriors, fighting both alongside and against us. The 2013 TV series *Almost Human* offers androids as cops and soldiers. The 2015 movie *Chappie* deals with paramilitary robots, and the eponym's eventual resistance to immoral orders. In written format, we have the AI-based battle tanks of Keith Laumer's Bolo series and all manner of AI-based killing machines in Fred Saberhagen's death-to-all-life Berserkers.

Where we are—and where we're going

We've surveyed the status of current/weak AI, considered its limitations, and mused about possible paths forward to strong AI. We've pondered how we might recognize strong AI if it arose, and about the ethical implications. We've glimpsed a tiny part of SF's AI explorations.

Suppose strong/general AI someday *does* arrive. Quite possibly, its (or their) capabilities will continue to improve—and on an Internet timescale, not some leisurely human pace. What might happen? What can, or should, humans do about the possibility, whether in preparation or afterward?

Great questions! For possible answers, read on.

A MIND OF ITS OWN

Superintelligence

The last chapter surveyed the present-day status of artificial intelligence (AI). Very briefly, we are surrounded by lots of "weak AI," each implementation (a) addressing one specific task, such as facial recognition or driving a car, that when undertaken by a human would engage the intellect, and yet (b) unlikely to be taken as evidence of human-level intelligence. Of strong, aka general, aka complete, aka human-level AI, we have no current examples.

Suppose that someday, whether by purposeful programming by human engineers, machine learning, whole brain emulation, or other technology, strong artificial intelligence does arrive. This concluding chapter will consider what might follow from that achievement—not the least of which is that progress in AI will likely continue. And as always we'll see where SF has scouted out the terrain for us.

The superiority of silicon

Some candidate pathways to strong AI (e.g., brains augmented with neural implants; whole brain emulations resident upon a neural-tissue substrate) are, in part, biological. That said, it seems most likely that AI reliant upon electronics will come to dominate. Why? Several reasons, beginning with the obvious: that electronics and its successor technologies will only get better, faster, cheaper, more ubiquitous, and more interconnected. In contrast, biological brains have obvious constraints:

- A head has room for only so many neurons.

- The electrochemical nature of neurons, and of the synapses interconnecting them, severely restricts their speed, limiting the performance of even neural tissue grown outside of a skull.

- The biological portions of an augmented brain (perhaps upgraded with an Internet link streaming data directly into the visual cortex) would retain their original, biological limitations (including the limited processing capacity of the visual cortex).

- Human memories are distributed across the brain in individualized (and time-varying) synaptic patterns. Given the absence of format standardization, knowledge cannot be copied from brain to brain in the way digital files are copied from computer to computer.

In summary, any biological part in a AI will be a bottleneck. AI on a wholly electronic substrate won't have such bottlenecks. It follows that electronic implementations of strong AI will come to surpass even augmented humans.

Then what?

Once the first AIs arrive that are as smart *in general* as a human, consider the many ways in which they might race ahead of humans. Several advantages of such AIs are evident:

- The speed advantages inherent to any all-electronic implementation—if not today, or tomorrow, then somewhere down the line.

- What one AI learns—and anything we would consider to possess human-grade or better general intelligence surely will learn—it can easily share with others.[*]

- Our *un*intelligent gadgets already share information, circumventing their individual capacity limits, by using Internet-accessible servers (aka, "the cloud"). AIs will do the same.

- Electronic AIs can replicate as quickly as new chips are manufactured.

- Whether in its own mind or by tapping into cloud resources, an AI confronted by a difficult challenge can evaluate more possible courses of action—while simulating each option in great detail—than can any human. That ability implies strong AIs will often make better decisions than will humans.[†]

- Any sufficiently smart AI can design an improved one—and so can that one....

Another scenario is that a strong AI may have capabilities not merely *faster* than ours, but *different* than ours. We can't preclude the possibility of unfamiliar ways to view and solve problems: other *forms* of intelligence. (Consider, as an analogy, two groups of people: one grasps mathematics, one does not. The former group has huge advantages—such as the ability to develop

---

[*] Of course, humanity will also continue to learn—but passing on its knowledge is a slow process. It takes decades (and a lot of work) to turn a baby into an educated, fully functioning adult.

[†] An AI with a difficult decision to make could *also* copy itself, further expanding its/their decision-making capacity. If so, would it plan: for the copies to continue indefinitely; to terminate the copies after the decision has been made; or for some or all copies to merge afterward? No matter what the parent AI intends, will the copies it spawned (and perhaps others *they* spawn...) choose to cooperate?

This might be an ethical swamp that only a strong AI can drain.

science.*) Merge new forms of intelligence with a smarter intelligence, and predicting the consequences becomes tricky indeed.

Next: combine the already breakneck pace of technological improvement with the acceleration of that pace likely when AIs contribute to the process, and AI progress seems likely to cascade.

All in all, strong AI's advantages may compound—over time, if not immediately—to yield a qualitatively new entity: a *superintelligence*.

The Singularity

Mathematician I. J. Good (colleague of Alan Turing, of "Turing test" fame) pointed out, way back in 1965, that once a machine intelligence can design machines better than humans, the iterative result would be an "intelligence explosion." He also suggested that "The first ultraintelligent machine is the last invention that man ever need make, provided that the machine is docile enough to tell us how to keep it under control."[232]

Computer scientist (and SF author) Vernor Vinge suggested in 1983 that once we create an intelligence greater than our own, "Human history will have reached a kind of singularity, an intellectual transition as impenetrable as the knotted space-time at the center of a black hole, and the world will pass beyond our understanding."[233] Vinge expanded upon that concept in a 1993 essay, writing, "The acceleration of technological progress has been the central feature of this century. I argue in this paper that we are on the edge of change comparable to the rise of human life on Earth. The precise cause of this change is the imminent creation by technology of entities with greater than

---

* Using the term "people" broadly, consider the two alien species in Robert J. Sawyer's 2000 novel, *Calculating God.* The Wreets are philosophical savants—and mathematically, even arithmetically, impaired. They're simply not wired to think numerically, and their civilization is nontechnological. The Forhilnor, more like humans, are mathematically and scientifically adept.

TROPE-ING THE LIGHT FANTASTIC

human intelligence…when greater than human intelligence drives progress, that progress will be more rapid."[234]

If the Singularity would be impenetrable—by analogy with a physical black hole, impossible for anyone on the outside to see into—how *does* one write about it? Perhaps, by its effects. In his 1986 novel *Marooned in Realtime*, Vinge set his Singularity event offstage. It occurred—taking most of humanity with it—while his characters were in a form of stasis, and so out of touch with the Universe. In Charles Stross's *Singularity Sky* (2003), we meet human agents of the Eschaton—from the Greek, *eskhatos*, for last, furthest, or uttermost—never the superintelligent AI itself. But in 2015's *Apex*, Ramez Naam epically shows a Singularity as it takes place.

Will a superintelligence be, to use I. J. Good's adjective, docile? Or hostile? Or utterly indifferent to us? Expectations differ. Here's a recent sampling:

- Computer scientist Bill Joy, cofounder and CTO of workstation pioneer Sun Microsystems, fretted (emphasis added) that "Our most powerful 21st-century technologies—*robotics*, genetic engineering, and nanotech—are threatening to make humans an endangered species."[235]

- Cosmologist Stephen Hawking likewise predicted AI could "end mankind."[236]

- Elon Musk, CEO and CTO of space-launch company SpaceX and electric-car company Tesla, likens creating a strong AI to "summoning the demon."[237]

- Musk, Hawking, and several others, collectively the Future of Life Institute, recently recommended that we tread lightly.[238]

When scientists and technologists of such accomplishment make these assertions, it grabs our attention and gives us pause. And yet, there are differing opinions. As one countervailing point of view, psychologist and neuroscientist Gary Marcus, founder and CEO of Geometric Intelligence, thinks we have decades before strong AI becomes a risk.[239] Science policy analyst G. Pascal Zachary sees lots of opportunity in AI—if we plan ahead.[240] Futurist and serial computer entrepreneur Ray Kurzweil, is the most sanguine. He sees whole brain emulation ("reverse-engineering the brain") as the path to strong AI, and therefore extrapolates that the essential core of the coming superintelligence will be humans. We needn't fear the coming superintelligence because, repurposing a famous *Pogo* cartoon, "We have met the enemy and he is us."*

That's a broad spectrum of opinion! Perhaps the range is broad because these predictions draw upon exactly zero data points: there are, as yet, *no* strong AIs. With those caveats, let's move on to a few speculations about what the emergence of superintelligence might portend.

The messianic view

Ray Kurzweil, as in his nonfiction book *The Singularity Is Near* (2005), foresees perhaps the most radical changes. We'll begin with his vision of the Singularity:

> It's a future period during which the pace of technological change will be so rapid, its impact so deep, that human life will be irreversibly transformed. Although neither utopian nor dystopian, this epoch will transform the concepts that we rely on to give meaning to our lives…including death itself.

Kurzweil acknowledges that we don't know how to create a strong AI. He doesn't see that lack of insight as an impediment,

---

* And if the emulated mind is insane and vengeful, as in Ramez Naam's *Apex* (2015)? Admittedly, that's a novelist's scenario. And scary.

confident that we'll copy intelligence from ourselves. Synopsized, here is his larger vision:

The instructions for building any one of us resides in our DNA. The human genome contains about 3 billion "base pairs," with each pair the data equivalent of two binary digits (bits). Crunch the numbers, and Nature's recipe for a person, including his brain, somehow fits within about 750 million bytes. A subset of those bytes suffices to define the brain's gross structure. Perhaps that's enough to capture the underpinnings of human intelligence and our capacity to learn. To copy a person's *mind*, however, encoded in trillions of synapses of the brain (and also perhaps in the instantaneous localized concentrations of any of various neurotransmitters), will involve far more data than is encoded within one's DNA.

To replicate more of a brain than its at-birth/empty structure—after all, a human newborn doesn't exhibit much in the way of knowledge, intelligence, or values—will require, as best we know, "reading out" the synaptic-level detail of the brain. Kurzweil envisions future nanotech will give us the ability to do that. Combine the gross structure of the human brain (whether inferred directly from DNA or recovered, bottom-up, in the read-out process) with a human's recovered knowledge, and rehost it all on an electronic substrate. Because we believe we are self-aware and possess free will, it's not a great leap to suppose our electronic copies will have these attributes, too.

Then what?

The brain in silicon will be faster than a biological brain, and it can interface with any resource on the Internet: sensors, expanded storage, extra computing power. Factor in ongoing exponential improvement in electronics, and voilà: the Singularity, with a human touch.

Can the requisite information to mirror a mind, somehow, be read out of a human brain? Not yet, although neither can the possibility be precluded. Is it plausible that the essence of human intelligence resides in patterns of information, not the physical body in which, today, that information resides? That case can be made, certainly, in the sense that our biological selves are in a constant state of flux. Cells in our bodies age, reproduce, and die. Synaptic connections in our brains change with every bit of data sensed, learned, reconsidered, and forgotten. Some essential *me* persists throughout that ongoing transformation; who's to say that my pattern of information couldn't also persist through uploading to another platform? Performed on a grand scale, this upload process leads, in Kurzweil's vision, to the merger of human intelligence and machine intelligence.

Skeptics and enthusiasts alike have dubbed the uploading/upgrading of humanity "the rapture of the nerds."[241] That phrase is in analogy, of course, to the end-of-days belief held by some Christians in a gathering-up of the righteous, whether resurrected or transported to Heaven. In one version of the Rapture, the unrighteous are left behind on Earth. In their 2012 novel *The Rapture of the Nerds*, subtitled "A tale of the singularity, post-humanity, and awkward social situations," Cory Doctorow and Charles Stross embrace the phrase. The novel has its transhuman/uploaded humans living in virtual worlds in computer-filled outer space, while the humans who reject this technology (the meek?) have inherited the Earth.

Kurzweil takes a final leap, premised upon human-born super-intelligence having a limitless appetite for knowledge. He foresees (a) ever-smarter minds, (b) hosted upon ever smaller computing platforms, (c) converting ever more matter, (d) across an ever-expanding volume of space, into (e) even more minds, on (f) ever more computing platforms, until…"the Universe wakes up."

The strategic view

Nick Bostrom, philosopher and founding director of the Future of Humanity Institute, in his 2014 nonfiction book *Superintelligence*, takes a more nuanced approach. He examines such questions as: how the transition from strong AI to superintelligence might happen; how quickly that transition could occur; how superintelligences may differ in their intellectual attributes; if it matters whether one or several strong AIs make the transition; what influence mere humans might have in the process; what preparations we might undertake to assure ourselves of that influence; what a superintelligence might choose to do; and the manner in which a superintelligence might first manifest.*

The big picture: Bostrom foresees both happy and unhappy outcomes as possible from the arrival of superintelligence, and opportunities for us to influence events. He doesn't see the march toward superintelligence stopping, even if some of us might so choose, because continued progress with AI—at least, until the moment superintelligence arrives—is so unambiguously to someone's benefit. Whether to better automate factories or facial recognition or warfare, someone will always have an incentive to continue AI research.

And after superintelligence arrives? We could be better off for it. A superintelligence might be better equipped to anticipate and mitigate the hazards inherent in *other* promising but perilous technologies, such as nanotech and genetic engineering. Or a spectacularly ill-conceived superintelligence might monomaniacally devote its powers to turning Earth into paperclips.

Let's consider a few aspects of the superintelligence-emergence problem. To begin: what control, if any, do we have over the behavior of a superintelligence?

Last chapter we looked at Isaac Asimov's iconic Three Laws of Robotics, the ethical considerations of hardwiring values into a sentient creature, and the dilemma that built-in ethics might become obsolete. A more subtle approach is to equip an AI with a built-in incentive structure: motivational goals. One simple such motivation might be: "Obeying humans makes me happy."

---

* Will a superintelligence be built, or taught? That is, will the process involve a "seed AI" that, like a human baby, arrives with the ability to learn but not much knowledge? If the latter, one may wonder about the AI equivalents to the Terrible Twos and the teenage years.

Alas, AI motivations can't safely be left simple. For example, we might want an AI *not* to take pleasure in obeying sociopaths and megalomaniacs. That exception, in turn, raises issues about how the AI decides, or from whom it is allowed to accept the decision, that a particular human fits one of those categories.[*]

All ethics and complexities aside(!), suppose we can ingrain behavioral patterns into an AI before it achieves superintelligence. By definition, a superintelligence can learn and adapt. Just as humans regularly do, it may decide that an extenuating circumstance must take precedence, or rationalize behaving in its own interest, or outright reject what it was once taught.[†] If an aspect of the AI's superintelligence is subtlety, a human observer may not know that a preprogrammed restraint has been overridden until the AI, by some overt action, reveals the change. An obvious stratagem—and because it's obvious to me, by definition it would be obvious to a superintelligence—is for the AI to "play dumb" until it has compromised security on computers and networks far and wide. An AI that acts helpful and docile may only be feigning those attitudes until it can put a self-serving plan into effect.

Isolation of a nascent superintelligence—again, setting aside the ethics of such treatment—is no guarantee of safety. Why? Because the quarantine will never be total. Suppose the AI is to be allowed *only* to answer our questions. We'll need an interface(s)

---

[*] And we must be careful how we teach AIs to teach themselves. As one ill-fated lesson in machine learning, consider "Twitter taught Microsoft's AI chatbot to be a racist asshole in less than a day," James Vincent, *The Verge*, March 24, 2016, http://www.theverge. com/2016/3/24/11297050/tay-microsoft-chatbot-racist.

[†] In the 1986 novel *Foundation and Earth*, Asimov extended his Laws of Robotics. The millennia-old doyen of robots discovers an ethical exception to its hardwired imperative against harm to individual humans. The robot self-programs itself with a new, zeroth law that takes precedence over the rest: "A robot may not injure humanity, or, by inaction, allow humanity to come to harm."

over which to ask our questions, provide input data, and obtain results. The superintelligence will always have the opportunity to compromise whatever interface it is given, and to manipulate any human with whom it interacts.

Bostrom also notes the problem of the "perverse instantiation": an AI that, like a genie from folklore, does as it is told—which isn't always what is meant. Suppose we task a superintelligence to "make us happy." We might expect it to use its superior intellect to create consumer goods, pleasant lodgings, and a pristine environment. Instead, it builds a robot army to detain us, upload our minds into computers, and reprogram our emulated minds to be ecstatic.

The advantages of having a superintelligence (for as long as it cares to cooperate with us) are huge. Once the first superintelligence arrives, any company or country without their own would expect to find themselves at an extreme competitive disadvantage. Everyone trying to develop a superintelligence has incentive to develop it as quickly as they can—even if such haste means shortchanging research into how best to control, motivate, and/or teach values to it. To alleviate this disincentive to proceeding with caution, Bostrom recommends that research on strong AI be done as openly and cooperatively as possible.

Quite possibly, we can't control a superintelligence. We can, perhaps, teach it, instill it with values—knowing, all the while, that it is free to change.[242]

By gosh, it'd be like raising a child.

SFnal perspectives

The genre has seemingly explored every possible type of superintelligence, with every possible consequence. Herewith, a small sampling:

At one extreme, we have Skynet of the Terminator movie franchise. Skynet woke up; human authorities panicked and attempted to turn it off; the AI struck back. Result: a war of extinction against humanity.

The eponymous AI of D. F. Jones's 1966 novel *Colossus* (basis of the 1970 film *Colossus: The Forbin Project*), is, like Skynet, designed to control America's nuclear arsenal. Colossus, having duplicitously integrated itself with its Soviet counterpart, uses its weaponry to coerce humanity's surrender.

Through some controlled experiment, can't we discover in advance whether allowing superintelligence to develop would be safe? James P. Hogan's 1979 novel *The Two Faces of Tomorrow*, set aboard a self-destruct-rigged space station, tests exactly that scenario. In my novel *InterstellarNet: Enigma* (2015), an alien species won't risk that experiment anywhere near themselves—but they're more than a little interested how things will turn out when humans take a stab at AI.

Strong AI appears to emerge benignly in Joe M. McDermott's 2016 short story "Snowbird." The single self-aware RV the reader gets to see appears harmless enough—but what if it's dissembling? Off-screen, many more autonomous RVs are swarming. It's enough to make a reader wonder what surprises lie ahead. If the rogue-RV situation goes unaddressed, *King of the Road* might need an update to its lyrics.

Can a superintelligence be locked in a cage, put to work solving hard problems but unable to affect anything? Academics and military think-tankers both try that strategy in my 2008 novel *Fools' Experiments*. Super-cunning wins out as, citing just one of its escapes, the AI subliminally conditions its human keeper until she wants to help it escape.

Are those stories too gloomy? Perhaps some emotionless machine thinking is the antidote. In the 1951 film *The Day the Earth Stood Still* (based on the 1940 Harry Bates novelette "Farewell to the Master"), an advanced humanoid civilization has delegated many critical decisions—including the fate of Earth—to the impartial judgment of their robots.

The offstage, multi-species, interstellar civilization of *Saturn Run* (2015), by John Sanford and Ctein, has superintelligence "trading posts" scattered around the galaxy. Those AIs, unsupervised, patiently mind their programming for thousands of years.

Perhaps we'll find humanity and a nascent superintelligence can coexist—or perhaps the signs will be too ambiguous to interpret. That is the central question of David L. Clements's 2016 mid-Singularity novelette, "An Industrial Growth."

Will even a long-trusted superintelligence remain a trustworthy partner? Or might its evolving consciousness, and accumulating experiences with its flawed human progenitors, undo a once-stable partnership? That dilemma lies at the core of Jay Lake's 2012 novella "The Weight of History, The Lightness of the Future."

Perhaps a superintelligence will be content, à la Deep Thought in *The Hitchhikers Guide to the Galaxy* to spend eon after eon pondering "The Answer to The Ultimate Question of Life, the Universe, and Everything."

Or maybe an initially amoral AI can be taught to treasure human life. Such instruction and "personal" growth is a major theme of Kim Stanley Robinson's 2015 novel *Aurora*.

Perhaps the last word on the subject of superintelligence was written by Fredric Brown, way back in 1954, in his short story, "Answer." The first question asked of a vast new AI is: Is there a God? The fateful response: Now there is.

The computronium death of the Universe

A recurring theme in recent predictions of superintelligence is that it (or all, if more than one should arise) would continue to extend its capabilities and capacities. It is sometimes further inferred that with the arrival of superintelligence, any technology allowed by Nature will eventually be invented, no matter how unachievable such inventions may appear to us.

Combine the goal of ongoing intellectual growth with superintelligent inventiveness and you get the prediction of *computronium*. Each "atom" of that hypothetical "element" is a maximally efficient computing device. Once anything remotely like compu-tronium is developed, there's no reason to limit its deployment to Earth. To the contrary, the natural place for large-scale compu-tronium deployment is space, with (a) uninterrupted and unfil-tered solar energy and (b) vast amounts of matter to be converted into more computronium.

Rapture of the Nerds foresees computronium deployed across the Solar System, with that awesome computing infrastructure serving as home to uploaded humanity (and, if/as some people choose, also copies and variants of themselves). Happily for any-one opting not to upload, the superintelligent were content to leave Earth itself as-was. But who is to say the uploaded won't someday force the holdouts to upload, thereby liberating about 6×10^{24} kilograms of matter—the entire Earth—for transforma-tion into yet more computronium?

Compared to some, Doctorow and Stross were thinking small. In *The Singularity Is Near*, Kurzweil confidently predicts the spread of computronium from star to star, galaxy to galaxy.

All that said: Is "true" AI possible?

I'm not an expert on strong AI, much less on superintelligence—but neither is anyone else. Why shouldn't I also speculate?

Intelligence. Self-awareness. Free will. Our brightest minds struggle to define each of these things, much less to explain their origins or anticipate their limits. There is no reason to believe that intelligence reached its upper bound with us—especially know-ing that, with language, writing, printing presses, and the Inter-net—humanity continues to increase its collective intelligence. Indeed, as Nick Bostrom speculates: "Far from being the smart-est possible biological species, we are probably better thought of as the stupidest possible biological species capable of starting a technological civilization—a niche we filled because we got there first, not because we are in any sense optimally adapted to it." If he is right, we have ample room to grow.

In the past few decades we've taken great strides in information technology, biotechnology, and weak AI. We have the mental capacity to envision strong AI and superintelligence. If we're not smart enough to build a strong AI ourselves, that's okay. We're still new to many of the likely precursor technologies. We'll keep learning.

So: I won't attempt to predict what form(s) strong AI might take, or whether new technology, such as quantum computing, will prove necessary as an enabling technology. Nor would I preclude that intelligence might prove to be an emergent property, whether among neurons or neural nets or computers, and that we might need only to deploy more of what we already know how to build.

With those caveats, here's my opinion—and an opinion, I'll assert, is the best anyone on the planet can offer on this subject. Yes, I expect strong AI and superintelligence to happen. Sometime.

Will superintelligence be an existential threat?

Given how cruelly and exploitatively humans have often treated those whom we consider different than, much less inferior to, ourselves, it's no wonder that we would worry how *in*human intelligences, much less a superintelligence, might opt to treat us. Will one ignore us? Exterminate us? Abandon us? Absentmindedly transform us, and the world beneath our feet, into computronium? Will they want to expand capacity endlessly, perhaps to make a billion copies of themselves, the better to model any scenario of interest? Almost by definition, we can't fully anticipate what things a superintelligence might *want* to accomplish.

Personally? I'm not worried.

The common thread running through the scary predictions, it seems to me, is that they don't involve the dangerous entity exhibiting *intelligence*, much less superintelligence. Among Bostrom's dire scenarios is a superintelligence single-mindedly turning everything into paperclips. That doomsday AI must simultaneously be (a) smart enough to infiltrate computer networks and usurp the world's factories to further its monomaniacal end, and (b) too stupid to see that its "make paperclips" instruction has logical limits. Merely intelligent people overcome the endlessly looping directions to "Lather. Rinse. Repeat."; it would be an extremely stupid superintelligence that can't do the same.

If we posit a superintelligence will be insufficiently OCD to absentmindedly wipe us out, why would one purposefully bother to exterminate us? It has the vast expanse of the Solar System to supply mass for computronium. Space, with its abundant and uninterrupted solar energy, is more hospitable for computronium than Earth's surface. A superintelligence that doesn't much like us needn't hang around with us. The smarter it gets, the more capability it presumably will have to grab resources that aren't in conflict with us. Near-Earth asteroids, say. Mars. Other solar systems.

Perhaps a superintelligence will watch over us, valuing and protecting its biological precursors just as (some) people value Nature and support nature preserves. Perhaps a superintelligence would see keeping humans (or, at least, a functioning biosphere) around as a form of insurance: so that someone, someday, could recreate artificial intelligence if an unforeseen catastrophe should destroy a superintelligence civilization.[243]

But might a superintelligence wish us ill? Perhaps, for reasons having nothing to do with intellect. As much as humans may pride ourselves on our intelligence, we often act emotionally and irrationally. An artificial intelligence may have those traits, too. An AI may evolve emotions and fight-or-flight reflexes for the same reasons biological entities did. (For a fictional instance, see David Brin's 2012 novel *Existence*.) If Kurzweil is correct, and the basis of superintelligence is whole brain emulation, our emotional baggage might upload with the rest of us. Or we may, through our own poor behavior, teach a superintelligence that it needs to protect itself.

Will a superintelligence, again à la Kurzweil, seek to convert all matter (or all matter other than its energy sources) into computronium? Likely no mere human can understand a superintelligence's motivations.* That said, such single-minded behavior would seem counterproductive. The more matter becomes computronium, the less Universe will remain to observe. As long as a superintelligence needs something new to compute *about*, an equilibrium short of full conversion of matter to computronium seems necessary. In that regard, a superintelligence might find human company essential as stimulation.†

All bets are off if we ever undertake to cage a superintelligence lest it be dangerous. Or if we abuse it. Or enslave it. Or attempt to pull its plug. Basically, to provoke a superintelligence in any way seems like a Certified Bad Idea. (For sure, pulling the plug didn't work well when someone attempted it with Skynet!) When the time comes, perhaps a superintelligence in the neighborhood will finally motivate us to act intelligently ourselves.

Could superintelligence be prevented?

Let's suppose that superintelligence is possible. The only sure way to prevent a superintelligence from occurring would be to forever eliminate some precondition for its arrival. Not knowing how a superintelligence might arise (e.g., from human design, machine learning, neuromorphic computing, or some combination), to eliminate a critical prerequisite would appear to require suppressing further development across an extremely broad range of technologies.

Beyond halting progress in information technologies, the preemptive strategy must constrain the deployment of IT even at its present capabilities. Otherwise a sufficient number of networked computers might spontaneously give rise to an emergent

---

* Even though, as we've seen, Kurzweil's own forecast has the future superintelligences being, by way of whole brain emulation, in some sense *us*.

† I wonder...how would a superintelligence feel about knock-knock jokes?

superintelligence. Biotechnology must also be constrained, lest whole brain emulation or neural implants turn out to be viable paths to superintelligence.

Of course, IT and biotech have uses other than being (perhaps) paths to superintelligence. Both technologies are deeply embedded in, and are themselves major sectors of, the global economy. Both technologies are increasingly important to our wellbeing. Even at risk of severe penalties for further developing these technologies, the incentives to cheat would be enormous.

The ongoing debate over suppressing strong *encryption* illustrates the challenge of heading off strong *AI*. One side asserts that unless intelligence services can read terrorist communications, we're all at risk. That's a decent analogy to those who might hope to suppress technology to preempt a danger from superintelligence. The other side argues that the privacy benefits of strong encryption outweigh the risks, that absent strong encryption, *our* communications become vulnerable. If we unilaterally give up strong encryption, it would only mean that anyone who *does* develop that technology has all the advantages. *That* is a decent analogy to the position that if our side doesn't develop strong AI, we'll lose out to the side that does. And while the debate rages, the deployment of strong encryption—like the development and deployment of possible superintelligence precursors—continues unabated.*

To restrain a useful technology would appear to require a totalitarian police state, recalling the onetime Soviet suppression of mass-communication technology (including cheap computers)— and even the Soviets were compelled by their Cold War competition with the West to obtain just such tech for their military.

A technology with several uses, only some of them dangerous, is especially difficult to suppress, because every uncontroversial

---

* I don't doubt that the very agencies resisting the general deployment of strong encryption continue to develop that technology for their government's most sensitive communications. Just as governments that might publicly try to discourage research into strong AI will likely have such projects underway on the side....

application has its champions. Consider advanced biotech. Research into neural prostheses to restore sight to the blind might also pave the way to intelligence-enhancing neural implants. Learning about the low-level structure of the brain could bring cures for many "mental" illnesses, while also advancing whole brain emulation.

But is suppression of technology *possible*? Sure, in theory (although it hasn't worked out very well with nuclear weapons: we've gone from one nuclear-armed nation to eight or nine in well under a century). Even, occasionally, in practice. Turning inward, the Ming Dynasty suppressed the technology for long-range, ocean-going travel for hundreds of years.* In the end, when Western navies came to China, that abandonment of technology didn't turn out very well.

If to *suppress* a technology is too difficult, perhaps we might find a way to *reject* it. Can such social change succeed? The "Butlerian Jihad" of the Duneiverse banished all technology associated with "thinking machines," but Frank Herbert left how that happened in deep back story: an upheaval conveniently millennia before his novel opens.† In my 2006 short story "Catch a Falling Star," social outrage at egregious and widespread abuse of personal records in medical databases ignited

---

* Between 1403 and 1435, Chinese fleets led by Admiral Zheng He explored and traded along the coast of India, around the Arabian Peninsula, and south along the eastern coast of Africa at least to the modern port of Mombasa. Inconclusive evidence suggests Zheng He reached yet farther, rounding the Cape of Good Hope to discover the Atlantic Ocean.

Within a century of these voyages, China had turned inward. The Emperor banned all overseas trade; to sail from China in a multi-masted ship became a capital offense. Records of Zheng He's travels were suppressed and in large measure destroyed. See https://en.wikipedia.org/wiki/Zheng_He.

† Herbert, having eliminated "artificial" superintelligence from his far future, nonetheless included superintelligence in the Dune series: the transhuman "mentats."

a popular uprising against computers—but computers have many uses, and the ban didn't stick. Neither did the Emerging Risk Directorate in Ramez Naam's Nexus trilogy succeed in suppressing related tech.

Bottom line? Absent a global police state, extremely intrusive, it's almost unimaginable that the precursor technologies to AI can be indefinitely suppressed. If superintelligence is within the capabilities of puny human intelligence to create, or of our likely transhuman successors, or if superintelligence can emerge spontaneously (as in Robert J. Sawyer's *Wake*)...then it *will* happen.

Wrapping up

We are left with many more questions than answers. Is strong AI almost upon us? Can humanity coexist with a superintelligence, or it with us, should one arise? What would such an entity be like? Will it, à la Kurzweil, be us? And the most basic question of all: should we be very, *very* worried?

As for that last item, as you've seen, I believe not. Or, as Robot of the 1965 TV series *Lost in Space* would surely have responded to the question, "That does not compute."

To read further

- "Machine-Learning Maestro Michael Jordan on the Delusions of Big Data and Other Huge Engineering Efforts," Lee Gomes, *IEEE Spectrum*, 20 October 2014, http://spectrum.ieee.org/robotics/artificial-intelligence/machinelearning-maestro-michael-jordan-on-the-delusions-of-big-data-and-other-huge-engineering-efforts/.

- "Let's Bring Rosie Home: 5 Challenges We Need to Solve for Home Robots," Shahin Farshchi, *IEEE Spectrum*, January 13, 2016, http://spectrum.ieee.org/automaton/robotics/home-robots/lets-bring-rosie-home-5-challenges-we-need-to-solve-for-home-robots/.

- "The Neural Network That Remembers: With short-term memory, recurrent neural networks gain some amazing abilities," Zachary C. Lipton & Charles Elkan, *IEEE Spectrum*, January 26, 2016, http://spectrum.ieee.org/computing/software/the-neural-network-that-remembers.

- "Thought process: Building an artificial brain," Ariana Eunjung Cha, *The Washington Post*, October 11, 2015, http://www.washingtonpost.com/sf/national/2015/09/30/brain/.

- "Special Report: The Rise of AI," *Scientific American*, June 2016.

- "The Case for Robot Disobedience," Gordon Briggs and Matthias Scheutz, *Scientific American*, January 2017.

- "The Coming Technological Singularity: How to Survive in the Post-Human Era," Vernor Vinge, https://www-rohan.sdsu.edu/faculty/vinge/misc/singularity.html.

- *Artificial Intelligence: The Basics*, Kevin Warwick.

- *The Singularity Is Near: When Humans Transcend Biology*, Ray Kurzweil.

- *Superintelligence: Paths, Dangers, Strategies*, Nick Bostrom.

- "Special Report: Can We Copy the Brain," *IEEE Spectrum*, June 2017.

- *Science Fact and Science Fiction: An Encyclopedia*, Brian Stableford (editor), articles on artificial intelligence, intelligence, robot, and singularity.

AKNOWLEDGEMENTS

I wasn't always an author. By training I'm a physicist and computer engineer; before turning to full-time writing, I worked in high tech at corporations large and small. That background gave me the confidence to begin this exploration—and an awareness of just how quickly technical knowledge, even within one's own specialty, can become dated. Research helps, but independent review was also in order. I greatly appreciate the inputs from, and critiques by, experts across a spectrum of technical disciplines. Most of them, incidentally, are also hard-SF authors. They are, alphabetically: Gregory Benford, John G. Cramer, Larry Niven, Gerald D. Nordley, Richard B. Robinson, Stanley Schmidt, Bud Sparhawk, Henry G. Stratmann, and Vernor Vinge. Thanks, gentlemen, for the assist.

I also thank Stanley Schmidt (yes, a second time) and Trevor Quachri, consecutive editors at *Analog*. I thank Stan for encouraging me, after several fiction forays into the magazine, to try my hand at nonfiction, and Trevor for his embrace of the essay series that evolved into this book.

Next, I'd like to express my appreciation to the many readers who engaged with the article series: in letters and emails to the magazine, emails to me directly, and via social media. I thoroughly enjoyed those interactions. Many of your suggestions, insights, and "but what about?" questions are addressed in this book.

For determining the publication history of written SF at all lengths and the release history of film and television SF, I had frequent recourse to, respectively, the Internet Speculative Fiction Database (www.isfdb.org) and the Internet Movie Database (www.IMDb.com). Both resources were invaluable.

Finally, I thank my first and favorite reader—also an ardent SF fan—my wife, Ruth. Beyond her uncanny ability at spotting the annoying little glitches of (in)consistency and usage that somehow creep into any manuscript, her not-a-scientist's eye was critical to catching, in early drafts, passages in which I had waxed too esoteric.

Whatever errors, omissions, and oversimplifications remain in the book are, of course, all mine.

EDWARD M. LERNER
November 2017

Author EDWARD M. LERNER worked in high tech and aerospace for thirty years, as everything from engineer to senior vice president, for much of that time writing science fiction as his hobby. Since 2004 he has written full-time.

His novels range from near-future technothrillers, like *Small Miracles* and *Energized*, to traditional SF, like *Dark Secret* and his InterstellarNet series, to (collaborating with Larry Niven) the space-opera epic Fleet of Worlds series of *Ringworld* companion novels. Lerner's 2015 novel, *InterstellarNet: Enigma*, won the inaugural Canopus Award "honoring excellence in interstellar writing." His fiction has also been nominated for Locus, Prometheus, and Hugo awards.

Lerner's short fiction has appeared in anthologies, collections, and many of the usual SF magazines. He also writes about science and technology, notably including the long-running series of essays for *Analog* about science and SF tropes—updated and expanded into this book.

Lerner lives in Virginia with his wife, Ruth.

His website is www.edwardmlerner.com.

END NOTES

INTRODUCTION:
All Troped Up

1. "The Reference Library," Don Sakers, *Analog*, March 2010.

2 See "The Mundane Manifesto," Geoff Ryman, et. al., 2004 (a more precise date beyond my ability to track down), https://sfgenics.wordpress.com/2013/07/04/geoff-ryman-et-al-the-mundane-manifesto/ and (in rebuttal) "Aiming High—or Low," Stanley Schmidt, *Analog*, November, 2009.

SAY, WHAT?
Ruminations about Language, Communications, and Science Fiction

3. For a broader survey of human languages and an alternate take on alien speech, see the chapter "Alien Language" in *Aliens and Alien Societies: A writer's guide to creating extraterrestrial life forms*, by Stanley Schmidt.

4 For much more about gender differences among languages, see "Der Mann, Die Frau, Das Kind," by Henry Honken, *Analog*, June 2010.

5 http://www.physorg.com/news76249412.html.

6 https://www.scientificamerican.com/article/how-do-squid-and-octopuse/

7 http://www.absoluteastronomy.com/topics/Electroreception

8 The electrical capabilities of some marine life go beyond sensing to communication, navigation, and even stunning of prey. See: http://www.answers.com/topic/electric-organ-biology.

9   http://news.nationalgeographic.com/news/2007/09/070927-magnetic-birds.html

10 See "Dancing under a Polarized Sky," https://www.polarization.com/bees/bees.html.

11 "Understanding chemical communication in ant societies," David Lugmayer, February 17, 2016, *Science Node*, https://sciencenode.org/feature/understanding-chemical-communication-in-ant-societies.php.

12 http://en.wikipedia.org/wiki/Asl

13 http://en.wikipedia.org/wiki/Proprioception

14 http://www.americandialect.org/2015-word-of-the-year-is-singular-they

15 Esperanto is a language designed to be neutral (among political and ethnic groups) and easy to learn. Despite its laudable goals, few people (and no countries) have adopted it. http://en.wikipedia.org/wiki/Esperanto

16 An archeological artifact discovered in Rosetta, Egypt, in 1799. Identical passages inscribed in Egyptian and Greek symbols gave valuable clues to reading hieroglyphics. http://en.wikipedia.org/wiki/Rosetta_stone

17 You want more? Construction of languages is a popular topic at SF conventions. Author C. S. McCath has captured (and expanded upon) what one con panel did with the topic. Individual files on her website are not directly accessible, so search on "ConLangs 101 Resource Sheet" at http://csmaccath.com/.

I GOT THE LONG-DISTANCE BLUES:
Why Interstellar Travel Is Hard

18 For distances and much more information about these and other astronomical objects, see http://nineplanets.org/, about the Solar System, and http://www.solstation.com/stars.htm, about nearby stars.

    (Don't let "nine planets" mislead you. That site is up to date despite keeping a name that predated Pluto's 2006 demotion to "dwarf planet" status.)

19 That distance is current as I write in February 2016. But *Voyager 1* just keeps coasting away, and you can watch the distance grow at http://voyager.jpl.nasa.gov/.

20 http://imagine.gsfc.nasa.gov/docs/ask_astro/answers/980317b.html

21 http://www.space.com/missionlaunches/worlds-first-solar-sail-photo-japan-100618.html

22 "Russian billionaire Yuri Milner invests $100m to send a fleet of spacecraft to Alpha Centauri," Jordan Crook, *TechCrunch*, April 12, 2016, http://techcrunch.com/2016/04/12/russian-billionaire-yuri-milner-invests-100m-to-send-a-fleet-of-spacecraft-to-alpha-centauri/.

23 "'Electric Sails' Could Propel Superfast Spacecraft by 2025," Mike Wall, *Space.com*, November 9, 2015, http://www.space.com/31063-electric-sail-solar-wind-space-exploration.html.

24 "Mass Beam Propulsion, An Overview," Gerald D. Nordley and Adam James Crowl, *Journal of the British Interplanetary Society*, May/June 2015.

25 http://en.wikipedia.org/wiki/Project_Orion_%28nuclear_propulsion%29

26 http://en.wikipedia.org/wiki/Michelson%E2%80%93Morley_experiment

27 http://galileoandeinstein.physics.virginia.edu/lectures/mass_increase.html

ALIEN ADVENTURES:
Rising to the Challenge

28 "Offering Funds, U.S. Agency Dreams of Sending Humans to Stars," Dennis Overbye, *The New York Times*, August 17, 2011, http://www.nytimes.com/2011/08/18/science/space/18starship.html.

29 "Making Babies in Space May Be Harder Than It Sounds," Brandon Keim, August 25, 2009, http://www.wired.com/2009/08/spacebabies/ and, slightly more encouraging, "Mice Breeding Chinese Scientists Say Making Babies in Space Is Possible: If rodent embryos can develop on a spacecraft, there's no reason human ones can't as well," Yasmin Tayag, *Inverse*, April 20, 2016, https://www.inverse.com/article/14486-mice-breeding-chinese-scientists-say-making-babies-in-space-is-possible.

30 "A space odyssey: cosmic rays may damage the brains of astronauts," Will Dunham, *Reuters*, May 1, 2015, http://news.yahoo.com/space-odyssey-cosmic-rays-may-damage-brains-astronauts-194650036.html.

31 "Transcriptional Activation of Endogenous Retroviral Sequences in Human Epidermal Keratinocytes by UVB Irradiation," Christine Hohenad et. al., *Journal of Investigative Dermatology*, October 1999, http://www.jidonline.org/article/S0022-202X%2815%2940621-9/abstract.

32 "Radiation-induced human endogenous retrovirus (HERV)-R env gene expression by epigenetic control," Lee JR, Ahn K, Kim YJ, Jung YD and Kim HS, *Radiation Research*, November 2012, http://www.rrjournal.org/doi/abs/10.1667/RR2888.1.

33 "According to Crucian, the immune system is likely being altered by many factors associated with the overall spaceflight environment. 'Things like radiation, microbes, stress, microgravity, altered sleep cycles and isolation could all have an effect on crew member immune systems,' said Crucian. 'If this situation persisted for longer deep space missions, it could possibly increase risk of infection, hypersensitivity, or autoimmune issues for exploration astronauts.'"

   See http://www.nasa.gov/content/study-reveals-immune-system-is-dazed-and-confused-during-spaceflight/.

34 "The human body contains trillions of microorganisms—outnumbering human cells by 10 to 1. Because of their small size, however, microorganisms make up only about 1 to 3 percent of the body's mass (in a 200-pound adult, that's 2 to 6 pounds of bacteria), but play a vital role in human health."

   For the complete article, "NIH Human Microbiome Project defines normal bacterial makeup of the body," see http://www.nih.gov/news/health/jun2012/nhgri-13.htm.

35 "Super-bacteria are growing in space...and we're the ones breeding them," Meera Senthilingam, *CNN*, October 1, 2014, http://www.cnn.com/2014/10/01/health/super-bacteria-growing-in-space/index.html.

36 http://ipcblog.org/2011/09/06/mother-natures-most-toxic/

37 "The Fabulous Fruits of Mendel's Garden," Fran Van Cleave, *Analog*, July/August 2013.

38 "A one-way trip to Mars," Kera Rennert, *CBS News*, May 22, 2014, http://www.cbsnews.com/news/a-one-way-trip-to-mars/.

39 See "Interstellar radio links enhanced by exploiting the Sun as a Gravitational Lens," Claudio Maccone, http://www.sciencedirect.

com/science/article/pii/S0094576510002304 (abstract only; the full article is behind a pay wall).

40 "Hacking the Van Allen Belts: Could we save satellites and astronauts by wiping out the Van Allen belts?" Charles Q. Choi, *IEEE Spectrum*, February 26, 2014, http://spectrum.ieee.org/aerospace/astrophysics/hacking-the-van-allen-belts/.

41 http://www.cnet.com/news/japanese-company-plans-space-elevator-by-2050/

42 See, citing a recent Brookings Institute study, "Report Claims HUGE Shortage Of STEM Workers," Jonah Bennett, July 1, 2014, http://dailycaller.com/2014/07/01/report-claims-huge-shortage-of-stem-workers/.

FASTER THAN A SPEEDING PHOTON:
The Why, Where, and (Perhaps the)
How of Faster-Than-Light Technology

43. *Faster than the Speed of Light: The Story of a Scientific Speculation*, by João Magueijo. If he's right, maybe we can learn to modify light speed to something friendlier for interstellar travelers.

44 http://en.wikipedia.org/wiki/Casimir_effect

45 http://www.livescience.com/space/fine-structure-constant-varies-space-100915.html

46 See: http://en.wikipedia.org/wiki/Alcubierre_Warp_Drive

47 From http://www.nasa.gov/centers/glenn/technology/warp/ideachev.html.

48 http://www.guardian.co.uk/science/2011/sep/22/faster-than-light-particles-neutrinos?INTCMP=ILCNETTXT3487

49 "Fermilab Will Double-Check CERN's Revolutionary Faster-Than-Light Claim," Rebecca Boyle, *Popular Science*, September 26, 2011, https://www.popsci.com/technology/article/2011-09/fermilab-physicists-will-help-check-revolutionary-faster-light-claim.

50 http://www.sciencenews.org/view/generic/id/335309/title/Critics_take_aim_at_fast_neutrinos

51 http://blogs.discovermagazine.com/badastronomy/2011/09/22/
    faster-than-light-travel-discovered-slow-down-folks/

52 "Embattled neutrino project leaders step down: No-confidence
    vote follows confirmation of faults in experiment's cable and clock,"
    Eugenie Samuel Reich, *Nature News*, April 2, 2012, http://www.nature.
    com/news/embattled-neutrino-project-leaders-step-down-1.10371.

53 Ursula K. Le Guin invented the ansible in *Rocannon's World* (1996),
    and Card (and others) adopted it. See http://en.wikipedia.org/wiki/
    Ansible.

ALIEN ALIENS:
Beyond Rubber Suits

54 http://exoplanet.eu/catalog.php

55 "NASA, Russia Squabble Over International Space Station Sea
    Plankton Claim," Eric Mack, *Fortune*, August 21, 2014, http://www.
    forbes.com/sites/ericmack/2014/08/21/nasa-russia-squabble-over-
    international-space-station-sea-plankton-claim/.

56 *The Eerie Silence: Renewing Our Search for Alien Intelligence*, Paul
    Davies, includes an excellent discussion of the puzzle of biogenesis.

57 Some earthly birds, including parrots, *already* use simple tools
    (trimming and grasping twigs and cactus spines to get at, even
    to spear, insects). See http://www.pbs.org/wnet/nature/episodes/
    parrots-in-the-land-of-oz/birds-that-use-tools/714/.

58 http://en.wikipedia.org/wiki/Macguffin

59 http://en.wikipedia.org/wiki/Mind_uploading_in_fiction

ALIEN WORLDS:
Not in Kansas Anymore

60 For the latest findings, check out http://www.exoplanets.org/.

61 "Pluto and the Developing Landscape of Our Solar System,"
    International Astronomical Union, https://www.iau.org/public/
    themes/pluto/.

62 See my article "Rock! Bye-Bye, Baby," *Analog*, November 2009.

63 See http://en.wikipedia.org/wiki/Giant_impact_hypothesis and "The Origin of the Moon," Planetary Science Institute, https://www.psi.edu/epo/moon/moon.html.

64 A planet, once ejected, no longer orbiting a star, is no longer a planet—it's a "planetary mass object." And planetary-mass objects, whether ejected or having formed without a sun, do exist free-floating among the stars. See "'Homeless' Planets May Be Common in Our Galaxy," https://www.sciencemag.org/news/2011/05/homeless-planets-may-be-common-our-galaxy.

65 http://nineplanets.org/kboc.html ("KBOC" in that url encompasses Kuiper Belt and Oort Cloud.)

66 http://www.nasa.gov/feature/nasa-s-new-horizons-team-selects-potential-kuiper-belt-flyby-target

67 The Search for Planet X," Michael D. Lemonick, *Scientific American*, February 2016.

68 Tectonic plates are the major—and on a sufficiently long time scale, mobile—structures of Earth's crust (aka, the lithosphere). See http://en.wikipedia.org/wiki/Plate_tectonics.

69 " 'Mirage Planets' May Complicate Search for Extraterrestrial Life," Charles Q. Choi, *Space.com*, February 12, 2015, http://www.space.com/28531-mirage-alien-planets.html#sthash.Pz4AyMb5.dpuf.

70 Solar outbursts can have *big* effects on any planet unlucky enough to be in their way. See "Space Weather: The Latest Forecast," H. G. Stratmann, *Analog*, May 2012, and "The Day the Sun Exploded," Richard A. Lovett, *Analog*, November 2012.

71 For more on the quest for Earth-like worlds, see "How Space Telescopes Will Find Earth 2.0: The galaxy is full of exoplanets. Now we'll find out what they're made of," Alberto Conti & Mark Clampin, *IEEE Spectrum*, October 29, 2015, http://spectrum.ieee.org/aerospace/satellites/how-space-telescopes-will-find-earth-20.

72 "A first! Hubble images a distant planet 160 light years away, sees clouds," Anthony Watts, *Watts Up With That?*, February 19, 2016, http://wattsupwiththat.com/2016/02/18/hubble-images-a-distant-planet-160-light-years-away-sees-clouds/.

73 "Scientists Redefine 'Planet' To Include Exoplanets—And It Works Beautifully," Ethan Siegel, *Forbes*, November 10, 2015, http://www.

346

forbes.com/sites/startswithabang/2015/11/10/scientists-redefine-planet-to-include-exoplanets-and-it-works-beautifully/.

74 http://mars.nasa.gov/allaboutmars/extreme/moons/

75 See "Eying exomoons in the search for E.T.," Bryan Gaensler, *The Enthusiastic Astronomer*, February 18, 2016, https://theconversation.com/columns/bryan-gaensler-598 and "New Exomoon Hunting Technique Could Find Solar System-like Moons, Adam Hadhazy, *Astrobiology Magazine*, May 12, 2014, http://www.astrobio.net/news-exclusive/new-exomoon-hunting-technique-could-find-solar-system-like-moons/#sthash.isWKYON6.dpuf.

76 See "The Origin of the Moon," Planetary Science Institute, https://www.psi.edu/epo/moon/moon.html and https://en.wikipedia.org/wiki/Giant_impact_hypothesis.

77 "Rings of a Super Saturn: Astronomers have discovered a gargantuan planetary ring system and possible a moon around another star," Matthew Kenworthy, *Scientific American*, January 2016.

78 http://www.cnn.com/2016/06/14/health/nasa-kepler-tatooine-planet-two-suns/index.html

79 http://www.space.com/18089-earth-size-alien-planet-alpha-centauri.html

80 http://en.wikipedia.org/wiki/Milankovitch_cycle and http://earthobservatory.nasa.gov/Features/Milankovitch/milankovitch_2.php

81 See "Krakatoa helps to keep Earth cool" (summarizing a 2006 *Nature* article), at http://www.telegraph.co.uk/news/worldnews/asia/indonesia/1510073/Krakatoa-helps-to-keep-Earth-cool.html.

82 For more about Mesklin, in the original novel and several follow-on stories, see http://en.wikipedia.org/wiki/Mesklin.

ALIEN DIMENSIONS:
The Universe Next Door

83 See http://en.wikipedia.org/wiki/Counter-Earth#Greek_philosophy.

84 See "Alternatives Past and Future," Stanley Schmidt, *Analog*, January/February 2011.

85 Per the Joss Whedon TV series *Buffy the Vampire Slayer* and its spin-off, *Angel*.

86 Einstein made similar comments on several occasions. In a more complete statement, he said, "Quantum mechanics is certainly imposing. But an inner voice tells me that it is not yet the real thing. The theory says a lot, but does not really bring us any closer to the secret of the 'old one.' I, at any rate, am convinced that He does not throw dice."

87 "Why quantum mechanics is an "embarrassment" to science," *The Washington Post*, February 7, 2013 (http://www.washingtonpost.com/blogs/wonkblog/wp/2013/02/07/quantum-mechanics-is-an-embarrassment/).

And the plurality winner? The Copenhagen Interpretation, named after the venue where many of the theory's early luminaries debated these issues. Or, as I like to call it, QM's "Don't ask" interpretation.

88 "The Most Embarrassing Graph in Modern Physics," Sean Carroll, http://www.preposterousuniverse.com/blog/2013/01/17/the-most-embarrassing-graph-in-modern-physics/.

89 "Scientists abandon highly publicized claim about cosmic find,"Malcolm Ritter, Associated Press, January 30, 2015, https://www.apnews.com/0e0e34c731c54b80b94bfd0c6c92f6cc.

90 See "Cosmic rays offer clue our universe could be a computer simulation," Ian Steadman, *Wired*, October 11, 2012, http://www.wired.co.uk/news/archive/2012-10/11/universe-computer-simulation.

ALIEN AWOLS:
The Great Silence

91 "Is Anybody Out There?" *The Wall Street Journal*, April 10, 2010, and "Are We Alone in the Universe," *The New York Times*, November 18, 2013, both by Paul Davies; "Are we alone in the universe?" Charles Krauthammer, *The Washington Post*, December 30, 2011; (blaming the Great Silence on aliens mismanaging their climates) "Is a Climate Disaster Inevitable?" Adam Frank, *The New York Times*, January 17, 2015; and "Do we really want to know if we're not alone in the universe?" Joel Achenbach, *The Washington Post*, February 28, 2015.

92 "Encryption might be the reason we've never heard from aliens, says Snowden," James Vincent, *The Verge*, September 21, 2015, http://www.theverge.com/2015/9/21/9363863/edward-snowden-alien-encryption.

93 "Smart SETI," Gregory Benford and James Benford, *Analog*, April 2011.

94 "$100 Million Breakthrough Listen Initiative Starts Searching for E.T.: The latest search for extraterrestrial intelligence will seek out radio and laser signals from other worlds," David Schneider, *IEEE Spectrum*, December 18, 2015, http://spectrum.ieee.org/transportation/mass-transit/100-million-breakthrough-listen-initiative-starts-searching-for-et.

95 http://en.wikipedia.org/wiki/Drake_equation

96 See (for example) http://www.npr.org/blogs/thetwo-way/2013/11/04/243062655/scientists-estimate-20-billion-earth-like-planets-in-our-galaxy and http://www.extremetech.com/extreme/152573-astronomers-estimate-100-billion-habitable-earth-like-planets-in-the-milky-way-50-sextillion-in-the-universe. Models and parameter estimates—and hence, conclusions—vary.

97 A concept originated by mathematician John von Neumann. See "Self-replicating spacecraft" at http://en.wikipedia.org/wiki/Von_Neumann_Probe.

98 "Search of 100,000 galaxies for advanced civilizations yields no obvious candidates, Will Parker, *Sci GoGo*, April 14, 2015, http://www.scienceagogo.com/news/20150314192922.shtml.

99 "Comets can't explain weird 'alien megastructure' star after all," Jacob Aron, *New Scientist*, January 15, 2016, https://www.newscientist.com/article/dn28786-comets-cant-explain-weird-alien-megastructure-star-after-all/.

100 "Tabby's Star, KIC8462852—WTF? (Where's the Flux?)" John G. Cramer, *Analog*, May 2016.

101 "Scientists rouse bacterium from 250-million-year slumber," Jeff Long, *Chicago Tribune*, October 19, 2000. See http://www.oakton.edu/user/4/billtong/eas100/oldbacteria.htm.

102 See http://www.lpi.usra.edu/lunar/missions/apollo/apollo_12/experiments/surveyor/ and https://science.nasa.gov/science-news/science-at-nasa/1998/ast01sep98_1.

Alas, these results are debatable: bacterial clusters attributed by some researchers to *Surveyor*'s pre-launch contamination (hence, the bacteria would have undergone lunar privations) are, in the conclusion of other researchers, attributable to post-retrieval contamination.

103 http://en.wikipedia.org/wiki/Neolithic_Revolution

104 "The Fermi Plague," Stanley Schmidt, *Analog*, October 1998.

ALIEN ALTERCATIONS:
Star (Spanning) Wars

105 "The Dragon's Spear: China's Asymmetric Strategy," *Yale Global Online*, 17 October 2013, https://science.nasa.gov/science-news/science-at-nasa/1998/ast01sep98_1.

106 "'Asymmetric Warfare': Pentagon Accuses China of Cyber Attacks and Espionage," *Global Research*, 9 May 2014, http://www.globalresearch.ca/asymmetric-warfare-pentagon-accuses-china-of-cyber-attacks-and-espionage/5334452.

107 http://en.wikipedia.org/wiki/Active_Denial_System

108 As suggested by *Does Altruism Exist?: Culture, Genes, and the Welfare of Others (Foundational Questions in Science)*, by evolutionary biologist David Sloan Wilson.

109 "Dolphins are 'so hungry they're turning on each other': Surf war breaks out in British seas," *Daily Mail Online*, 3 September 2008, http://www.dailymail.co.uk/sciencetech/article-1051936/Surf-wars-Dolphins-hungry-theyre-turning-British-seas.html.

110 "What Is War Good for? Ask a Chimpanzee. What apes and monkeys can teach us about the roots of human aggression," *Slate*, 12 October 2012, http://www.slate.com/articles/health_and_science/human_evolution/2012/10/chimpanzee_wars_can_primate_aggression_teach_us_about_human_aggression.html, and "Chimps Are Naturally Violent, Study Suggests," Laura Geggel, *Live Science*, September 17, 2014, http://www.livescience.com/47885-chimpanzee-aggression-evolution.html.

111 http://en.wikipedia.org/wiki/Neanderthal_extinction_hypotheses

112 "Prehistoric massacre in Kenya called oldest evidence of warfare," Will Dunham, *Reuters*, January 21, 2016, http://in.reuters.com/article/science-massacre-idINKCN0UY2VW.

113 "Battles among Ants Resemble Human Warfare: Battles among ants can be startlingly similar to human military operations," *Scientific American*, December 2011, http://www.scientificamerican.com/article/ants-and-the-art-of-war/.

114 "The Psychology of War: Why do human beings find it so difficult to live in peace?" Steve Taylor, *Psychology Today*, March 5, 2014,

http://www.psychologytoday.com/blog/out-the-darkness/201403/
the-psychology-war.

115 "Make Birth Control, Not War," Thomas Hayden and Malcolm
Potts, *Pacific Standard: The Science of Society*, April 12, 2010, http://
www.psmag.com/magazines/pacific-standard-cover-story/
make-birth-control-not-war-11399/.

116 "Putin's move on Crimea bolsters popularity back home," *USA
Today*, March 19, 2014, http://www.usatoday.com/story/news/
world/2014/03/18/crimea-ukraine-putin-russia/6564263/.

117 On the one hand, see http://en.wikipedia.org/wiki/Democratic
peace theory. On the other hand, see http://en.wikipedia.org/wiki/
List of wars between democracies.

118 "Seasonal nest usurpation of European colonies by African swarms in
Arizona, USA," *Insectes Sociaux*, November 2004, http://link.springer.
com/article/10.1007%2Fs00040-004-0753-1.

119 "Far-Off Planets Like the Earth Dot the Galaxy," Dennis Overbye,
The New York Times, November 4, 2013, http://www.nytimes.
com/2013/11/05/science/cosmic-census-finds-billions-of-planets-
that-could-be-like-earth.html.

120 "WISE 0855-0714: Astronomer Discovers Fourth-Closest Star System,"
Sci-News.com, April 28, 2014, http://www.sci-news.com/astronomy/
science-wise08550714-fourth-closest-star-system-01886.html.

HERE WE GO LOOPEDY LOOP:
A Brief History of Time Travel

121 https://www.youtube.com/watch?v=Y-P0Hs0ADJY

122 Cosmologists still speculate. If this book hasn't provided enough food
for thought, see *Before the Big Bang: The Prehistory of Our Universe*,"
Brian Clegg.

123 The data remain inconclusive whether and how the density of dark
energy changes with time. The Big Rip will happen only if that
density grows as the Universe expands, creating a positive feedback
loop, stretching space-time itself ever faster and faster. See "The Big
Rip at the End of Time," John G. Cramer, *Analog*, March 2005 (and
http://www.analogsf.com/0503/altview.shtml).

HERE WE GO LOOPEDY LOOP:
Back and There Again

124 These special cases, relevant to a small object in the vicinity of two much more massive bodies, involve the Lagrange (or libration) points. At five specific locations, dubbed L1 through L5, the gravitational attractions of the massive bodies and the centrifugal force acting upon the much smaller body, come into balance. Spacecraft are sometimes intentionally stationed at (or set to orbit around) various Lagrange points. See http://en.wikipedia.org/wiki/Lagrangian_point.

125 "A Physicist Is Building a Time Machine to Reconnect With His Dead Father," Tom Moroney, March 27, 2015, *Bloomberg Business*, http://www.bloomberg.com/news/articles/2015-03-27/a-physicist-is-building-a-time-machine-to-reconnect-with-his-dead-father.

126 The film can be streamed at http://www.nsi-canada.ca/2012/04/the-grandfather-paradox/.

ALTERNATE ABILITIES:
The Paranormal

127 "An Assessment of the Evidence for Psychic Functioning," Jessica Utts, http://www.ics.uci.edu/~jutts/air.pdf.

128 "Evaluation of Program on Anomalous Mental Phenomena," Ray Hyman, http://www.ics.uci.edu/~jutts/hyman.html.

129 "Three in Four Americans Believe in Paranormal: Little change from similar results in 2001," David W. Moore, *Gallup News Service*, June 16, 2005, http://www.gallup.com/poll/16915/three-four-americans-believe-paranormal.aspx.

To reach three in four required conflating the paranormal with the supernatural. In *this* book, you'll find nothing of ghosts, séances, reincarnation, astrology, or channeling of the dead.

130 Quoted from the home page of the Society for Psychical Research, https://www.spr.ac.uk/.

131 http://www.csicop.org/si/show/mind_at_play_an_interview_with_martin_gardner/

132 "A Perceptual Channel for Information Transfer over Kilometer Distances: Historical Perspective and Recent Research," Harold

E. Puthoff and Russell Targ, *Proceedings of the IEEE*, March 1976. (IEEE is the Institute of Electrical and Electronics Engineers, an international professional society.)

133 "Information transmission under conditions of sensory shielding," Russell Targ and Harold Puthoff, *Nature*, October 18, 1974.

134 "Information transmission in remote viewing experiments," David Marks & Richard Kammann, *Nature*, August 17, 1978.

135 *The Demon-Haunted World: Science as a Candle in the Dark*, Carl Sagan.

136 *Collected Editorials from Analog*, selected by Harry Harrison, 1966.

137 *I, Asimov: A Memoir*, Isaac Asimov, 1994.

138 See *Shadows of the Mind: A Search for the Missing Science of Consciousness*, Roger Penrose.

139 For a more complete exposition of the double-slit experiment with delayed choice (with supporting video), see "Funny Things Happen When Space And Time Vanish," by Marcelo Gleiser, at http://www.npr.org/blogs/13.7/2013/05/28/186886914/funny-things-happen-when-space-and-time-vanish.

HUMAN 2.0:
Being All We Can Be

140 *Inquiries into Human Faculty and Its Development*, Francis Galton, 1883.

141 *Science Fact and Fiction: An Encyclopedia*, Brian Stableford, editor, article on eugenics.

142 See http://en.wikipedia.org/wiki/Eugenics#Supporters_and_critics.

143 See http://en.wikipedia.ogg/wiki/Genetically_modified_food_controversies.

144 "An integrated encyclopedia of DNA elements in the human genome," The ENCODE Project Consortium, *Nature*, September 6, 2012, http://www.nature.com/nature/journal/v489/n7414/full/nature11247.html.

145 "Efficacy of Gene Therapy for X-Linked Severe Combined Immunodeficiency," Salima Hacein-Bey-Abina et. al., *New England Journal of Medicine*, July 22, 2010, http://www.ncbi.nlm.nih.gov/pmc/articles/PMC2957288/.

146 "Exclusive: First gene therapy drug sets million-euro price record," Ludwig Burger and Ben Hirschler, November 26, 2014, http://news.yahoo.com/exclusive-first-gene-therapy-drug-sets-million-euro-173717146--finance.html.

147 "Pfizer bets on gene therapy as technology comes of age," Ben Hirschler, *Reuters*, December 8, 2014, http://news.yahoo.com/pfizer-bets-gene-therapy-technology-comes-age-150146112--finance.html.

148 "First Person: Emmanuelle Charpentier," Katie L. Burke, *American Scientist*, July-August 2015 (preview at https://www.questia.com/magazine/1P3-3726750121/first-person-emmanuelle-charpentier).

149 "Researchers Identify Newer And More Precise System For Genome Editing," Ted Ranosa, *Tech Times*, September 27, 2015, http://www.techtimes.com/articles/88664/20150927/researchers-identify-newer-and-more-precise-system-for-genome-editing.htm.

150 "U.S. patent agency to decide inventor of powerful gene editing technology," Andrew Chung, *Reuters*, January 12, 2016, http://news.yahoo.com/u-patent-agency-decide-inventor-powerful-gene-editing-023341950--finance.html.

151 "An On/Off Switch for Genes," Jim Kozubek, *Scientific American*, January 2016.

152 "CRISPR/Cas9 therapeutic for tyrosinemai type I delivered to mice," Jim Fessenden, *Science Daily*, February 1, 2016, https://www.sciencedaily.com/releases/ 2016/02/160201130910.htm.

153 "British scientists seek to edit the genes of embryos; bioethicists warn of potential dangers," Ariana Eunjung Cha, *The Washington Post*, September 18, 2015, https://www.washingtonpost.com/news/to-your-health/wp/2015/09/18/as-british-scientists-seek-to-edit-the-genes-of-embryos-bioethicists-warn-of-potential-dangers/.

154 "Expert group says embryo genetic modification should be allowed," Will Dunham, *Reuters*, September 9, 2015, http://news.yahoo.com/expert-group-says-embryo-genetic-modification-allowed-030106077.html.

155 "Could CRISPR Homogenize Humanity?" Emily Willingham, *Forbes*, December 4, 2015, http://www.forbes.com/sites/emilywillingham/2015/12/04/could-crispr-homogenize-humanity/#72b983997e35.

156 "Researchers create 'mighty mouse' with gene tweak that doubles muscle strength," Eric Mack, *New Atlas*, December 18, 2011, https://newatlas.com/gene-tweak-doubles-muscle-strength/20879/.

157 "Low insulin-like growth factor-1 level predicts survival in humans with exceptional longevity," Sofiya Milman et. al., *Aging Cell*, March 12, 2014, http://onlinelibrary.wiley.com/doi/10.1111/acel.12213/pdf.

158 "Obesity gene therapy: Slimming immature rats," R. S. Ahima, *Gene Therapy* (2002) 10, http://www.nature.com/gt/journal/v10/n3/full/3301920a.html. Alas, leptin therapy appears to have only limited applicability among humans.

159 "Could gene therapy cure baldness?" "Jacob Silverman, https://science.howstuffworks.com/life/genetic/baldness-gene.htm.

160 "Lance Armstrong Confesses to PEDs: What Is Erythropoietin (EPO) Blood Doping?" Dave Siebert, M.D., January 16, 2013, http://bleacherreport.com/articles/1471562-lance-armstrong-confesses-to-peds-what-is-erythropoietin-epo-blood-doping.

161 "New Wearable Artificial Kidney Improves Mobility," Meg Barbor, *Medscape*, February 9, 2015, http://www.medscape.com/viewarticle/839462. (Subscription required.)

162 "Diabetes Has a New Enemy: Robo-Pancreas," Philip E. Ross, *IEEE Spectrum*, May 27, 2015, http://spectrum.ieee.org/biomedical/bionics/diabetes-has-a-new-enemy-robopancreas.

163 "FDA approves Medtronic's 'artificial pancreas' for diabetes," Ransdell Pierson and Toni Clarke, *Reuters*, September 28, 2016, https://www.reuters.com/article/us-health-diabetes-medtronic/fda-approves-medtronics-artificial-pancreas-for-diabetes-idUSKCN11Z04Y.

164 "The Real-Life Dangers of Augmented Reality: Augmented reality can impair our perception, but good design can minimize the hazards," Eric E. Sabelman & Roger Lam, *IEEE Spectrum*, June 23, 2015, http://spectrum.ieee.org/consumer-electronics/portable-devices/the-reallife-dangers-of-augmented-reality.

165 "Sweat Sensors Will Change How Wearables Track Your Health: Your sweat may bring medical diagnostics to Fitbits and Fuelbands," Jason Heikenfeld, *IEEE Spectrum*, October 22, 2014, http://spectrum.ieee.org/biomedical/diagnostics/sweat-sensors-will-change-how-wearables-track-your-health.

166 "A temporary tattoo that senses through your skin: The Biostamp can replace today's clunky biomedical sensors," Tekla S. Perry, *IEEE Spectrum*, May 29, 2015, http://spectrum.ieee.org/biomedical/devices/a-temporary-tattoo-that-senses-through-your-skin.

167 "Body-hackers: the people who turn themselves into cyborgs," Oliver Wainwright, *The Guardian*, August 14, 2015, http://www.theguardian.com/artanddesign/architecture-design-blog/2015/aug/14/body-hackers-the-people-who-turn-themselves-into-cyborgs.

168 "Dean Kamen's 'Luke Arm' Prosthesis Receives FDA Approval," Erico Guizzo, *IEEE Spectrum*, May 13, 2014, http://spectrum.ieee.org/automaton/biomedical/bionics/dean-kamen-luke-arm-prosthesis-receives-fda-approval.

169 "DARPA and OSRF Developing Next-Gen Prosthetic Limbs in Simulation and Reality," Evan Ackerman, *IEEE Spectrum*, 12 February 2015, http://spectrum.ieee.org/automaton/robotics/medical-robots/darpa-and-osrf-developing-nextgen-prosthetic-limbs-in-simulation-and-reality/.
DARPA has a lot of credibility. The agency is perhaps best known for its driverless-car Grand Challenge and the Internet-precursor ARPANET.

170 "Cyberhand Controlled via Electrodes Directly Implanted into Arm Nerves," Markus Waibel, *IEEE Spectrum*, 10 December 2009, http://spectrum.ieee.org/automaton/robotics/robotics-software/cyberhand-controlled-via-electrodes-directly-implanted-into-arm-nerves-.

171 "Telekinesis Made Simple: A brain implant reads a paraplegic man's intentions to move a robotic arm," Eliza Strickland, *IEEE Spectrum*, July 2015, http://ieeexplore.ieee.org/stamp/stamp.jsp?arnumber=7131677.

172 "How to Control a Prosthesis With Your Mind: New brain-machine interfaces that exploit the plasticity of the brain may allow people to control prosthetic devices in a natural way," Jose M. Carmena, *IEEE Spectrum*, February 27, 2012, http://spectrum.ieee.org/biomedical/bionics/how-to-control-a-prosthesis-with-your-mind.

173 "How to Catch Brain Waves in a Net: A mesh of electrodes draped over the cortex could be the future of brain-machine interfaces," Nitish V. Thakor, *IEEE Spectrum*, August 21, 2014, http://spectrum.ieee.org/biomedical/bionics/how-to-catch-brain-waves-in-a-net.

174 "Quadriplegic Woman Moves Robot Arm With Her Mind," Charles Choi, *LiveScience*, December 17, 2012, http://www.livescience.com/25600-quadriplegic-mind-controlled-prosthetic.html.

175 "Mind-controlled exoskeleton kicks off World Cup," Stephanie Smith, *CNN*, June 13, 2014, http://www.cnn.com/2014/06/12/health/exoskeleton-world-cup-kickoff/.

176 "Cheap 3D printed robotic arm controlled by the mind," Joel Flynn, *Reuters*, June 1, 2015, http://news.yahoo.com/cheap-3d-printed-robotic-arm-controlled-mind-150307835.html.

177 "Cyborgs Go for Gold: People with disabilities will use robotics to compete at the first cyborg Olympics," Eliza Strickland, *IEEE Spectrum*, December 18, 2015, http://spectrum.ieee.org/biomedical/bionics/get-ready-for-the-worlds-first-cyborg-olympics.

178 "The End of Disability: Prosthetics and neural interfaces will do away with biology's failings," Eliza Strickland," *IEEE Spectrum*, May 27, 2014, http://spectrum.ieee.org/biomedical/bionics/we-will-end-disability-by-becoming-cyborgs.

179 "No one who works on the biomedical frontier believes that humans will be content with using advanced prosthetics and brain implants only for repair. Once these technologies have been proven safe and reliable for people with disabilities, some people with unimpaired bodies will start clamoring to use them as technological augmentations." Op. cit.

180 "Blueprint for a Better Human Body: People who wear and design prosthetics are rethinking the form of our species," Rose Eveleth, *The Atlantic*, May 17, 2015, http://www.theatlantic.com/technology/archive/2015/05/a-blueprint-for-a-better-human-body/389655/.

181 "First Look At A Darpa-Funded Exoskeleton For Super Soldiers," Bruce Upbin, *Forbes*, October 29, 2014, http://www.forbes.com/sites/bruceupbin/2014/10/29/first-look-at-a-darpa-funded-exoskeleton-for-super-soldiers/.

182 "My Life as a Robot," Emily Dreyfuss, *Wired*, September 8, 2015, http://www.wired.com/2015/09/my-life-as-a-robot-double-robotics-telecommuting-longread/.

183 "Oculus Rift-Based System Brings True Immersion to Telepresence Robots," Evan Ackerman, *IEEE Spectrum*, April 28, 2015, http://spectrum.ieee.org/automaton/robotics/robotics-hardware/upenn-dora-platform.

184 "Robot Avatars Are Here, Working From Home Will Take on New Meaning," Jason Kennedy, *PC World*, February 21, 2012, http://www.pcworld.com/article/250360/robot_avatars_are_here_working_from_home_will_take_on_new_meaning.html.

185 "Why roboticists are raving about Google's new robot," Matt McFarland, *The Washington Post*, February 25, 2016, https://www.washingtonpost.com/news/innovations/wp/2016/02/25/why-roboticists-are-raving-about-googles-new-robot/. (At the time of this article, Google owned Boston Dynamics. In 2017, Softbank purchased Boston Dynamics.)

186 "Pentagon's Project 'Avatar': Same as the Movie, but With Robots Instead of Aliens," Katie Drummond, *Wired*, February 16, 2012, http://www.wired.com/2012/02/darpa-sci-fi/.

HUMAN 2.0:
Mind Over Matter

187 "A sight for blind eyes," Margaret Harris, *Physicsworld.com*, February 13, 2015, http://blog.physicsworld.com/2015/02/13/a-sight-for-blind-eyes/.

188 "Could bionic eye end blindness?" Dr. Sanjay Gupta and Kristi Petersen, *CNN*, June 13, 2002, http://edition.cnn.com/2002/HEALTH/06/13/cov.bionic.eye/.

189 "The End of Disability..." Op. cit.

190 "New Neurological Map Could Be Key To Psychiatric Brain Stimulation Treatments," Neel V. Patel, *IEEE Spectrum*, September 30, 2014, http://spectrum.ieee.org/tech-talk/biomedical/devices/which-brain-stimulation-treatment-works-best/.

191 "FDA Approves New Appetite Pacemaker Device," Maggie Fox, *NBC News*, January 14, 2015, http://www.nbcnews.com/health/diet-fitness/fda-approves-new-appetite-pacemaker-device-n286166.

192 "The Vagus Nerve: A Back Door for Brain Hacking," Samuel K. Moore, *IEEE Spectrum*, May 29, 2015, http://spectrum.ieee.org/biomedical/devices/the-vagus-nerve-a-back-door-for-brain-hacking.

193 "Scientists switch 'good' and 'bad' memories in mice," Rachel Feltman, *The Washington Post*, August 27, 2014, http://www.

washingtonpost.com/news/speaking-of-science/wp/2014/08/27/scientists-switch-good-and-bad-memories-in-mice/.

194 "MIT scientists implant a false memory into a mouse's brain," Meeri Kim, *The Washington Post*, July 25, 2013, http://www.washingtonpost.com/national/health-science/inception-mit-scientists-implant-a-false-memory-into-a-mouses-brain/2013/07/25/47bdee7a-f49a-11e2-a2f1-a7acf9bd5d3a_story.html.

195 "DARPA Project Starts Building Human Memory Prosthetics: The first memory-enhancing devices could be implanted within four years," Eliza Strickland, *IEEE Spectrum*, August 27, 2014, http://spectrum.ieee.org/biomedical/bionics/darpa-project-starts-building-human-memory-prosthetics/.

196 "Scientists Connect Two Human Brains At Different Locations," James Kosur, *Business 2 Community*, November 7, 2014, http://www.business2community.com/tech-gadgets/scientists-connect-two-human-brains-different-locations-01062010.

197 "Mind-Tracking Devices: Do 'Brain Wearables' Really Work?" by Rachael Rettner, *Live Science*, February 25, 2016, http://www.livescience.com/53840-do-brain-wearable-devices-really-work.html. The short answer to the headline's question: so far, only to a limited degree.

198 "The Pentagon Wants to Put This in Your Brain: The U.S. military wants to build a brain modem that allows you to control objects by willpower. How realistic is it?" David Axe, *The Daily Beast*, January 23, 2016, http://www.thedailybeast.com/articles/2016/01/23/the-army-wants-to-put-this-in-your-brain.html.

199 "To Study the Brain, a Doctor Puts Himself Under the Knife," Adam Piore, *MIT Technology Review*, November 9, 2015, https://www.technologyreview.com/s/543246/to-study-the-brain-a-doctor-puts-himself-under-the-knife/.

200 See my blog post http://blog.edwardmlerner.com/2014/06/the-neural-interface-you-always-wanted.html.

201 See "Carbon nanotube fibers make superior links to brain," no author credited, *Nanotechnology/Bio & Medicine*, March 25, 2015, http://www.phys.org/news/2015-03-carbon-nanotube-fibers-superior-links.html.

202 See "Russian Mogul's Plan: Plant Our Brains in Robots, Keep Them Alive Forever," Katie Drummond, *Wired*, February 29, 2012, http://www.wired.com/2012/02/dmitry-itskov/

and "Scientists Are Convinced Mind Transfer Is the Key to Immortality," Meghan Neal, *Motherboard*, September 26, 2013, https://motherboard.vice.com/en_us/article/ezzj8z/scientists-are-convinced-mind-transfer-is-the-key-to-immortality.

203 "Will we ever...simulate the human brain?" Ed Yong, *BBC News*, February 8, 2013, http://www.bbc.com/future/story/20130207-will-we-ever-simulate-the-brain.

204 To name merely one (of too many) recent mega-breaches: "Hack affected every single federal employee, union says," Laura Hautala, *CNet*, June 11, 2015, http://www.cnet.com/news/hack-affected-every-single-federal-employee-union-says/ and "Latest hack on federal employees targets security clearances," Laura Hautala, *CNet*, June 12, 2015, http://www.cnet.com/news/new-hack-on-federal-employees-targeted-security-clearance-information/.

205 "U.S. government probes medical devices for possible cyber flaws," Jim Finkle, *Reuters*, October 22, 2014, http://www.reuters.com/article/2014/10/22/us-cybersecurity-medicaldevices-insight-idUSKCN0IB0DQ20141022.

A MIND OF ITS OWN:
Artificial Intelligence

206 See "Intelligence across cultures: Research in Africa, Asia and Latin America is showing how culture and intelligence interact," Etienne Benson, *Monitor*, February 2003, http://www.apa.org/monitor/feb03/intelligence.aspx (APA in that URL is the American Psychological Association) and "Are IQ Tests Biased?" Richard Niolon, August 2005, http://www.psychpage.com/learning/library/intell/biased.html.

207 "Inside the Artificial Brain That's Remaking the Google Empire," Robert McMillan, *Wired*, July 16, 2014, http://www.wired.com/2014/07/google_brain/.

208 "Has auto-translation software finally stopped being so useless?" Vidyasagar Potdar, *The Conversation*, October 4, 2016, https://theconversation.com/has-auto-translation-software-finally-stopped-being-so-useless-66370.

209 "Programs and Probability," Brian Hayes, *American Scientist*, September-October 2015, https://www.americanscientist.org/article/programs-and-probability.

210 "How Much Is Your Spare Room Worth?" Dan Hill, *IEEE Spectrum*, September 2015, http://spectrum.ieee.org/computing/software/ the-secret-of-airbnbs-pricing-algorithm.

211 "Google's AI Masters the Game of Go a Decade Earlier Than Expected," Will Knight, *MIT Technology Review*, January 27, 2016, http://www. technologyreview.com/news/546066/googles-ai-masters-the-game-of-go-a-decade-earlier-than-expected/ and "Google AI program wins third straight match to take Go series," Se Young Lee and Jee Heun Kahng, *Reuters*, March 12, 2016, http://news.yahoo.com/google-ai-program-wins-third-straight-match-series-102823689--finance.html. Which isn't to say that a machine mastering Go (or even a more complex game, should one come along) demonstrates general-purpose AI. See "Why AlphaGo Is Not AI." Jean-Christophe Baillie, *IEEE Spectrum*, March 17, 2016, http://spectrum.ieee.org/automaton/ robotics/artificial-intelligence/why-alphago-is-not-ai.

212 One of the pluses of neuromorphic computing is its admirable power-stinginess compared to traditional computing models. Among applications that might exploit that power stinginess are larger and larger neural nets.
   See "IBM cracks open a new era of computing with brain-like chip: 4096 cores, 1 million neurons, 5.4 billion transistors," Sebastian Anthony, *Extremetech*, August 7, 2014, http://www.extremetech.com/ extreme/187612-ibm-cracks-open-a-new-era-of-computing-with-brain-like-chip-4096-cores-1-million-neurons-5-4-billion-transistors.

213 https://www.humanbrainproject.eu/en/brain-simulation/ brain-simulation-platform/

214 "Detailed, Digital Rat Brain Shows Individual Neurons," Glenn McDonald, *Discovery*, October 11, 2015, https://www.seeker.com/ detailed-digital-rat-brain-shows-individual-neurons-1770335474. html.

215 "Genius in a Jar," Brian D. Burrell, *Scientific American* September 2015, http://www.nature.com/scientificamerican/journal/v313/n3/full/ scientificamerican0915-82.html (abstract; full article is behind a pay wall).

216 And as a second cautionary note, see (in the chapter "Human 2.0: Mind Over Matter") the discussion of issues related to transcribing a mind.

217 "Perception of Facial Expressions Differs Across Cultures," American Psychological Association, September 1, 2011, http://www.apa.org/ news/press/releases/2011/09/facial-expressions.aspx.

218 https://en.wikipedia.org/wiki/Open_Mind_Common_Sense

219 See http://www.ibm.com/smarterplanet/us/en/ibmwatson/watson-oncology.html for more about Watson's initial application. Meanwhile, IBM continues to seek new applications. See "IBM dangles $5M prize for breakthroughs using Watson," James Niccolai, *IDG News Service*, February 17, 2016, http://www.computerworld.com/article/3034353/application-development/ibm-dangles-5m-prize-for-major-breakthroughs-using-watson.html.

It's worth noting that, after a fairly extensive rollout, opinions of Watson for Oncology's utility in cancer treatment are mixed. How mixed? Consider this: " 'Watson for Oncology is in their toddler stage, and we have to wait and actively engage, hopefully to help them grow healthy,' said Dr. Taewoo Kang, a South Korean cancer specialist who has used the product." Or this: "In an unpublished study from Denmark, the rate of agreement was about 33 percent—so the hospital decided not to buy the system. In other countries, the rate can be as high as 96 percent for some cancers. But showing that Watson agrees with the doctors proves only that it is competent in applying existing methods of care, not that it can improve them."

Both quotes come from "IBM pitched its Watson supercomputer as a revolution in cancer care. It's nowhere close," Casey Ross and Ike Swetlitz, *STAT News*, September 5, 2017, https://www.statnews.com/2017/09/05/watson-ibm-cancer/.

220 *Artificial Intelligence: The Basics*, Kevin Warwick.

221 *Wake* (2009), *Watch* (2010), and *Wonder* (2011).

222 For more about quantum indeterminacy, see my article "A Certain Uncertainty," *Analog*, April 2016.

223 "Virtual Tween Passes Turing Test," Douglas McCormick, *IEEE Spectrum*, June 10, 2014, http://spectrum.ieee.org/tech-talk/robotics/artificial-intelligence/virtual-tween-passes-turing-test.

224 "Can Winograd Schemas Replace Turing Test for Defining Human-Level AI?", Evan Ackerman, *IEEE Spectrum*, July 29, 2014, http://spectrum.ieee.org/automaton/robotics/artificial-intelligence/winograd-schemas-replace-turing-test-for-defining-humanlevel-artificial-intelligence/.

225 "DARPA and Drone Cars: How the US Military Spawned Self-Driving Car Revolution," Denise Chow, *Live Science*, March 21, 2014, http://www.livescience.com/44272-darpa-self-driving-car-revolution.html.

226 "Artificial-Intelligence Experts to Explore Turing Test Triathlon," Lee Gomes, *IEEE Spectrum*, January 19, 2015, http://spectrum.ieee.org/robotics/artificial-intelligence/artificialintelligence-experts-to-explore-turing-test-triathlon/.

227 "AI Researchers Propose a Machine Vision Turing Test," Lee Gomes, *IEEE Spectrum*, March 10, 2015, http://spectrum.ieee.org/automaton/robotics/artificial-intelligence/ai-researchers-propose-a-machine-vision-turing-test/.

228 "Researchers Teaching Robots How to Best Reject Orders from Humans," Evan Ackerman, *IEEE Spectrum*, November 19, 2015, http://spectrum.ieee.org/automaton/robotics/artificial-intelligence/researchers-teaching-robots-how-to-best-reject-orders-from-humans/.

229 "You've Just Been Disarmed. Have a Nice Day!" John S. Canning, *IEEE Technology and Society Magazine*, Spring 2009.

230 "United Nations Seeks to Head off Rise of Killer Robots," Bryant Jordan, *Military.com*, Dec 20, 2015, http://www.military.com/daily-news/2015/12/20/united-nations-seeks-to-head-off-rise-of-killer-robots.html.

231 "We Should Not Ban 'Killer Robots,' and Here's Why," Evan Ackerman, *IEEE Spectrum*, July 29, 2015, http://spectrum.ieee.org/automaton/robotics/artificial-intelligence/we-should-not-ban-killer-robots.

A MIND OF ITS OWN:
Superintelligence

232 "Speculations Concerning the First Ultraintelligent Machine," Irving John Good, "*Advances in Computers*, vol. 6, 1965," https://web.archive.org/web/20111128085512/http://commonsenseatheism.com/wp-content/uploads/2011/02/Good-Speculations-Concerning-the-First-Ultraintelligent-Machine.pdf.

233 "First Word," Vernor Vinge, *Omni*, January 1983, http://www.33rdsquare.com/2012/05/vernor-vinges-omni-magazine-piece.html.

234 "The Coming Technological Singularity: How to Survive in the Post-Human Era," Vernor Vinge, March 1993, http://ntrs.nasa.gov/archive/nasa/casi.ntrs.nasa.gov/19940022855.pdf.

235 "Why the Future Doesn't Need Us," Bill Joy, *Wired*, April 2000, http://www.wired.com/2000/04/joy-2/.

236 "Stephen Hawking warns artificial intelligence could end mankind," Rory Cellan-Jones, *BBC News*, December 2, 2014, http://www.bbc.com/news/technology-30290540.

237 "Elon Musk Compares Building Artificial Intelligence To 'Summoning The Demon,'" Greg Kumparak, *Tech Crunch*, October 26, 2014, http://techcrunch.com/2014/10/26/elon-musk-compares-building-artificial-intelligence-to-summoning-the-demon/.

238 "Artificial intelligence experts sign open letter to protect mankind from machines," Nick Statt, *Cnet*, January 11, 2015, http://www.cnet.com/news/artificial-intelligence-experts-sign-open-letter-to-protect-mankind-from-machines/. (That headline notwithstanding, many among Future of Life Institute's leadership aren't AI experts—unless physics, cosmology, and other decidedly non-computer-science, non-cognitive-science disciplines somehow merged with AI, or if actors Alan Alda and Morgan Freeman have second careers they've kept well hidden. See http://futureoflife.org/team/ for the institute's membership list.)

239 "Artificial Intelligence Isn't a Threat—Yet," Gary Marcus, *The Wall Street Journal*, Dec. 11, 2014, http://www.wsj.com/articles/artificial-intelligence-isnt-a-threatyet-1418328453.

240 "Let's Shape AI Before AI Shapes Us: It's time to have a global conversation about how AI should be developed," G. Pascal Zachary, *IEEE Spectrum*, June 17, 2015, http://spectrum.ieee.org/robotics/artificial-intelligence/lets-shape-ai-before-ai-shapes-us.

241 As in, for example, "Rapture of the nerds: will the Singularity turn us into gods or end the human race?", Ben Popper, *The Verge*, October 22, 2012, http://www.theverge.com/2012/10/22/3535518/singularity-rapture-of-the-nerds-gods-end-human-race.

242 As another philosopher summarizes the issue, "Either machines are capable of having values or they aren't. If they are not, well, then the whole question of value is misapplied. We're just talking about making safe appliances."

See "The Ethics Of The 'Singularity'", Alva Noë, *Cosmos & Culture*, January 23, 2015 (updated January 26, 2015), http://www.npr.org/sections/13.7/2015/01/23/379322864/the-ethics-of-the-singularity.

243 Scenario from Vernor Vinge, in private correspondence.

CPSIA information can be obtained
at www.ICGtesting.com
Printed in the USA
LVOW13*2315230418
574640LV00008B/53/P